D0336749

Dictator

www.**rbooks**.co.uk

Also by Tom Cain

The Accident Man
The Survivor
Assassin

Dictator

TOM CAIN

LOND S • JOHANNESBURG

TRANSWORLD PUBLISHERS
61–63 Uxbridge Road, London W5 5SA
A Random House Group Company
www.rbooks.co.uk

First published in Great Britain
in 2010 by Bantam Press
an imprint of Transworld Publishers

A CIP catalogue record for this book
is available from the British Library.

ISBNs 9780593062340 (cased)
9780593062357 (tpb)

Addresses for Random House Group Ltd companies outside the UK
can be found at: www.randomhouse.co.uk
The Random House Group Ltd Reg. No. 954009

The Random House Group Ltd supports The Forest Stewardship
Council (FSC), the leading international forest-certification organization. All our
titles that are printed on Greenpeace-approved FSC-certified paper carry the FSC logo.
Our paper procurement policy can be found at
www.rbooks.co.uk/environment

Typeset in 11/14pt Caslon 540 by
Falcon Oast Graphic Art Ltd.
Printed and bound in Great Britain by
Clays Limited, Bungay, Suffolk

2 4 6 8 10 9 7 5 3 1

Mixed Sources
Product group from well-managed
forests and other controlled sources
www.fsc.org Cert no. TT-COC-2139
© 1996 Forest Stewardship Council
FSC

Dictator

Part 1
Ten Years Ago

1

Carver sat astride the girl's broad hips and ran his cool green eyes over her naked torso. Her belly was by no means fat, but it had a proper female curve to it. Her breasts were full and weighty. Her features were anything but delicate: the nose a little too big, the jaw perhaps too heavy. But her mouth was a vivid slash of blood-red lips that parted to reveal strong white teeth, and her eyes were bright with spirit and life.

He leaned forward, reached out his right arm and very gently, experimentally, allowing barely any contact between her skin and his, brushed his hand across her left nipple. She shivered and gave a little gasp as it hardened against his palm. She threw her arms back on the pillow, the wrists crossed above her head as if tied by invisible cords to his bedframe. Her fists had clenched at Carver's first touch. He smiled and gave her other breast exactly the same treatment.

Then, he placed a hand on each breast, a little more firmly now. Taking all the strain in his back and stomach, so that his hands did not press down too hard, he lowered his head and let his lips and tongue play where his hands had just been. He felt her hips move beneath him and tightened the grip of his thighs, restricting her movements and increasing her frustration. She moaned as he took one of her nipples between his teeth and toyed with it, biting her with delicate precision, just enough to hurt a very little.

Now Carver ran his hands down both sides of her ribcage till they settled in the dip of her waist. His mouth delivered weightless kisses to the undersides of her breasts and the downy, peachy skin that surrounded her belly button. He explored that with his tongue for a second, tickling her, and then shifted position so that his arms moved off her body on to the mattress, taking his weight as his legs slipped between hers and slowly but inexorably forced her thighs apart. She put up a token, playful resistance. She was strong, but he was stronger. They both knew this was a contest he was always going to win.

His mouth brushed against the thin strip of pubic hair, just a few wisps to toy with as she tilted her pelvis to bring herself closer to him. There was another moan now, a little louder this time, in anticipation of the feel of his tongue inside her. She moved her own hands down to his head, almost cradling it as she ran her fingers through his hair, trying to guide him to her, but Carver wasn't in any hurry. Instead of carrying on down, he teased her a little, kissing the insides of her thighs, right at the very top, so that he was breathing in the smell of her, feeling her heat.

His own hips were moving now and he could feel his hardness between his body and the sheets. He was frustrating himself as much as her, but that was just part of the fun, seeing who could hold out the longest. Her fingernails were digging into his scalp, scratching the skin, urging him on. The moment was getting closer. He placed his lips against her, tasted her for the first time, and then . . .

And then a thought suddenly dropped, unbidden and unwanted, into his brain: he had absolutely no idea at all what the woman beneath him was called.

The realization hit him like a bucket of ice-cold water, killing the moment stone dead. Had he really come to this? A drunken pick-up in a crowded club; going through the motions of a cynical, anonymous fuck: was this his idea of a great night out? He'd always thought he was better than that.

He shrivelled with disgust and self-loathing and pushed himself away from her.

She must have thought this was just another one of his teases because for a couple of seconds she didn't react. Then she raised herself on her elbows.

'What's the matter, baby?' she said.

Her accent was Italian. It didn't help him remember her name any better.

She giggled enticingly. 'Come back here. What you do feels so good, so hot. Don't be mean, boy. Don't stop now.'

Carver ignored her. He sat on the edge of the mattress and rubbed a hand across his eyes. Now that the buzz of sexual excitement had gone, he was just another sleepless man at half-past four in the morning, on the cusp between intoxication and the inevitable hangover.

He got to his feet, taking a moment to get his balance before padding through to the kitchen.

'Hey! Where you going, leave me here?' she shouted after him, then muttered something in Italian. It didn't sound like much of a compliment.

He stopped in the corridor and turned back towards the bedroom door. 'You want some coffee?'

She gave him the finger.

Carver shrugged and continued on his way. As he poured water into the coffee-machine he could hear her stomping and cursing in the distance, letting him know how she felt as she searched for her discarded clothing and got dressed.

He looked out at the rooftops of the Old Town as they turned from black to battleship grey in the first watery light of the false dawn. It struck him that he was ravenously hungry. He hadn't eaten anything last night, and he wasn't about to eat now. There was nothing in the fridge apart from an old half-empty bottle of Sancerre and an ancient lump of Gruyère now roughly the consistency of heavy-duty plastic and thickly encrusted with green and white mould.

The coffee-machine was making gurgling noises that suggested the water had boiled. Carver slid a cup under the spout. The cup still had the dried brown remnants of yesterday morning's multiple espressos in it. What the hell, boiling water would kill any germs, no need to bother washing it now.

By the time he'd poured his coffee and left the kitchen, she was making her way to the door.

'What your problem?' she sneered when she noticed him watching her. 'Can't do it? No woody? Puh!'

He downed his espresso and opened the door for her. 'Here, allow me.'

'Oh thank you, Mr English Gentleman.' The sarcasm was laid on with a spade.

'Just before you go,' Carver said, putting an arm across the open door. 'What's my name?'

She gave him a withering look. 'I don' know. Don' care. Never wanna see you again.'

'So we're even.'

He let his arm fall and she walked past, not even sparing him a backward glance. He closed the door behind her and wandered back to the coffee-maker, wondering when it was that he'd let it all slide. Not just the girl, everything.

Stupid question. He knew exactly when it had happened. He could date it to the second. Another woman walking through the same door, the finality as it closed behind her, ripping out his heart.

Even now, months later, there were moments when Carver thought he saw Alix Petrova again. All it took was a flash of gold hair in the sunlight that caught his eye, but was not hers; a waft of her scent on the air, but sprayed on another woman's body; a voice that sounded like hers but came from another's mouth.

No matter how often it happened, he was helpless to stop the surge of hope, or the crushing pain when those hopes were dashed.

Carver pulled on some clothes and went out in search of a bakery that would sell him a couple of slices of pizza or a croque-monsieur. Both maybe. He'd need the energy because as soon as he'd eaten and showered he planned on driving up into the mountains. He was going to run through woods and across meadows, run till he'd burned the alcohol from his body and the poison from his soul. And tomorrow he'd do it again.

It was time he got his edge back, time he regained focus. But all the physical fitness in the world would only get him so far.

What Samuel Carver really needed was a job, an assignment that would allow him to exercise his very particular, deadly skills. And several thousand miles away, in the landlocked African state of Malemba, that need was about to be met.

2

On the Stratten Reserve in southern Malemba, hard by the South African border, a black rhino cow was standing placidly in a grove of acacia trees, close to the pool on the banks of a slow-flowing river where she liked to drink. The game wardens who had followed her progress like doting godparents since her birth fifteen years ago called her Sinikwe, just as they named all the key animals – the rhinos, elephants and big cats – on the reserve.

She looked up as she heard a squeal from Fairchild, her calf, who was discovering to his cost that while acacia leaves were tender and delicious, they grew on branches protected by vicious thorns. The youngster had suffered no serious damage, however, and his hunger soon overcame his pain. He returned to the acacia, but a little more cautiously this time, a lesson learned. Two other calves were feeding nearby, Sinikwe's two-year-old daughter Lisa-Marie, and her cousin, Kanja, whose mother Petal had wandered to the pool to slake her thirst.

A dirt road ran by the grove, near enough to enable tourists to sit in their open-sided trucks and photograph the rhino and other species that clustered there. The animals had become accustomed to humans and no longer fled at the first sound of an engine, unless they were actually on the road when a truck appeared. In that case the safari-goers got to enjoy the sight of a fully grown rhino's massive backside heading away from them at thirty miles an hour in a rolling, waddling, fat-man gait – a sight as comic as that of a rhino charging towards them would be terrifying.

But the eight men crammed into the battered old Toyota Hilux pick-up – two in the cab, six packed tight in the back – were not tourists. Dressed in a motley jumble of jeans, army fatigues, football tops and sleeveless T-shirts, and aged from eighteen to forty, their only common denominator was the AK-47 assault rifle each of them carried.

Sinikwe looked up again as the truck drove by the grove. Her ears gave an edgy twitch. But the truck kept moving and its noise faded away, so she returned to browsing for food.

The truck came to a halt downwind from the grove, so she did not smell the men as they dismounted and walked back towards her. The feeble eyesight with which rhinos are cursed meant that she did not see them either as they crept up to the acacia grove and raised their weapons to fire.

A rhino has no natural predators. The biggest danger they face is each other: roughly one-third to a half of all rhinos die from injuries sustained as a result of fighting other rhinos. Thick hide and a sharp horn will deter any other natural threat. But they are powerless against a brutal volley of automatic weapons fire like the one that ripped through the acacia grove that day, tearing skin and flesh, cracking bones and shredding leaves and branches.

Sinikwe was the first target. She died with a high-pitched scream of terror that could be heard over the brutal chatter of the guns before she and they fell silent, leaving her punctured body, garlanded with the crimson rosettes of its wounds, lying on the blood-spattered earth.

All but one of the other rhinos fled, suffering no more than minor injuries. But Fairchild, frozen by terror, overwhelmed by the sound and smell of the guns and baffled by his mother's sudden stillness, remained by the bush where he had been feeding. Then he slowly crept towards Sinikwe's body, mewling and squeaking in a plaintive attempt to rouse his parent.

A single sharp order was barked by one of the men. Two of the others slammed fresh magazines into their AK-47s. There was another, much briefer burst of firing. Then Fairchild, too, lay dead.

The men got to work with machetes. One group hacked the full-grown horns off Sinikwe and the much shorter, immature growths off Fairchild. The others, some wielding axes, attacked the rhinos' feet until their work was cut short by another order.

The men stepped away from the mutilated corpses, keeping Sinikwe's longer front horn, their most valuable trophy, but leaving the rest for the carrion feeders who would soon be drawn to the slaughter. They made their way back to the Hilux. And silence fell again upon the grove.

3

Zalika Stratten kept hoping that her father would rescue her. Later, she knew, he would ruffle her hair with his strong brown fingers, their skin as rough as bark, and tell her, 'Don't you worry too much about what Mummy says. She means well. She just worries about you, that's all.' But Zalika didn't want 'later'. She wanted him to stand up now and say, 'Stop it, Jacqui. That's enough.'

Dick Stratten ruled his own vast personal kingdom – not just the reserve, but farms and ranches all over the country, filled with people who depended on him for their work, their homes, even the food in their bellies. Why couldn't he rule his own wife? Why did he have to sit there, chewing on his lamb chop and very deliberately looking out at the view from the terrace while he ignored the argument going on right next to him at the table?

And why wouldn't her mother leave her alone?

'Honestly, darling,' Jacqui Stratten was saying, 'it really wouldn't hurt, just once in a while, to put on a pretty dress. If you just took off those ghastly trainers and put on some heels, or paid a tiny little bit of attention to your make-up, it would make such a difference.

You have such lovely blue eyes, they're much your best feature, but no one will notice unless you make some effort to show them off. As for your hair, René keeps asking me when I'm going to bring you along to the salon. He's longing to give you some proper highlights. He says it would absolutely transform you.'

'I don't want highlights,' Zalika snapped back. 'Sitting for hours with my hair wrapped up in tinfoil, getting bored out of my mind while that horrible old man fusses about with his fake French accent – that's my idea of total hell.'

'Well you're never going to get a boyfriend if you carry on with those attitudes, that's for sure,' her mother replied.

'I don't want a boyfriend.'

'Oh don't be silly. You're a seventeen-year-old girl, of course you want a boyfriend. When your brother was your age, he was absolutely surrounded by girls. But then, Andrew's never had any trouble making the best of himself.'

Zalika rolled her eyes. 'Here we go again with my oh-so-perfect brother . . .'

'Well, have you seen how many letters he's had since he got back from New York, all obviously written by girls? All my friends there could talk about was the impression he was making. Every pretty little thing in Manhattan wanted to know him.'

'God, Mummy, don't you have any idea what Andy's like? He'll be giving all these silly Americans his big stories about going on safari, pretending that he rides on elephants and fights lions single-handed, and they'll all be dreaming that he'll take them away to Africa and planning what they're going to pack. Then as soon as he's got inside their pants, he's off telling the exact same stories to some other girl. That's what he does. Don't pretend you haven't noticed.'

'Honestly, Zalika, you really do talk utter nonsense sometimes. And you shouldn't be so mean about your brother. After all, he's the one who worked hard enough to get a place at Columbia Business School. To judge by last term's reports, you'll be lucky to pass a single A level. And I'm sure you're not stupid, really. You'd have a good mind if only—'

'The plane!' shrieked Zalika, ignoring her mother and switching straight from furious indignation to utter delight with the speed only a teenager can muster. She leapt to her feet and ran away, dashing from the shade of the thatched veranda and down the steps, her long, slender, butterscotch legs racing out on to the rich-green lawn while Jacqui Stratten called after her, 'Zalika, Zalika! Don't leave the table!'

Frustrated by her daughter's sudden departure, Jacqui turned her attention to her husband. 'That girl will be the death of me. And you could have done something to help, my darling, instead of sitting there stuffing your face while your daughter was being so rude.'

Dick Stratten didn't respond. He had long since learned that there were times when nothing a husband said could possibly be right. It was best just to let his wife have her say and get things out of her system.

Out on the lawn, Zalika stopped in mid-stride and spun to face her parents, still sitting at their lunch. 'Look!' she cried, flinging one hand back up at the sky. 'Can't you see? It's Andy! He's back from Buweku! He's brought Moses home!'

Stratten frowned as he peered out towards the horizon, following the line of his daughter's arm.

'My God, the girl's right,' he said. 'I must be going blind in my old age.'

Now he rose too, stepping up to the wooden rail that ran round the edge of the veranda, the evident strength and fitness of his body giving the lie to his claims of decrepitude.

'Oh, you're not so bad . . . not for such a very old man,' said Jacqui, teasingly.

They'd met when Dick was thirty and she a girl of eighteen, just a year older than Zalika. His family and friends, all stalwarts of white Malemban society, had been appalled: she was too young and, even more importantly, too common for the heir to the Stratten estates. Dick didn't care what anyone else thought. His view of the world was shaped far more by the law of the jungle than the niceties of social convention. As far as he was concerned, Jacqui Klerk was the most desirable female he had ever clapped eyes on and he was damn well going to have her as his mate. Twenty-six years later, they were still together and that youthful animal passion had deepened into a lifelong partnership.

'Don't be too hard on the girl,' Stratten said.

'Oh I know,' his wife sighed. 'It's just, well, I worry that she's going to turn into a wallflower if she doesn't make a bit more of an effort. All one can see now, looking at her, is a mass of drab mousey hair and that great big Stratten nose.'

'It's a very splendid nose,' said Stratten with exaggerated pride.

'On a man like you, darling, yes it is. But not on a young girl. I know Zalika means "wondrously beautiful" in Arabic, but we have to accept our daughter will never be that. She could be a great deal less plain, though, if only she accepted even one of my suggestions.'

'I don't think she's plain at all.'

'Of course not, you're her father.'

'Anyway, I'm sure it's just a phase. She's trying to work out who she really is. It's natural for her to rebel a little bit, all children do it.'

'Andrew didn't.'

Stratten gave her a quizzical, not to say sceptical look. 'Maybe you just didn't see it. In any case, you are famously the most beautiful and best-dressed woman in the whole of southern Africa' – Jacqui Stratten glowed in the warm light of her husband's compliment – 'so she's rebelling against you by pretending to take no interest at all in how she looks. The second she finds a boy she really likes that will all change, just you wait.'

Jacqui mused on the problem as she watched Zalika take a few more paces across the grass. As the plane drew closer she started waving her arms above her head. The girl's frantic gestures were answered by a waggle of the plane's wings. She squealed with delight then ran away again across the grass, calling out as she went, 'I'll go and meet them at the strip!'

Zalika disappeared out of sight of the veranda. Not long afterwards came the sound of an engine starting up and the arid scrunch of tyres on dusty gravel.

Jacqui's thoughts turned to the boys her daughter was rushing to meet. Her son Andy – how handsome he was becoming, she mused proudly – and his lifelong friend Moses Mabeki, the son of the family's estate manager. Moses was Andy's equal in looks, with a finely sculpted bone structure made all the more apparent by a shaven head, and full lips framed by a close-cropped beard. But as the horn-rimmed spectacles round his liquid brown eyes suggested, he took a much more earnest approach to his studies. Moses had attended the University of Malemba before being offered a graduate place at the London School of Economics' Department of Government. As the first member of his family ever to receive a college education, he had no intention whatever of wasting it on girls and parties.

Dick Stratten had insisted on paying the young man's tuition fees and living expenses. 'Moses is like a son to me too,' Stratten had told the boy's father, Isaac Mabeki, as they shared one of the bottles of thirty-year-old Glenfiddich they polished off from time to time, talking not as master and loyal servant but as one man to another. 'I know he will do great things for this country one day. With your permission, it would be my pleasure and an honour to help him on his way.'

Moses had spent the past three years in London, returning to Malemba only for occasional visits. Now, with his masters degree completed, he was coming home for good.

The roar of the Cessna's engines as it passed low over the house and made its final approach to the landing strip roused Jacqui Stratten from her reverie. She blinked, gave a little shake of the head and thought for a second. Yes, there would be time. Then she smiled at a servant who was hovering a few feet from the table. 'Coffee, please, Mary,' she said. 'Mr Stratten and I will have a cup while we wait for the boys to arrive.'

4

The seventy-four-year-old man sitting behind his mahogany desk in a lavishly appointed office in Sindele had begun his career as a village schoolteacher, working in the same modest school where he had been given his own early education by Anglican missionaries. Had his life followed its expected course, Henderson Gushungo would now be retired, a respected member of his little community, spending his days sitting under a shade-tree, talking to the other old men, grousing about the way the world had changed and indulging his grandchildren.

Gushungo, however, had had other, more radical ideas. He'd joined the resistance movement against the white minority who ruled his country as though it were still a colony of the British Empire. Like Nelson Mandela in South Africa, he'd burnished his reputation among his people and radicals around the world by going to prison for his beliefs. Unlike Mandela, he'd emerged from jail filled with a lust for revenge, not reconciliation. For years he had fought a war on two fronts: publicly against the whites, and privately against his competitors within the liberation movement.

Now he held the entire country's destiny in his hands. Having been Prime Minister, he had promoted himself to President, never submitting himself to any election whose result was not certain before a single vote had been cast.

Gushungo liked to call himself the Father of the Nation. But he was a very stern and cruel parent.

His soldiers were fighting in the jungles of the Congo. His henchmen were forcing white farmers off their properties and forcibly cleansing hundreds of thousands of black Malembans from areas where, in his increasingly paranoid imagination, they might constitute a serious opposition to his continued rule. His demoralized opponents, unable to remove him themselves, prayed that God would do the job for them. But the old man had no intention of meeting his maker any time soon. His hair was still thick and black, his face remarkably unlined, his posture erect. His mother had lived past one hundred. He still had a long way to go.

One of the phones arranged to the right of his desk trilled.

'It has begun,' said the voice on the other end of the line.

'Excellent,' said Henderson Gushungo. 'Let me know when the operation has been completed.'

5 ————————————————————

When he met Moses Mabeki at Buweku airport, Andy Stratten had greeted him with the words 'Sawubona, mambo!' In Ndebèle, the Zulu dialect widely spoken in southern Malemba, it meant 'Greetings, king!'

Moses had grinned as they bumped their clenched right fists against each other, then held them up to their hearts. Yet there was a serious truth behind Andy's lighthearted greeting. To the vast majority of the Malembans who lived and worked on the Stratten lands, Andy was not the true aristocrat, Moses was. He could trace his bloodline back to Mzilikazi, founder of the Ndebele tribe, a man who combined a genocidal craving for the slaughter of his enemies with a statesman's gift for leadership. The land over which they'd flown on the journey down to the Stratten family compound was territory Mzilikazi himself had conquered, a hundred and sixty years earlier. So it had surprised no one that Moses studied the art of government during his years in London. As Andy often told his friend, 'One day, I will run the Stratten estates. But you will run the whole damn country.'

It had taken a little over half an hour for the Cessna to reach its destination.

'Just look at that, hey,' Andy had said when he spotted the girl frantically waving on the lawn. 'I tell you, man, my sister's the craziest chick in the whole of Malemba.'

Moses had laughed. 'Don't be cruel. Zalika has a good heart.'

Stratten brought the Cessna in to land with practised ease. By the time he was slowly taxiing to a halt, Zalika was arriving, trailed by a plume of dust, just a few yards away. She'd barely stopped the open-topped, olive-green Land Rover before she'd flung the handset down on to the passenger seat and was scampering towards the two young men emerging from the plane.

'Moses!' she shrieked delightedly, flinging herself at him and wrapping her arms round him. 'It's so great to see you again!'

'You too,' he said, patting her on the shoulder and smiling at her puppy-like enthusiasm.

'Don't I get a hug too?' asked Andy.

'Of course not,' his sister replied, 'I saw you at breakfast. You'll have to be away for much longer than a few hours if you want a cuddle from me.'

Andy looked at his friend. 'Like I told you, the girl's crazy.'

'And my brother,' said Zalika, 'is an arrogant, self-opinionated pig!'

The insult might have been more effective had not happiness been radiating from the girl like the warmth from an open fire.

They climbed into the Land Rover, Zalika slammed it into gear, and as the young men clung on for dear life she raced back up to the house.

6

The southeastern quadrant of Africa, from the equator to the Cape of Good Hope, contains some of the world's most spectacular landscapes. But between those highlights lie countless miles of open savannah, which is a technical way of saying 'an awful lot of dry grass, interrupted by the odd bush or tree' – a harsh but not entirely unjustified description for much of the land on the Stratten Reserve. The glory of it lay in its animal inhabitants. And on days when the Big Five animals – lion, leopard, rhino, elephant and Cape buffalo – declined to make themselves visible, prosperous middle-aged tourists soon became hot, sweaty and disgruntled.

That was the situation facing a guide called Jannie Smuts as he drove his tourist-filled truck on a so-far fruitless safari. His customers had seen warthogs by the score, a few unimpressive varieties of deer and one listless giraffe. But that hardly amounted to value for the very large sums of money they'd paid for their African holiday. Smuts himself was endlessly fascinated by the marvels of the African sky: so dazzling with stars at night; so lurid at sunrise and sunset; so capricious in its ability to switch from limitlessly clear blue to massed ranks of mountainous thunder-clouds, seemingly in an instant. He could see, however, that 'Why don't you folks look at the sky?' wouldn't go down too well, par-ticularly since the truck's canvas sunshade prevented them from actually seeing it.

He could feel the disappointment starting to mount behind him on the passenger seats. But as he pulled to a halt half a kilometre shy of the acacia grove and stood up and turned to face his customers, he felt confident he could turn things round.

'I've got something pretty special for you now, folks,' he said, his voice lowered, almost whispering, to create an air of tension and expectancy. 'Just round the corner there's a special spot where rhino like to gather to feed and drink. With any luck they'll be there right now, and let me tell you, this is a sight worth seeing. And about time too, eh guys?'

There was a ripple of relieved laughter. Smuts grinned back, then sat back down in the driver's seat and got the truck underway again.

They were still a couple of hundred metres from the grove when Smuts caught sight of jackals feasting on a giant grey carcass. He cursed under his breath and prayed that none of his customers had spotted what was going on. He braked again, hopped down to the ground and grabbed his rifle.

'Just a minute, folks. I just want to see if any of our rhino buddies are in the area. Just don't leave the truck, hey? Don't want anyone getting lost.'

The laughter was a little more nervous this time, the tourists sensing there was something not quite right here.

Smuts was gone barely a minute. When he returned to the vehicle his face had lost all its good humour. He did not say a word to his passengers. Instead he picked up his radio and spoke in Afrikaans, not wanting anyone else in the truck to understand as he reported the presence of poachers.

Then he started up the engine again, pulled the truck into a three-point turn and headed back the way they had come.

'Sorry about that, folks!' Smuts shouted as he drove away. 'Looks like our rhino buddies aren't available. But don't worry, this is a big reserve. And sooner or later we'll find where its animals are hiding!'

7

When the news came through that poachers had killed Sinikwe and Fairchild, Dick Stratten's first instinct was to go and investigate the incident himself. The younger men, however, were having none of it.

'Come on, Dad, let me do it,' Andy pleaded. 'I could use some excitement.'

'That's what worries me,' growled his father. 'I don't want any excitement, just someone to go and see what's happened. If there's going to be any action, any poachers getting scrubbed, I want some police right there so it's all above board.'

'Please, Mr Stratten, do not concern yourself,' said Moses. 'I am sure that no one will come to any harm.'

'But Moses, dear,' said Jacqui, 'you must be tired after such a long flight from London. Wouldn't you rather rest?'

'It's all right, Mrs Stratten, I'll be fine. I slept very well on the plane. This will make me feel as though I have properly come home. Besides, you have been very generous to me. I would like the chance to be useful to you, to show my appreciation for all that you have done.'

'Fair enough,' Dick Stratten conceded. 'Take a couple of the boys with you. I want all four of you armed. But you are only to fire in self-defence. Do you understand me? I don't want you arsing about, trying to act like John Wayne.'

'John who?' Andy said with a grin.

'You know exactly what I mean, young man. Be careful out there.'

'Please, darling,' said Jacqui, 'do what your father says. And come back safe.'

Andy Stratten kissed his mother's head as he passed her. 'We will, Mum, no worries,' he said, and then, to Moses, 'Hey, boet, let's cut!'

The two friends bantered back and forth as they drove out to the site where the shootings had been reported. But the conversation stopped when they came upon the mutilated corpses of the two rhinos.

'Bastards!' hissed Andy. He turned to Moses. 'Welcome back to Africa. Not a lot has changed.'

'Not yet, no,' Moses agreed. 'Come, let us see what happened here, and where the killers went.'

The four men began examining the crime scene, tracking every footprint across the grove, noting the patterns of cartridge shells as carefully as police forensics officers. Tracking spoor was a skill Andy had learned from his first footsteps. To the Ndebele it was a heritage that stretched back through countless generations to the very dawn of humankind.

Moses spoke to the two other black Africans, then addressed Andy. 'So, we are agreed: eight men, armed with AK-47s, but only seven of them fired. The eighth man stood here, watching the whole scene.'

'The leader,' said Andy, 'giving orders.'

'I would think so, yes.'

'OK, so let's see where they went. I know we promised the old man there'd be no heavy stuff, but if I find the bastard who ordered this, he's a dead man.'

'Yes, and then what will happen?' Moses asked. 'Nothing good for you, that is for sure. So you must calm that hot Stratten blood. We will follow these men. We will find them, observe them, call in their position and wait for the police. Then, maybe, you can have your revenge. But for now we just follow the spoor.'

The poachers had made an attempt to cover their tracks and set false trails, but the failure of their deceits merely added to the confidence of the men following them. It was not long before they found the spot where the Hilux had been left. The tyre-tracks clearly showed how the poachers had turned off the road and left their vehicle screened by mopane scrub. They had not turned back on to the road, though, when they left the scene. Instead, they'd kept going away from it, deeper into the scrubland.

'They headed for the river,' said Andy. 'They must be nuts.'

'Perhaps they thought they could cross it,' Moses suggested.

'There are fords, but not here. They can't be that stupid, can they?'

Moses shrugged. 'Not stupid, perhaps, but desperate. We should be careful. Maybe we should stop here. There are eight of them, remember.'

'Stop? No way. I will have these fuckers, mark my words.'

Moses said nothing. But his knuckles whitened around his gun and his eyes darted nervously around as they made their way through the mopane bushes that rose as high as ten feet to either side of the path forced through the undergrowth by the heavily laden pick-up.

No one was talking now. The air was still and close, heavy with the resinous, turpentine smell of mopane seeds, and the men's shirts were gummed to their backs with sweat. The visibility was poor in every direction, every sightline blocked by trunks, branches and foliage. The men bowed their heads low, looking ahead of them at ground level, below the foliage, hoping to catch sight of a poacher's feet or his shadow.

Even Andy Stratten's demeanour lost its bullish confidence. His

father had fought in the vicious civil war that led to the trans-
formation of the white-ruled former colony of British Mashonaland
into an independent Malemba governed by its own people, but his
son had been spared that pitiless conflict. For all his talk of revenge
he had never gone after human prey, nor been a target himself.
Fear was gripping him by the throat and twisting his bowel and
guts.

Then, with barely a warning, they were through the scrub and
standing by the banks of the river. There, sure enough, was the
Hilux, its front wheels and bonnet half underwater, its cab tilting
down towards the river, only its rear wheels still finding some
purchase on the damp red soil of the bank.

'Fuck!' Andy Stratten exclaimed. 'I hope those dumb munts can
swim.'

His relief had made him forget himself: he'd used the white
Malemban slang for a black man. No sooner had he said it than he
realized his offence.

He was starting to stammer an apology to Moses when the sound
of his voice was drowned by two sharp bursts of gunfire. The two
estate workers had no time to cry out, still less raise or fire their
weapons as the bullets from the AK-47s dropped them where they
stood.

The poachers emerged from the mopane scrub, just a few paces
away, screaming and gesturing at Andy and Moses to drop their
weapons. Then their leader stepped on to the open ground on the
riverbank. His eyes hidden behind a pair of fake designer shades,
he walked up to Andy Stratten and jabbed a finger hard at his
chest.

'Now who's the dumb munt?' he said.

Then he stepped back and got out of the line of fire as the order
rang out and the guns started chattering again.

8

They called themselves war veterans, men who had served in the endless string of conflicts, at home and abroad, that plagued Malemba along with so many other African countries. They were psychologically scarred by their experiences, filled with rage and convinced of their entitlement to land and money in compensation for their services to the state.

When they'd finished their deadly work, they pulled the Hilux back out of the river, restarted the engine and made their way back to the acacia grove. There, the raiding team split in two, four of the men taking the Strattens' Land Rover as they headed towards the estate house. They paused once along the way to meet another pick-up filled with more armed veterans, then, reinforced, they sped towards their destination.

Zalika Stratten had tried to protest when her father ordered her into the family's underground shelter, hidden beneath a workshop some distance from the main house. Contact had been lost with Andy and his men. Word had come in from an outlying village of a truck of armed men on the move. In a country inured to armed insurgency, people were used to preparing for the worst. Like many white women in southern Africa, Zalika had taken every self-defence and weapons training course she could get. It was a given among her race and class that they, too, were an endangered species.

'I know how to handle a gun,' she insisted, 'let me fight!'

Her father was having none of it. 'For once in your life, Zalika, do as you are told!' he shouted, grabbing her by the arm and half-dragging her towards her only hope of safety.

'Come on, darling, you know this is for the best,' said Jacqui. 'Daddy doesn't want to have to worry about us.'

The shelter was well supplied with food, water, basic survival gear and even a couple of rifles. The women clambered through a hatch and down a ladder into the underground chamber, then looked up at Stratten, who was on his haunches above them.

'You know the drill,' he said. 'Stay here. Do not make any noise. Do not use any of the torches or lanterns. If all goes well, I will come for you. If it does not, then wait until nightfall, and try to get out under cover of dark.'

'Oh Dick!' cried Jacqui, her composure finally starting to crack.

'It's all right, my dear,' said Stratten, trying to keep his own fear from his voice. 'Don't you worry now. Everything's going to be just fine.' He paused for a second, forcing his emotions back under control, then said, 'I love you both so very, very much,' before he closed the hatch.

'Daddy!' shouted Zalika in the darkness. But her father was already gone.

Down in the shelter, the women were aware of the trucks' arrival. They heard the firing of the guns, the screams of the fearful and the wounded, and the frenetic shouts of the fighting men. Then, as swiftly as a passing storm, the gunfire abated and the screaming gave way to a few agonized moans, swiftly silenced by single shots. Finally came a crash as the workshop door was barged open, followed by four quick, confident footsteps heading straight for the hatch.

For a fraction of a second hope flickered in the women's hearts as they stood in the darkness, each gripping a rifle. Whoever was up there was not blundering around. They knew exactly what they were doing. That could only mean Dick Stratten, or one of the very few family retainers who were trusted enough to know about the shelter.

Then the hatch was flung open and a disembodied voice – a refined, educated voice – commanded them, 'Put down your guns. They are of no help to you now. My men have hand-grenades. If you do not leave the shelter within the next ten seconds, unarmed, holding on to the ladder with both hands, they will blow you to pieces. Ten . . . nine . . .'

'You two-faced little shit,' hissed Jacqui Stratten. Then she gripped the ladder and called 'We're coming up!' as she stepped up into the beam of light coming through the open hatch.

Zalika Stratten followed her mother. Before she'd reached the top of the ladder, strong hands reached down to grab her, pull her upwards and dump her on the workshop floor. She landed by a man's feet, clad in expensive, barely worn safari boots.

She heard the man's voice bark, 'Take the mother away.'

Zalika raised her face and looked Moses Mabeki in the eye as he said, 'Your brother is dead. Your father is dead. Your mother will soon be dead. You, however, are coming with me.'

9

Two weeks later, a man named Wendell Klerk phoned Carver and summoned him to a meeting at a hotel on the northern shore of Lake Geneva. Klerk did not say what he wanted to discuss. He did not need to. He merely barked, 'Be there in thirty minutes,' and hung up without waiting for an answer.

Carver was intrigued. Klerk was as familiar a figure in the gossip columns, invariably attached to the latest in a long line of beauty-queen blondes, as he was in the business pages. Born into a working-class white family, one of two children of a railway worker and his socially ambitious teacher wife, Klerk had fought on the losing side in the civil war and left the country soon after British Mashonaland's rebirth as Malemba. He'd settled in Johannesburg, South Africa, from where he'd built an international business empire whose interests included gambling, hotels, construction and mining – 'from casinos to coalmines' as one reporter had put it. Klerk was known as a tough operator. Over the years both journalists and hostile politicians had accused him of corruption, bribery and even ties to organized crime. But none of the charges had stuck. If anything, they had just made the public warm to Klerk as a tough but likeable renegade.

In recent weeks, however, Klerk had been in the news for very different reasons. Carver assumed that was the reason for the call. Out of curiosity, if nothing else, he wanted to know what Klerk had in mind.

Twenty-seven minutes later, Carver walked into the reception of a modern low-slung building faced in brick and terracotta rendering that made it look more Moroccan than Swiss. He was led by one of the staff across the ground-floor reception area, out past a swimming-pool ringed with unoccupied sun-loungers and down into a tunnel which passed under the main road that ran along the lakeshore. At the far end of the tunnel a jetty stretched out across the water. A long, thin wooden motorboat that resembled a Venetian water-taxi was moored at the far end.

The boat belonged to the hotel, whose insignia was embroidered on the pennant that fluttered from its stern. But the man standing at the open wheel in front of the covered passenger cabin was not one of the standard white-jacketed hotel boatmen. He wore the global uniform of the upmarket heavy: black suit, tie, shades and shoes; white shirt; earpiece; a gun invisibly but unquestionably secreted somewhere about his person.

Carver was patted down, then ushered into the cabin where Wendell Klerk was waiting. Klerk's short, stocky, powerful body, with its snub-nosed peasant's face and tightly curled black hair, looked as incongruous as a cannonball deposited on the elegant quilted seating. The two men shook hands, then sat in silence as the boat was cast off from the shore and motored out on to the lake.

Klerk looked out through a porthole. Evidently happy that they had travelled far enough to be out of earshot of any shore-based surveillance, he turned his black-brown eyes on Carver and asked, 'You know who I am, ja?'

'Of course.'

'So you are aware of my interest in a certain kidnapping case.'

'Sure, I watch the news. You're the Stratten girl's uncle – her mother's brother.'

'In that case you can work out why I wanted to see you.' Klerk's voice was a deep, guttural rumble.

Carver nodded. 'Your sister was killed and your niece was kidnapped. With the father and the brother both dead, that left only you to get her back. I assume you hired one of the top security firms to handle the negotiations to recover her. Clearly they've not succeeded, so now you're thinking it's time for Plan B. Money's not an issue for a man of your resources and you must have some very powerful, well-connected friends. Some of them could have been involved with the organization I used to work for. Maybe you were in it yourself. Either way, I'm assuming my name came up. Right?'

Klerk nodded. 'Close enough. So let me tell you the situation. The kidnappers are moving every few days, but my people have been tracking them wherever they go. It isn't hard to do. Nothing stays secret in Africa for long, not if you're willing to pay. I have not told the authorities because I do not trust them either to keep the information secret, or act on it appropriately. Instead, I want you to get my niece Zalika Stratten out of there. She must be recovered unharmed. Her safety is the only reason I have not sent my people in after her long before now. They are good, but – how can I put it? – they lack subtlety. That is why I have come to you.'

'Maybe so,' said Carver, 'but however subtle I might be, the guys who have your niece aren't likely to let her go without a fight. Even if she doesn't get hurt, they will. And I don't want to end up rotting in an African jail.'

'I understand. But you can rest assured that if any of the kidnappers are made to pay the price for their actions, I will not care, and nor will the police. I will make sure of that.'

Klerk rubbed his fingers together to indicate that a willingness to pay would, once again, be the key. Then he looked at Carver, appraisingly.

'How tall are you?' he asked.

'Five eleven.'

'Weight?'

'About one seventy-five in pounds, a little under eighty kilos.'

'Light heavyweight,' said Klerk. 'That'll do. You keep yourself in shape?'

Carver gave a silent prayer of thanks for the hundred-plus miles of hard cross-country running he'd put in over the past fortnight. 'Yes.'

'Fully recovered?'

So Klerk knew about the torture Carver had endured in the chalet outside Gstaad and the havoc that had wreaked on his mind.

'I'm fit for action, yes,' said Carver.

Klerk looked at him again like a jeweller examining a stone under his glass, searching for hidden flaws. 'Yes, I believe you are,' he finally replied. 'Right, I'm sure we can work out a financial package, you and I. My people will get you all the details we have about the kidnappers' current location. That just leaves two things you must know. The first is that Zalika Stratten is all the family I have left. I have never been able to have children, Mr Carver. I always hoped there would be someone to carry on my work when I am gone, keep my business alive. Zalika is my only hope and I will stop at nothing, absolutely nothing, to get her back. Whatever you want, you will have. Understood?'

'Absolutely. What's the second thing?'

'The terms on which we do business,' said Klerk. 'I am a tough, mean bastard, Mr Carver. My sister got all the looks and social graces in our family and I got nothing but the will to win. But I am also a man of my word. You do right by me and you have nothing to fear. On the other hand, if you even try to screw with me I will not forget it and I will get even, however long it takes. So, now that you know what kind of a man you are dealing with, are you still interested?'

'Yes,' said Carver.

'Good. When can you leave?'

'When's the next flight?'

10

The eastern border of Malemba resembles a crudely drawn semi-circle, ringed by its neighbour Mozambique much as a spanner grips a nut. About fifty miles inside Mozambique, astride the river Zambezi, lies the town of Tete.

Carver arrived there at nine in the morning after a twenty-hour journey from Geneva, changing planes twice en route. He was expecting to be hit by a physical blast of heat and humidity as he stepped from the plane: Tete is only sixteen degrees south of the equator, well within the Tropic of Capricorn. He knew too that Mozambique was one of the poorest nations on earth, devastated by more than a decade of armed struggle against its former Portuguese masters, and a fifteen-year civil war that had killed almost a million people. Yet the air was pleasantly warm and dry, and the small terminal building, which rose from the runway tarmac in a series of whitewashed blocks topped by sharply angled roofs, was surprisingly clean and well maintained.

He'd cleared passport control and customs and walked out into the arrivals area when a short, wiry, moustachioed white man wearing a faded safari shirt over a pair of khaki shorts came up to him, pulled a cigarette from his mouth and asked 'You Carver?' in an abrasive colonial accent.

Carver said nothing.

'Flattie Morrison,' said the man, chucking the glowing butt on to the floor and grinding it under the heel of an ancient walking boot before sticking out his right hand. 'Howzit? We've been expecting you.'

'Samuel Carver.'

Morrison turned and led the way through a crowd of people, exchanging greetings in what Carver presumed was the local dialect; shooing away anyone who looked as if they were about to try to sell something; cursing and occasionally swatting the children who constantly darted around them.

'The munts here are all right, but they are the worst fucking thieves in the whole of Africa,' Morrison said, shoving a diminutive boy out of the way. 'They will jack the clothes off your back and you will not even notice until you feel the wind on your arse. What the hell, hey? They have no economy, so if they want some kite, what else can they do?'

'Kite?'

'Money . . . greenbacks!' Morrison rolled his tongue round the word with enormous relish then grinned, his upper lip spreading in a flat line across his face, exposing a line of gleaming white teeth below his grey-flecked ginger moustache. He tapped his right cheek. 'See this smile, hey?' he said, then clipped another child with the back of his hand without slowing his stride or pausing for breath. 'That is why they call me Flattie. In Malemba, a flattie is a crocodile. And he gives you a great big smile just like this . . . right before he kills you. Hahaha!'

They walked out to Morrison's car, a battered old Nissan Sunny, its once red paint faded to a washed-out pink, streaked with rust and punctuated with dents and holes.

'Sorry if the wheels are a bit rough for your taste,' said Morrison, getting in the driver's side then leaning across to shove open the passenger door. 'No point having a fancy new car here, boet. The munts strip it like fucking vultures on a corpse, and if it breaks down out there in the bush, there's no bugger qualified to fix it. But this old heap? A baboon could learn to service it.'

After a couple of failed attempts, the engine coughed into life like an elderly man waking from an afternoon nap, and they headed out of the airport towards the city.

'So,' said Morrison once they were on the open road, 'you are here to get the girl, hey?'

Carver nodded. 'That's the plan.'

'By whatever means necessary.'

'Something like that. So, you got the gear I asked for?'

Morrison grinned. 'Mr Heckler and Mr Koch are in the building, and so are all their friends, stripped, checked, reassembled and in perfect working order.'

'I'll be the judge of that.'

'Quite right. Never trust another bugger to check your weapon. So, they told me you were a Royal Marine, hey?'

'Yeah.'

'Regular bootie or SBS?'

'That's not something I talk about.'

Morrison gave a slightly narrower, slyer smile. 'Ja, you were SBS, I can tell. Did you see action, may I ask? Contacts with the enemy?'

'Yeah, I've had contacts.'

'Good. Because let me tell you, I don't want to fuck about with any more plum-in-mouth so-called experts in fancy suits who don't know how to fight. "Conflict resolution" they call it, "a negotiated settlement". Bullshit, man! They're just sitting on their fat backsides in the bar of the Zambezi Hotel making bloody telephone calls to Mabeki, the treacherous, ungrateful black bastard, while that poor little chibba Zalika Stratten is all alone, scared out of her fucking mind, wondering why no one's come to get her.'

'She hasn't been moved in the past twenty-four hours?'

'Nah, still in Chitongo. It's a village up by the Cahora Bassa dam, just another back-country shithole. Now me, I'd go and get her myself. Fuck, I've killed enough of them in my time. Wasted more than a hundred gooks, way more. Rebels, their women, children . . . hell, you see something moving in the elephant grass, you don't stop to ask questions, you just empty your magazine before the other fucker bends you over and gives you one right up the nought. But sometimes, hey, sometimes you should not have fired . . .'

Morrison's voice trailed away. For a moment Carver could have sworn he was welling up. But then Morrison coughed, wiped a hand across his flushed, scarlet face, whispered, 'Christ,' to himself and went on, 'So, anyway, I offered to do it, but the boss said, "No, Flattie. We must have a man who is more clinical than you. In, out, no mess, that is the plan."'

Carver wondered what kind of kid Morrison had been before someone stuck some pips on his shoulder, put a gun in his hand and sent him off into the bush to destroy anything he found, himself included. The man was barely keeping it together. But Carver wasn't about to judge. The ghosts of his own dead haunted him too, visiting him in nightmares that left him sweat-soaked, wide-eyed and fighting to hold back the screams. Anyone who'd truly been to war was scarred by the experience. If they told you any different they were lying.

'How come you work for Klerk?' he asked. 'You don't seem the corporate type.'

Morrison broke into a chuckle that ended in a wheezing cough. 'You mean, why does a man like him put up with a crazy old bastard like me, hey? Well, I will tell you. I used to be his company commander. Klerk was just a corporal back then. After the war, well, let's just say that our lives took very different courses. But we were comrades. We fought side by side. You don't forget a thing like that.'

They drove down a broad avenue, the tarmac hardly visible beneath a thick coat of dust whose red-ochre colour seemed tinted by all the bloodshed it had absorbed. Tall palms poked up between the trees on either side.

'We could not put you up at the Zambezi because we don't want those other useless buggers knowing what's really going on,' said Morrison, pulling up in front of a dilapidated attempt at an American-style motel. 'This place will have to do. Don't worry, though, you won't be stopping here long.'

Morrison walked into a lobby whose mint-green paint was mottled with black stains of mould. He had a brisk, argumentative shout at the man behind the reception desk then led Carver to his room.

'Sling your gear in there, then we will cut into town,' he said, standing by the open door as Carver went into the room and slung his bag on an ancient, sagging bed beneath a grimy grey mosquito net. 'You need a good meal inside you. I must have more smokes. We will go through tonight's entertainment. Then I suggest you get a couple of hours' rest. We take off at fifteen hundred hours, on the bloody dot.'

As Carver was on his way back out, Morrison stepped into his path and stuck a hand into his chest to stop him.

'I want you to make me a promise, hey,' Morrison said, and there was no trace of humour now. 'Promise me, swear on your mother's life—'

'I don't have a mother.'

'On her fucking grave then, I don't care. Just swear that you will get that girl out alive. This is Africa and there is no negotiation here, just taking and killing, the way it has always been. These kidnappers will never give that girl back, never. They intend to take the money and then kill her anyway. So you get her out, Mr Carver. You get her out, or believe me, she will die.'

11

The chopper was flying northeast out of Tete, following the Zambezi upstream towards the Cahora Bassa dam. At first the river flowed calm and wide, a mile from bank to bank at some points. But then the gradient steepened, the river narrowed, and the force of water within it increased. The valley became deeper and the hills on either side of the river closed in, becoming first bluffs then cliffs that plunged hundreds of feet down to boiling, frothing rapids whose surface disappeared from time to time beneath a fine mist of spray. The helicopter had been flying high above the river, but now it swooped down, plunging between the precipitous rockfaces of the gorge: a metallic dragonfly skimming the surface of the river, swooping right and left as it followed the twists and turns of its course.

Carver wanted his approach to be as fast and discreet as possible and the unpopulated, inaccessible ravine provided a route that led directly to his target out of sight of prying eyes. It also threatened a far greater danger of death en route. One flick of a rotor-blade against the valley walls, one touch of the landing gear against an

outcrop of rock and he, Morrison and the pilot would all be sent
spinning to their graves. But he had ridden plenty of helicopters at
absurdly low levels en route to missions whose odds were near
suicidal. It was not so much that he felt no fear, simply that he had
learned to park it in a distant, sealed-off area of his mind, while his
conscious thought was directed to the job in hand.

Beside him, Flattie Morrison's cigarette was clamped at one end
of a crocodile smile that was even wider and toothier than usual.

'This is the life, hey?' Morrison shouted over the clatter of the
rotors, made even louder by the echoes resounding off the rock
walls on either side. 'Feels like old times! Fuck, man, the closer I
get to the Reaper, the more I feel alive. You know what I'm talking
about?'

Carver said nothing, but he couldn't argue. There was nothing
on earth so charged with pure adrenalin as the excitement that
came with the risk of oblivion. But that too had to be kept in check,
every ounce of nervous energy reserved for the moment when it
was most needed.

'Yeah, you know all right,' said Morrison. He looked at his watch.
'Not long now till we get there. You want to check anything, go
through the plan again, this is the time to do it.'

They went over the timeline of the next nine hours one more
time. The success of the mission depended on perfect coordination: the simultaneous arrival of two elements at a given
point, timed to the last second.

'OK,' said Morrison, once the details had been confirmed. 'One
last thing: if anything goes wrong and you need an emergency evac,
just get on the comms and say "Flattie". Whisper it, shout it,
fucking yodel it, doesn't matter, we'll be on our way. But one thing
you should consider. We will be parked at an LZ just across the
river. It will take us eight minutes to reach the extraction point, and
I don't have to tell you, eight minutes is a fuck of a long time if
you're getting your arse shot off in a firefight. So think about that
before you call, hey? Right, now we must get out of here before we
hit the dam like a bug on a windscreen.'

No sooner had Morrison spoken than the helicopter lurched upwards and hurtled up the cliff-face, past the bare rock towards the luscious carpet of greenery at its summit. Then they were escaping the grasp of the gorge, and for a second Carver caught a glimpse up ahead of the mighty Cahora Bassa dam, whose five-hundred-and-sixty-feet-high concrete walls held back the Zambezi, confining the river within a man-made lake more than a hundred and eighty miles long. Then the pilot swung left over a range of hills, skimming the trees as closely as he had the water, before dropping again and bringing the chopper in to land at the centre of a minuscule clearing with the precision of an experienced big-city driver squeezing into a tiny parking space.

'Out you get!' shouted Morrison as the helicopter's skids kissed the ground.

Carver jumped down, holding the Heckler and Koch MP5 sub-machine gun he had specified, and a kitbag was thrown after him.

Morrison gave him a thumbs-up and then the helicopter rose and sped away over the trees.

'Mr Carver!'

Carver turned at the sound of the voice and saw a tall African man in faded blue trousers and a loose, short-sleeved white shirt gesturing at him to follow.

'My name is Justus Iluko, but everyone just calls me Justus,' said the man when Carver had caught up. 'Come with me, please. I work for Captain Morrison. I fought with him in the war of liberation,' he added, by way of explanation.

'On the same side?' Carver asked.

Justus laughed. 'Oh yes! All the soldiers were black in our company. Just the officers and NCOs were white. Some of them . . . pah!' He shook his head dismissively. 'But Captain Morrison, he was square with us. He never made any man do anything he would not do himself. We trusted him and we followed him, you know?'

Carver nodded.

'Mr Klerk, too,' said Justus. 'He was a mighty warrior. When he fought, no one could defeat him!'

Carver followed Justus through the trees to a dirt track on which an ancient VW van was parked. He climbed up into the passenger seat. Justus got in the driver's side and set off.

'I knew Miss Zalika too, when she was just a little baby girl. When the war ended, before he started his own businesses, Mr Klerk got me a job as a game warden on the Stratten Reserve. I was only there for three years, but I remember Miss Zalika being born. We were all given the day off and plenty of beer to drink!' Justus laughed at the memory. 'Sometimes Mrs Stratten took her children for picnics and one of us drove them out on to the reserve and watched over them in case any lions or other dangerous animals came, but they never did. Those were good days. No more war, everyone with so much hope for the future . . .'

His voice trailed away, and for a while the only noise came from the VW as it lurched and rattled along the potholed track. Justus looked around, then nodded as he spotted a familiar landmark. 'Just thirty minutes and we will be in Chitongo.'

'Has Morrison briefed you on the plan of action for tonight?' Carver asked.

'Of course. The captain is a very thorough man. He always told us about the importance of proper preparations. He does not like to leave anything to chance.'

Five minutes' worth of intensive questioning proved that Justus was right. Morrison might have his problems, to put it mildly, but he still retained the organizational skills that had made him a company commander whose men trusted him to lead them into action and out the other side. Meanwhile, Justus was evidently the kind of reliable, level-headed fighting man who made any officer's life a lot simpler. That didn't make tonight's mission any less difficult, but at least it tilted the chances of success marginally in their favour.

Once he had satisfied himself that he was in good hands, Carver leaned back in his chair and looked around. Hanging from the rearview mirror were a string of beads, a St Christopher medal and a photograph of a laughing woman with her arms round two small children, a boy and a girl, both in their neat white school shirts.

'Your family?'

'Oh yes,' said Justus, the warmth of his smile conveying the love, pride and happiness he felt. 'That is my wife Nyasha, who has blessed me with her affection for twelve years now, and my son Canaan – he is eight – and my daughter Farayi, who is six.'

'They look like great kids. You're a lucky man.'

'Yes, I am very, very lucky. Do you have a family, Mr Carver?'

'No, not yet.'

'So you have never found the right woman to take as your wife?'

Carver grimaced. 'A couple of times I thought I had. Never quite worked out.'

'That is sad,' said Justus, shaking his head. 'To have a good woman who gives him strong, healthy children is the greatest satisfaction a man can have. You know, sometimes when I am tired from working too long, or the jobs I must undertake do not please me, I ask myself, "Why do I do this?" Then I look at that picture and I know. I do it for them.'

'So where do you live?'

'I have a small farm, about twenty miles from Buweku. The country there is very beautiful: rolling hills, so green that my cattle grow as fat as hippos, and with earth so rich that all you have to do is throw seed upon the ground and any crop will grow. I am building a house there. Soon it will be finished. Then I will go to my wife and say, "I have given you many rooms. Now you give me more children to fill them all!" '

Carver laughed along with Justus, admiring but also envying the straightforward convictions by which he seemed to lead his life. Carver would probably earn more from this one night's work than Justus could hope to make in his entire life. But that didn't make him richer in the things that really mattered.

He brushed the thought from his mind as if swatting an irritating fly. He had more immediate problems to worry about than his lack of women or kids.

Justus, too, was getting back to business. He pulled the car up by the side of the road and said, 'We are getting close to Chitongo and it is most important that no one sees you arrive.' He turned in his seat and looked towards the rear of the vehicle. 'Please lie on the floor at the back, Mr Carver. I have provided a blanket to cover you.'

'OK.'

A minute later they were on the move again, Samuel Carver huddling under an ancient tartan picnic blanket as he was driven into battle.

12

Zalika Stratten had long since lost track of where she was. She thought she'd heard voices a couple of days ago talking in Portuguese. That suggested she might be somewhere in Mozambique. Beyond that, though, this was just another bare mattress shoved into the corner of another room, with another uncovered bucket to squat over. The windows were boarded over and the door in the centre of the wall opposite her mattress was locked, with a guard permanently stationed outside. There was no bulb at the end of the wire that hung from the ceiling. The only light came from the cracks between the planks nailed to the window frame.

Zalika's feet were chained together, just far enough apart that she could shuffle across her room, but too close to allow her to walk properly, let alone run. Her jeans and shoes had been taken away and all she had to wear now were the T-shirt and underwear she'd been wearing when she was captured.

They gave her two meals a day, feeding her on a basic diet of maize-meal porridge, with an occasional treat of salty, bony fried fish, or a meat stew that consisted of a couple of lumps of in-determinate gristle adrift in a plateful of grease. From time to time she'd be handed a small plastic basin filled with cold water and a bar of gritty pale-grey soap with which to wash herself. She did her best but her hair was matted and greasy, there were black rings of dirt beneath her fingernails and she was permanently damp and prickly with sweat.

Just as airline passengers getting off a long-distance flight have no idea how disgusting the air onboard smells to ground-crew getting on, so Zalika's senses had long since become accustomed to the rank odours of sweat, urine, excrement and stale food that hung in the airless atmosphere of her solitary cell.

Yet Mabeki himself seemed not to care about her plight. She barely recognized her brother's smiling, impeccably mannered friend in the fierce, embittered ideologue who from time to time came into her room. He paced up and down, his voice ranging from a sinister, low-pitched calm to rabid fury while she huddled on her mattress, as defensive as a curled hedgehog, her knees pulled up to her chest and her arms wrapped round them.

This was virtually the only human contact left in Zalika Stratten's life: her meals and bucket were delivered and removed in total silence by guards who ignored any attempt of hers to make conversation.

In the near-darkness, Mabeki was as insubstantial as a wraith. Only his words seemed real. Again and again he repeated the arguments that justified his actions, building up a portrait of her father and family, layer by layer, that flatly contradicted everything she had ever believed.

'Richard Stratten was an oppressor, an imperialist. How can it be right for one man to have so much land, so much money, so much power when countless millions have so little? How can it be right for the white man to give the orders, while the black man can only say, "Yes, boss! No, boss!" and do his bidding?'

'But my father was a good boss,' she argued. 'All our workers had running water and electric power.'

'There is no such thing as a good boss,' Mabeki spat back. 'There are only the rulers and the oppressed. You talk about running water and power as though they were luxuries for which the workers should be grateful. They are basic human rights. And running water means more than a tap in every village. Power means more than a few bare lightbulbs.'

'What about your father? Isaac did not think Dad was a bad man. He was devoted to him.'

'Is that what you think? Then you are a fool. Your eyes have been closed all your life. Do you imagine that my father came back to our meagre hovel, with its four bare walls of breezeblock and its corrugated iron roof, and felt affection for a man who lived in mansions built on land that our ancestors ruled as kings? Do you think he was grateful when your father declared that he would pay for my education? That money was made from land stolen from its rightful owners – stolen by the white man from the black!

'And tell me, Zalika, since your father was such a fine man: what did he do for all the workers on his farms and his game reserves who suffered from HIV? Did he get them treatment, the latest drugs? No, they were worked until the disease became so bad that they could not work any more. Then they were dismissed and left to die, while new workers were hired in their place.'

Some days Mabeki updated her on the latest development in the negotiations he was conducting from his satellite phone with the hostage rescue consultants brought in by Wendell Klerk. 'Your uncle does not wish to spend any of his money to free you,' he said one time. 'You could be at his house in Cape Town right now, or in London, or on his country estate, or even sunbathing at his place in the Bahamas if he had simply paid what I asked. Do you want to know what price I put on your head?'

'No,' said Zalika, trying to sound as though she meant it.

'It was five million dollars, US. That is roughly one-tenth of one per cent of Mr Klerk's estimated personal assets. It is a fraction of what he paid to get rid of his last wife, the beauty queen, after just three years of marriage. What was she, Miss Austria?'

'Czech Republic,' said Zalika, before she could stop herself.

'Thirty million he gave her to go away, or so the newspapers said. And all I want is five. Not for myself, but for my people. This money will be used to dig wells and buy tractors, medicines, solar electricity panels, schoolbooks, pencils. It will do far more good working for Africa than it ever could in Mr Klerk's bank account, and yet . . . and yet, he will not pay it. He tells his people to bargain with me, to drive the price down. He threatens to walk away and leave you to your fate. I am sorry, Zalika, but he does not think you are worth saving.'

For his part, Moses Mabeki looked forward to his conversations with Zalika Stratten with keen anticipation. He derived great pleasure from seeing her humbled, stripped of all comforts, breathing the stench of her own filth. He enjoyed this daily proof of his newfound power almost as much as he had enjoyed giving the order to shoot Zalika's brother dead; or pouring diesel fuel down a funnel into her father's throat until it drowned him; or giving her mother to his men to do with as they pleased; or even the exultant moment when he faced his feeble, lickspittle father and took a machete to the treacherous body with which he had so willingly served the Stratten family. Hearing the pain and bafflement in Zalika's voice when he had told her those lies about his father – that, too, had been something to relish. But what he was planning to do later this very night . . . well, that, he thought, he might enjoy even more.

13

They were keeping Zalika Stratten on the top floor of a two-storey building – one of the few in the village – that occupied the north-east corner of a crossing where two dirt roads intersected. In the classic fashion of a colonial African building, a ground-floor colonnade ran along the main facade and round the corner facing the road, providing shelter for passers-by. Above it on the first floor ran a covered open-air walkway, with a waist-high balustrade for the building's occupants. The ground floor was occupied at one end by a shebeen – an illegal bar, whose clientele neither asked nor answered questions about one another's business – and a half-empty excuse for a local store at the other. Upstairs there were three very basic apartments, all now occupied by Mabeki and his men. A stairway bisected the front of the building, connecting one walkway with the other.

Justus had installed himself in a derelict building directly across the street, having given the family who occupied it ten US dollars – almost certainly more than they could expect to earn in a month – to let him use it as an observation post.

Shortly after midnight, three hours before the operation was due to begin, Justus was scanning the target building's facade with a pair of military-specification thermal-imaging binoculars. They reacted to temperature rather than light so that hot-spots showed up in colours that ranged from a warm red through orange and yellow to white-hot. A human body glowed white on a cold night at close range. If the line of sight was clear, visual identification of individuals was possible at ranges of a mile or more. But through the walls of the room in which Zalika was being held, people showed up as little more than vague orange blurs. That was enough, though, to allow Justus to discern Zalika's body, lying on her mattress, just as it had enabled him to detect the man who had brought her evening meal. When, shortly afterwards, she had got up to use the bucket, he had turned his imager away to check the other apartments.

Now Justus was checking in with Carver, who was lying flat on the roof of a garage directly behind the target building. He was dressed in black, with a black balaclava hiding his face, and had melted into the shadows beneath the second-storey wall behind which Zalika was being held. It rose windowless for ten feet above him, its surface covered with a faded, crumbling painting of a giant Coca-Cola bottle.

The night air was filled with music, the raucous voices of hard-drinking men and the shrieks and laughter of the working girls coming from the shebeen. Carver had to put his finger to his earpiece as Justus spoke to hear his words distinctly.

'Mabeki brought five of his men with him into Mozambique,' Justus said. 'Three of them are downstairs in the shebeen right now. One of the other two is in the inner hallway of the apartment, outside Miss Stratten's room. The other is on duty as a sentry on the walkway. There is one figure in the adjacent apartment. I believe this is Mabeki. He . . . wait, he is moving. He is leaving the apartment and I think he is going to the room where Miss Stratten is held. Yes, he is entering it. Now he is going to the bed. Miss Stratten must have woken. She is sitting up. Mabeki is doing something down at her feet. Oh, I see, he is loosening her chain. Maybe he is about to move her.'

On the garage roof, Carver tensed, sensing that all his carefully calibrated plans were about to be rendered irrelevant. Well, he was used to that. He just had to work out when to go in, and – even more important – when to call Morrison. Whatever happened, he aimed to be in and out of the building in under sixty seconds. That left seven long minutes before the chopper arrived. He had to find a way to buy time. Then he heard Justus's voice in his earpiece again.

'No, he is not moving her. He is bending over her. Now he is on the bed. Oh no, he is on top of her. She has raised her hands. I think she is trying to fight him, but . . .'

'Flattie!' hissed Carver.

'We'd already fired up the engine,' said Morrison. 'On our way.'

'Mr Carver, this is very bad,' said Justus.

'Yeah, I get it,' Carver replied. 'Now listen, I need you to distract the sentry on the walkway. I don't care what you do, just make sure all his attention is focused on you. Got that?'

'OK . . .'

Carver stood up, quickly flexed his neck, shoulder and back muscles, then picked up a length of nylon rope attached to a grappling hook that he had placed beside him on the roof. He stepped back, threw the hook over the top of the wall above him and tugged on the rope until the hook caught on the roof parapet. It took him a matter of seconds to abseil up the painted Coke bottle and over the parapet on to the flat roof above. His MP5 sub-machine gun, fitted with a noise suppressor, was slung across his back. He also carried a knife, three grenades and a pair of black nylon pouches strapped to his hips. In them were two fifteen-round magazines, a powerful torch, an emergency flare in case he needed to mark his position for an incoming chopper, some nylon fishing wire and a basic first-aid kit.

Keeping his head down, he padded across to the front of the building and peered over the parapet down to the street. Justus was standing by the side of the road with a bottle in his hand, trying to strike up a conversation with the sentry. They were speaking in an African dialect, but Carver had no trouble getting the wheedling, drunken tone of what Justus was saying or the annoyance in the sentry's voice. Perfect.

He moved to the side of the building, away from the point where the two men were talking, and climbed back over the parapet on to a narrow ledge that ran all the way round the facade of the building, providing additional shelter for the walkway below. Carver crouched down, placed his hands on the ledge and then lowered his legs and body over the side till he was hanging by his fingertips, suspended outside the walkway. A single lightbulb provided enough illumination for him to look all along it, straight towards the sentry who was now leaning on the balustrade, gesticulating at Justus down below.

Carver rested his feet against the balustrade, pushed them away and then swung them back towards the walkway, letting go of the ledge above and dropping over the balustrade, down on to the floor. He landed noiselessly on rubber-soled boots, swung his weapon up to his shoulder and put two bullets through the sentry's head before the man even knew he was there.

Having checked that the sentry was dead, Carver smashed the light with the stock of his gun, plunging the walkway into darkness. Then he peered over the balustrade and signalled to Justus to get the van and drive it round the side of the building. The Malemban nodded and ran off.

For a moment, the noise from the shebeen dipped and Carver could hear a muffled female scream coming from inside the building. Carver prided himself on his ability to remain calm and dispassionate, but there was a difference between being professional and being a robot. The sound of that voice awoke a primal male instinct in him to defend and avenge a female in distress.

There was a door from the walkway into the apartment where Zalika Stratten was being held. Carver kicked it open and advanced into the building, his gun raised and ready to fire.

14

Moses Mabeki had planned on taking his time. This was a self-indulgence to be savoured. Then he heard the crash of the outside door slamming open and the jolt of shock and fear that flooded his nervous system made sex the last thing on his mind. He rolled off Zalika and, all but sightless in the darkness of the room, scrabbled on the floor for his trousers and the Chinese-made Norinco pistol that he'd jammed into one of the pockets. His fingers tried to extract the gun from the fabric wrapped round it and finally, after an eternity of fumbling, it was in his right hand.

Mabeki heard a shout of alarm from the guard in the hall. It was suddenly cut short, ending in a strangled cry of pain followed by the thud of a body slumping against the door to the room. Somebody was out there, he realized. They were willing to kill. And he was next.

Still kneeling on the floor, Mabeki fired three rounds in the rough direction of the door, the sound of the shots almost deafening in the small, echoing room. Behind him, Zalika was raising herself on her elbows. Mabeki didn't want her crying for help. He turned back to the mattress and gave the girl a hard backhanded slap to the face. She whimpered in pain.

'Quiet!' he whispered. 'Not a sound!'

He could just about see the outline of her nodding head. There was a sniff as she tried to control her tears, then Mabeki heard a scraping sound as the body was dragged from the door by the unseen predator.

He shot again, twice more. This time there was a wordless shout from beyond the door and more stumbling footsteps, followed by the sound of a body against a hard surface. Whoever was out there had been hit, but how badly?

Mabeki needed to find out, but he wasn't leaving the safety of the room with just his gun to protect him. Zalika Stratten would be his shield. He got to his feet, then, still holding the gun in his right hand, he bent down and grabbed Zalika with his left, making her wince as he clamped his fingers round the soft flesh of her upper arm.

And then he heard another sound from beyond the door.

15

The bullet that hit Carver as he tried to dodge to one side of the door had struck him a glancing blow beneath his left armpit and spun him across the hallway. There was a lot of blood and it hurt like hell. Every breath ended with the sharp stab of a broken rib. But aside from that, he was still in one piece and more pissed off than ever. The blasts from Mabeki's gun would surely have been heard down in the shebeen. No matter how drunk they were, his people were bound to investigate.

Carver strode back to the door, the face behind his balaclava clenched in furious determination, and kicked hard. The flimsy door with its rusty hinges and half-rotten wood flew open.

Ahead of him and to the right, Carver could see Mabeki, dimly illuminated by the light from the hallway. He was bending over the mattress, dragging Zalika Stratten to her feet with one hand while holding a gun in the other. He wasn't wearing any trousers and the sight of his bare legs only underlined the obscenity of what he'd been about to do to the girl.

Mabeki let go of her. His head and shoulders were rising back up and turning towards Carver. He was bringing his pistol to bear.

Carver put his first bullet though Mabeki's jaw, which exploded, showering Zalika Stratten with blood and fragments of flesh and bone. As the impact sent Mabeki staggering backwards, Carver fired again, hitting him in the upper torso.

Mabeki was thrown to one side. He lay still as the blood, just one more liquid shade of black, pooled round his body and spread across the floor.

The girl started screaming. She was huddled on the bed, shaking uncontrollably. Somehow, her pitiful vulnerability affected Carver far more than the shattered body on the floor.

'Time to go,' he said, his voice sounding far harsher than he intended.

She looked up, eyes wide with horror at the sight of the masked, faceless figure looming over her.

'Come on!' Carver insisted.

Zalika did not move, just pointed at the body and sobbed, 'Is he dead?'

'I certainly hope so,' Carver replied, holding out a hand. 'Now, please, get up. We've got to get out of here before his mates arrive. Your uncle's expecting you.'

That seemed to do the trick. Zalika took Carver's hand and let him pull her up. But then she stiffened, unable to move any further, still transfixed by the sight of Mabeki's body. Carver tightened his grip on her wrist and started running, dragging her with him, forcing her to follow him out of the room, past the body in the corridor towards the outside walkway.

'Stay here,' he mouthed as they reached the door to the walkway.

He let go of Zalika's hand and inched out into the open. People were starting to spill out of the shebeen on to the street. He could not see them, but he could hear them, just as he heard the sound of heavy boots clattering up the concrete stairs. The silhouette of a heavy-set man appeared a few paces down the walkway and swayed slightly as he took his bearings. Carver dropped him with a single headshot. There were no more footfalls on the steps.

Carver gestured with his cupped left hand, ordering Zalika out on to the walkway. 'This way,' he said. 'Stick tight to the wall.'

He led her away from the two dead men, through the shadows to the side of the building till they reached the place where he'd jumped on to the walkway less than a minute earlier.

A shout came from the street below, followed by more excitable, angry voices. They'd been spotted.

Carver muttered a curse. Then his spirits rose as he heard the coughing and spluttering of the VW van and saw it pull up directly beneath them. Justus got out and dashed to the side of the building. He raised his arms and said, 'Let her down, I will catch her.'

Carver manhandled the terrified girl to the balustrade and then, wincing as the pain from his cracked rib sliced through him, lifted her up and over it. He let go of her arms and watched as she fell six or seven feet into Justus's arms. The African buckled under Zalika's weight, but kept her from hitting the ground.

As he pulled himself and the girl to their feet, Justus turned his head then looked back up at Carver and shouted, 'Quick, they are coming!'

Carver vaulted over the balustrade and fell to the ground, unable to stifle a sharp cry of pain at the impact. He looked up to see Justus bundling Zalika into the back of the VW and closing the rear passenger door behind her. Beyond them about fifteen or twenty men were rounding the corner of the building, the pitch of their voices rising as they saw the car and its would-be occupants. Their advance slowed as they saw Carver straightening with the gun in his hand. He raised the MP5 to point at the crowd. The men came to a halt, looking at one another as if seeking guidance. None of them appeared to be armed.

Carver heard the sound of Justus starting up the VW behind him. He moved back very slowly towards the vehicle, keeping his eyes and gun fixed on the crowd.

It was the movement that alerted him, an anomalous shift in the pattern of limbs, bodies and faces captured on the edge of his peripheral vision that told him someone was aiming a gun. Carver flicked his eyes to a man in the second rank aiming an AK-47. He was using his companions as cover, assuming Carver would be reluctant to shoot unarmed civilians.

Carver fired anyway, aiming three bursts over the crowd, but keeping the shots as close as he dared to their heads. They scrambled to get out of the way, and their movement was just enough to knock the man with the AK-47 off his aim, sending his first burst harmlessly wide.

Now, though, the stampede worked against Carver, preventing him from getting a clean shot on his target. He fired his last two rounds fractionally high again, just to discourage anyone from getting closer, then dived into the VW as Justus floored the pedal and sent the vehicle moving with surprising speed down the street, away from the men who were now getting to their feet behind them.

'Kill the lights!' shouted Carver.

He pulled off his balaclava and stuck a fresh magazine into the MP5 as they raced away into the purple-black night.

16

He was known as Killaman. He was thirty-eight years old and he'd been a soldier for twenty-five of them. It was he who had led the poaching expedition to kill the rhinos and lure the Strattens into the trap. Mabeki may have been the brains behind the operation, and President Gushungo's consent had been required for it to go ahead, but Killaman had been the senior fighting man.

It had taken him a matter of seconds to exit the shebeen, race up the stairs, find his four fallen comrades and work out what had happened. His fury at the incompetence that had allowed one man to penetrate their defences and steal their most precious possession had swiftly given way to the realization of a golden opportunity.

Killaman gathered up the weapons lying by the bodies, shoved Mabeki's pistol into the waistband of his trousers, and slung the straps of the AK-47s round his left shoulder. He retrieved the keys of the Hilux truck from the tabletop where they had been thrown when they'd first arrived in Chitongo. Then he went back outside and looked down at the men milling around in the road, some staring into the distance, others arguing about what to do next, the rest standing about aimlessly.

Among the milling rabble was the man who had fired at Carver, another member of the kidnap gang, who went by the name Silent Death. He was looking up at the building, waiting for Killaman to tell him what to do next. The rest were swiftly losing interest, now that the excitement seemed to have passed. Soon they would all return to the shebeen and the moment would be lost.

A series of pillars that supported the roof ran down the balustrade about ten feet apart. Killaman grabbed hold of one of them with his right hand and pulled himself up on to the balustrade so that everyone down below could see him, swinging his left arm up and making the guns hanging from it clearly visible.

'Get the truck . . . go!' he shouted at Silent Death, throwing the keys down to him. Then he turned his attention to the crowd. 'Comrades!' he cried. 'Listen to me now!'

Killaman waited until every face had turned towards him and an expectant hush had fallen.

'Something very precious that belongs to me has been taken – a white girl. I will offer ten thousand American dollars to any man who helps me recover this girl. Fifty thousand to anyone who kills the white man who stole her from me. I have guns for you to shoot, I have a truck for you to ride in. Now, who will join me?'

There was a clamour of volunteers. A couple of fights broke out as men competed for Killaman's attention. He picked the four meanest-looking individuals he could find. Then he ordered them into the Hilux, clambered in next to Silent Death and set off in pursuit of the VW van and its passengers.

17

There was a football pitch on the edge of town, out beyond the last houses. On the road leading up to it, just behind one of the goals, stood a large warehouse used for storing food sent to the area by aid agencies. To one side of the pitch, by the halfway line, was a small stand made of scaffolding with a dozen rows of seats to hold a couple of hundred spectators. Directly opposite, on the far side of the ground, a motley collection of concrete buildings, little more than tin-roofed huts, provided changing rooms and an office. The playing area itself comprised an area of flat, beaten-down earth without a blade of grass upon it, surrounded by a few wooden poles topped by rudimentary floodlights. Carver had taken one look at the aerial photographs of the village and picked it immediately as his extraction point.

His plan had been to coordinate his arrival there with that of the helicopter. That way there'd be no hanging around. The chopper would touch down, the girl would be bundled aboard, swiftly followed by Carver, then they'd be off again. Now he had time to kill. And what bothered him was the possibility that time might kill him first.

'Pull up over there,' Carver said, as Justus got to the warehouse. He pointed towards a padlocked door, above which a security light gave off enough of a weak, flickering glow to illuminate the van and draw any pursuer's eye. Just raising his arm made the cracked surfaces of his broken rib grind together, sending another agonizing jab into his chest.

Carver gave Justus the torch. That hurt too. Everything hurt. There were painkillers in Carver's medical kit, but any dose strong enough to make him forget his ribs would by definition dull his senses and lessen his effectiveness. It was better to hurt and stay alive than be drugged up and die.

'Take her over to the huts,' he said. 'One of them is painted pale blue. I'll meet you inside it.'

The girl looked from Carver to Justus and back again. Carver had tried to explain to her that they were all working for her uncle Wendell Klerk, but she was still mentally paralysed by the unrelenting traumas she'd been forced to endure.

'It's OK,' he said. 'You'll be safe with him.'

'Have no fear, Miss Zalika,' said Justus, grinning, as he pulled out from beneath the dashboard a weapon that looked like an oversized black pistol. 'This is a very powerful shotgun. No one gonna get you now.'

'Go,' said Carver. 'I'll be right behind you.'

Justus got out of the VW, walked round to the passenger door and took Zalika's hand, helping her out. She gave one last look towards Carver then let Justus lead her away.

Carver watched them go. He spent about a minute more in the VW van. Then he grabbed his gun and walked across to the warehouse door. He put a single bullet through the padlock and freed the chain that secured it. Then he opened the door. An alarm began to ring. Carver did not seem concerned. Another twenty seconds passed as he stood by the half-open door. Finally he took a step back, looked at the opening, nodded to himself and loped away towards the changing rooms.

Not far away, he could hear the growl of an approaching engine. Carver picked up his pace.

18

Four men had been picked to go with Killaman, but twice as many clung on to the Hilux as it set off after the VW van. Many of those who had been left behind then dashed off to their homes to pick up weapons of their own. After a lifetime of conflict, almost all had some form of military experience, either for government or rebel forces, or even both. Many had kept hold of old weapons. They grabbed whatever they could find then started running after the departing vehicles. They didn't care that the cars had left them far behind. They could run for hours if the need arose. And the tens of thousands of dollars at stake provided all the incentive they required.

Most of the men carried regular knives and guns. One, though, had a long thin tube on his shoulder. At the rear end it flared like the mouth of a trumpet. At the front the tube appeared to swell, before tapering to a point. This was the unmistakable silhouette of an RPG-7 grenade-launcher, a weapon beloved by terrorists, guerrillas and freedom fighters the world over for its ability to take out small buildings, armoured vehicles and even helicopters. It was, by some distance, the most precious single item in the entire village.

As Killaman's forces converged on Carver, Justus and the girl, a Bell JetRanger was skimming over the hills to the west of the Zambezi.

'For fuck's sake, man, can't you make this heap fly any faster?' Morrison was shouting at the pilot.

'Forget it, Flattie, I'm maxing it already,' he replied. 'And if you keep yelling in my ear, putting me off my stroke, I will make a mistake and hit a tree or a fucking power line. And then we will all be dead. But I tell you what, boet, it will be worth it just to get a little peace. Ek se, you are one loud item.'

19

Silent Death was driving the Hilux that was leading the pursuit of Carver, Justus and the girl. He had followed the road the VW had taken, but had been too far behind to catch sight of his prey. Then he heard the shrill clamour of the warehouse alarm. He looked across at Killaman and asked, 'Is that them?'

'Slow down,' Killaman ordered him. The commander leaned out through the passenger window, almost like a dog sniffing the air. He pulled his head back inside the cab and nodded. 'Yes, the warehouse. They are there. Follow them.'

Silent Death turned off the main road and drove down a short incline towards the warehouse.

'Stop!' snapped Killaman.

Up ahead, both men could see the VW parked by the warehouse. There did not appear to be anyone in it.

'Right,' he went on. 'Let us make these drunken apes earn their money.'

He got out and faced the men in the back of the truck. 'I need two volunteers,' he said. Then he pointed at two of them in quick succession. 'You and you. Check out the van.' Killaman illustrated his orders with hand signals, to ensure that there could be no possibility of misunderstanding.

Both men glanced across the expanse of open road between them and the van. There was no cover at all aside from the wooden poles that supported the lights round the football pitch or carried power cables to the lights and the warehouse. The poles were very slender and at least fifteen metres apart. The men looked back at Killaman, eyes wide.

He grinned. 'So you lose your enthusiasm. OK, no money for you. I will choose someone else.'

The men immediately leaped down from the Hilux and set off nervously down the road.

'Make sure that the van is always between you and the open door,' Killaman called after them. 'If there is anyone inside the warehouse, they will not be able to shoot you. If anyone fires from the van, we will cover you.'

The men seemed to take heart. As Killaman and his remaining troops took up positions behind the Hilux and those with weapons aimed them towards the VW, the two unwilling volunteers jogged more purposefully to the first pole. There was no response from the van. The men emerged from behind the pole and started running again. Still nothing.

When they had got to within twenty metres of the van without any sign of hostile activity, the men relaxed. They stopped running and dodging and just walked straight towards the VW, their guns held diagonally across their bodies, ready to be used in an instant if required.

Ironically, their comrades left behind at the Hilux now became more tense. It was bad enough thinking that two of their number might be killed. Even worse, however, was the possibility that they might survive and be the first to get to the woman and the bounty she would earn them.

The driver's door was nearest to the two men's line of march. They walked right up to it. One of them pressed his face to the glass and tried to peer into the interior of the van. He put his hand to the handle and tugged. It was unlocked.

Back at the Hilux, Killaman suddenly realized what was about to happen. He shouted, 'Do not . . .'

Before he could finish the sentence, the car door had swung open. There was a length of fishing line, invisible in the darkness, inside the VW. One end was tied to the inside door handle. The other end was attached to the pin of one of Carver's grenades, which was jammed against the runners beneath the passenger seat. As the door moved, the line pulled tight and the pin was tugged out of the grenade.

'. . . open the door!'

Killaman's voice drowned out the faint chink of the pin hitting the metal sill at the bottom of the door. The two men jostled each other in their eagerness to get inside the vehicle. One of them said 'Hey!' in protest at being pushed out of the way.

And then their voices and their lives were obliterated by the deafening blast of the grenade that blew them both to pieces and sent shrapnel from the grenade, fragments of the VW and minced human body parts back up the way they'd come, rattling and splattering against the side of the Hilux and scaring the hell out of the men cowering behind it.

'Get up, you cowards!' Killaman screamed. 'You gutless sons of jackals and hyenas! Follow me!'

He walked towards the burning VW, not looking round, trusting in his own powers of command as Silent Death and the other men traipsed after him.

The flames were casting an orange glow across the dirty white walls of the warehouse. Killaman walked straight past the VW and up to the warehouse door. There he stopped. He put out a hand behind him, palm up, stopping his men in their tracks. They looked on with a mix of fear and curiosity as Killaman got down on his haunches, looked very carefully at the opening, and then smiled.

In the light from the fire, the nylon filament stretched from the door to the warehouse wall was clearly visible. Killaman under-stood exactly how the booby-trap had been rigged; he had done it often enough himself. The grenade would be by the wall somewhere.

He gently raised his left hand and took hold of the line, close to the door. He pulled it taut, towards the wall, lessening the tension on the pin of the grenade. Then he reached into his trouser pocket and took out the black handle of a flick-knife that had served him well in many a bar and backstreet fight. He pressed the switch and a vicious six-inch blade sprang from the handle.

Killaman cut the fishing line between his hand and the door. He let go of the line and swung the door fully open. There was a light switch on the wall near him. When he turned it on, the empty warehouse was fully illuminated. And so was the grenade just inside the entrance, tied to a sand-filled firebucket with the same kind of fishing line that had linked its pin to the door.

Killaman took the grenade, then turned back to his men.

'There is no one here,' he said.

He looked around, trying to sense where the girl and her rescuers might have gone. His eyes caught a glint of flickering amber caused by the firelight playing on the crossbar of the nearest goal. Killaman thought about the football pitch. It suddenly struck him why anyone needing a speedy extraction would head in its direction.

He was grinning when he spoke again to his men: 'But they are not far away.'

20

In the darkness of the concrete changing room, Carver spoke over his communications system. 'Where are you, Morrison?'

'Ten clicks out from you, a little over three minutes' flying time. Can you give us your exact position?'

'We're by the football pitch, as planned. Did you see the explosion just now?'

'Nah man, there is still a ridge of hills between us and you. It'll be a couple of minutes before we can establish visual contact.'

'OK, well, when you get over the hills, you should see the fire from Justus's van.'

Morrison's laughter, filled with the savage glee coursing through him at the promise of combat, cackled in Carver's earpiece. 'What? You fucked up his precious Kombi? Ah shit, that must be one unhappy munt.'

'He's fine. So's the girl. Now listen, there's a cluster of small buildings approximately one hundred and twenty metres northeast of the burning van. That's where we are. The closer you can get to that the better. There's a lighting pole by the corner of the pitch.

Your pilot doesn't want to get his disc anywhere near that. Other than that, nothing to worry about.'

'Apart from all the buggers trying to kill us, you mean.'

'Yeah, apart from them.'

The helicopter wasn't the only thing being drawn towards the fire. The men running from the village, whose numbers had swollen as news of the night's excitement spread, picked up their pace as they followed the route of the two vehicles off the main road and down towards the warehouse. Some of them were shouting. A couple fired their guns in the air.

The noise distracted Killaman, just as he was issuing orders to his men. He was not happy to see what was coming towards him. The last thing he needed was an ill-disciplined rabble getting in the way and complicating an operation that was already difficult enough as it was. Then he saw the silhouette of the grenade-launcher. That changed everything.

'Stop!' he shouted, bringing the village men to a halt just short of the flaming VW. He pointed at the man with the RPG. 'You! Come here. I have special need of you.'

The man stepped forward, a huge grin across his face, proudly carrying the weapon that had long been his pride and joy.

'The rest of you form a line right across the football pitch over there. All the way across, evenly spaced.'

Killaman motioned to Silent Death to organize them.

'You will proceed at walking pace down the pitch,' he said once the line had been formed. 'The rest of us will follow you. You will look very carefully for any sign of the white girl and the men who took her. Do not be alarmed if one of you is shot. That will simply demonstrate that we are getting close.'

It was a clear night with the moon almost full. Carver had Justus's thermal-imaging binoculars slung round his neck, but he did not need them to spot the men coming down the football pitch, making progress with the sluggish inexorability of zombies.

The building where he, Justus and Zalika were holed up con-sisted of one main changing room with slatted wooden benches pressed up against the walls along the longest sides. At one end, crude breezeblock partitions had been used to create a rank-smelling toilet cubicle and a shower area whose rusted shower-heads and dusty tiled floor suggested it had long been unused. There were no windows, just a simple skylight to provide illumination, with half the glass missing from its panes. The only access came from a single doorway, directly opposite the shower, accessed via a porch recessed into the building.

Carver had left the other two inside and was now crouched in the porch. It gave him just enough cover to be able to observe what was happening out on the playing field without giving away his own position. Soon, though, the enemy would be on him.

There was a crackle in his earpiece, followed by Morrison's voice: 'With you in about a minute. We have a visual on the van. Looks like you've got company.'

'Are you armed? Can you give me any suppressing fire?'

'Oh ja, don't you worry about that.'

Carver could hear the faint sound of the approaching chopper now. He raised the binoculars to his face and swept as much of the horizon as he could manage without exposing himself to sight. It took two passes before he spotted the helicopter, coming towards him at tree-skimming height over open country beyond the far side of the pitch. The course would bring it directly over the stand at right angles to the direction in which the line of men was going, but slightly behind it. Carver could see exactly what Morrison had in mind. He was going to run along the line, getting a clear shot at every single one of them.

By the time the chopper arrived, though, it might be too late. The nearest men were barely twenty metres away from the shack now. In a matter of seconds they would be on him. It was time to adjust the odds a little bit more in his favour.

Carver could not afford to waste a single round. He aimed at the man at the nearest end of the line and fired a single shot. The bullet hit its target in the right temple and exploded out of the back of his head. Before he had even hit the ground, Carver had traversed and fired at the second target a further ten metres away. It took two rounds to put him down, and the time wasted by the second of those shots allowed man number three to shout out in warning and fling himself to the ground as another bullet fizzed through the air where his body had been. The man had not seen Carver, but just from the way his comrades had been killed he had a general idea of where the shots must have come from. He also had a gun.

He emptied an entire magazine blazing away at the cluster of buildings by the side of the pitch.

Carver ducked back inside the porch.

The helicopter sounded louder in the distance. Very soon it would be over the field. Now all he had to do was make sure that he, Justus and, most importantly, Zalika were still alive when it got there.

21 _____

Carver's movement caught Killaman's eye. He did not panic. He had come there to watch a football match a couple of days earlier and knew the layout of the ground and its buildings. Nor was he going to be forced into anything hasty or ill-considered by the sound of the helicopter engine. He had already factored that element into his calculations.

Lying on the ground, he summoned Silent Death to drag himself across the dirt towards him, then explained what he wanted. 'They are in the building nearest us, the home changing room. See it?'

Silent Death followed his commander's pointing finger and nodded.

'Good,' said Killaman. 'So this is what you must do.'

A few seconds later, Killaman's ragtag platoon started blazing away at Carver's position again, forcing him to stay hidden as Silent Death rose from the ground and padded away, body bent almost double, jogging off the side of the football pitch and making a sweeping flanking movement round the back of the buildings.

*

In the changing room, Justus was trying to keep Zalika Stratten from descending into total nervous collapse. Her whole body was shaking, and though she seemed to be trying to speak between her sobs, it was impossible to make out what she was saying.

'It's all right, Miss,' he kept repeating. 'Not long now. Soon have you out of here.'

If this had been his own daughter, he would have wrapped her in his arms and stroked her hair to calm her. But he did not dare do that now. Just the touch of a man could send this girl over the brink.

There was a reason Silent Death had acquired his name. Even among men who took great pride in their ability to melt into the scenery, move undetected and attack without warning, his talents stood out. Tonight, however, his prey had no means of seeing him, and with so many gunshots and the ever-increasing clatter of a helicopter engine to cover them, a herd of elephants could have walked up to the building unheard. Carver, positioned in the porch, had no idea that one of the enemy was just a few feet behind him, moving round the back of the shack and climbing with feline agility up its wall.

Silent Death reached the roof and looked down through the skylight into the changing room. He pulled the pin from the grenade Killaman had given him and dropped it through the broken glass, on to the concrete floor of the changing room. Then he slid to the edge of the roof and jumped back down to the ground.

'Grenade!' shouted Justus as the metal sphere, not much bigger than a cricket ball, skittered across the concrete.

He grabbed Zalika, all previous inhibitions dropped in an instant.

Justus knew he had less than four seconds to save their lives. But faced with mortal danger, the mind has a remarkable ability to slow the passage of time, and it seemed to Justus that he had an age in which to consider his options.

He saw at once that the grenade was intended not to kill them –

Zalika was too valuable for that – but to drive them out into the open, where she could be recaptured. There was no point trying to throw the grenade back out through the skylight. The risk of missing the gap in the broken glass was too great.

That left only one option.

With one hand clinging to his gun and the other wrapped round Zalika, Justus ran for the shower cubicle. He took three quick strides and then dived, throwing them both through the gap in the breezeblock partition. The air was driven from his lungs as they hit the tiled floor. Gasping for breath, Justus rolled away from the opening, still clinging on to the girl.

The grenade exploded, filling the empty changing room with white-hot shards of shrapnel that destroyed the wooden bench and cut into the breezeblock walls like a million deadly wasp stings.

The shower room was sheltered from the worst of the blast. Even so, it left Justus deafened and dazed. His mind, so sharp and fast just seconds before, now seemed incapable of functioning at all, and his eyesight was dulled by the thick cloud of choking dust that filled the air.

Outside, Silent Death scampered back up the wall of the building and contemplated the hole where the skylight had been before the grenade blew it away. Watching out for the ragged, saw-like edges of the shredded corrugated iron, he clambered across the roof and slipped noiselessly down through the hole into the fog of dust.

Justus did not hear him come. He simply saw the outline of a gun-barrel emerging through the dust by the entrance to the shower, followed by a man's arm. Operating now on pure fighting instinct, without any conscious thought Justus wrenched his shotgun free from the weight of Zalika's body, raised it one-handed and fired.

The concentrated blast of a twelve-gauge cartridge ripped Silent Death's left hand clean away, taking his AK-47 with it. Now he was not so silent. He screamed in pain, though the high-pitched cry of agony was little more than a whisper to Justus's battered eardrums.

Justus scrambled to his feet, pumped another round into the chamber of his gun and stepped over to the gap in the breezeblock partition. Through the slowly clearing cloud of dust he could see Silent Death bent over, his right hand clinging to a ragged stump of arm from which a geyser of blood was pumping.

Justus put him out of his misery with a second round that hit Silent Death in the chest, lifted him off his feet and flung him against the wall like a doll thrown by an angry child.

From outside there came the sound of another detonation, followed by the angry chatter of small-arms fire.

Justus hurried back to find Zalika slowly rising from the floor. He could see her eyes widen as she spotted the severed hand, still clinging to its weapon, lying on the floor. He got down on his haunches and looked directly at her.

'Are you hurt?' he asked.

Zalika shook her head.

'Good.'

Justus helped her to her feet and led her back into the ruined changing room. In the faint moonlight there was no colour anywhere, just a ghost world of black and grey. Zalika's hand went to her mouth at the sight of the intruder: his lolling head; his staring sightless eyes; the dark gaping hole that had been punched into his body.

The two of them made their way towards the door.

Justus opened it a fraction and peered out through the crack, expecting to see Carver waiting for him in the porch.

There was no one there.

Somewhere out in the darkness a man was screaming. Not far away a blazing flare was belching crimson smoke across the field. The helicopter's approach was getting louder with every second.

But Samuel Carver had gone.

22

Seconds after Killaman sent Silent Death on his mission, he arranged a distraction to keep Carver's attention away from anything that might be happening in the building behind him. He sent a man running directly across Carver's line of fire. His orders were simple: run like hell till you are level with the porch, throw yourself to the ground, then fire at the man in the doorway, who will now be completely exposed to your shots.

The man started running.

Carver took aim like a punter at a shooting gallery and hit his target before he could dive to the ground.

A second man ran the gauntlet.

He had flung himself forward, like a rugby three-quarter diving for the try-line, when Carver's shot caught him in the side, ploughing into his intestines. He lay on the ground, screaming in agony and crying out for his mother.

After that, there were no more runners.

Through the man's screams, Carver could hear Morrison's voice in his earpiece again: 'We got problems. First, you are in severe danger of being outflanked.'

'I'd noticed.'

'Second, there is a man on the ground, behind the first line of troops, carrying an RPG. He hits us, we're fucked.'

'Can you get him first?'

'Too risky. You will have to do it.'

'Where is this guy?'

'Right in the middle of the field, the centre circle, behind the first line of men.'

'And where are you?'

'Holding pattern, six hundred metres out.'

'Then come on in.'

'Nah way, man.'

'Just do it, now. That's an order.'

If Morrison had any reply to that, Carver didn't hear it. From behind him came the echoing blast of a grenade going off in a confined space. What the bloody hell had happened in there?

There was no time to answer that question now. The chopper would come in at around fifty metres a second. Anyone who knew how to operate an RPG would wait until it was between one and two hundred metres away, almost impossible to miss, before they opened fire. That gave Carver an absolute maximum of ten seconds, probably less. Saving the chopper was his immediate priority. And that meant no distractions.

He took the emergency flare, pulled the tag and hurled it out on to the field, throwing blind. The moment it was gone, he took out his last grenade, counted two, stepped out of the porch, thanked God for the hellish red smoke now drifting between him and the enemy, and threw.

He ducked back inside the porch. Half a second later, the grenade detonated.

Before the sound of the explosion had died away, Carver was up and running.

A modern anti-personnel grenade will kill any unprotected

human within a five-metre radius, and either kill or severely wound anyone within fifteen. Carver had therefore given himself a thirty-metre-wide window of opportunity.

He was going flat out, forgetting the pain from his rib, the choking billows of chemical smoke from the flare and the weight of the weapon in his hands. He paused, turned to face a threat, raised the MP5 and fired twice at a shadowy target. Then he was off and running again.

Carver burst out of the smoke and saw a knot of men ahead of him, apparently unharmed by the grenade. They were shouting, bringing their guns to bear on him. Behind them he could just make out the grenade-tipped barrel of the RPG, and beyond that the outline of the helicopter coming in low and flat over a copse of trees.

He did not stop running, shooting as he went. He was beyond any rational thought, entirely caught up in the frenzy of battle. He was dimly aware that he'd taken a hit in his left arm, though there was no pain there as yet.

He saw two of the men in front of him go down.

He sensed rather than heard the click as the firing pin of his gun came down on an empty chamber.

He felt the cracking of broken bones as he smashed the stock of the MP5 into the face of the last man standing between him and the grenade-launcher.

And then he was throwing himself with an inarticulate scream of rage at the man crouching on one knee holding the RPG, and a jet of flame was shooting from the rear end of its barrel, scorching Carver's skin as he hit the man and his weapon. He knocked them both to the ground, smashing his own head against the metal body of the launcher and sending the RPG shooting low across the football field before it hit the modest little stand and blew it to smithereens.

Over the next few seconds, Carver lay dazed and winded on the ground, battered by the downdraft that told him the helicopter was landing. He was aware of the RPG operator wriggling out from under him and running away as fast as his legs would carry him. He did not, however, see Killaman emerge from the tangle of bodies behind him, drag himself upright, pull out the flick-knife and stagger towards his unprotected back.

23

Before the skids of the helicopter's undercarriage had hit the ground, Justus was racing across the open ground towards it, urging Zalika to keep pace with him as he went. He tried to keep his body between hers and anyone who might still be out there, but only a few wild, aimless shots were fired in their direction. The downdraft had cleared away the smoke from the flare and it looked as though whoever had been attacking them had lost the will to fight.

Flattie Morrison was standing in the open doorway of the helicopter firing bursts at the retreating figures to speed them on their way. He stopped shooting and reached one hand down to help Zalika up into the passenger compartment.

Justus was next in line. He turned his head to look back across the football pitch.

'Get in!' Morrison shouted.

Justus ignored him. Instead he sprinted away from the chopper, back towards the remaining whispers of smoke.

Morrison made Zalika comfortable, then, still standing, turned back to follow Justus's progress.

Now he knew what his old comrade had seen. Right in the middle of the pitch a black-clad body Morrison instantly recognized as Carver's was lying face-down, moving slightly, as though retching or gasping for air.

Behind the body, another man was staggering towards it with a knife.

Two more steps and the knife would be plunged into Carver's defenceless back. Justus stopped some forty or fifty metres away from the knifeman, raised his shotgun, took aim and fired; pumped more rounds into his chamber; pulled the trigger until his magazine was empty and his target blown away.

Morrison gave a wry smile. His wartime lessons had clearly left their mark: fire till the last round is gone. And only then ask questions.

Justus jogged up to the knifeman's dead body, gave it a quick look, then bent down and helped Carver to his feet. He draped Carver's right arm across his shoulder and the two of them staggered back across the field.

Morrison raised his gun and swept it from side to side, looking for any possible threats to the two men, but none came. The field behind them was empty, save for the bodies of the dead and those too wounded to walk, crawl or drag themselves away.

Now Justus and Carver were by the helicopter door, and Morrison was taking Carver and hauling him aboard.

So he only had one hand on his gun. And his eyes were focused on Carver, not the field.

He did not see the man lying not far from the changing-room building – the man Carver had hit and wounded barely a minute earlier – summon up the last of his strength, raise himself to his elbows, point his gun and fire.

'Fuck,' said Flattie Morrison, almost in surprise.

Then he keeled forward, half in and half out of the helicopter, blood seeping across the back of his shirt.

Justus raised his gun, holding it like a pistol, but there was no need to fire. The wounded man had already slumped back to the ground.

Justus dropped the shotgun and grabbed hold of Morrison's body. By the time he had dragged it inside the cabin, the pilot had already taken off and was heading for the hills and the safe embrace of the Zambezi river gorge.

Carver looked round the cabin. Zalika was strapped into one of the seats, still disoriented but physically unharmed. Morrison was either dead, or about to be. Justus looked exhausted, caught by the comedown that hits a fighting man when the adrenalin has drained away. He raised a hand and smiled weakly when Carver caught his eye.

'Nice work,' said Carver.

Then he, too, slumped back, mentally and physically spent but – the only thing that mattered – still alive.

24

The first light of dawn was glowing on the eastern flanks of Table Mountain as the executive jet began its approach into Cape Town. The doctor Wendell Klerk had sent with it had formally pronounced Flattie Morrison dead before they took off from Tete. In the first hour of the flight he had administered sedatives to Zalika Stratten and done what he could to stitch up the wound in Carver's left bicep, and ease the pain in his ribs.

Before the sedatives had sent her under, Zalika had asked to speak to Carver.

In the cramped aisle of the passenger compartment, he crouched down beside the head of the settee on which she had been laid out.

'I just wanted to say thank you,' she began.

'That's all right. I'm sorry it turned out the way it did. You shouldn't have had to go through something like that. But we didn't have a choice. We had to move in when we did.'

She reached up and gripped Carver's wrist. Her voice was an urgent whisper and there was an anxious, pleading look in her sapphire eyes. 'I understand. But please, I'm begging you, please don't tell my uncle, you know, that Moses took his clothes off and . . . you know. It's just, well, it's not something I want to talk about.'

Carver said nothing. He thought of the report he was due to write, accounting for all of his actions. He'd attacked ahead of schedule, and that would be hard to explain if he didn't mention that Mabeki had been about to sexually assault Zalika. But surely she had the right to some privacy. If she didn't want people to know, why should he make an issue of it?

'Don't worry,' Carver said, 'I won't tell a soul. Ever. That's a promise.'

She looked at him with sleepy eyes and nodded, as if satisfied he was telling the truth. Then she sank back down on to the settee. Her eyelids slowly fell shut. And as she drifted off to sleep, Carver was sure that he could detect, for the very first time, the faintest hint of contentment on Zalika Stratten's face.

When Carver arrived in Cape Town, the news of Zalika Stratten's rescue had not yet hit the South African media. But the *Cape Times* was running a story from Sindele. A Malemban government spokesman had announced that all the Stratten family properties in Malemba had been appropriated by the state, including their many farms and the Stratten Reserve. The farmlands would, the spokesman said, be divided between thousands of war veterans and their families. The reserve, however, would continue to operate as a tourist attraction and a valuable source of foreign currency. 'In honour of its importance to the economy, and the great value that he places upon our country's natural heritage, President Gushungo, the Father of the Nation himself, will personally supervise the transfer of the reserve into the people's hands. He will be using the Strattens' former estate house, and the land around it, as his personal head-quarters during this process.' When questioned, the spokesman assured reporters that the President's occupation of what had been, arguably, the most beautiful private home in Malemba was a purely temporary issue. In time, it too would be handed over for the benefit of all the people of Malemba.

*

As Carver was driven away to give Wendell Klerk his account of Zalika's rescue, his mind turned to Justus Iluko. They'd said good-bye at Tete airport.

'Thanks,' Carver had said, 'you know . . .'

He hadn't spelled it out. Both men knew that Justus had saved his life. There was no need to make a big deal about it.

'No problem,' Justus had replied.

'Keep in touch, yeah?'

'Sure,' the Malemban had said, though his smile suggested he thought it was pretty unlikely.

Carver had given him a contact number anyway, and Justus had responded with the address of his family farm. It hadn't seemed significant at the time. But now, sitting in the limo riding into Cape Town from the airport, Carver realized he'd been given a chance to show his appreciation for everything Justus had done.

Carver's first thought was simply to wire him a hundred grand in US dollars – just a fraction of his own fee for the job. But it didn't take five seconds' thought to realize that in a small rural community in Malemba that kind of money would cause as many problems as it solved. People would look on their newly rich neigh-bour with a festering mixture of envy, greed and resentment. Far better to give him, say, ten up front, but then set up a discreet trust fund for the children to make sure they got a good education. Justus would prefer that too: those kids meant everything to him. Carver made a mental note to call his banker as soon as he got back to Geneva.

Shortly after dawn, the first police arrived in Chitongo and set to work examining the building where Zalika Stratten had been held, the warehouse and its surroundings, and the area around the foot-ball pitch. A uniformed constable was picking his way through a group of four bodies, all lying within metres of one another, when he stopped and frowned as a fractional movement caught his eye. He got down on his knees next to a body and leaned over it, his head tilted so that one ear was just above the body's mouth. Then he gasped, jumped back up to his feet and shouted out, 'Doctor, doctor! Over here! One of them is still alive!'

Part 2
Now

25

The second time Wendell Klerk summoned Carver, he phrased it as an invitation: a weekend at Campden Hall, his estate in Suffolk, seventy miles north of London. 'I'm having a few people over. I think you'd enjoy it,' he said. 'If there's a better chef or a finer wine-cellar in any private home in England, I've yet to see them. And I've got a shooting set-up that's second to none.'

Whatever the reason Klerk was so keen to see him, Carver didn't think it had much to do with good company or fine wine. But the Mozambique assignment had given him a lot of respect for the man. In a business filled with double-crossing bastards, Klerk had told it straight, kept his word and paid in full when the job was done. That was a decade ago now, but there was no harm in at least listening to what he had to say.

'Sounds good,' Carver said.

'Excellent. You still based in Geneva? I'll send a plane to pick you up.'

The plane duly arrived one Friday afternoon in May, and a uniformed chauffeur driving a Bentley Arnage limousine collected

Carver from the airport and drove him to Campden Hall. A butler opened a front door that nestled beneath the portico of classical Ionic columns that dominated the building's Palladian facade. When Carver stepped into the marble-floored grand hall, from which a double staircase rose through the heart of the house, one of the most striking women he had ever seen in his life was waiting there to greet him.

She walked towards him with a click-clack of teetering patent black heels and a smile that proclaimed there was nothing, absolutely nothing in the whole wide world that could possibly delight her more than saying hello to Samuel Carver. Her glossy auburn hair floated around her shoulders like a slow-motion close-up in a shampoo commercial. Below the breasts that pressed against the soft cream silk of her blouse a broad black belt – patent, to match her shoes – emphasized the slenderness of her waist, while an apparently demure knee-length black pinstriped skirt was somehow cut to suggest every inch of the long, slender thighs sheathed in sheer black stockings that swayed beneath it.

'Hello, I'm Alice, Mr Klerk's personal assistant,' she said.

Her voice was soft, pliant, almost submissive; but for a fleeting moment Carver caught a much sharper glint in her hazel eyes and the hint of an ironic twist to the corners of her mouth. Alice, he decided, knew precisely the effect she had on men and liked to play with it a little.

She paused, as if daring him to make some cheap crack about the nature of the assistance she offered, then went on: 'Mr Klerk is so sorry he can't be here to meet you himself. He's tied up on a call. But if you follow me, I'll do my best to make you feel at home.'

Alice turned and led the way across the hall, proving as she went that her rear view was almost as good as her front. She showed him into a richly decorated drawing room that, in a nod to long-gone imperial traditions, combined very English proportions and furniture with rugs, paintings and objects suggestive of wilder, distant lands.

'Can I get you a drink, Mr Carver?' Alice asked.

'Scotch, please, Blue Label if you've got it.'

'Of course. Ice? Soda water?'

'No thanks, neat will do fine.'

She pressed a button on one of the side-tables and a second later the butler reappeared and was given Carver's order.

'Terence will bring your drink in a moment,' Alice said as he departed. 'I'll go and see what Mr Klerk is getting up to. I'm sure he won't want to keep you waiting.'

She left with what Carver felt certain was a deliberate twitch of her pinstriped backside just before the door closed behind her. Less than a minute later, Terence entered with a silver tray on which stood two whisky snifters, a full lead crystal decanter and a small glass jug of water with two more glasses. He placed the tray on a table and poured out a glass of whisky and another of water. Then he stepped to one side, saying nothing, giving no indication whatever of how he expected Carver to proceed.

Carver could tell that Terence, like so many servants, was a crashing snob. This was his way of testing Carver's right to be served.

'Thank you, Terence,' said Carver, with charming condescension.

There weren't many times he thanked his adoptive parents for sending him off to the overpriced, emotionally stunting, frequently abusive confines of an old-fashioned private boarding school, but this was one of them. He had at least been taught how to conduct himself properly, and, when his education failed to provide the correct solution to a social problem, to have the self-confidence to fake one.

Ignoring the snifter, Carver took a sip of water to clear his palate. Only then did he lift the glass of whisky, gently swirl the honey-coloured liquid and take a long, appreciative sniff of its smoky, floral aromas. Finally he lifted the glass and took a sip. 'Perfect,' he said, once he had savoured its complex flavours. 'That will be all, thank you.'

Terence gave a fractional nod, acknowledging that Carver would now be treated as a gentleman rather than a mere hired hand, and disappeared once again.

Taking his whisky, Carver strolled across to the ornate marble fireplace that was the centrepiece of the room. It was flanked on either side by two mighty elephant's tusks that stood almost to Carver's full height.

Above the fireplace hung an oil painting at least five feet tall and wide enough to cover the entire chimney breast. It was a head-on portrait of a single bull elephant striding across the savannah. The artist had somehow perfectly captured not just its appearance, but its spirit. Carver could almost feel the earth tremble at the elephant's approach, as though it might at any moment break free from the imprisonment of the picture and step right out into the room.

'Magnificent, isn't it?'

Wendell Klerk's low rumble of a voice had, if anything, become even deeper in the years since Carver had first heard it.

He turned to look at his host. Klerk had acquired a few more lines on his face and the curly hair had gone from coal black to steely grey, but the man's pugnacious air of vitality and determination was undimmed.

'Good to see you again, Sam,' Klerk said, taking Carver's hand in a crushing grip. 'Glad you could make it. I want you to know that I have not forgotten what you did for me and my family. I can never repay you. Never.'

Carver gave a wry smile, thinking of the massive fee that had been deposited in his Geneva account. 'You made a pretty good stab at it, Mr Klerk.'

The tycoon laughed. 'Ja, that's true! But hey, call me Wendell. You are my guest, in my home. I don't want to stand on ceremony.'

Klerk went across to the table where the drinks had been left. He ignored the water, poured himself a deep measure of whisky, downed it in one and refilled his glass before rejoining Carver by the fireplace.

'David Shepherd did that for me – finest wildlife artist in the world,' Klerk said, looking up at the painting. 'What's really remarkable, he was working entirely from photographs. The old bull was dead. I had shot him – quite legally I should add. Those are his tusks: one hundred and eleven, and one hundred and thirteen pounds respectively. We were in northeast Namibia, the Caprivi Strip. I tell you, man, when I came back to Cape Town with those beauties, no one could bloody believe it. Mind you, they cost me the love of a fine young woman.'

'How so?'

'Her name was Renée. Beautiful girl, but she hated the idea of me shooting such a magnificent creature. I tried to explain that it is vital to cull the herds for conservation purposes. If elephant populations are allowed to expand too much, they will destroy their habitat through overeating. Then there is nothing left for them, or other animals, or even the human population, and that is when things turn nasty. It is far better for everyone to manage the elephants through controlled hunting. It even provides legal ivory so that there is less opportunity for poachers to make money.'

'What did Renée say to that?'

'She said she didn't care. Killing animals was wrong and she couldn't love a man who could slaughter a defenceless elephant. I said to her, try wandering up to an angry bull elephant and see how defenceless it is. How would you like one of those tusks jammed right through your guts?'

'I bet she didn't like that.'

'No, she certainly did not! But my argument still stands. Sometimes the herd must be culled. Sometimes the rogue male must be destroyed. Do you understand what I'm saying, Sam?'

'Sure.'

'Good,' said Klerk. 'Because there is someone I want you to cull.'

26 _____

Carver closed his eyes for a second and sighed. 'You know I don't do that kind of thing any more,' he said. 'I quit a long time ago.'

Klerk nodded. 'That's what I heard, yes.'

'So why are you asking?'

'Because this is a special case,' said Klerk. He placed his whisky glass on the mantelpiece. When he spoke again, his hands were in front of him, palms up in something close to supplication. 'Listen, I truly believe that what I am about to ask you to do will make the world a better place. You could be saving tens, even hundreds of thousands of lives. Millions of people will be freer, healthier and more prosperous.'

Carver took another sip of his drink. 'And how, precisely, will I do that?'

Klerk looked him straight in the eyes. 'By killing that mad, tyrannical old bastard President Henderson Gushungo of Malemba.'

'Why bother? The man's in his eighties. He'll die soon anyway.'

'That's what people said when he was in his seventies,' Klerk replied. 'But in the past ten years, while people have waited for him to go, the whole country has fallen apart. We're talking an annual inflation rate of eleven million per cent. It is literally cheaper to wipe your arse with Malemban dollars than buy toilet paper. You know, they just printed a one-hundred-trillion-dollar note, and it's worth less than the scrap of paper it's printed on.'

'Is that why you want him dead, to lower the rate of inflation? You sure the reason isn't more personal than that?'

'You know, Carver, that's what I like about you: there's no bull-shit. Ja, I admit it, I'd like to see Gushungo dead for what he did to my family. He ordered the attack on the Stratten Reserve. The deaths there were down to him and he must pay for them in his own blood. That debt is long overdue. But I mean what I say about the shit he's heaped on Malemba, too.'

Klerk's right hand was clenched now, just the index finger stick-ing out, jabbing at the air between them as he spoke.

'My homeland used to be the breadbasket of Africa, but vast areas of rich, fertile farmland·are now just dust and weeds. The only thing stopping mass starvation is food aid from the West. The average life expectancy is just over forty-five years. More than one person in ten has HIV. There's been an epidemic of cholera. And on top of all that, the people have to put up with oppression, rigged elections, forced eviction from their homes and resettlement in squalid camps miles from bloody anywhere. I tell you, man, it's a disaster.'

'I get it,' said Carver. 'The man's an evil tyrant. But that's what they said about Iraq. And killing Saddam didn't do much good, did it? You take out the bastard at the top, you don't get a sudden out-break of peace and love. You just get some other bastard taking his place. Or even worse, a whole bunch of other bastards all fighting for the top spot while innocent civilians get caught in the crossfire. And if you do it illegally it just makes matters even worse. Why would Malemba be any different?'

'Because there is an alternative: a genuine democrat waiting for the chance to govern the country properly and peacefully. I presume you've heard of Patrick Tshonga, head of the Popular Freedom Movement?'

'Is he that guy who keeps winning elections without ever getting power, the one whose son was killed in a light aircraft? The authorities said the crash was an accident, as I recall.' Carver gave a short, humourless laugh. 'Oh yeah, I know all about that kind of accident.'

Klerk took out his mobile phone and pressed a speed-dial number. 'Could you bring in our other guest please, my dear? And the laptop, too, if you don't mind.'

The two men waited in silence for a minute or so. Then the door opened and Alice walked in, holding the slender aluminium body of a MacBook Air under one arm like a futuristic evening-bag. She was accompanied by a tall, powerfully built black man whose shaved head was dusted with a stubble of greying hair. His huge shoulders seemed to strain at the fabric of his suit and his neck bulged over the collar of his shirt. He looked like a retired NFL player, the kind of guy who'd played in the trenches, slugging it out on the line of scrimmage. If he'd been allowed to claim his country by solitary combat, the President wouldn't have stood a chance.

'Good evening, Mr Carver,' he said. 'My name is Patrick Tshonga. I have the privilege of leading the struggle for democracy in Malemba. I presume Mr Klerk has already made the request that was the reason for inviting you here tonight?'

'Yes, he has,' said Carver as the ever reliable Terence slipped into the room bearing more glasses and fresh supplies of whisky. 'And I was about to tell him how I used to think I was making the world a better place by taking out the bad guys. Then I realized that it made no difference. The world carried on just like it had before. And I had more deaths on my conscience.'

Klerk gave a snort of disgust. 'Don't get wishy-washy on me now, man. You weren't this squeamish when you rescued my niece. You plugged plenty of the bastards then, and a bloody good thing too.'

Tshonga accepted the whisky that Terence offered him, gave a nod that indicated both thanks and dismissal, then said, 'No,

Wendell, Mr Carver has a point. It is one thing for us to wish an evil man dead, it is quite another to be the one who actually has to kill him. But think of all the people who have died because of this man. Do they not deserve retribution? Think of the people who will die because of him. Do they not deserve to be saved? On their behalf, Mr Carver, I implore you, rid the world of this monster.'

'Suppose I did. Suppose you and your party took power. What then? Any way you dress it up, you're planning the murder of a head of state. Doesn't sound like a good precedent to be setting if you plan on taking his job. Someone might decide to get rid of you the same way. And you claim to be a democrat. What kind of democrat becomes president by assassination?'

'The kind who has discovered that it's not enough to win elections,' said Tshonga. 'I have tried to do this in the proper fashion. I have fought elections honestly, even though Gushungo sends his thugs to disrupt my rallies and attack my supporters; even though his men threaten and intimidate voters; even though the final counts are corrupt; even though it cost me my son. I have done that and won a majority, against all the odds. But then he refuses to accept the result. He denies the truth. He spits in the face of the electorate. And no one has the power to stop him. Believe me, Mr Carver, if there were a way to remove the President by legal means, I would find it and pursue it. But there is not. I have therefore been forced to conclude that the only way to save the lives of our people, who are dying every day of disease and starvation, is to kill the man who is causing all this suffering. And if you think that is wrong, I would ask you: why is it worse to kill one evil man, so that innocent people can be saved, than to let him live and condemn those people to death? Why are their lives worth so much less than his?'

'That's a very powerful argument, Mr Tshonga,' said Carver. 'But I don't hear you making it in public. I don't see the rest of the world's politicians nodding their heads and agreeing. None of you people can afford to be seen to support the assassination of a national leader. So you're asking me to do something you don't even have the guts to talk about outside this room.'

'You are right, Mr Carver, I cannot get up in public and say that the President should die. But that does not make any difference to my argument. It is still better to cause one evil leader to die than to let an entire nation perish.'

Carver nodded, taking the point. 'Maybe, but what about you, Klerk? Don't even try to tell me you're doing this for the good of humankind. What's in it for you?'

'Tantalum,' Klerk replied, with typical bluntness. 'You know what that is?'

'Sounds like some kind of designer drug,' said Carver.

Klerk laughed. 'Well, there are certainly people who are addicted to it. But they are industrialists, not junkies. Tantalum is a very hard, very dense metal. It is a superb conductor of electricity and heat, and incredibly resistant to acid. Mixed with steel, it makes alloys of unusual strength and flexibility. You could say it is a wonder-metal.'

'That's the science lesson,' said Carver. 'How about the economics?'

Klerk smiled. 'Ah, yes, the money. Well, tantalum is particularly useful for the manufacture of components for the electronics industry. There are currently two main producers: Australia and the Congo. But the tantalum mined in the Congo is stained with blood, just like their diamonds. No one would use it if they could get tantalum more easily and acceptably somewhere else.'

'And you think there's tantalum in Malemba?'

'I know there is,' said Klerk. 'There used to be a tantalum mine at a place called Kamativi. It closed about fifteen years ago. But I believe there's still more tantalum down there – a helluva lot more.'

'So you organize the death of the President and get the tantalum in return? Well, it makes a change from liberating countries for oil . . .'

'Is that really such a bad thing, Mr Carver?' asked Tshonga. 'You know, a man in my position receives a great deal of sympathy for his plight. Many important people tell me how they weep for my country. But then they do nothing for us. So I appreciate Mr Klerk's honesty. He makes no secret of what he wants. If he reopens the mine, yes, he will make a great deal of money. But he will also employ many thousands of workers and bring hundreds of millions of dollars into the country to help my government restore our country to health. That sounds to me like a fair deal. I believe the people will think it is a fair deal, too.'

'This is good business all round,' said Klerk. 'So here's my proposition, Sam. I have set up a holding company to handle the tantalum project. I will give you five per cent of its shares if you agree to do the job. Of course, these shares are worthless . . . now. But if you succeed then the mine will be reopened and soon your stake will be enough to set you up in luxury for the rest of your life. And if that isn't enough incentive, I've got one last card up my sleeve.'

Klerk looked away from Carver towards the far corner of the room. Alice had opened a large walnut cabinet to reveal a flatscreen TV, to which the MacBook was now connected. She was standing just in front of the cabinet, holding a remote control.

'Come with me, Sam,' said Klerk, walking across towards her. 'It's time we became reacquainted with a long-lost friend.'

27

A Quick Time file appeared on the TV screen and Alice pressed 'play'. It was video footage, handheld, taken from the crowd at a political rally in Malemba. President Gushungo was giving a speech, ranting at the evils of white politicians in Britain and America. The camera, however, did not linger on him long. Instead the image zoomed and focused on a figure standing just behind the President, to his right-hand side: a tall, bespectacled man in an expensively tailored black suit, cut to fit his scrawny, emaciated frame.

He appeared to be paying little attention to the speech; all his concentration was on its audience. His head kept turning from side to side in a series of jerky, staccato movements as he looked out across the sweaty, jostling mass of people, observing their reactions, scanning them like a malevolent spider seeking out its prey.

The man's posture was twisted by his right shoulder, which was hunched and curved in towards the side of his face. But the feature that caught Carver's eye and which he then gazed at with a mixture of repulsion and compulsive fascination was the lower half of his face. What was left of it.

His jaw was twisted, misshapen and bereft of muscle control, so that his mouth kept flopping open. His cheeks had caved in like those of an old toothless codger, except that this was much worse, because the man's skin was ridged and pitted with great welts of scar-tissue. His lips twisted up to one side in a vicious parody of a smile, revealing an expanse of vivid pink gum, a single, sharply pointed white canine tooth and a gaping black hole where his molars should have been.

Carver heard a high-pitched gasp and turned to see Alice stripped of her cool self-possession as she fought to control her emotions.

'I'm sorry,' she said, blinking back tears. 'It doesn't seem to matter how many times I see this, I still can't seem to take it.'

Carver looked at Klerk. 'What the hell happened to that guy?'

'You did,' said Klerk. 'That's Moses Mabeki, the man who kidnapped Zalika Stratten. It was your bullets that made him the fine figure of a man he is today.'

'Mabeki?' Carver's mind went back to the room above the she-been and the man he'd left lying in a spreading pool of his own blood. 'Last time I saw him he was dead.'

'Plenty of people in Malemba believe he still is. They don't believe he's human. They think an evil spirit took up residence in Mabeki's dead body, brought it back to life and then used it to spread death and suffering wherever he went.'

'It is not an unreasonable opinion,' said Patrick Tshonga. 'One would not wish to believe that an ordinary man could be as cruel and as bloodthirsty as Moses Mabeki.'

'You've obviously not met the same people I have,' said Carver.

'Oh no, Mr Carver, trust me, I know all about the evil that men do,' said Tshonga. 'I would just prefer it if we could blame evil spirits rather than human nature for their actions.'

'So what exactly has Mabeki been up to?'

'You name it,' said Klerk. 'Moses Mabeki is the man who does the President's dirty work. If the President is an African Hitler, Mabeki is his Heinrich Himmler. He runs the secret police and approves their use of torture, coercion and brutality. He plans the war veterans' attacks on the few white farmers who have not yet fled their lands, just as he planned the attack on my sister and her family. He organizes the forced expulsions of hundreds of thousands of people from their homes and villages. Then he makes certain that there is not enough food for them on the lands where they are forced to settle. They say he likes to see people starve, you know. He cannot eat solid food himself – everything has to be pulped like baby food, or sucked through a straw – and he resents anyone who can.'

'Sounds like I should have finished him off when I had the chance.'

'Ach, don't beat yourself up about it, man. You were there to rescue my niece. You used the force necessary to achieve your objective. No blame attaches to you.'

'Big of you,' said Carver.

'On the other hand, if you were to remove Mabeki at the same time as the President, you would be doing me a great personal favour.'

'And you would be liberating the people of my country from his wickedness,' Tshonga interjected. 'More importantly, you would remove one of the great obstacles to peace and democracy in Malemba. There would be little purpose in getting rid of the current President if his most able understudy were still able to continue his regime. If Mabeki succeeds to the presidency, the tyranny under which we have suffered for the past twenty-five years will seem like a golden age compared to what he would inflict, and the opportunity to establish a truly democratic government and a free society will vanish.'

'And you won't get your tantalum mine, will you, Klerk?' said Carver.

A broad smile crossed Klerk's face. 'And your shares will be worth nothing, Sam. It seems our interests coincide, financially and personally. I want my revenge for what this man did to my family, and if you are half the man I take you for, you will want the satisfaction of completing the job you started all those years ago.'

'Satisfaction doesn't come into it,' said Carver. 'There are only two things that interest me. Can I do the job? And, can I live with myself after I've done it?'

He felt a gentle pressure on his arm, the touch of Alice's hand.

'Please, Mr Carver, take the job,' she said. Her voice was urgent, anguished. 'So many people have died. So many more are suffering. Surely it's a good thing to try, at least, to help them.'

'All right, suppose I did. People only hire me when they want total deniability. Whatever happens to Gushungo or Mabeki, you can't afford to have it traced back to you. If I do the job – if – rest assured you'll get that deniability. But I'll need full logistical back-up, some way of getting close to the President and a cover that will stand up to thorough examination. And that's before we even talk about when, where and how the whole thing goes down.'

'Of course,' said Klerk, 'that goes without saying. In fact, I have had one of my associates working on this project for some time now, finding out everything there is to know about the President's movements, his security arrangements and the layouts of every one of his residences and offices on three different continents. We have people on the inside, supplying us with information. A dossier has been prepared that contains everything you could possibly want to know. If there is any further information that has somehow been omitted, we will get it for you. If there is anything you need to do your work, anything at all, we will provide it. My sole condition, and this is as much for your good as anyone else's, is that my associate should work with you during the planning process and accompany you on the mission itself.'

'On a job like this I prefer to work alone. Simplifies things.'

'I understand,' said Klerk. 'Nevertheless, I insist.'

'So who is this associate, then?'

Klerk gave a wry half-smile. 'My niece, Zalika Stratten.'

'Are you out of your mind?' Carver snapped. 'You're asking me to put my balls on the line, not to mention the future of an entire bloody country, and all the billions you plan to make from that tantalum mine, and I'm supposed to do this at the same time as nursemaiding some screwed-up schoolgirl who's got bugger-all training, experience or competence for this kind of work?'

Klerk's smile broadened. 'She's not a schoolgirl any more, Sam. She's a grown woman of twenty-seven. She's highly intelligent, extremely fit, a qualified pilot and a first-class shot. I guarantee that her bushcraft skills are at least as good as yours, probably better. And no one on earth knows more about the President, or Mabeki, than she does.'

'That's just the problem, though, isn't it? Mabeki knows her too. He'd recognize her the moment he clapped eyes on her.'

'Really?' said Alice. 'You didn't.'

28

Zalika slipped off the auburn wig and removed the tight stocking cap beneath it, revealing a head of pale brown hair, highlighted with streaks of blonde. She shook her head and scrunched her hair with her fingers, then grinned at him. 'Still don't see it?'

She tilted her face forward and lifted her index finger to her eyes, removing the hazel-coloured contact lenses that had covered them. When she raised her head again, her eyes were a deep jewelled blue.

'How about now?'

Now Zalika's whole face slipped into focus. She'd had some work done on her nose, Carver reckoned – it was much less prominent than before – but that aside, the teenage girl he'd met a decade ago was clearly visible in the woman who stood before him. And yet she'd changed utterly.

'Yes,' said Carver. 'Now I see it.'

'Superb!' laughed Klerk, clapping his hands with delight. 'Zalika, my dear, that was a magnificent performance. I apologize, Sam. It was hardly fair to play such a cheap trick on the man who saved Zalika's life. But the best way to convince you that she could fool someone else was if you had already been fooled yourself.'

Zalika gave a little pout of mock contrition, then she took a couple of steps towards him until she was close enough to reach out and take his hands in hers.

'Will you forgive me?' she said, looking him in the eye.

The knowing, teasing look had returned to her smile, but much more openly now that she did not have to play at being Alice the sexy secretary. Carver suddenly felt a very strong urge to wipe that smile off her face, whether by kissing her or slapping her he didn't much care.

She gave his hands a little squeeze, as if she knew just what he was thinking, and leaned forward to kiss him, very delicately, on the cheek.

'Yes,' she said, 'of course you will.'

She'd asked one question, but she'd answered another one altogether.

'Good,' said Carver. 'I'm glad we're agreed on that.'

A silence fell on the room, eventually broken by a harsh, guttural cough. Zalika spun round, saw Klerk with his fist to his mouth and frowning as if in deep discomfort. She burst out laughing. 'God, Wendell, I've never seen you looking embarrassed before!'

'Not at all,' growled Klerk, clearing his throat. 'I just wondered if you could stop flirting for five seconds and demonstrate to Mr Carver here that you really do know as much about President Gushungo as I just said you did.'

'Of course,' said Zalika. 'I'd be delighted.'

She picked up the remote control and turned back to the TV, clicking her way through a series of menus until she came to a PowerPoint file titled HG-HK.ppt. She clicked it open and a picture of Henderson Gushungo appeared on the screen.

'Just in case we'd forgotten who we were dealing with,' Zalika said.

Now she was all business.

'Before we go any further,' she continued, 'I just want to explain how we – well, I actually – arrived at the location that was chosen for this operation. The obvious place to attack Gushungo, of course, is Malemba itself. But it is also the least suitable. The President has the nation's entire armed forces to call on as personal protection. His secret police are everywhere. He still has a lot of allies, men who know that their only hope of staying in power is to keep the old man alive as long as possible. We also have reliable information suggesting that Gushungo has at least four doubles. Their basic role in life is to take a bullet that's meant for him, so it would be depressingly easy to take out the wrong man and kill some innocent lookalike instead of the real thing. And if that were not bad enough, the total collapse of the country's infrastructure would make it a hard place to leave in a hurry. Of course we could organize a fast extraction if we had to. But the state Malemba is in makes everything much more complicated and much less reliable than you'd want it to be. So if Malemba's no good, when does Gushungo go abroad?'

She clicked the remote control and a new picture appeared of the President standing in front of a giant Bedouin tent, shaking hands with a man wearing vivid purple silk robes, a matching pill-box hat and impenetrable black shades.

'There are still some states willing to welcome Gushungo. This is him meeting Gaddafi in Libya last year. He also had the brass nerve to attend an EU summit on relations with Africa in Lisbon. Officially, the European nations are opposed to his regime. All his bank accounts within the EU and even Switzerland have been frozen. But it's very difficult for them to prevent a head of state entering a European nation, particularly if he's been invited to attend a multinational meeting, or an event held by an inter-national organization like the United Nations. So here he is in Rome, for example.'

Now the picture on the screen showed Gushungo, surrounded by a scrum of bodyguards and photographers, standing in front of the Colosseum.

'He went to a UN conference there and talked about the need to preserve global food supplies and meet the threat of climate change,' said Zalika. 'This from a man who has reduced his country to a desert! When I think of how our farms used to be when I was a girl: the land looked after so beautifully; wonderful crops every year; plenty of work for everyone . . . and now it's all gone. It makes me so angry.'

'You are not alone, my dear,' said Tshonga. 'We all feel the same way.'

'Thank you, sir,' she said. 'Anyway, there are opportunities when the President makes these visits. But the host countries give him the same protection they provide for any head of state. These days all the western nations have excellent special forces, the Middle Eastern and Asian ones, too. I'm sure you could find a way past them if you had to, Sam. But again, it adds to the risk. Which left me with one final option.'

Another picture appeared on the screen. It was blurry, taken at long distance with an extreme telephoto lens. It showed a close-up of Gushungo wearing a dressing gown, leaning on a balcony.

Click.

Now the picture expanded and revealed that the balcony was on the top floor of a slender four-storey building perched on a hillside, with similar constructions on either side.

'This is dear old Henderson, beloved Father of our Nation, sunning himself at his new holiday home,' said Zalika. 'It's in Hong Kong. And that's where we're going to get him.'

29

Before Carver could respond to what Zalika Stratten had said there was a tentative, barely audible knock on the door.

'Come!' barked Klerk.

The door opened to reveal a woman in a short strapless red cocktail dress. She was very blonde, very tanned and very thin. As she walked across to Klerk, she smiled in a way that was simultaneously dazzling yet also somewhat tentative, as if she were not quite sure of how she would be received. She stepped up to Klerk and lightly placed her right hand on his chest then kept moving round him as if marking out an invisible boundary to ward off any competitors. She left her hand where it was as she stepped behind him so that her fingers ended up draped over his right shoulder, revealing long, perfectly manicured nails painted in the same scarlet shade as her dress. The diamond and ruby ring on the fourth finger was a mugger's wet dream.

She gave Klerk a proprietorial peck on the left cheek and said, 'When do you think you'll be ready for dinner, sweetie? Jean-Pierre is totally stressing out. He's making us individual cheese and black truffle soufflés and he says they have to be served straight from the oven.'

'Ten minutes,' said Klerk. 'Let this be a warning to you, Sam: when I have made you very, very rich, you too will have to deal with temperamental chefs and beautiful, highly strung women.'

Klerk turned back to the blonde. 'My dear, this is Mr Samuel Carver, who is about to do me a very great personal favour by sorting out a problem with our African operations. Sam, meet Brianna Latrelle, my fiancée, who hopes that I'll do her an even bigger favour by setting the date for our wedding before I die of old age.'

'Pleased to meet you, Brianna,' said Carver, shaking her hand.

Up close, he could see that there were fine lines beneath the make-up on Brianna's pretty face. No wonder she wanted to seal the deal with Klerk. She had to be in her late thirties at least. She needed to land her man soon, before someone younger and fresher stole him away.

'Hello, Sam,' Brianna replied, with another all-American cheer-leader smile.

She looked at Zalika, as if noticing her for the first time. 'Zalika, honey,' she said, kissing her on either cheek. 'You make the cutest little secretary. But aren't you changing for dinner?'

'I'm so sorry, Bree,' said Zalika. 'I've been working so hard I just haven't had time. And anyway, your dress is so stunning, I'm sure I couldn't compete.'

The compliment was sweetly made. But Carver detected some-thing much more hostile beneath the surface: each word was like a dagger covered in candyfloss. These two women were anything but friends.

'Right then, that's enough chit-chat,' said Klerk. 'Brianna, my dear, go and tell Jean-Pierre he can start cooking his precious soufflés.'

'Of course, my love,' Brianna said, giving Klerk another little kiss before she left.

Klerk turned his attention to Zalika. 'Gushungo,' he said. 'Hong Kong. Please continue.'

'Last year, the President paid more than five million dollars for this bolt-hole in Hong Kong,' said Zalika, snapping straight back into business mode. She'd been totally convincing in the role of Alice the sexy secretary. Now she was equally at ease as a serious, intelligent professional, delivering a well-prepared briefing with all the key facts at her fingertips. Carver had to admit that he'd under-estimated her.

'The location is no accident,' she continued. 'For the past fifty years, the Chinese have been working hard to extend their influence over post-colonial Africa, presenting themselves as fellow strugglers against Western imperialism. The deal is always the same. The African nations sell the Chinese the natural resources they can produce and in return the Chinese help install basic infra-structure: roads, railways, power supplies, ports, pretty much anything a modern nation needs, really.

'Every year, thousands of African students go to Chinese universities. Of course, the irony is that the average Chinese is even more racist towards Africans than a white would be. They call the students "black devils". Oddly enough, Gushungo doesn't seem to mind. He's spent years and years ranting about the evils of white people, but he's never said a word against the Chinese. Why? Because they let him put his money in their banks and buy property on their territory. And they do something he likes even more than that: they buy his diamonds.'

Another series of images flashed up on the screen: hordes of men and women, carrying spades and pickaxes and caked in dust and grime, clustered in a series of giant open trenches.

'This is the Chidange diamond field in eastern Malemba,' said Zalika. 'It's an area of forest that's potentially the single richest source of diamonds in the world. The stones are just lying in the dirt, right up to ground level. So it could be worth billions of dollars a year to the Malemban economy, but it's never been properly mined or exploited. Until a few years ago, De Beers, the huge South African company that dominates the global diamond market, had the mining rights. They were planning a proper full-scale operation there. But in 2006 the rights were passed to an English company, and then, just a few months later, seized by the government.

'Naturally, no government run by Henderson Gushungo could ever do something as complex as set up a diamond mine. So the diamonds just lay there, waiting for someone to take them away. Which is what happened. Thousands of people came to Chidange, hoping to make their fortunes. Well, Henderson couldn't have that. He didn't want anyone taking his rocks. So he sent in the troops. They went in without warning, firing from helicopter gunships, shooting to kill. No one knows exactly how many people died; dozens certainly, maybe even hundreds. The forests were littered with bodies for miles around. When the killing was over, the whole area was sealed off and all the survivors were forced to fill in all the holes they had dug. They weren't given any food or water. If they died, they were just thrown into the holes. Anyone who was still alive after all that was then forcibly removed from the area and driven away for resettlement. Then, when no one else was left, Gushungo allowed a new group of diggers into the area – people he trusted, members of his political party. The operations started up again, and all the stones went straight to Henderson Gushungo and his closest associates.'

'Including Moses Mabeki,' Tshonga interjected.

'So they're blood diamonds,' said Carver.

'Exactly,' said Zalika. 'And one of the reasons Gushungo has bought a place in Hong Kong is that he thinks he can sell his diamonds there. He's trying to put a deal together with the Chinese government. They have an almost unlimited need for industrial-quality diamonds. But the best stones, millions of dollars' worth of uncut diamonds, he wants to sell separately. Well, I say "he" wants to sell them, but that's not quite right. Because the real brains behind this scheme is not Henderson Gushungo at all, but his wife.'

The contrast between the images of the desperate, filthy prospectors at Chidange and the woman who now appeared on the screen could not have been more acute. She appeared first as a young bride, resplendent in a flowing, lacy white wedding dress, smiling and waving at the camera with Gushungo standing in formal morning dress beside her. Then came another image, evidently taken a few years later. The wedding dress had been swapped for a black outfit, and her face had hardened: her mouth was set in an expression of tight-lipped disdain, her eyes invisible behind dark glasses whose frames were studded with crystals.

'This is Faith Gushungo, Henderson's second wife,' said Zalika. 'And there's no point getting rid of him if you don't get her as well.'

Carver didn't like the way the conversation was heading. 'Just how many people am I supposed to be hitting? First we had Gushungo, then Mabeki, now the wife. Who's next? Any kids you want me to get rid of? Pets, maybe?'

Klerk looked to the heavens and sighed. He pulled out a BlackBerry and pressed a speed-dial letter. 'Terence, it's Mr Klerk. Tell Jean-Pierre to take his soufflés out of the oven. We could be a little late for dinner. Tell Jean-Pierre, if he's got a problem, take it up with Miss Latrelle. She can deal with it.'

Klerk put the phone away. 'Carry on, Zalika. You were about to tell Sam about Faith Gushungo. Fascinating woman. Let us hope she'll soon be burning in hell, hey?'

'She doesn't believe she will,' said Zalika. 'She's Faith by name and faith by nature: a devout Christian, just like Henderson. They spend six days a week doing nothing but evil, then they say their prayers on Sunday, take communion and think that everything's forgiven. They make their bodyguards do it, too. The whole household comes to a standstill. It's so hypocritical it makes me sick. This is a woman who's ordered the construction of a new presidential palace, which will cost at least twenty million dollars. She goes on shopping trips to London, Paris and Milan, blowing hundreds of thousands more at a time when the country is desperately short of foreign currency to buy food or oil for its people. And she's got the nerve to claim that she's religious.'

'So Mrs Gushungo's Africa's answer to Imelda Marcos,'

said Carver. 'It isn't pretty, but it's hardly a capital offence.'

'Imelda Marcos . . . and Lady Macbeth,' Zalika countered.

'Perhaps I can explain,' said Patrick Tshonga. 'You understand, Mr Carver, that Henderson Gushungo is a very elderly man. His ability to retain command of the country is remarkable, but still he is mortal and his faculties are diminished. Faith, however, is still a young woman, in the prime of life. She is filled with energy. She is also filled with hatred, spite and malice. These days, when the veterans seize property or attack people who are deemed to be opponents of the government, as like as not they are doing it on Mrs Gushungo's orders, not the President's. She has built vast estates from all the farms she has appropriated. And in every case, it is not just the white owners who have been forced to flee. All the people who worked for them are evicted also, their possessions are seized and their homes are given to Mrs Gushungo's supporters. And you will note that I say "Mrs Gushungo's supporters". These people owe their loyalty to her, not her husband. She has built up an entire power-base of her own. She knows that her man will soon be gone, either because he dies or is finally removed from office. And when that day comes, she does not intend to go with him. No, Faith Gushungo will stay and fight for power for herself.'

'So where do Hong Kong and the diamonds fit into all this?' asked Carver.

'Simple,' said Zalika. 'They're Faith's Plan B. If it all goes wrong and she gets kicked out along with her husband, then she's got somewhere to go and a very large amount of money, she hopes, to keep her in comfort and idleness when she gets there.'

'And what does it all have to do with us?'

Zalika smiled. 'Well, the Gushungos have a hard time getting any bank to take their business. So when they're in Hong Kong they keep their diamonds at home. Now, what if someone tried to steal those diamonds?'

'The robbery might go wrong, people might get hurt and no one would suspect a political motive,' said Carver. 'It's an excellent idea . . .'

'Thank you,' said Zalika, giving an ironic little bow.

'. . . but I might have one that's even better.'

'Really? What might that be?'

She looked him straight in the eye, challenging him.

'I don't know yet. I'll tell you when I get it.'

'So, Sam,' said Klerk, cutting through the growing tension, 'you will accept my offer?'

'I don't know that, either,' said Carver. 'I'll give you my answer tomorrow afternoon, right here, seventeen hundred hours. You happy with that?'

'It sounds like I don't have a choice. Ja, I can live with tomorrow afternoon. Before the meeting we will go shooting. Then we will talk. Meanwhile, let's eat.' He glared at Carver and Zalika. 'You two can sort out your differences over Jean-Pierre's damned truffle soufflés.'

30

There was a time when Severn Road might easily have been a desirable neighbourhood in the stockbroker belt of Surrey. The substantial houses, set amid croquet lawns, tennis courts and shrubberies, had all been built in the 1930s. They had steeply gabled roofs, half-timbered mock Tudor facades and verandas on which privileged ladies, burdened neither by jobs nor household chores, could comfortably take their tea. The men who owned them had all been educated at the same small group of private boarding schools and shared identical, unquestioned assumptions about their innate superiority, the lesser status of anyone unfortunate enough to be black, brown, yellow or French, and the utter deviousness of Jews.

Yet Severn Road lay not in southern England but southern Africa, in what had once been a suburb of Fort Shrewsbury, capital of British Mashonaland. Its houses were built for the families of the colonial administrators, army officers and businessmen who ran this particular outpost of Empire, as well as the native servants who tended to their needs. For half a century, nothing changed. Then a civil war was fought and lost and British Mashonaland became the independent state of Malemba. Fort Shrewsbury changed its name to Sindele and the white inhabitants of Severn Road made way for a new governing class of African bureaucrats, lawyers and entrepreneurs. By and large, they kept on the servants who had once waited upon their country's white masters. They even retained some of the old furniture, left behind as the whites fled for the old country. The new bosses were, in some respects, just the same as the old ones.

So another twenty years went by, and Severn Road remained as exclusive and comfortable as it had always been. Then Henderson Gushungo made his fateful decision to cleanse his nation of the white farmers and entrepreneurs he hated with such a burning passion. The economy promptly collapsed, the notionally democratic government became a tyrannical dictatorship, and Severn Road was changed beyond all recognition. The houses were stripped of their contents as the people who lived in them sold everything they could, simply to make a few instantly worthless Malemban dollars. Then they were subdivided as rooms were rented out. Families half-a-dozen strong were crammed into bedrooms intended for a single pampered child; grand living rooms became makeshift dormitories; floorboards were lifted for firewood; crude sheets of plastic were nailed over holes in roofs whose tiles had not so long before been kept in immaculate repair.

Mary Utseya and her baby son Peter had been sharing part of the old dining room at No. 15 Severn Road with three other women and their children for the past four months, ever since Mary's husband Henry, a soldier in the Malemban army, was killed in action in the Congo. She had been forced to leave the married quarters where she and Henry lived. With the government in no shape to pay her a widow's pension, Mary had no way of renting a place of her own and had counted herself fortunate that a friend had offered her a few square feet on the dining-room floor.

Within a week or two of Mary's arrival at Severn Road there had been a presidential election. Loudspeaker vans filled with armed men had driven down the street warning the inhabitants of the terrible consequences of voting for the treacherous Popular Freedom Movement and its lying, unprincipled leader Patrick Tshonga (who was, they added, a notorious homosexual and soon to die from AIDS). Mary was not registered to vote at the nearby polling station and had no means of getting back to her old neighbourhood, so she did not vote. Had she done so, however, she would certainly have sided with the rest of Severn Road's people, who overwhelmingly ignored the threats of Gushungo's thugs and voted for Tshonga. They knew that they were wasting their time, since Gushungo would never accept the result. But they voted anyway.

Now, on a Friday night in May, with the ground still damp from an afternoon downpour, they were going to pay for their impudence.

The operation was carried out with a brutal ruthlessness honed by constant repetition: many, many people had already suffered the fate that awaited the people of Severn Road. The two ends of the road were blocked. Patrols were posted in neighbouring streets to catch anyone who tried to escape over back walls and garden fences. Then the military trucks arrived, one for every house. The trucks were organized in groups of four, three soldiers to a truck, each group under the command of a sergeant.

They did not bother to knock. Front doors were kicked or if necessary blown open. Warning shots were fired into the ceiling to cower the inhabitants, the muzzle flashes blazing in the gloomy interiors, where the only light came from the occasional gas or meths-fuelled lantern. Soldiers went in shouting at the tops of their voices and swinging their gun-butts with indiscriminate abandon. If they were lucky, the people crammed into the houses had time to grab a few belongings and even some food or water before they were herded at bayonet point on to the trucks, but many clambered into the bare open-topped cargo bays with nothing more than the clothes on their backs.

Mary Utseya was relatively fortunate. She managed to sling a canvas bag across her shoulder and stuff it with a bottle of milk, a couple of biscuits and a clean nappy-cloth for baby Peter. All she kept for herself was a small framed picture of her dead husband Henry. It had been taken on his last leave home before he died. He was dressed in his army uniform, smiling proudly at the camera as he showed off the corporal's stripes he had just been awarded.

It was only when one of the soldiers grabbed her upper arm and shoved her up on to the truck that Mary noticed that his uniform carried exactly the same regimental insignia as Henry's. These men were his old comrades, his brothers in arms.

'Did you know Henry Utseya?' she babbled, hoping she might somehow get better treatment if the soldier knew her man had belonged to his unit. 'Please! He was in your regiment. He was killed in—'

Mary was silenced by a slap to the side of her head. The blow sent her spinning across the floor of the cargo bay. She dropped Peter, who started crying, bawling with the banshee volume that even the tiniest baby can generate. Her face still stinging, her mind dazed and her vision blurred by the soldier's slap, she scrabbled half-blindly around the truck, desperately trying to get to her baby before the soldier silenced him for good. She bumped into an old man, who lashed out at her with his boot. A woman started screaming. More people kept being shoved over the tailboard into the cargo bay, terrifying Mary, who felt sure her child would be trampled.

At last her outstretched hands felt Peter's cotton blanket, tightly curled hair and soft, warm skin, and she clutched him desperately to her breast. Then the truck's ignition key was turned, its engine coughed into life, and they rumbled off into the night.

A black Rolls-Royce Phantom was parked by the turning into Severn Road. It had been stretched to more than twenty-two feet in length and fitted with armour plating by Mutec, a specialist carriagemaker in Oberstenfeld, Germany. From behind tinted, bulletproof windows, its passengers watched as the trucks went by.

'Let that be a lesson to them,' said Faith Gushungo. 'Have you allocated the properties yet?'

She was sitting in one of four passenger seats, arranged in two facing pairs behind the divider that separated them from the driver, guaranteeing total privacy.

Moses Mabeki gave a jerky twitch of his brutally distorted head. 'Of course,' he said, the last word dissolving into a drooling slur.

'And the new owners are aware that the trucks will come for them, too, if they ever question their loyalty to our cause?'

Mabeki's laugh was a hacking cough. 'Oh yes, they know, and they believe it, don't worry about that.'

'And the diamonds: you have a buyer lined up?'

'Yes. They're offering ten million. I will make them pay twelve.'

'Twelve million dollars,' purred Faith Gushungo with something close to ecstasy. 'All for us.'

'It will almost double our holdings,' said Mabeki.

'You're sure Henderson doesn't know that we control the accounts?'

'He does not know that we control the country. Why would he know about the accounts?'

Faith laughed. She reached out to stroke Mabeki's face, feeling the hard, shiny knots of scar-tissue under her fingertips. His terrible ugliness appalled her. The drops of spittle that fell from his lips on to the palm of her hand disgusted her. Yet they thrilled her, too, and she felt herself melting with desire for him.

'You are my beast,' she whispered.

She ran her hands over the whipcord muscles beneath his suit and lowered her head over his body. Moses Mabeki's face had lost all its beauty and his shoulder was a twisted wreck. But he was still a man, for all that.

31

The dinner was as magnificent as Klerk had promised. The truffle soufflés were almost as light as the air around them. The main course was a leg of tender pink roast spring lamb, served with fondant potatoes and a fricassee of baby vegetables picked barely an hour earlier. For dessert they ate fresh strawberries and cream, dusted with ground black pepper to bring out the sweetness of the fruit. All the ingredients came from Campden Hall's own home farm. Even the truffle had been found in one of the patches of woodland that dotted the estate. Only the wines had been imported, and for Carver, the journey from Geneva was entirely justified by the chance to sample the 1998 Cheval Blanc, a red wine from the Bordeaux commune of St Emilion, which accompanied the lamb. He wasn't a man who sat around thinking of pretentious adjectives to describe what he was drinking. It was simpler just to say that the wine tasted even better than Zalika Stratten looked.

No one talked about Malemba, or Gushungo, let alone the reason why Carver was a guest at the meal. It was as if there were an unspoken agreement to keep the conversation light and trivial.

After the meal, the diners began to drift upstairs to bed. Carver's room was on the same corridor as Zalika's. They went up together.

'Well, this is me,' she said, stopping outside her door.

They stood opposite each other, so close that it would take only the slightest inclination of their heads to join in the kiss that would open the door and take them both inside. The tension between them mounted. Then Zalika leaned across and gave Carver an innocent peck on the cheek. He did not move as she turned the handle, half-opened her door and then paused at the entrance to her room. She looked him in the eyes. And then she was gone.

Before long, only Tshonga and Klerk were left downstairs. They discussed their impressions of the afternoon's discussion over brandy and cigars. Then the Malemban called it a day, leaving only Klerk behind.

In the small hours of Saturday morning, when all but one of the inhabitants of Campden Hall were lost in sleep, a mobile phone was used to contact a number in Malemba.

'Carver arrived here today,' the caller said. 'We offered him the Gushungo assignment. He hasn't accepted yet.'

The voice on the other end of the line was hard to make out. The reply had to be forced through a lazy mouth filled with spittle and incapable of precise speech: 'Did you make sure he was tempted as I suggested?'

'Oh yes. He knows you are still alive. We told him this is his chance to finish the job he started ten years ago.'

'Did he like that idea?'

'Hard to say. He wouldn't commit himself.'

Moses Mabeki gave a long, rattling sigh, like a hiss from an irritable venomous snake.

'I want them all dead: Gushungo, his bitch wife and Carver. All of them.'

'Relax. He'll take the job. It's just a matter of time.'

'Good. Everything we planned depends on that.'

'I'm well aware of that,' said the caller.

Then the phone snapped shut, the call ended, and within three minutes every bed in Campden Hall was occupied once again.

32

Wendell Klerk didn't like to be hurried on a Saturday morning and saw no need to hurry his guests. The staff were on hand from the crack of dawn to provide anything anyone might want, but the first set event of the day was a midday brunch.

'So, Sam, are you ready to shoot some clay pigeons?' Klerk said, emphasizing his words with jabs of a sausage-laden fork.

Zalika smiled at Carver. 'My uncle is very proud of his shooting ground. He had to bulldoze half of Suffolk to make it.'

'At least half!' said Klerk. 'Patrick, will you be joining us?'

Tshonga smiled and shook his head. 'No, Wendell, I have never had any skill with a gun. While my brothers were fighting for freedom in the bush—'

'Ja, fighting me!' Klerk interrupted.

'I was studying law. All these years later, I am still happy just to read while others play with guns.'

'Fair enough,' said Klerk. 'Brianna is not a great fan of shooting either, are you?'

'Well, it's not as boring as golf,' Brianna sighed.

Carver laughed. So the plaything had a sense of humour hidden away inside that doll-like figure. There was more to her than met the eye. She had that, at least, in common with Zalika.

'Very good,' said Klerk, sounding rather less amused. 'So now we three who will be shooting must agree on the stakes. What do you say, Sam, how about the two losers each give the winner ten thousand US?'

'If you like,' said Carver, unenthusiastically.

'Not enough for you? What if we make it fifty grand each?'

'Honestly, Wendell, can't you see Sam's not interested in money?' Zalika said.

'He was the last time I paid him.'

'Well of course, that was business,' Zalika insisted. 'But if we want to get him interested today, it has to be something more personal. Now, I seem to remember that yesterday he called me, and I quote, a "screwed-up schoolgirl who's got bugger-all training, experience or competence for this kind of work". Sorry, Sam, but that's not the sort of thing a girl forgets in a hurry. So my wager is this. I bet you can't beat little schoolgirl me in a straightforward head-to-head shooting match. And I'm not going to put any money on it because I know that if you, the great Samuel Carver, action hero extraordinaire, can't shoot better than a helpless, weak and feeble female, you'll lose something – well, a couple of things, actually – that say more about you than cash ever can.'

'Ahahaha!' Klerk burst out laughing. 'You're really putting your balls on the line here, my man! Don't be fooled by this kid. She's a Stratten. She was blasting away all over the family estates when she was still in nappies.'

'You're on,' said Carver.

Zalika smiled. 'Excellent.'

One by one the others drifted away until Carver and Zalika were alone in the room. She sat herself down next to him and pulled her chair right over to his. Then she leaned forward so close it seemed to Carver that her sea-blue eyes were not just looking at him but through him, and very softly said, 'If you want to take me, you'll have to beat me first. And believe me, Carver, I won't make it easy.'

33

The open trucks came rumbling down the dirt track that snaked between the rolling hills of south-central Malemba, throwing up a choking cloud of parched red earth over the tightly packed huddles of fearful, half-starved men, women and children crammed into their cargo bays. A horn blared from the leading vehicle and a uniformed soldier with sergeant's stripes on his arm and his eyes hidden behind fluorescent yellow-framed sunglasses got out of the driver's cabin. He slammed the door behind him and lifted his AK-47 assault rifle one-handed into the air. He fired off a volley of shots then shouted, 'Move! Move! Clear the way!'

Ahead of him the track was blocked by more people: a horde that stretched away to either side, covering the rolling ground as far as the eye could see. There were more than thirty thousand of them, covering a barren wasteland that had once been occupied by flourishing crops and cattle made sleek and contented by lush green grass. Camps like this had sprung up all over the country, filled by families ejected from rural villages, estates seized from their white owners and urban neighbourhoods, just like Severn

Road, that had dared to vote against Henderson Gushungo. Officially, the forced eviction and transportation of hundreds of thousands of people was known as resettlement. In reality, it was more like a form of ethnic cleansing, except that Gushungo terrorized members of his own tribe as willingly as he did those from other social and ethnic groups. Once moved, the people were simply dumped, without food, water or shelter, and left to fend for themselves. That they were doing so on land that belonged to other Malembans did not concern Henderson Gushungo in any way at all.

A two-storey house, constructed of breezeblocks with a corrugated iron roof, stood like an island in this ocean of humanity, some fifty metres from where the trucks had stopped. All around it, wisps of smoke rose from smouldering cooking-fires and women sat before huts and tents cobbled together from whatever scraps of rag, wood and corrugated iron they or their men could find. Here and there small children with legs like fragile twigs and bellies as swollen as honeydew melons tried to play. But they had no energy to run or jump; no toys for imaginary tea-parties or battles; no light in their round, enquiring eyes.

There was a slow, tired, hungry ripple of movement in front of the line of trucks and a few metres of track were cleared. The trucks rumbled forward again until they were swallowed up in the ocean of humanity and had to stop once more, some thirty metres now from the house. The man with the gun, who had been walking beside the leading truck, kicking people out of his way, fired another burst into the sky, and again a path through the throng, shorter and narrower this time, briefly appeared. When even this progress had reached its limit, the man accepted the inevitable. He turned round to face the line of trucks and shouted, 'Enough, we stop here! Get them out!'

A dozen or so more soldiers spilled from the trucks' cabins. They went round to the backs of the cargo bays and opened them up, screaming 'Get out!' to the people inside, prodding them with the barrels of their AK-47s and lashing out with the butts at anyone who dared protest, or even ask where they were or what was going on.

Mary had learned her lesson the previous night. She said nothing. She just held Peter tight, hoping that he would keep quiet. It made no difference. One of the soldiers smashed her in the face with his gun, just for the hell of it. He laughed and pointed Mary out to his mates as she fell to the ground, one hand still clinging to her baby, the other clasped to her face, blood seeping out between the fingers.

'Stop that!'

The shout came from the building. A boy in his late teens and a girl of about the same age – brother and sister by the look of them – were standing in the open front door. They seemed a little healthier and better-fed than the rest of the people around them and they carried themselves with the confidence of young people who have been raised in the belief that anything is possible and have yet to discover the limitations and dangers of that particular delusion.

It was the boy who had shouted. Now he was walking through the people towards the truck, moving with the purposeful stride of a warrior prince. He ignored the soldiers and went straight to Mary Utseya, crouching on his haunches beside her and wrapping a consoling arm round her shoulders.

The boy looked up at the soldier who had hit Mary. 'Shame on you,' he said with dismissive contempt. 'A real man has no need to hit a defenceless woman.'

The soldier took a step forward and the boy sprang to his feet to meet him. They stood opposite each other, glaring, barely a pace apart.

'This woman needs help, her child too,' the boy said. He turned his head towards his sister and called out, 'Farayi, come and give me a hand.'

The girl ran towards him, picking her way through the crowds with the sure-footed grace of a young gazelle. She took hold of Mary's elbow, gently guiding her as the boy lifted her to her feet.

'We're taking her to the house,' the boy said.

He turned to lead the two women in that direction. They'd only taken three shuffling steps towards their destination when the sergeant's voice rang out again: 'Where you going, boy? You stay right here.'

The boy hissed at his sister, 'Keep going. Ignore him.'

She hesitated for a second. 'Canaan, do what he says.'

The sergeant ignored them both. He had his own way of resolving tricky situations. He slammed a fresh magazine into his AK-47, took careful aim and fired a three-shot burst. Mary Utseya seemed to dance in the two kids' arms, then her body slumped to the ground as the boy and girl jumped aside, away from any more shots.

Peter was left lying on the ground between them. He started to cry. The sergeant walked up to the small bundle wriggling on the bare red earth. He aimed his gun at it then lowered the barrel. No need to waste a bullet. He raised his right foot high in the air, bringing his knee up almost to his chest, then slammed it down, crushing the baby's skull with one blow of his boot heel.

'Now you got no reason to go to the house,' the sergeant said, rubbing his boot in the dirt to scrape the fragments of skull and brain matter off its sole.

He pointed his index finger at four of his men. 'You, you, you, you.' He jerked a thumb at Canaan and Farayi. 'Seize them. They are rebels. They are trying to sabotage our mission. They must come with us.'

'No!' The simple word was dragged out into a long, wailing cry of despair as a third person came out of the house, a middle-aged woman, her once-elegant features ravaged by exhaustion and stress. 'You will not take my children!' she shouted, hurrying towards the trucks.

'Stay away!' the sergeant shouted, but she kept going.

'Do what he says!' Canaan cried, struggling to free himself from the soldiers who had him in their grip.

His words were drowned by the chatter of the gun.

As Nyasha Iluko – wife of Justus Iluko, mother of Canaan and Farayi – lay on the ground, twitching in her final death-throes, the sergeant walked up to Canaan and jabbed him in the chest with the burning-hot barrel of his gun. 'You see, young man? This is what happens when you meddle in another man's business. These two women, this child, they all died because of you.'

34

Wendell Klerk's gamekeeper Donald McGuinness was a wiry Scotsman who combined an impeccably polite manner with a sharp, sceptical look in his eye that suggested he was a very easy man to get along with, but a very hard one to impress.

'If ye'll just follow me, please,' he said in a soft Highland burr, leading Carver, Klerk and Zalika down a set of stairs that led to a subterranean hallway off which there were two doors. One of them led to the wine-cellar of which Klerk was so proud. McGuinness ignored it. He went directly to the second door, to one side of which was a keypad. McGuinness punched in a number.

Klerk looked at Carver. 'I think you're going to like this,' he said.

Carver heard the sound of a lock being released. The door swung open. It was solid steel and hefty enough to resist anything short of an artillery shell. McGuinness stood aside to let them through, and Carver followed Klerk and Zalika into a room about forty feet long and fifteen wide. Three of the walls were wood-panelled and decorated with photographs, prints and oil paintings that depicted shooting scenes, dogs and artful arrangements of dead game. The fourth was taken up with a gigantic cabinet. Its lower portion consisted of a series of twin-door wooden cupboards, rising some three feet from the floor. Above them, the rest of the cabinet was set back behind a narrow shelf, covered in green baize. This upper section rose to the ceiling and was fitted with toughened, shatterproof glass. Behind it, a long line of guns marched the full length of the room.

The majority of them were shotguns, presented in matched pairs. Beyond them came a much smaller selection of rifles for use in target-shooting or stalking deer. There must have been at least a hundred weapons, enough firepower to equip a company of soldiers, and their quality was as striking as the quantity.

Klerk was smiling more broadly than at any time in the entire weekend, clearly delighted by Carver's evident appreciation of his collection. 'Pretty impressive, hey?' he said. 'And look here . . .' Klerk opened two of the low cupboard doors to reveal a metal cabinet that looked like a small safe. Above its door, a digital readout showed the figure 68.5. 'That, my friend, is a climate-controlled ammunition store. The temperature is constant. The air is dessicated to prevent any moisture corrupting the cartridges and their contents. When you fire my ammunition, Sam, you get the best bang my bucks can buy!'

Carver got the feeling that this was not the first time Klerk had used the line, but he was impressed nonetheless.

'So,' Klerk continued, 'let us choose our weapons. I'll have my usual gun, please, Donald.'

McGuinness unlocked one of the panes of glass and slid it open. He took out a supremely beautiful double-barrelled twelve-bore shotgun engraved with an image of a pair of pheasants taking to the air. Around the birds, the gun's action was decorated with an intricate swirling pattern of stylized leaves and flowers. In the midst of them a scroll bore the words 'J. Purdey & Sons'. The Mayfair-based gunsmiths, founded in 1814, were to shotguns what Rolls-Royce were to cars: the ultimate example of traditional British craftsmanship and luxury. Their products were priced accordingly: a gun like Klerk's, Carver reckoned, must have cost seventy thousand pounds at the absolute minimum. It was as much a work of art as a firearm.

Klerk turned to Carver. 'What will you have, Sam?'

'I'll wait my turn,' he said. He looked at Zalika. 'Ladies first.'

Carver was acting the gentleman, but his intention was far less chivalrous. He wanted to see what kind of weapon Zalika chose. It would be the first clue as to the kind of opponent she was likely to be.

If Zalika was aware of the game Carver was playing, she gave no sign of it. She strolled along the full length of the cabinet, looking at the guns as casually as a woman eyeing up fruit on a market stall. Carver expected her to stop by the lighter, small-bored ladies' guns, whose barrels were typically twenty-eight inches long. She ignored them. Instead, she pointed at a twelve-bore Perazzi MX2000S with thirty-inch barrels. 'That one, please, Donald,' she said.

Carver wondered for a moment whether she was putting on an act. The Perazzi was a serious competition gun, used by Olympic-level shots. It was entirely bare of fancy decoration. This was a gun that had no need to look pretty. Its only purpose was to shoot straight. It was his kind of weapon.

With gun-barrels as with skis, beginners go short for easier control, while experts go long for greater performance. Zalika frowned at the gun McGuinness was holding out to her. 'Pity it's only got thirty-inch barrels,' she said.

'Not to worry, Miss,' McGuinness replied, placing the gun carefully on the green baize shelf. 'I should have some thirty-twos available as well. I'll get them fitted right away.'

'Thank you, Donald,' said Zalika with a gracious smile. 'Would you mind putting full and three-quarter chokes in them, please?'

'Certainly, Miss.'

Carver's face remained impassive, but his mind was racing. The choke was a fitting placed into the end of the gun-barrel that restricted the blast of pellets from the cartridge, compressing them into a much tighter spread. This gave the gun much more hitting power, particularly at a distance. But it also placed a huge premium on the shooter's accuracy because there was far less margin for error than a wider spread of pellets allowed. Zalika Stratten was either a seriously good shot, Carver decided, or she was playing her own personal game of bluff, raising the stakes without the hand to back it up. One way or the other, she was certainly ready to compete with him before a single shot had been fired.

So far he'd thought of her challenge to him as little more than a game, just another flirtation on the way to an inevitable conclusion. But it struck him now that he really wanted to beat her very much indeed. It wasn't just because she'd made that a condition of having her. It was the fact that she'd been playing him, one way or the other, ever since he'd stepped inside the house, and now he'd had enough. Carver was not a man who sought either conflict or competition. But if anyone insisted on taking him on, then they were going to pay for it. It was time he taught Miss Zalika Stratten a lesson she wouldn't forget.

'And you, sir?' McGuinness said, interrupting Carver's train of thought.

'I'll take a Perazzi too,' Carver said.

'Longer barrels?' McGuinness asked.

'Sure.'

'How about choke?'

Zalika had gone to one extreme by being so specific, Carver decided to go to the other. 'I'll just take it as it comes, thanks,' he said.

He was pleased to see Zalika's brow crinkle into a frown. She would, he hoped, be wondering why he could afford to be casual about his gun. Was he really that good, that confident of victory?

'Interesting choice you made,' Carver said.

'I've always liked the trigger-pull on the Perazzi,' she said. 'It's got a nice, even weight. Very crisp, don't you think?'

Klerk was watching the two of them with detached amusement. 'Come,' he said, 'let's get out of here. We've chosen our weapons. Time we went and used them.'

35

A Range Rover was waiting for them outside the front door. McGuinness loaded the guns and cartridge bags into the back then drove them down one of the private roads that criss-crossed the estate until they came to a massive earthwork, at least thirty feet high, extending in either direction as far as the eye could see. The road led to a tunnel through the earthwork.

When they emerged into the open again, Carver could see that the ground fell away into a gigantic bowl that must have been at least fifty feet deep. The land within was laid out like a golf course, with patches of open grass separated by copses of trees, hedgerows, man-made hills and valleys and even a stream that fed into a small lake. But instead of golf tees, fairways, bunkers and greens, each individual section of land was equipped with a selection of different stands for guns to fire from; traps to launch clay pigeons; a selection of what looked like watchtowers, or mobile telephone masts; and a rifle range.

'Impressive,' said Carver.

'Thank you,' said Klerk. 'I've taken elements from the finest shoots in the British Isles and reproduced them right here. Different landscapes, different types of game, we've got them all.'

McGuinness drove them down to the bottom of the bowl and parked the car. He handed each of the three competitors their gun, a cartridge bag and a set of ear-protectors. Then he stood before them and, abandoning his usual deference, spoke to them as the man who, as keeper, would be taking responsibility for the shoot.

'You will each be shooting ten clays per stand, at five separate stands,' he said. 'So you each have fifty-five rounds: fifty for the competition and five spares in case any shots have to be retaken. Guns will be carried broken and unloaded. Ear-protectors must be worn while shooting is taking place. I will keep score and act as referee. Does anyone have any questions? No? Well, in that case, if you would please follow me, we will go to the first trap.'

'Do you shoot much?' Klerk asked Carver as they walked away. 'For sport, I mean, rather than business.'

'Every now and then. Been a while since I shot any clays.'

Carver wasn't paying too much attention to Klerk. He was watching Zalika, who was walking ahead of them. She'd put her hair back into a ponytail and changed into jeans and a Beretta ladies' shooting vest. The vest, in theory a purely functional garment, was cut to follow every curve of her upper body and to stop just high enough to reveal the contours beneath her jeans. As she walked, the sway of her body seemed designed to tantalize, giving Carver just a hint of the pleasures in store if he was man enough to match her challenge.

Zalika half-turned to look at him over her shoulder, a teasing smile on her face, and for a second Carver felt another surge of anger at her blatant tactics and irritation at himself for falling for them so easily. She'd meant to distract him, and it had worked. It was time to concentrate on the matter in hand: winning the shooting match.

They were walking through heather now. A short way ahead of them, Carver saw three circular butts, or shooting hides, constructed of dry-stone walls, topped with turf. Ahead of the butts the heather-covered ground rose gradually, simulating the slope of a grouse moor.

'Thought we'd start with grouse,' said Klerk. 'We'll be shooting one at a time from the centre butt. Sam, why don't you shoot first, hey?'

It was an obvious tactic to put Carver at a disadvantage. The other two had shot there a hundred times and knew all the quirks of the land and the positions of the traps from which the clays would be fired like miniature black Frisbees, precisely 108mm across. As the newcomer, Carver would have benefited hugely from watching the others go first. Instead, he would have to shoot sight unseen, trust his reactions and hope for the best.

Carver transferred ten cartridges from his cartridge bag to a pocket of his shooting vest then walked into the butt. He closed his eyes and breathed deeply for a few seconds, trying to clear his mind of everything but the thought processes required to hit a small, fast-moving target. Then he loaded two cartridges into the twin barrels of his gun and raised it to his shoulders.

McGuinness was standing behind him, slightly to one side, holding a control box.

'Would you like to see a pair, sir?' he said.

He was offering to release two of the clays before the shooting began so that Carver could see where they came from and at what distance and angle they flew. The obvious response was, 'Yes please.' But some perverse refusal to be seen to need outside help prevented Carver from doing the sensible thing. Instead he replied, 'No thanks, I'm fine.'

He concentrated his vision on the air just above the artificial moor, directly in front of him, and said, 'Pull!'

McGuinness pushed a button on his control box and Carver heard the sound of a spring being released as the trap slung the first clay pigeon into the air. Then came the fluttering whirr of the clay as it cut through the air. It came low and fast from a point about forty yards away, just as a real grouse would do, flying towards him but slanting right-to-left across his line of fire.

Carver fired.

The clay pigeon kept flying, entirely untouched, until gravity pulled it to earth.

He'd missed.

Appalled by his stupidity and incompetence, he barely heard the release of the second clay, was late getting back into position, and missed that one as well.

Carver could not remember the last time he'd felt so humiliated, so exposed. Behind him, the other three stood in stunned, embarrassed silence for several seconds until Klerk called out, 'Jesus Christ, Carver, you ever fired a gun before in your life?' It was meant as banter, pulling his leg. But there was nothing funny about Carver's shooting. It wasn't just that he had missed. He had done so like a rank amateur.

He ejected the first two cartridges from his gun, resumed his stance and called 'Pull!' once again. This time he hit both clays. They broke into a few large fragments – a sure sign that he'd not struck them dead-centre – but they were hits nonetheless. So were the next three pairs. Carver walked away from the butt with a score of eight out of ten. He only cared about the two dropped shots.

Klerk went next. He shot with the metronomic style of a man who has spent a lot of time and money on lessons from an excellent teacher. Technically, he was faultless, but he wasn't a natural marksman. Even so, he too scored eight, and seemed perfectly happy to have done so.

Now it was Zalika's turn. She didn't just hit the first pair of clays, she dusted them, striking them so perfectly that they disintegrated in mid-air, vanishing in what looked like little puffs of smoke.

When she broke open the gun, she caught the cartridges one-handed as they sprang from the barrels before placing them in a little bin that stood inside the butt. The catch was a nice touch, Carver thought, a clever, deceptively casual way of letting him know how at ease she was around guns. He noticed something else as Zalika reloaded: she rotated her cartridges in the barrels so that the writing on the brass base of each shell was the right way up. It was a telling little ritual, designed to prepare her for action, like a tennis player bouncing a ball, or a golfer practising his swing.

It worked. Zalika vaporized the next four pairs as efficiently as she had the first. She walked away with a perfect ten. If it wasn't obvious before, Carver knew for sure now that he had a fight on his hands – one he could easily lose. If he were going to stand any chance at all he had to shed the look of a loser and regain some sense of authority.

As they walked away to the next stand, he asked McGuinness, 'Just out of curiosity, what chokes have I got?'

'Quarter and cylinder,' the gamekeeper replied.

'Interesting,' said Carver.

He hoped he sounded relaxed, even a little blasé. But inside he was cursing himself. A quarter-choke was the least restriction available; 'cylinder' meant an entirely clear barrel. That gave him a much wider spread of shot. At short range that was an advantage; it might have been the only reason he'd been able to hit any clay at all in that disaster of a first round. But the further the shot went, the more holes opened up in the air between the scattered pellets and the tougher it became to get a kill. If they had to shoot at clays flying high, or any distance away, Carver was going to be in trouble.

36

'So, we've shot grouse, now it's time for partridge,' said Klerk as they reached the second stand. It was much simpler than the grouse butt, just a basic square of wooden fencing, hip-high, with a bin for used cartridges attached to the shooter's side. All the effort had been devoted to creating a classic, mature hedgerow of bushes and trees directly in front of the stand that looked as though it had been a part of the landscape for centuries. Carver marvelled at the effort and cost that must have gone into locating, transporting and replanting the mix of dogwood, spindleberry and hawthorn hedging, as well as the oak and chestnut trees that stood among them.

From behind the hedgerow, Carver heard the noise of a motor starting up followed by a quieter, whirring sound. Somewhere back there at least one mechanized platform was rising into the air, taking with it a trap. So the clays, like the birds they were imitating, would emerge from behind the hedge at a variety of heights.

'Simultaneous pairs,' said McGuinness, indicating that both clays would be released at the same time. 'Mr Klerk to go first.'

Now the strike order had rotated in Carver's favour. This time he would be the last to shoot.

Klerk took his place behind the fencing and called 'Pull!' for the first pair.

The clays emerged from behind the hedgerow, passing over one of the oak trees and rising higher into the air as they flew towards Klerk, angled left-to-right this time. They flew at different heights and on marginally differing courses, adding to the challenge of shooting them both in quick succession.

Klerk tracked the clays as they sped through the sky, swinging his gun round clockwise from twelve o'clock almost to three before he fired. Again his technique was well-schooled and effective. He scored nine out of ten.

Zalika demonstrated once again that she was more gifted than her uncle. She dismissed the first four pairs with her usual accuracy, firing earlier, so that the clays were hit when they had barely passed two o'clock. When the final pair appeared, she destroyed the ninth clay with calm efficiency. But as any serious shot knows, the last bird is often the hardest. It may be a matter of mental fatigue, for even the sternest concentration can slip. Or perhaps complacency is the greater danger, a fractional relaxation brought on by the certainty that the tenth will go down just like the last nine have done. In any event, many a competitor has been undone right at the end of a hitherto perfect sequence. And that was what happened to Zalika Stratten. She looked incredulously at the final clay as it kept flying long after the last echoes of her shot had faded away, then snapped her hand irritably round her cartridges as they sprang from the barrels of her gun.

So the girl was human, after all.

Zalika had given Carver an opening. He had to make sure he took full advantage.

This time there were no distractions. He did not look around. He did not think about anything but the clays. While the others had been shooting he had studied the clays' flight patterns, noting precisely where they first appeared, relative to the oak tree, taking his mark from one specific branch. He dusted the first four pairs by the time they reached one o'clock.

As McGuinness pressed the control-button for the fifth time, Carver's eyes narrowed, his jaw clenched slightly, and in a moment of pure focus he felt as though the whole world had slowed down around him, so that the clays seemed to be drifting as big and lazy as two black balloons and he had all the time in the world to bring them down. He shot them both before anyone else had even realized they were there, when they'd barely passed twelve on that imaginary clock.

As he placed his cartridges in the bin and turned round to face the others, Carver noticed a wry half-smile on McGuinness's lips. The gamekeeper caught his eye and gave a fractional nod of acknowledgement.

Zalika's lead had been reduced to one. Carver was back in the game.

37

'Now let's bash some bunnies,' said Klerk.

The third stand wasn't based on anywhere fancy. There's nothing fancy about shooting rabbits, no matter where you are. But that doesn't make rabbit clays any less of a challenge.

They came out of the trap upright, presenting the full face of the clay to the shooters as they scooted along the ground, bouncing up when they hit a bump, or a thick tuft of grass. McGuinness released the clays on report – in other words, pressing the control for the second clay as soon as he heard the first shot – coming first from the right, then from the left.

Zalika went first and shot flawlessly. She swivelled her gun to the right to pick up the first clay, tracked it until it was directly in front of her, then fired. Without pausing, she kept the gun moving to the left, locked on to the second clay, followed it back into the centre and fired again. She scored two hits, then four, six, eight, ten.

When she had finished, she caught the last two spent cartridges, disposed of them and walked away from the stand as though she had never done anything easier in her life. Memo to Carver: whatever you've got, I can handle it.

Carver matched her easily enough for the first four pairs. But the first clay of the final pair took a wicked bounce and he missed. The tenth clay was dusted without any trouble, but he was still left cursing his luck. So much for making a comeback: he was back to two behind.

Klerk shot eight. He was out of the running now, but for all his natural, ferocious competitiveness, he wasn't bothered. It was enough for him to watch the other two struggle for supremacy.

'Walk with me a moment,' he said to Carver as they moved on to the next stand. He nodded towards Zalika, who was chatting to McGuinness. 'Impressive young woman, isn't she?'

'Certainly seems to be,' Carver agreed.

'I'll tell you something, though: this is all new. For years after the kidnap, Zalika was dead to the world, completely blank. She had no energy, no passion. She hardly said a word to me, surly all the time.'

'Not surprising. She had an incredibly traumatic experience, lost her whole family.'

'Survivor guilt, the shrinks called it. Christ knows I paid for enough of them. Bought her anything she could possibly want. Nothing worked, she was stuck in the past. Then this whole Gushungo business started. Now she's a new woman. Take yesterday, playing the secretary – she'd never have done that before.'

'Sounds like it's given her a purpose in life.'

Klerk nodded. 'Ja, that's exactly what I think, too. She wants to get her hands on that bastard Mabeki. That's what's driving her, you mark my words. That and having you about the place.'

'I'm not so sure about that.'

'Trust me, she insisted on you being involved. But I'll tell you what, you had better beat her today or she will be severely disappointed. She will hold you in contempt.'

Klerk put such relish into the word 'contempt' that Carver could not help but smile.

'One more reason to beat her, then,' he said.

For the fourth test of skill, they stopped in front of a grassy path, three paces wide, that ran between two high blackthorn hedges, one of which was somewhat taller than the other.

'You ever seen a walk-up before?' Klerk asked Carver.

Carver shook his head. 'Nope.'

'Well, the idea is very simple. You walk steadily down the path. The first clay of each pair is fired without warning, then the second one on report. I tell you, man, some of these bastards fly over the hedge, some run along the ground – there's no way of knowing what's going to happen, particularly if you go first.'

'Which I'll be doing,' said Carver.

'Ja, so I see!' Klerk laughed. 'In any case, you are allowed to stop walking to reload. But then you must get on the move again. The two people who are not shooting walk behind the one who is. When we get to the end of the walk, we turn round, come back to the start and repeat the whole process.'

Carver liked the look of the walk-up. It was like being on patrol, knowing that a contact was imminent, ready to shoot the instant danger approached. Wherever the clays came from – left or right, high or low – it made no difference. Carver knew from the first pace he took down the walk that he was going to score ten, and he was not disappointed.

'Ten straight hits,' said Klerk as they turned to stroll back to the start. 'I'm impressed. Donald's the only man ever to have straighted the walk-up before now. And I have to follow you.'

Carver walked directly behind Klerk as he fired his ten shots, scoring six hits. How was he to know the custom that the next person down the walk-up followed the shooter, so as to get a clear sight of what was in store? Except that Carver did not have to be told that: it was obvious. And so was the irritation that possessed Zalika Stratten as she walked behind him, forced to watch his backside, when she could and should have been taking mental notes on her uncle's shooting. Good: let her be distracted for once.

Carver spotted a very slight twitch in her neck – a sign of tension at last – as she loaded her opening two cartridges. It didn't seem to affect her, not at first anyway. She hit the first two pairs and reloaded. The fifth clay came straight up the walk, low and fast. She missed. But before Zalika could curse, or Carver silently cheer, the second clay was released, or what was left of it. The clay had broken in the trap and was now just a scattering of fragments.

'No bird,' called McGuinness. 'The pair will be fired again.'

A smile spread across Zalika's face. She had been reprieved.

But then McGuinness finished his sentence. 'However, may I remind you, Miss Zalika, that was a pair on report, and the rules of clay pigeon shooting state that the score for the first bird is counted. I am afraid the miss still stands.'

It said a lot for her strength of mind that she did not let the disappointment distract her. She shot the pair again and hit both times, even though the first counted for nothing. The final two pairs were also disposed of. It was a remarkable recovery, and Carver admired the sheer guts Zalika had displayed. But the fact remained that she had dropped a shot. The gap had come down to one. As they walked to the final stand there was still everything to play for.

38

The stark metallic structure loomed over the shooting ground like a watchtower at a POW camp. But there were no guards standing at its summit, armed with searchlights and machine guns. Instead, two traps were slowly rising up pulleys attached to the outside of the tower, making Carver more uneasy with every second they kept moving.

'Think of this as a very steep hillside,' said Klerk. 'The beaters are about to flush the pheasants off the top of the hill and they're going to fly right over us, just begging to be shot.'

'How high are the traps going?' Carver asked.

'One hundred and forty feet.'

At that range, the widely scattered shot from Carver's gun would be far less effective than the tight, heavily choked patterns Zalika would be punching through the air. Just as the competition reached its climax, she would have a major advantage. It was down to him not to make it a decisive one.

'That's some pretty serious shooting,' he said.

Klerk laughed mischievously. 'Oh ja, this is the bloody black run all right. And we've added a little complication, haven't we, Donald?'

'Aye, that we have. I've loaded the traps with midi clays. They're ninety millimetres across instead of the standard one-oh-eight.'

Klerk slapped Carver on the back. 'No worries for you, eh? I've seen you shoot. I'm sure you'll blow them out of the sky. I know Zalika will, that's for sure.'

'Maybe,' Carver replied, doing his best to sound completely unconcerned. 'But not before you've gone first.'

The clays were released in simultaneous pairs this time, but from two separate traps, meaning that they flew towards Klerk at slightly different heights and angles, forcing him to change his aim between shots. He coped well enough, and his score of seven was more than respectable in the circumstances. But he was really just the warm-up act before the main attractions.

Zalika was second up. She walked up to shoot with her usual air of calm self-control. Her breathing was steady. She lined up the cartridges with her standard ritualistic precision.

Everything seemed fine, yet something wasn't quite right. She hit the first pair, but only by striking the back edges of the two clays.

Now she faced a real test of character. When a good shot makes a very slight mistake there is always the temptation to over-compensate. It's very easy, having shot the back of a clay, to aim further ahead of its flight and miss the next one entirely to the front. The best and bravest thing to do is nothing at all. You're still hitting the clays, so why change anything?

Carver could just imagine the battle going on in Zalika's head. It was visible in her movements, too: the very slight shake in her hands as she slipped the cartridges into the barrels, the fumbling as she rotated them till they faced the right way.

She was tough: she gutsed it out and hit both the next clays. Now there were just six left for her in the entire competition. She was still a shot up. If she could close out the last three pairs she'd win and Carver could do nothing about it. But the tension was rising, no matter how hard she fought to keep it at bay.

After the fourth shot had been fired, Zalika paused just a second too long, staring at the ground, and she took a long, deliberate breath. When she broke open the barrels she was still lost in her thoughts. She made no attempt to catch the used cartridges but let them fall to the ground. When the new cartridges went in, she did not even look at them, still less line up the writing on their bases before snapping the gun shut again.

Carver knew that she was on a knife-edge. 'Miss one, miss one,' he whispered soundlessly to himself.

Zalika did not oblige. She hit the fifth clay all right, but the sixth came out broken, prompting McGuinness to call 'No bird!' again.

If anything, this seemed to relax Zalika. She looked far less concerned as she once again discarded the used cartridge, replaced it with a new one and then lined up both cartridges to her satisfaction.

She'd got her routine back again. She'd returned to the zone.

The third pair was replayed. This time Zalika missed the first clay but hit the second. She smiled to herself, blessing her good fortune: when she'd made a mistake, it didn't matter. Carver could see that she'd remembered McGuinness's words about the rules of clay pigeon shooting stating that the score for the first bird is counted. On that basis, the first bird was a hit, the hit stood, and she was still one up, just four shots left.

Carver saw the confidence flooding back into Zalika as she dusted the next pair. She was in the final straight now, the finishing line in sight.

The final pair were released. Over they came, the right-hand clay slightly higher than the left, the angle between them widening all the time. Zalika hit the right one first then swung her gun in an arc towards her left shoulder. The swing was smooth, her movements controlled, both her eyes open to give her optimum vision and depth perception.

And yet she missed.

Carver couldn't believe it. He'd have put any money in the

world on Zalika getting the pair. Yet, for the second time, she'd been let down by the final shot in a sequence. Zalika looked equally incredulous, staring at the untouched clay as it continued its gentle arc to the ground as if she could dust it by sheer force of will. She gave a final shake of the head, then snapped the gun open, caught the cartridges with an irritated snap of her fingers and hurled them in the bin before turning and walking back towards the others.

As she walked past Carver, her eyes blazing with defiance, she hissed, 'Well, you still can't beat me,' quietly enough that only he could hear.

Carver said nothing. He had no intention of getting ahead of himself. The end result was just a distraction. He had a job to do first.

He strode towards his firing position not hoping he would shoot well, or even believing that he would. He demanded it.

He banished all thoughts of Zalika, dismissed any worries about the height and size of the clays, or the fact that he'd be firing with unrestricted barrels that would spray his shots across the sky like confetti. He concentrated purely and simply on the element he could control: the quality of his shooting.

The first four clays were obliterated.

When the third pair flew from the traps, Carver hit the first clay smack in the middle, but only caught the leading edge of the second, very nearly missing to the front. Now he was the one who had to fight the temptation to change his technique, the one who had to have faith enough to stick with what he'd been doing.

Carver felt the pounding of his heart against his chest and the itchy stickiness of sweat beneath his armpits. He told himself to get a grip.

'Pull!' he called.

The clays were flung from their traps, and at that precise moment the wind, which had blown steadily all day, suddenly flurried. The gust only lasted for a second or two, but it was enough to disturb the flight of the clays. The right-hand one slowed in mid-air and lost height, making the left clay appear to race away from it. Now their courses were radically different, and Carver had to adjust his shot in mid-swing as he locked on to the dropping clay. Somehow he managed to hit it and then jerk his gun left and up, his sights scrabbling across the sky to find the other clay.

Where the hell had it got to?

His spine was arched like a tightly pulled bow and the weight of his head was so far back that he was almost toppling over when he finally found his target. He had no balance, no stillness. He was as ragged as hell.

Carver fired.

The crack of the shot slapped the summer air like a palm to a face, closely followed by a frustrated cry of 'No!'

Zalika Stratten had not been able to contain her frustration at Carver's absurd good fortune. The clay had been blown to pieces. Somehow, he'd got everything wrong about the shot except the end result.

After that, the last pair was a formality. Carver came away with a perfect ten.

'So we tied,' said Zalika, coldly.

'You sure?' Carver replied.

She frowned at him uncertainly. But before she could say anything else there was the sound of a polite cough.

'I have the scores,' said McGuinness.

He was holding the score cards in one hand, divided into boxes for each pair of clays. The shots were marked down as 'kills' and 'losses', a diagonal line across a box indicating that both shots had been kills.

'Mr Klerk, you came third. I've never seen you shoot so well, sir. Good enough to win, I reckon, nine times out of ten. And you, Miss Zalika, well, I cannae imagine how anyone could shoot like you did and not come out on top.'

She gave a weary smile. 'Thank you, Donald.'

'But the winner,' he continued, 'is Mr Carver by one.'

'What?' Now Zalika's eyes blazed with furious energy. 'That's not possible! It was a tie!'

'I'm afraid not, Miss. You lost two shots in the final five pairs.'

'I know, but one of them was in the pair that I had to reshoot. It didn't count. You said so yourself: the score from the first bird is counted. I killed the first bird.'

'Aye, so you did. And the score is counted . . . when you are shooting on report. But these pairs were simultaneous. And I'm afraid the rules are very clear, Miss. If a "no bird" is called in a simultaneous pair, the score for the other bird does not count. You start from scratch when the pair is released again. And you lost the first bird of that pair, as well as the very last bird of all. When Mr Carver killed all ten, he overtook you.'

Zalika sighed. 'I see.' She switched her attention back to Carver. 'So you win, then.'

'Yes.'

'But only on a technicality.'

'A win is a win. That's how it works.'

She narrowed her eyes and stared at him. 'You knew that rule all along, didn't you? When I said you couldn't win, you knew.'

'Yeah, I knew I had the beating of you. But I still had to get all ten.'

The look in Zalika's eye was as cold as bare steel on a frosty morning. But as she turned and walked away from him, Carver swore he could see the beginnings of a smile spreading across her face, almost as though she, not he, were the real winner.

39

Justus Iluko had spent the day at a UN World Food Programme supply centre, trying to persuade officials there to double the size of their deliveries of maize to the refugee camp that had sprung up on his farm. 'You bring enough food for ten thousand people, but there are many times that number now. You must send more,' he begged.

The official's name was Hester Thompson. She could not remember the last time she had stepped into a hot bath, or grabbed more than four hours' sleep. Her greasy, unwashed hair was pulled back into a bedraggled ponytail, held in place by a rubber band.

She looked at Justus through eyes made red by fatigue and dust. 'We don't have more food,' she said. 'The UN has cut its food aid budget. We're giving you all we've got.'

'But people are dying of starvation. There is no fresh water, no sanitation. Yesterday we had twenty new cases of cholera, but we have no doctors, no medicine to treat them.'

'I understand, and I sympathize, really I do. But even if I had all the money in the world to spend on food it wouldn't make any difference because your government—'

'They are not *my* government,' Iluko snapped. 'They are hyenas, feeding on my country's corpse.'

Thompson sighed wearily. 'Whatever, the Gushungo regime refuses to import more than a hundred thousand tons of maize into Malemba. The President says he does not need any more than that. In fact the minimum amount required to keep this country alive is close to six hundred thousand tons. Last week we cut our basic maize allowance to five kilos per person, per week. That works out at six hundred calories a day. And yeah, I know, that's a starvation ration.'

'So you will not help . . .'

'Not unless I suddenly develop superpowers, no.'

Justus drove home empty-handed. He tried to call his family from the Toyota Land Cruiser he had bought, second-hand, with half the money Samuel Carver had sent him a decade earlier. There was no reply.

When Justus finally returned home he discovered the reason for their silence. Overwhelmed by grief and rage, he screamed out curses against Henderson Gushungo, and cried out to God for vengeance. As the sun set behind the western hills, he began digging Nyasha's grave, completing the task by the light of a torch. She was buried wrapped in a blanket, and as a handful of refugees gathered round him, Justus said a few prayers to speed his wife's soul on its way. When he asked the people what had happened to his children, no one knew. They had been taken away, two more recruits to the ranks of the disappeared. What difference did it make where they had disappeared to?

Late that night, in a brief moment of calm before the tears and fury consumed him again, he thought of the one man on earth who might be able to help him. He had always kept in touch with Carver, marking every Christmas with a long letter detailing his children's progress as they made their way up the school ladder. Less regularly, Carver had replied, but the Englishman had always shown him friendship and respect. Justus could not afford to make an international mobile phone call, but what did that matter now?

He had a number for Carver. So he dialled it and hoped for the best.

40

Twenty-four hours after Carver's arrival, he was back in Klerk's drawing room, standing in front of the elephant painting. But this time he had his back to the charging tusker. His attention was focused on Wendell Klerk, Patrick Tshonga and Zalika Stratten. Carver wasn't normally given to public speaking. But he had to admit he was getting a buzz out of feeling the anticipation in the air. He knew the answer they all wanted from him. But he was going to make them wait till he was good and ready to give it to them.

Terence had provided drinks, as always. Carver swilled his whisky in the glass, putting his thoughts in order as he watched the motion of the golden liquid. Then he said, 'A long time ago, a couple of years before I went into Mozambique to get Zalika, I spent some time in a clinic near Geneva. I'd done a job that started going wrong right from the start, and only ended up worse. I imagine you knew about that, Mr Klerk.'

He nodded. 'I was aware you'd been in a bad way, ja.'

'Well, then, I'm sure you also knew that my case was handled by a psychiatrist called Geisel, Dr Karlheinz Geisel. Once I started functioning a little better – stopped being a vegetable, basically – we used to have therapy sessions. He said he had a problem with making me better. He was worried that once I was well, I'd just go back to doing things that he thought were morally inexcusable. So it troubled his conscience, feeling like he was my enabler.'

'And your point is?'

'I've spent the weekend listening to you three going on about your precious land of Malemba. Now you're going to listen to me.

'Geisel and I got into the whole question of killing. How did it feel? Could you ever justify it? I came up with an imaginary situation for him. Suppose you're put in a time machine and taken back to Germany, 1936. You're at the airport in Berlin. Adolf Hitler is getting on a plane. Someone sticks a detonator in your hand and tells you that there's a bomb on the plane. All you have to do is push the switch, the bomb goes off and Hitler dies. No World War Two. No Holocaust. Trouble is, there are other people on the plane. Nice, clean-living folk: the crew, a couple of pretty stewardesses, maybe some cute, smiley little blond kids from the Hitler Youth. So if Adolf dies, they die too. Question: do you push the button?'

'Of course!' snapped Klerk. 'A few lives against tens of millions. What's the problem?'

'Geisel had a problem,' said Carver. 'He wasn't the one who was going to kill all those millions. But he was going to kill all the people on the plane. Their deaths would be down to him. So he wanted time to think about it. I said, "You don't have time. You've got to do it now or never." Then I gave him all this macho crap about how he'd screwed up the job. It was too late, the plane just took off, and now Hitler's alive and seventy million people are going to die. I remember I told him, "That's why I don't waste too much time worrying about the things you like to worry about. In my line of business, there isn't time." '

'That's the right attitude,' said Klerk, approvingly.

'No it isn't. That's the attitude that ends up with people in black uniforms with silver skulls on their caps and SS badges on their shoulders, shoving Jews into cattle trucks: "Don't worry. Don't think about morality. Just obey your orders and do the job." See, it took me a while to grasp that Geisel was right. None of us ever knows what the consequences of our actions will be down the line. All we can look at is what's in front of us, and ask ourselves, "Is this the right thing to do, right here, right now? Can I justify it to myself?" Maybe I'm going soft in my old age, but as much of a mad, genocidal, fascist bastard as Gushungo is, I can't justify killing him in cold blood. So my answer is that I'm not going to take your job, Mr Klerk . . . Mr Tshonga . . . Zalika. You want the old bugger dead so much, you go and kill him. See how that works for you.'

Klerk shook his head in disbelief and disgust. 'You telling me that you've lost your nerve, Carver?'

'No, just my interest in other people's dirty laundry.'

'Please, Sam, it's not like that,' Zalika pleaded. 'This is a matter of principle, of saving lives. It's totally justifiable.'

'You think so? From where I'm standing it looks like one man who wants power, another man who wants money and a woman who wants revenge for a ten-year-old crime, and, oh, while we're at it, can I have all my land back? All those dying, suffering people you keep going on about aren't the reason for killing Gushungo. They're the excuse.'

'So what about everything I told you yesterday?' Klerk asked. 'You going to throw all that back in my face?'

'What, that killing Gushungo and Mabeki will do more for Zalika than any shrink ever could? Like it's some kind of therapy? Trust me, it isn't.'

'I see. Well, if that's what you think, Carver, there's no purpose in extending your stay here any further. Terence will arrange a taxi to take you to the airport. I'm sure there will be a flight that's going somewhere near Geneva.'

'Thanks. That's all I need. I appreciate the hospitality, Mr Klerk. It was good seeing you again. You too, Zalika. Mr Tshonga, I wish you the best of luck with your next election.'

Tshonga gave a gentle, knowing smile. 'Thank you, Mr Carver. But somehow I do not think it will come to that. I believe I have not seen the last of you.'

'I wouldn't count on it.'

'Think about it, Sam,' Zalika urged. Then her voice turned much harder as she added, more like an ultimatum than a request, 'Think very carefully about what you're throwing away.'

Carver had thought about that. He'd very nearly discarded all his rational, carefully marshalled arguments for turning down the job, just for the chance to be next to Zalika Stratten. It had taken a serious effort of will to turn his back on everything she had to offer. He had no answer for her now; no explanation that would justify his rejection of her.

Klerk, meanwhile, having got nowhere playing hardball, tried the softly-softly approach. 'There are still a few days before the Gushungos fly to Hong Kong. If you change your mind, the offer's still open.'

Carver nodded in acknowledgement. 'I'll find my own way out,' he said.

41

Carver didn't leave Campden Hall quite as quickly as he'd anticipated. Just before he got to the front door, he heard a low, urgent
voice behind him: 'Mr Carver! Please! Wait!'

He turned to see Brianna Latrelle striding towards him, her head
darting from side to side as she made sure there was no one else
around to see her.

'Did you agree?' she whispered again, even more quietly, when
she'd caught up with Carver. She reached out a slender brown arm
and grabbed his wrist in a surprisingly strong grip. 'Whatever they
asked you to do, did you agree?'

'I'm leaving,' said Carver. 'I have a plane to catch.'

'So you said no?' She relaxed her hand a fraction and her
shoulders dropped as the tension in them abated. 'I hope so . . . for
your sake.' Her hand tightened again. 'I don't know exactly what it
is you guys have been talking about. But just the way everyone's
been acting, it gives me a real bad feeling. Before you arrived,
Wendell and Tshonga were shut away for hours, no one else
allowed near the room. Then Zalika, dressing up like that, faking

you out . . . I can't tell you why it bothers me. I mean, Wendell has meetings all the time. Why should this be any different? I guess it's just my female intuition. Silly, huh?'

Carver removed her hand from his arm as gently as he could. Brianna Latrelle meant well, but she wasn't in any position to know what had really been going on.

'I've got to go,' he said, not unkindly.

By the time he'd walked through the doors, he'd already put Brianna Latrelle out of his mind and switched his attention to his travel plans.

The last flight out of Luton to Geneva was already about to leave by the time Carver's taxi pulled away. He went online, checked the schedules and found a British Airways flight out of Heathrow leaving in two hours' time. There were seats left in business class. Carver bought one and checked in online.

Heathrow Terminal Five was a hundred and eleven miles from Klerk's front door. He took four fifty-pound notes from his wallet.

'Yours if you get me there in eighty minutes or less,' he told the driver, who was called Asif.

The money made no difference. There were roadworks on the M11 with a forty-mile-an-hour limit and speedcams. Then they hit traffic on the M25. Asif clocked a hundred and twenty trying to make up for lost time, but arrived fractionally too late for Carver to make the plane. He gave him the two hundred anyway, and got another ticket at the airport: a Swissair flight to Zurich.

By the time he got there, the only way of getting to Geneva was the train. It left at four minutes past eleven and arrived a little before half-past two in the morning. Carver caught a cab from the station to the Old Town, went up to his apartment and was asleep before his head hit the pillow.

He had turned off his mobile as he got on the Zurich flight and had not bothered to turn it back on. He had a feeling Zalika might call him to try to persuade him to change his mind about the Gushungo job, or just give him hell for saying no. His refusal of Klerk's offer must have felt to her like a personal rejection. She'd offered herself and he'd walked away. She wasn't likely to be too happy about that. And if he told her the truth, that his decision was nothing personal, it was only likely to make matters worse.

It wasn't till he woke up around nine that he finally opened up his connection to the outside world again and heard Justus's message.

And his first reaction was that he'd made a mistake. It wasn't Zalika playing tricks. It was Wendell Klerk.

42

They came back for Justus Iluko in the morning. He wasn't surprised. Even the ignorant apes who ran the local branch of the National Intelligence Organization, the secret police who enforced Gushungo's never-ending campaign of fear and oppression, would have worked out that if they had a man's children, they would not be safe until they had him too. Justus let them come. He took it for granted that he was a dead man. And he reasoned that the nearest jail was at Buweku, some thirty miles away. Canaan and Farayi were almost certainly being held there. If he were taken to Buweku too, that would be his best chance of getting close to them, however fleetingly, before they all vanished for good.

All he wanted was to speak to Carver first. Justus knew that there was nothing his friend could do now. But perhaps, if he could only tell Carver what had happened, that might, in the end, give him some hope of revenge.

'I know you're a ruthless bastard, Klerk, but I never thought you'd stoop that low.'

'What the fuck, Carver – what's this "stoop that low"? What are you talking about, man?'

Carver stopped pacing round his living room and spoke with steely clarity. 'I'm talking about the message I got from Justus Iluko.'

'Justus who?'

'Iluko. He worked for you, remember? You fought together in the war. He helped me get Zalika away from Moses Mabeki.'

'Ah shit, that Justus. Sure I remember him. Good man, quit working for me a while back. But what's this about a message?'

'He called me last night – someone who claimed to be him, anyway. The connection was crap and the guy's voice was shot to hell, could have been anyone. He said his wife was dead and his kids had been taken by Gushungo's men. He was begging me to help. So you're telling me this isn't some stunt you're trying to pull, faking some tragedy with a family I know, trying to get me to change my mind? Because it's a helluva bloody coincidence. I walk out on you and a few hours later, hey presto, there's one of your old employees calling me up—'

'Hey, I swear, I had nothing to do with it. And to prove it, I'll get my guys in Malemba to check this out, find out what the fuck's going on. All right?'

There was a bleeping in Carver's ear.

'Hang on,' he said, 'someone on the other line. Shit, it's Justus's number. I'll call you right back.'

'Samuel, is that you?'

The voice on the other end was tight and high-pitched with anxiety and the reception was terrible, but now that Carver could hear him live he was in no doubt: this was Justus Iluko.

'Yeah, I'm here. What's happening?'

'They are coming for me. They killed my wife and took my children. Now they are here for me too.'

Down the line, Carver could hear shouting and a hammering noise – someone trying to batter down a door. He felt a desperate sense of helplessness and guilt at his inability to change any of what was about to happen.

'Is there anything I can do?' he asked, though he knew it was a futile question.

'Do not worry about me, I am a dead man,' came the reply. 'But please, Sam, I beg you, if there is anything you can do for my children . . . anything . . . I . . .'

Justus's final words were drowned in the crash of the splintering door and a cacophony of heavy boots and raised voices as the room was invaded and Justus was seized.

There was one last despairing cry of 'Sam, please!' then a brief burst of feedback and static before the line went dead.

Carver stood alone in his Geneva flat, surrounded by all the possessions and comforts that many years in a lucrative trade had bought him, shamed by the ease of his existence; shamed, too, by his initial scepticism about Justus's call. While Carver had been tucking into breakfast and shooting at clay pigeons on Klerk's estate, Justus and his family had been torn apart, their lives destroyed on a madman's whim. He thought back to the psychiatrist Karlheinz Geisel, who had baulked at the idea of doing something that would cause the death of a few specific individuals, even if it might save many more faceless, unknown people. Now Carver faced the precise opposite situation: people he knew would die if he did not do something. There was a moral imperative to act.

The children whose education Carver had supported and whose father had saved his life were imprisoned, facing interrogation, torture, even execution. Every year Canaan and Farayi had sent him hand-drawn cards at Christmas, along with letters earnestly describing their progress at school. In the past few years, childish descriptions had given way to growing maturity. He had seen them blossom as individuals with minds and opinions of their own, young people of the kind Malemba desperately needed if it had any hope of recovering from the devastation wrought by Henderson Gushungo. How could he stand by and let such promise go to waste?

Justus had begged Carver to do something for his children, but it had to be something effective: no cheap gestures, no grandstanding, but something that would make a difference. He had to give the Iluko kids, and others like them, the best chance of surviving now and prospering in the future. And there was only one way a single individual could do that.

Carver went over everything he had been told about Malemba and its ruling élite. An idea began to take shape in his mind. It grew clearer and more strongly defined as he went online and looked at maps and aerial views of Hong Kong. Then he surfed websites dealing with tropical medicine and marine biology. He took out a notepad and wrote down 'pyx', 'patten', 'cruet', 'chasuble', 'lavabo'.

Finally, Carver called Klerk.

'Justus Iluko was captured by Gushungo's men today,' Carver said. 'I heard it happen. His wife is dead. His kids are in jail. I need to know which one. Can your people find that out for me?'

'Sure,' said Klerk. 'But are you going to try and break them out? Don't waste your time, man. You're good, but one man against Gushungo's entire security forces? Forget it.'

'Thanks, but I worked that out for myself. Next question: your mining operations, do they employ chemists?'

'Of course. The best. We depend on them for a lot of our refining processes.'

'Excellent. Tell them I need someone to carry out' – Carver looked at the words on the laptop screen and took a deep breath – 'a synthesis that relies on the formation of a benzylhydrazide intermediate, subjected to methyl glyoxylate hemimethyl acetal and a Lewis acid, in order to construct a highly reactive azomethine imine which subsequently undergoes an intramolecular 1,3-dipolar cycloaddition reaction, leading to an advanced tetracyclic intermediate. They should end up with a substance that has the molecular formula $C_{10}H_{17}N_7O_4$.'

'Sam, what the fuck are you on about?'

'Something that will sort out that issue you've got in Hong Kong.'

'Really?' said Klerk. His whole attitude had changed in a single word. Suddenly he sounded a lot more interested.

'Yes, really. I've reconsidered my position. Let's just say I now have a strong personal interest in making sure the job is done as thoroughly as possible.'

'That's great news. Zalika will be delighted.'

'Good for her, but that's not the reason I'm doing this. I'll email you that synthesis along with the appropriate diagrams. Tell your people that if they want a full account they can find it in the *Journal of the American Chemical Society*, 1984, edition 106, page 5,594. They're also going to need flour, water and a basic guide to unleavened baking. And you'd better tell them to wear protective clothing when they work on this.'

'Might exposure prove dangerous to their health?' Klerk asked.

'Very.'

'That's good to know.'

'Now, I agree that the way to do this is by faking a diamond heist. The robbers come in, get rid of the inhabitants of the house, then take the stones at their leisure. The obvious time to do it is when the entire household is down on its knees taking communion – the one time in the week when their guard is down. The way this plays out, it will look like two separate groups of people taking advantage of a given situation. Gushungo leaves the country, that's when his opponents mount a coup to seize power. The cat's away, the mice play. That makes perfect sense. Meanwhile, he and the wife are carting millions of bucks' worth of diamonds around Hong Kong: frankly it's a miracle someone hasn't lifted them long before now. Is it a handy coincidence, both things happening at the same time? Yes. Can anyone prove there's a connection? No. I'll make sure they can't. And that would be a lot easier if your niece wasn't tagging along for the ride. So give me one good reason, aside from her making life miserable for Uncle Wendell if she doesn't get her way, that she has to be there.'

'Two reasons. First, because this is her job. She researched it. She planned it. She has a right to help execute it. And second, because you can't get the diamonds without her.'

'Why not?'

'The safe,' Klerk replied. 'It opens via a scanner which is set to recognize Faith Gushungo's finger and palm prints. They have to align the right way, too. And that requires a woman's hand. Yours would be too big.'

'And you know this about the scanner because . . . ?'

'Because one of the maids, young woman by the name of Tina Wong, is actually a former detective sergeant in the Organized Crime and Triad Bureau of the Hong Kong Police. She's working for us, been undercover in the house for the past three months. She can get you a set of Faith Gushungo's prints. She can make sure the front door is unlocked. The one thing she can't do is get the diamonds for you. She has to be on her knees, saying her prayers, same as everyone else. In any case, the Chinese, very petite. Her hand is too small.'

'But Zalika's got Goldilocks hands, I get it. I'll need to get her trained up first. You say you have plans of the house?'

'Yes.'

'You have outbuildings up at that place of yours in Suffolk?'

'Of course.'

'Right then. Get the target house mocked up inside a barn or something. Doesn't have to be anything fancy: chalk marks on the floor, some stairs and a first floor made out of planks and scaffolding. Just so long as the dimensions are right. Try and get a copy of the safe, or as near as dammit, too. We're not going to go in blasting on this. No guns, no smoke, no bombs. It's all about timing, and that has to be perfect. If Zalika shows me she can do it, she can come. Otherwise I'll take my chances with your undercover cop. All right?'

'Ja,' said Klerk. 'But now let me give you my condition for doing the job. I've got great things planned for that young lady, so you just listen to me. You brought her back safely once. You damn well bring her back again.'

'I'll do my best.'

'No, Carver, just do it.'

43

Within half an hour of Klerk and Carver ending their conversation, Moses Mabeki received another call from within the grounds of Campden Hall.

'That's good news,' he said. 'I had considered remaining in Malemba while the Gushungos went abroad, so that I would be well placed to respond in the event of any . . .' Mabeki chuckled to himself as he searched for the right words. 'Any unforeseen emergencies. But on reflection, I think the best course of action would be to accompany the President and First Lady to Hong Kong, so that I can offer any assistance that might be required there. Yes, that is certainly the better option.'

44

Carver was not a religious man, though there had been times when he was grateful for the words of comfort offered by military chaplains in the hours before battle, or at the gravesides of recently dead friends. But that afternoon he took a short drive out of town, along Route 1, parallel to the north shore of Lake Geneva. At the Nyon exit he turned left, away from the lake, up towards the village of Gingins. A little oasis of Englishness in the heart of Switzerland, it possessed both a cricket club and a beautiful old church where the Anglican parish of La Côte held a service at four o'clock every Sunday afternoon.

Carver took communion there for the first time in more than a decade. The words of the service, ingrained in him by years of compulsory religious attendance at school, came back to him with all the familiarity of an old friend encountered by chance after many years of absence. The ritual played out with comforting predictability, and the prayers retained a strange, potent poetry for all the many attempts of the Church's modernizers to strip them of their mystery and magic.

The moments of silence and contemplation enabled him to think about what he was planning to do. Was he committing a murder, he wondered, or casting out a devil? As always, however, Carver did not waste too much energy on metaphysical speculation. His focus had to remain on the here and now, and that meant concentrating on the words printed in the Order of Service he was holding in his hand:

> Grant us therefore, gracious Lord,
> so to eat the flesh of your dear Son Jesus Christ
> and to drink his blood,
> that our sinful bodies may be made clean by his body
> and our souls washed through his most precious blood,
> and that we may evermore dwell in him and he in us.
> Amen.

When the prayer was over and the vicar's preparations complete, Carver left his pew and joined the line of worshippers waiting for communion. Finally, he approached the altar and knelt to receive the bread and wine. He watched every movement the vicar made, noted the precise sequence of events and the words that accompanied each of them. And when the service was over, just to make sure he'd got it right, he drove straight back to Geneva, went out to evensong at Holy Trinity Church, which the locals called *l'église anglaise*, and took communion all over again.

45

For the rest of the day after Justus Iluko had been taken away, his house remained undisturbed. It was as if the violence and suffering that had occurred in its vicinity had created some kind of force field that held the mass of dispossessed who clustered around it at bay. It was not until the final light of the dying sun had been extinguished and the purple-black African night, heavy with the spicy scent of warm earth, had descended that the first scavengers started edging towards the walls of whitewashed concrete blocks.

This was no more than the law of nature in action. When an animal died in the bush, its carcass provided carrion for hyenas, vultures and all manner of insects until nothing remained but its bare bones. Even they provided marrow for truly enterprising scavengers. And so it was with the house. It too was a corpse from which the spirit of life had been extinguished. Its inhabitants had no more use for the beds on which they had slept, the tables at which they had worked and eaten, or the countless little possessions that spoke of a man and woman working together to raise the children they loved. This was neither a moral issue nor a sentimental one. Better that these belongings should be recycled for the benefit of those still alive and present than rot away to no purpose.

The larder was emptied of all its contents. The floorboards, joists, doors, window frames and shutters were taken for firewood and building materials. The corrugated iron panels were stripped from the roof. By dawn, only the walls remained. And with the rising sun came men with hammers, chisels and pickaxes to hack and chip away at the blocks themselves.

By noon, the house that Justus Iluko had built with such sweat and devotion, and occupied with such pride, had vanished as if it had never been. The land on which it stood was covered with brand-new huts and improvised tents, filled with the never-ending stream of people being transported to this once bountiful farm, now a dusty, barren hell.

46

As a religious man, Justus would not have described his new conditions in Buweku jail as hellish. They were more like a form of purgatory, a waiting room filled with other lost souls awaiting their day of judgement.

The cell to which he'd been taken was intended for all the remand prisoners who were awaiting trial. One of its sides faced a corridor and consisted of iron bars and crosspieces, so that the inmates were at all times visible to any passing guard. The other three sides comprised concrete walls into which concrete bunks had been fitted in three rows, rising several feet towards the roof. Justus had to reach up to grab the top bunk: it must have been seven feet off the ground. The only sanitation was a hole in the floor, ringed with cracked tiles, stained with the faeces of inmates from years and generations gone by. There was a solitary standpipe from which an intermittent dribble of water flowed, regardless of whether the tap was turned on or off. A single bare bulb, hanging from the ceiling in a wire-mesh cage, provided light to the cell, in theory at least. But it, too, worked only sporadically, and at times over which the men beneath it had no control whatsoever.

There were thirty-four men crammed into this hot, airless, fetid space. One of them was Justus's son Canaan. They hugged each other with a mixture of relief at being reunited, profound sorrow at the loss of Nyasha and the fierce desperation of men who know their days are numbered.

'Are you all right?' Justus asked, stepping back to look his boy in the eyes.

Canaan nodded. 'Yes, Father.'

Justus looked around at the eyes watching them, scanning them for signs of threat.

'Have you been treated well?' he asked.

Again his son nodded. This time he said nothing, just gave a nervous lick of his top lip. The boy's former princely demeanour had entirely disappeared and Justus felt certain he was hiding something, but knew that there was no point in pursuing the matter. If someone had attacked or abused him, it would only invite further trouble to mention it.

'Do you know what they have done with Farayi?' Justus asked. 'Is she all right? Have you seen her, or spoken to her?'

Canaan shook his head slowly. 'She is here somewhere, in a women's cell. But that is all I know.'

Justus nodded, trying to remain calm. He was Farayi's father. He should be protecting her, keeping her safe. Instead he was locked behind bars, unable to do anything to help his little girl. He sighed, then did his best to smile and put a cheerful tone in his voice as he asked, 'So, what have they been feeding you? Is the menu good at this establishment?'

Canaan shrugged, again saying nothing.

'The jailers,' Justus persisted, 'they must give you meals of some kind. I am sure the food is terrible, but—'

'There is no food, father.'

'No food? Don't be ridiculous! They must give you something.'

'The boy is right. There is no food.'

A man moved out of the shadows beneath one of the concrete

bunks, wincing as he got to his feet. His body was emaciated, his hair matted and grey.

'I see you are not familiar with the ways of our prison system,' he said. Not waiting for Justus to respond, he continued, 'The rules are very simple. All food must be brought to the jail by the friends or families of the men inside. In order to get it from the front door of the prison to these cells, a bribe must be paid to the guards. Sometimes this is money, sometimes it is food. They need to eat too, after all.'

'But we have no family,' said Justus. 'There is no one left to bring us food.'

'In that case,' said the man, 'prepare to starve.'

47

Early on the Monday morning, Carver flew back to England. Before he left Geneva, he stood by his kitchen island and reached into the wine rack that had been installed along one side. In the second row from the top, three spaces along, there was a hidden switch. He pressed it, then waited while the centre of the island's granite worksurface rose, revealing a metal frame containing a large plastic toolbox divided into six trays of varying depths.

Carver ignored the bottom tray, which contained his personal firearms: with a number of flights between now and the Gushungo job there was simply no point in bringing them along. In any event, he did not plan to do any shooting. Instead, he opened one of the shallower trays and removed an apparently random selection of items: a piece of wood, about six inches square, with a number of holes drilled through it; a set of AA batteries; and an assortment of nuts, bolts, washers and wires attached to crocodile clips.

From the kitchen he went to his bedroom wardrobe, took down a suitcase from the top shelf and picked out a couple of accessories he thought would come in handy: a pair of tortoiseshell spectacles with plain glass lenses and a short grey wig. When he was in the Special Boat Service, Carver had known another officer, not much older than him, who went prematurely grey in his early thirties. The officer's face, as if to compensate, remained unusually youthful and unlined. These contradictory signals made it very difficult for anyone who did not know him to judge his age. Carver was aiming for a similar effect.

All he needed now was an assortment of passports, driving licences, credit cards and SIM cards. He was ready to go.

He came in through Gatwick this time, rented a car at the airport and drove five miles to the West Sussex town of Crawley. On an industrial estate not far from the town's station he found a specialist suppliers called Vanpoulles and explained his particular requirements to a sales assistant, who was happy to go through Carver's list and recommend which of the various items he should purchase. Neither a chasuble nor a patten would be necessary, he was told.

Carver also mentioned that he was looking for a very particular kind of case to carry everything in, preferably second-hand and well worn-in. The salesman conferred with a colleague and mentioned an old customer who had just retired and might be able to supply just what Carver was looking for. He was down in Kent, not far from Tunbridge Wells.

The journey there and back took the best part of three hours, but was well worth the diversion. While he was there, Carver took advantage of Tunbridge Wells's reputation for being populated by elderly conservative gentlefolk. He went to a charity shop and found a lightweight dark-grey suit, tailor-made but just beginning to get a hint of that gloss around the elbows, knees and backside that comes from regular use. The trousers were cut for a man who ate more and exercised less than Carver, but a half-decent Hong Kong tailor would sort that out easily enough.

By late afternoon, Carver was battling the rush-hour traffic on the M25, heading up to Campden Hall. The tedious crawl round the eastern perimeter of London was enough to try the patience of a far more saintly man than him, but despite it Carver still felt that his day had been very well spent.

48

Faith Gushungo stormed into the kitchen of her Hong Kong property and screamed at the two servants cowering on the far side of the table in the middle of the room, stabbing a bejewelled finger at her underlings. 'My bedroom is a pigsty! I ordered you to have it spotlessly tidy when the President and I arrived, but the beds are not made! There is dirt everywhere! The bathroom is like an open sewer!'

She leaned forward, placing both hands flat on the table. In her red-soled Louboutin heels she stood over six feet tall, a giantess compared to the smaller figures of the Chinese women in their pale-grey uniforms and white aprons.

'But . . . but . . . I cleaned it, Missy,' the younger of the servants blurted out between sobs of fear and humiliation.

Faith Gushungo focused the full force of her disapproval upon the poor girl. Her voiced lowered in volume and pitch, but became all the more menacing as she replied, 'Oh really? You think you cleaned the room, do you? Well, listen to me, you little yellow monkey. You may be used to living in filth and squalor, but I am not. I demand the highest standards and I insist on absolute obedience from my staff. So unless you wish to lose your job, you will go to the room right now and you will sweep and polish and dust every single square inch of it to the standard expected. And you will not go home until I am satisfied with your work. Do I make myself clear?'

'Yes, Missy, yes . . . very clear. I will get everything I need, be there in one minute.'

'You had better be,' the First Lady of Malemba snarled, stepping away from the table. 'One minute, and not a second longer.' Then she turned on a stiletto heel and strode from the room, her heels clacking on the marble floor as she went.

Tina Wong waited until Faith Gushungo was out of sight and hearing, then placed a consoling hand on the back of the crying servant. 'I am sorry, little sister,' she said, speaking Cantonese Chinese. 'It is my fault that you had to endure such a terrible, undeserved humiliation.'

The servant stopped crying as quickly as she had begun. 'Do not worry, big sister. That evil witch cannot hurt me. It is bad enough to lose face from the shouts and screams of a civilized person, but much worse from a barbarian . . . and worst of all from an animal like that!' She gave a snort of disgust and picked up her cleaning things. 'I will go now and see if I can make that room of hers smell less foul.'

'Impossible!' said Wong with an encouraging smile as the younger woman departed.

When she was alone in the kitchen, Wong reached into the plastic bucket in which she kept her bottles of cleaning liquid and polish, her duster and her cloths, and took out a rolled-up piece of clear plastic. She peeled a protective backing layer away from it, then set the plastic down on the table, exactly where Faith Gushungo had placed her right hand. She then peeled it away from the table and covered it again with the protective layer.

After work, Wong took a train from Tai Po to Monkok, the heart of Kowloon, where the population is said to be packed together more tightly than anywhere else on earth. She went to the fourth floor of a rundown apartment building and knocked on a door covered in faded, peeling red paint. It was opened by a thin, bespectacled man wearing a tatty old white lab coat. He grinned when he saw it was Wong at the door and ushered his former Hong Kong Police colleague into the small apartment.

The perfectly maintained equipment inside was worth far, far more than the dingy property in which it sat. There were computers linked to every significant police database, scanners, laser printers, spectrometers, centrifuges – in short, the apartment was a miniature forensic lab.

The man took the plastic sheet Wong handed over to him and placed it on a scanner. Seconds later, a larger-than-life image of Faith Gushungo's handprint appeared on a thirty-two-inch monitor screen. The man looked at it for a second then turned to Wong with an even bigger smile on his face.

'Perfect,' he said. 'I will be able to give you exactly what you need.'

49

'Again!' Carver's command echoed around the cavernous interior of the barn.

From above him came the sound of Zalika Stratten's tired, frustrated voice: 'Oh for heaven's sake, what now?'

'You were blundering around like a herd of elephants up there. The idea, in case you hadn't noticed, is to do this without anyone being able to hear you.'

Zalika's face appeared, leaning over the railing that surrounded the crude platform that represented the Gushungos' master bedroom in Hong Kong.

'Are you suggesting I'm fat?'

'Not at all,' Carver replied, deadpan. 'Just clumsy and heavy-footed.'

'Oh!' Her voice went up an octave in sheer outrage. 'I'll kill you for that, Samuel Carver!'

'Not yet, you won't. We've got a job to do. So, one more time, from the top.'

Zalika stomped very deliberately across the planking, down the stairs and out of the barn. When she got outside, she walked precisely thirty-two metres, then stopped, stood still and waited.

In the barn, Carver started talking apparent gibberish: 'Bla-blah, yadda-yadda, waffle-waffle, now.'

Both he and Zalika were wearing miniature earpieces linked to their mobile phones. When she heard the word 'now' she started walking at a steady pace, came back in through the barn door and made her way – very, very quietly – up the stairs.

It was Wednesday afternoon. She'd been doing this for most of the last twenty-four hours, repeating the same apparently simple routine until it was grooved so deep that she could do the whole thing almost without thinking, as if she were operating purely by muscle memory. Carver had rounded up a handful of Klerk's staff to act as bodyguards and maids. They had no idea why they were getting involved in this strange game of make-believe, but it made a fun break from their daily routine. Every so often Carver used one or two of the staff to throw in variations. What if there was someone in the hall when Zalika walked in? What if she were interrupted when trying to get into the safe? What if she had to fight or talk her way out?

Carver was no longer surprised by the range of Zalika's abilities. The previous day, they'd sparred a little on a large judo mat, working on kicks, punches, blocks and throws. They'd gone at it hard, working up a sweat. When he'd complimented her on being able to keep up with him, she'd pulled a stray strand of hair off her face and, in between gasps for air, panted, 'Are you kidding? I'm a Stratten. I had my first self-defence class when I was six.'

When he'd commented on her amazing ability to come up with an almost infinite number of excuses, explanations and charming little deceits, she giggled and said, 'I'm a girl. I've been doing that all my life!'

Even in his guise as the tough taskmaster, Carver couldn't stop himself laughing. He could feel the two of them getting closer, heading towards a destination they both knew was inevitable. Just a few more run-throughs and he would be certain of her. Then they could relax and have some fun.

Zalika went through the operation again, and again, and then, after one more run-through, which was perfect, just as the previous half-dozen had in fact been, Carver said, 'That'll do it. Thanks, everyone.' And then, so that only Zalika could hear, 'You're ready. And you're going to be good. Bloody good.'

She smirked cheekily. 'But darling, I always am . . .'

They wandered back to the house together, and when Carver put his arm round her, Zalika nestled closer to him, moulding herself to his body.

Klerk watched them from the French windows to his drawing room as they ambled across the lawn.

'Hey, you two,' he called out, 'come over here. I've got some things that might interest you.'

Klerk ushered the two of them into the room and then handed Carver a sealed aluminium flask, roughly the size and shape of a packet of Pringles. The contents, however, were a lot less savoury.

'This is the recipe you asked for,' Klerk said. 'Flown in on my personal jet today. It was a rush-job, to put it mildly. But my boys are good. They say they got it right and I trust them. You can too. So now will you tell me what you're going to do with it?'

'Of course.'

Carver spelled out the key elements of his plan; the finer points of detail could wait till he and Zalika were in Hong Kong. At the end, Klerk nodded his assent.

'The timing is the key to it,' he said. 'Hong Kong is six hours ahead of Malemba. What time do you expect the job to be completed?'

'Around eleven-thirty on Sunday.'

'So that's about sun-up in Malemba: perfect. Most of the cops and soldiers will still be nursing the sore heads they got on Saturday night. I'm meeting Patrick Tshonga in South Africa tomorrow. I'll fill him in on what you've got planned. He's got senior police and military commanders loyal to him. They will make sure their men are rested and sober. Keep me posted over the next few days on any developments. I want to know exactly what you've got planned. When the job is completed, you will text OK, just that, to a number I will provide. That will be the go-signal. By breakfast time the country will be under new management.'

'I just hope Justus and his kids are alive to see it.'

'I've done something about that,' said Klerk. 'I put the head of security for my southern Africa operations, Sonny Parkes, on to it. He made a few calls, called in some favours and tracked them down to the remand cells at Buweku jail. Then he organized a lawyer for the family and some food – they don't get fed in the jails now, you know. He's a good man, Parkes, a man you can trust.' Klerk handed Carver a business card for one of his corporations with Parkes's name printed on it. 'His contact details are all on that. If you call him, he'll keep you posted on any developments. I have something else for you, too.'

A large, plain brown envelope was lying on a side-table. Klerk picked it up and pulled out a folder of documents.

'These are the contracts making you a five per cent shareholder in the Kamativi Mining Corporation. I've given you a non-executive directorship, too. You never know, one day you might want to settle down, find yourself a good woman and start earning a respectable living. I think you'd be a damn good businessman, Sam, if you ever put your mind to it.'

'Do you have a wife in mind for me, too?'

Klerk grinned. 'Ach, Sam, I'm not that crazy. You'll make your own choice on that score. Though I might make one suggestion . . .'

Klerk pointedly looked across the room at his niece.

'Wendell, stop that!' Zalika Stratten's indignation was mixed with laughter. She touched Carver's arm and said, 'Forgive my uncle, Sam. He has a terrible sense of humour.'

'Maybe I do,' rumbled Klerk, 'but the only men I've ever seen you with have been gutless, namby-pamby playboys. Not one of them has had the balls to stand up to you. But this man has your measure, young lady. And you know it.'

'Oh, don't be silly,' said Zalika, trying to cover her embarrassment.

Carver had never seen her flustered before. Suddenly she seemed softer, more vulnerable and, yes, more desirable. He wondered what she would be like as a wife, the mother of his children, and then had to suppress a laugh of his own. Klerk liked to portray himself as a simple, straightforward, hard-nosed businessman, but he was a cunning old bastard . . . and a sentimental one, too.

'Now be off with you,' Zalika was saying to her uncle. 'You've got to be on a BA flight to Jo'burg. You know how Brianna hates to be late. And they won't hold the plane for ever. Not even for you.'

Klerk kissed his niece goodbye, shook Carver's hand, wished them both luck and left.

'Fancy a swim?' asked Zalika, when she and Carver were alone.

'I don't have any swimming trunks.'

'Why would you need them?'

The pool at Campden Hall had a glazed roof, which retracted at the touch of a button, and walls whose glass panels slid away until the two swimmers were entirely open to the warm spring evening. The sky was still light and would be for a few hours to come, and the only noise to be heard was birdsong and the gentle whisper of wind through the trees.

Zalika dived into the water leaving barely a ripple on the surface, swam a length of fast front-crawl, performed the most outrageously sexy racing turn Carver had ever seen in his life – a tumbling, sparkling flicker of tanned wet legs and ass – and then returned to the end where he was still standing, watching her.

She rested her arms on the side of the pool. 'Aren't you going to join me?'

'Of course,' he said. 'Underwater combat is my specialist skill.'

'You'll have to catch me first.'

Carver was faster – just – and stronger, but she was elusive and agile. He was out of breath by the time he caught her, from the laughter as much as the exercise. But catch her he did, and hold her and kiss her with a pent-up passion whose intensity overwhelmed them both.

They stumbled in a tangle of intertwined limbs from the pool back to the house, Zalika clutching a towel to her gleaming wet body and squealing with laughter as they tried to get upstairs without being spotted by the staff. They stood for a while, wrapped in each other's arms beneath a steaming shower, and then tumbled into bed. And it seemed to Carver as though he was fighting Zalika as much as loving her. He wasn't sure whether this was just a hangover from his initial refusal to take the job she had so carefully researched, or a deeper, more intrinsic part of her personality. But she seemed compelled to resist him – wrestling as much as caressing him, fighting to be on top and raking her nails down his back – testing him to the very limit before she could finally relax into ecstasy and accept her own surrender.

50

London is arguably the most racially diverse city in the world. Heathrow handles more international passengers than any other airport, anywhere. It follows that there is nowhere on earth with as rich and concentrated a tapestry of ethnicities as the airport's over-crowded passenger terminals: they are their very own rainbow nation. It would take a very unusual human being indeed to warrant a second glance. So neither Samuel Carver nor Zalika Stratten paid any attention whatsoever to the tall, shaven-headed African standing by a suitcase a few steps away with a telephone pressed to his face as they checked in their baggage for the Thursday-morning Cathay Pacific flight to Hong Kong.

Carver's mind was torn between the beautiful woman standing in line next to him and the job he was preparing to undertake. He had never visited Hong Kong before and spent much of the flight engrossed in maps and guidebooks: partly a professional familiar-izing himself with the surroundings of his next mission, partly a tourist intrigued by one of the world's most fascinating cities, a tiny oasis of something approaching capitalist democracy within the great totalitarian monolith of communist China.

Although it was surrounded by a mass of small outlying islands, the heart of Hong Kong consisted of three sections. The first was Hong Kong Island, the site of the first British occupation in 1841 and still the political and financial heart of the city. Across Victoria Harbour, on the Chinese mainland, stood Kowloon, one of the most crowded places on the planet, where up to a hundred thousand people squeezed into every square mile. North of Kowloon, past a band of hills now preserved as a string of country parks and lakes, came the New Territories, land acquired by the British from the Chinese in 1898. Here, in the outlying district of Tai Po, was where the Gushungos had their bolthole. Carver took a good long look at the maps, memorizing every route in and out of Tai Po, by road, rail, air and sea.

The flight arrived at breakfast time on Friday morning. They checked in to a hotel on the Kowloon side of the water – the location chosen for ease of access to Tai Po. Once unpacked, showered and changed, they headed out into the city's incomparable atmosphere of energy, enterprise and tightly packed humanity, all jostling, arguing, bantering and sweating in the sweltering heat and humidity. Everywhere Carver looked, familiarity and strangeness collided with each other in a mesmerizing cultural confusion. Most of the signs were in Chinese characters that were totally incomprehensible to him. Yet among them English words would suddenly pop out: 'Tom Lee Music', 'Stockwell Securities', 'Classic Beauty', and even, on a shopfront that could have been pulled straight from an English high street, 'Body Shop'. More than a decade after the end of British rule, Pitt Street, Knutsford Terrace and Jordan Path still jostled for space with Tak Shing Street and Yan Cheung Road, traffic drove on the left, and the buses were double-deckers.

On one corner, there'd been some kind of incident in a grocery store. A handful of police were on the scene. They were all Chinese, but they wore olive-green short-sleeved tropical uniforms, with fatigue trousers tucked into gleaming black boots that could have come straight from a British Army quartermaster's stores, right down to their berets and cap badges. Carver passed one policeman speaking into his radio. A blizzard of Mandarin dialect was followed by 'Yes, sir. Over.'

Zalika insisted on stopping for a bite to eat at a white-tiled, neon-lit restaurant where the menu was in Chinese and they ordered by pointing at pictures of dishes and the numbers next to them. But the label on Carver's beer read 'Carlsberg'.

By then he'd already found a tailor to make the alterations to his suit trousers. Two hours later he had a car. He needed something that looked dowdy and unexceptional, but was still quick enough to get him out of trouble if any should arise. After twenty minutes online, a cab through the Cross Harbour Tunnel from Kowloon on to Hong Kong Island took him to the showroom of Vin's Motors in Tin Hau Temple Road, North Point, not far from the Happy Valley racecourse.

When Carver walked in, neatly dressed with a beautiful young woman on his arm, the salesman's eyes gleamed. Here, surely, was a man with the need and the means to impress. A fat commission would soon be on the way. His enthusiasm waned, to be replaced by disappointment, bafflement and then unfettered curiosity, as Carver spent a mere twenty-two thousand Hong Kong dollars – roughly seventeen hundred pounds – on one of the oldest, cheapest cars on the premises: a faded maroon-coloured 1998 Honda Civic EF9. It was a model beloved by petrolheads for the astounding horsepower the engineers at Honda had squeezed from its modest 1.6-litre engine – the most power per cc of any engine ever, some maintained.

That satisfied Carver's requirement for speed, but the downside was that Honda's stylists had tried to signal the car's capabilities by fitting it with red Recaro sports seats, a titanium knob on the gear-stick and fancy aluminium pedals. Carver politely requested that all these should be replaced by much drabber parts and bought a second, even shabbier Civic to provide them. He also asked for the bodywork to be scuffed and dented. The engine, meanwhile, had to be tuned to the highest possible spec, irrespective of the cost or number of components that needed replacing. He handed the salesman an incentive payment of twenty thousand Hong Kong dollars, cash, to make sure that the job was done within twenty-four hours. Then he answered all the questions he could see the man was dying to ask by winking and saying that a friend of his had just bought a new Porsche 911. He intended to turn up in his tatty old car, offer to race him, put a lot of money on the outcome, then watch his face as the Honda won. This, it was agreed, was a brilliant joke, and Carver was made to promise that he would come back on Monday and tell all the lads in the service department about the victory they had won for him.

'You're an excellent liar,' said Zalika as they left the showroom.

'That makes two of us,' said Carver. 'No wonder Klerk thought we were suited.'

51

Moses Mabeki was obliged to go back in time before he dialled the number. He had to remember the young man he'd been a dozen years ago and hear in his head the voice with which he'd spoken to his fellow students at the London School of Economics; the confident, even cocky sound of a handsome, well-connected kid whose biggest social problem was sparing enough time from his studies to accommodate all the girls who wanted to get to know him. It had been a mask, an act, just like the dutiful, grateful facade he presented to Dick Stratten, or the big-brother friendship he had with Stratten's son Andy. But that voice had served him well, and he needed to tap into it one more time.

'Johnny Zen, my man,' he drawled when he got through. 'Wassup?'

'Moses? Moses Mabeki?' asked his former LSE contemporary Zheng Junjie before breaking into laughter. 'Holy crap, it must be, what, ten years?'

'More,' agreed Mabeki. 'Lot of water flowed under my bridge. Yours too, I bet.'

'Well, you know how it is, man. You get a proper job. You get married, have kids. Suddenly you're an old fart. But I'm not complaining. I develop commercial property, and business has been good. How about you?'

'Well, I have no wife, no children. But no, I am not complaining.'

'No wife, eh? Ha! Typical Moses, too many women to choose from, I bet! So, what can I do for you, bro?'

Zheng, too, was putting on a face, a variation of the one he presented to all non-Chinese. To his parents' generation they were all barbarians, uncivilized peoples, and Africans like Moses Mabeki were barely human. Zheng did not share these prejudices remotely to the same extent – his generation, after all, coveted German cars, Italian designer clothes and Manhattan condominiums – but the innate sense of superiority remained, as did the absolute separation between the true self he reserved for his family and immediate community, and the face he presented to men like Moses Mabeki. They had been friends. There were aspects of Mabeki that Zheng respected, even envied. But they could never be equals.

In that respect, both men regarded each other in a very similar light. They were both intelligent enough to know it, too. Yet neither would ever let it get in the way of doing business to their mutual advantage.

'You remember, years ago, how we made each other a promise, an exchange deal?' Mabeki asked.

'Uh-huh,' grunted Zheng, noncommittally.

'We talked about our families, that I was the descendant of a king of the Ndebele and that your family were very powerful Tanka people in Hong Kong. I said that if you were ever in southern Africa and you needed something – something you could not get by conventional means – I would use my connections to help you.'

'Ye-e e s.'

'And if I came to Hong Kong, then you would do the same for me. You remember?'

'Of course. And I meant it.'

'Well, I am in Hong Kong and I need that favour.'

'I see. And what exactly is it that you need?'

'I need you to buy something from me. I need you to provide fast, private transportation. And I need you to help me remove a personal difficulty – no, an irritant. In exchange for this favour, I will make you richer by approximately five million dollars.'

'Excuse me for one moment. I have another call on the line. Just let me get rid of them.'

There was, of course, no other call. Zheng Junjie just needed time to think. If Mabeki was serious, and he suspected very strongly that he was, then this could be a chance to make his family a great deal of money and earn himself great face. On the other hand, it was clear that whatever Mabeki wanted could not be provided without the direct personal agreement of his uncle, known to all who knew him as Fisherman Zheng. He was a small, skinny, bald old man who ran a floating fish restaurant in Aberdeen harbour, on the south side of Hong Kong Island. He was also one of the richest, most powerful gangsters not just in Hong Kong, but all of southeast China. If the deal proved beneficial, Fisherman would be greatly pleased with his nephew. If it did not . . . well, that was not a possibility Zheng much cared to contemplate.

He got back on the line to Mabeki.

'I think you should come and have dinner with my family. You will propose what you have in mind. I will translate for you and help you make your case. I cannot promise that the deal will be acceptable. What I am doing to honour my promise is to make the introduction. The rest is up to you. Do we have a deal?'

'Yes.'

'Then meet me tonight at the fish market in Aberdeen. My family have a business there. It is marked by a large sign for Zhen Fang Seafood. I will be there at ten o'clock. Come alone.'

'See you then. And Johnny, there is something you should know. I have changed since you last saw me, changed a lot.'

Zheng laughed. 'Oh, we've all changed, Moses.'

'No,' said Mabeki, 'I can assure you, you have not changed like me.'

52

That evening, Zalika insisted on taking one of the Star Ferries trips round the harbour. Carver didn't mind going along for the ride. The Hong Kong shoreline was one of the world's most spectacular urban landscapes and the open deck of a ferry was as good a place as any to talk business undisturbed. An hour into the trip, though, and it was still all sightseeing and inconsequential, flirtatious chit-chat.

'I don't want to ruin the mood here,' he said, 'but we need to talk about Sunday.'

Zalika looked at her watch. 'Hang on,' she said, 'you're just about to discover why I dragged you on to this tourist-trap. Literally any second now. You've got to see this . . . Yes!'

A low, synthesized rumbling set to a pacy electro beat started pulsing across the water. Atop the towers on the Hong Kong side of the harbour, searchlights swept back and forth across the sky, as if searching for raiding bombers. Then the buildings themselves burst into life in a sort of electric firework display. One skyscraper was bathed in glowing blue. Sharp lines of pure white light zig-zagged up another soaring glass tower. A third building was transformed into a neon rainbow in a display that was simultaneously vulgar, absurd and completely irresistible.

'See!' Zalika exclaimed, grabbing Carver's arm and nestling against his shoulder. 'Isn't it amazing?'

'Yes, it is,' he agreed, suddenly feeling very old in the face of her unabashed enthusiasm. 'But the reason I'm on this boat is to have somewhere to talk business where we wouldn't be overheard. And I wouldn't mind getting on with it.'

She looked up at him with knowingly coy eyes. 'Humour me.'

Carver sighed and gave in to the pleasure of feeling her body against his and breathing in the scent of her hair while the lights danced across the water and the music whooshed, tinged and burbled to its climax.

When it was done, he said, 'OK, now we talk business.'

'Oh all right,' she replied, like a schoolgirl conceding that she had to do her homework.

Carver half-turned his body, so that they were face to face. He glanced over Zalika's shoulder to check that no one was close enough to overhear them, then leaned towards her as if lost in their own private lovers' world and said, 'So, run me through the whole deal between the Gushungos and their vicar again.'

'The Gushungos' nearest church is St George's in Tai Po,' she said. 'The vicar there is a Scotsman called Simon Dollond. He's in his mid-forties, much loved by his congregation, the British and the Chinese. And he wasn't exactly thrilled to discover that Henderson and Faith had just moved into his parish.'

As she filled in the details of the deal Dollond had struck with the Gushungos, Zalika spoke with the same efficient grasp of her subject as she had when briefing Carver about Malemba, back at Klerk's country house. As always, Carver was struck by her ability to switch moods – almost her whole personality, in fact – at a moment's notice. He decided to test it one more time. When she had finished, he pulled her even closer and gave her a long, passionate kiss. She switched to accommodate that, too, without any obvious difficulty.

'Mmmm,' Zalika whispered when he finally pulled his mouth from hers. 'That was nice. What made you so romantic suddenly?'

'I was just maintaining our cover,' he said, deadpan.

'Oh, I see,' she said. Then she frowned. 'Are you sure you maintained it quite enough, though? A few people might not have noticed.'

'You're right. Better make absolutely sure. Just to be on the safe side.'

When he came back up for air a second time, Carver asked, 'How did you find out all that stuff about the church?'

'Simple. Whenever I was in Hong Kong, I went to St George's. They have coffee and biscuits after the service every week, which is really just an excuse for all the old dears who go every week to hang around and have a good gossip. Once they'd got used to me being there, they chatted away perfectly happily, and of course they all knew about "dear, sweet Simon" and the wicked Gushungos and couldn't wait to tell me all about it.'

'Old women,' said Carver, 'they're the best spies in the world.'

'Not for you they aren't. This is strictly ladies-only.'

'Well then, thank you for betraying the sisterhood. So now I have a question. Can you go on the phone and sound like a black Malemban woman?'

'Depends who's listening. If I was talking to another Malemban, they'd know straight away. But if it's just a Brit or a Chinese, sure. I spent my entire childhood surrounded by Malemban nannies, cooks and housemaids. I know just how they sound.'

'Good, I hoped you'd say that.'

'Why?'

'Because you're going to give the nice Reverend Dollond a call on Sunday morning. And you're going to be a Malemban.'

'Oh, with him it'll be easy. Now, I've got something for you. Well, someone actually.'

Zalika tapped out a text. Seconds later, a Chinese woman in an anonymous outfit of T-shirt and jeans got up off a bench on the far side of the deck and, apparently paying no attention to either Carver or Zalika, made her way towards the railing, just next to them.

'I have what you need,' said Tina Wong, looking directly out across the harbour.

Carver and Zalika turned to face the same way – just three people in a line, looking out at the spectacular view.

Passing it in front of her, so that it could not be seen by anyone onboard, Wong handed Zalika an A4-sized padded envelope. Then, still not making eye contact, she said, 'So, are you going to kill these pigs?'

Carver did not reply.

Wong did not seem disappointed by his silence. For the first time she turned her head in his direction, fixed him with a penetrating stare, turned back again and nodded to herself. 'Yes, you can do this. Good.'

Now it was Carver's turn to speak: 'Are you working on Sunday?'

Wong nodded her head.

'Then just before the family and their bodyguards take communion, make sure the front door is unlocked. Can you do that?'

'Of course.'

'Good. And thank you for this.' Carver jerked his head towards Zalika's simple canvas shoulder-bag, which now contained the envelope. 'It's very important.'

'No problem. OK, enough sightseeing. It is beneath my dignity to look like a tourist.'

Wong left as casually as she'd arrived.

As she walked away, Carver asked Zalika, 'Are you sure you want to go through with this? You understand I'm not questioning your ability to do the job. It's just that this could get messy. You've had enough violence and death in your life. Are you sure you want more?'

There was no hesitation in her answer, not a flicker of doubt in her voice. 'Yes, I want more all right. I want to see what you've done. I want to spit on their dead bodies. Every single one of them.'

'All right. But you play it absolutely by the book.'

'Yes, sir.'

'And I'm getting you a phone with a tracking system, so if we get separated for any reason, I'll know where you are.'

'Whatever you say.'

'And if anything happens to me, you don't wait around to see if I'm all right, understand? Go straight to Hong Kong International. There's a fifteen-oh-five flight direct to London. Just get on it and go.'

'Absolutely.' She wrapped her arms round his waist and examined him thoughtfully. 'Thanks for having faith in me. My uncle was right. You're a good man, Samuel Carver.'

53

The Aberdeen fish market was deserted, the last traces of the previous day's catch all washed and swept away, yet the smell of fish still filled the air, as though it seeped from the polished concrete floor, the painted steel columns and girders and the corrugated iron roof. Zheng Junjie, the man once known as Johnny Zen, was standing beneath the bare neon lights of his family's stall, nervously sucking on a cigarette. He looked as though he'd grown a little soft around the middle since Moses Mabeki had last seen him. Maybe he'd been eating too much of his wife's home cooking or, more likely, having too many dinners out with his mistress. A sweet young concubine had always been considered an essential accessory for any Hong Kong businessman on the way to the top.

Mabeki had taken a cab down from Tai Po. He'd told the driver to drop him a few minutes' walk away from the Aberdeen Harbour fish market, at the foot of one of the high-rise apartment blocks that crowded into the narrow space between the hills of Hong Kong Island and the sea. They housed most of the local Tanka and Hoklo tribes, people who had for centuries inhabited floating villages of junks and narrow-boats, working and living almost entirely on the water. Now their descendants were pasty-faced property developers whose pastel-coloured Ralph Lauren polo shirts stretched across their bosomy chests and flabby guts. But then, Mabeki reflected, how different was he? His people had been cattle-herders and warriors, going where they wanted across the southern African savannah. Now most were happy with a cold beer and a Manchester United shirt. The white man's cruellest trick was not to conquer or even enslave, but simply to soften, weaken and corrupt every culture or people he encountered, until they lost the will to be themselves any more.

Mabeki made his way unobserved to within thirty feet of Zheng. He watched him take his cigarette out of his mouth, throw it down and grind it under his heel. Zheng looked around, checked his watch, then looked again. He did not look like a powerful man about to take charge of a tough negotiation. He looked like a frightened man wondering how he was going to explain to his superiors that he'd just let them down.

Mabeki let him sweat for a moment longer, then stepped out of the shadows and made his way between the large blue and yellow plastic containers from which the following morning's fish would be sold. He deliberately let his right foot knock one of them as he walked by. The noise made Zheng spin round and catch sight of his old university friend.

Over the years, Mabeki had become a connoisseur of people's reactions to his appearance, and Zheng's was a classic example. In the space of a couple of seconds his face registered alarm at the unexpected noise, relief that it came from Mabeki, shock and revulsion at the first sight of his face, and finally, after an all-too-evident internal struggle, a bland mask of impassive self-control.

'Hello, Johnny,' Mabeki said.

'Moses.'

They shook hands. Mabeki took a perverse pleasure from watching Zheng's attempts to find a safe, polite place to look. He had seen it so many times, the way people could not help themselves staring at the scars, craters and distorted flesh of his face, no matter how much the sight disgusted them. He knew, too, the questions they all wanted to ask and the mental contortions they went through trying to find the right words with which to frame them.

Zheng did better than most. 'I see what you mean,' he said. 'You have changed. May I ask what happened?'

'I was shot. A nine-millimetre parabellum round fired at extreme close range passed right through my mouth from one side to the other. I was left for dead by the man who shot me. His mistake.'

'Did you ever find him?'

'He is about to find me.'

Zheng nodded thoughtfully. 'I see. He is the problem you referred to?'

Mabeki gave a fractional nod of assent.

'Then you'd better follow me,' Zheng said.

They made their way out of the market and down to the water's edge. A flight of stone steps with a polished metal handrail led down from the quayside. A square-bowed boat whose sturdy wooden hull was buffered with old tyres bumped up and down against the bottom steps in the swell of the water. The deck, sheltered by a canvas roof stretched across a metal frame, was scattered with plastic buckets and boxes. An old woman in loose grey pyjamas with a large mushroom-shaped straw hat on her head was standing barefoot among them. When she saw Zheng she rattled off a high-pitched, hectoring volley of incomprehensible Chinese, pointing at Mabeki as she spoke. Zheng bowed respectfully and replied in a far more conciliatory style. The old woman spat disgustedly on to the deck, glared at Mabeki, then made her way to the stern of the boat.

A second later, the boat was reversing away from the steps. The old woman turned it round, miraculously avoiding all the other boats clustered by the quay, then set off across the bay. The fishing boats were crammed so tightly that Mabeki could barely see the water, yet the woman steered between them with an ease that came from a lifetime's practice, squeezing between hulls that seemed barely a hand's breadth apart and heading straight towards apparent dead ends that miraculously opened up at her approach.

They passed under a road bridge across the harbour and saw, not far away, the dazzling strings of fairy-lights and gaudily painted hull of the Jumbo Kingdom floating restaurant, where four thousand customers could dine at a single sitting, rise in tiers into the night air, a huge temple of gastronomy and greed.

'Impressive, isn't it?' said Zheng. 'I'm afraid our destination is much more modest.'

That, Mabeki soon realized, was an understatement. The old woman brought their little boat to a halt by the rectangular, barge-like hull of a far smaller, dingier restaurant, moored on the far side of Aberdeen Harbour, connected to the shore by a red-painted walkway. A rusty metal ladder hung down from the side of the hull. The old woman nestled the blunt bow of her boat against the foot of the ladder and gave a dismissive gesture in its direction.

'This is where we get off,' said Zheng.

'One moment,' said Mabeki.

Turning his back on Zheng, who was already stepping gingerly on to the ladder, he took a few paces towards the old woman and, speaking quietly but with infinite menace, told her in Ndebele that she was a dung-eating whore of a baboon with shrivelled-up breasts and a closed-up cunt as dry as an old gourd. He revelled in the fear that spread across the crone's incomprehending face as he loomed over her and let the poison of his malice fill her soul. In a louder, much friendlier voice, he switched to English and said, 'Thank you for bringing us here, grandmother.' Then he walked up to the bow and sprang with surprising athleticism, even grace, on to the ladder. A few seconds later, he was standing on the restaurant's deck.

'Let's go,' said Zheng.

He led Mabeki along a narrow walkway running down the side of the hull to the front entrance to the restaurant. There were no strings of fairy-lights here, just a scruffy, dimly lit interior where no more than a dozen tables were filled. The desultory hum of scattered conversations almost faded away as Mabeki walked by.

A white-jacketed waiter gave a respectful nod to Zheng as he walked to the back of the dining area, past the bar and through a door into a kitchen heavy with the smell of stir-fried food. Here, too, the atmosphere was half-dead. A handful of cooks were standing by one of the ranges, talking and smoking with the lassitude of men who did not expect to be taking many more orders that night. Zhen ignored them and led Mabeki to a metal door.

'Watch your head,' he said as he opened it and moved into a small store-cabin.

The walls were lined with metal shelves on which huge drums of cooking oil and soy sauce were crammed alongside cans, bags and glass jars of produce, packets of dried noodles and sacks of rice. A porthole, cut into the hull near the ceiling, had been opened to provide ventilation but the air was still thick with the cigarette smoke that rose from the four men sitting around a small wooden table, topped with a plastic cloth, in the middle of the cabin. All were as old as the woman who had piloted the boat. Dressed in a motley selection of sweaty, dirt-stained vests and tatty shirts, they looked like old dockside navvies, or lowly ship's crewmen. In front of them, the table was covered in ivory mah-jongg tiles marked with Chinese characters, piles of notes in an assortment of currencies, bottles of spirits and cheap plastic tumblers, all illuminated by the single bare bulb that hung above the table.

Zheng approached the oldest man at the table and spoke quietly in his ear. The man looked up at Mabeki, who caught not a trace of discomfort, let alone fear, in his eyes. So this was Fisherman Zheng. Well, he was a tough, cold-blooded old bastard, that was for sure. But Mabeki wasn't worried. He'd spent the past decade working for the biggest cold-blooded old bastard of them all. He'd fucked Henderson Gushungo's wife and got away with it. He'd changed their relationship day by day, inch by inch, until he was the real master and Gushungo his puppet. He was entirely confident that he could deal with this old Chinese gangster, too.

Fisherman turned his attention back to his nephew. They spoke for a few seconds, and then Zheng spoke in English to Mabeki:

'My uncle will hear your proposal. He wishes you to know, however, that nothing happens in Hong Kong without him knowing about it, or that he cannot discover within a matter of an hour or two. There is, therefore, no point in you trying to mislead or cheat him. It is very important, for your sake, that you understand this.'

Zheng lowered his voice. 'Seriously, Moses, you don't want to cross my uncle.'

Mabeki gave his own approximation of a smile. 'I understand, Johnny. So please assure your uncle first that I would never attempt to double-cross him, any more than he would think of double-crossing me. Also, inform him that I have spent the past ten years as the most trusted personal adviser of the President of Malemba, His Excellency the Honourable Henderson Gushungo, with the result that there is no threat he could possibly make that I have not both heard before and made myself. Further, tell him that no matter how many people he has had killed during his long and illustrious career, I have killed more in my relatively short one. And fourthly, please ask him, with all due respect for his age, dignity and position, to stop pretending that he cannot speak English, since I can see very clearly from his eyes that he has understood every word I have just said.'

Mabeki watched the anger flare in Fisherman Zheng's eyes, knew that he'd caught the old man red-handed, and added, 'As I thought. So, let me explain the deal I have in mind, which is in essence very simple. At around noon on Sunday, roughly thirty-six hours from now, I will sell you a consignment of uncut Malemban diamonds worth at least fifteen million US dollars for a mere eight million. In exchange for this discount, which is much greater than I would normally give to any middle-man, you will kindly do me two additional services. One of them is nothing, a mere delivery run. The second is more complicated.'

Mabeki took out his phone and brought a photograph up on the screen. It had been taken at Heathrow airport and showed a Caucasian male, full length, as he waited with his baggage by the Cathay Pacific desk. Mabeki flicked a finger across the screen and a series of further shots spun by, showing the man from varying angles and distances.

'The man in these pictures is called Samuel Carver. I want him dead. You will ensure that he dies at a time and place that I will specify. The killing will be carried out in such a way that no suspicion attaches to me. Do this and I will give you the bargain of a lifetime. So, do we have a deal?'

Fisherman Zheng sat silently as Mabeki ran through his proposal. Then he cleared his throat like a man gargling gravel and phlegm and spoke to his nephew in perfect English: 'Tell this African that the favours he asks can be granted with one wave of my hand. But tell him also that even the meanest beggar in Hong Kong knows about his precious diamonds and that no dealer would value them at more than a third of the figure he mentions. If I am to make a fair profit, I therefore cannot offer him more than two million dollars. That is my offer, and it is final.'

Moses Mabeki cast his eye over the three other mah-jongg players. 'One of you give me your chair,' he said. 'I can see that this will take some time.'

Fisherman Zheng barked an order. All three men left the room. Mabeki sat himself down, as did Zheng Junjie. Fisherman poured them all drinks from one of his liquor bottles. And so the negotiations began.

54

On Saturday morning, Carver set about acquiring the final pieces of equipment he would need for the Gushungo assassination. First, he went to a hobby shop that sold amateur rocket-making kits and bought a couple of cheap engines in the form of cardboard tubes like small fireworks, filled with fast-burning explosive powder. At a hardware store, he acquired some acetone paint thinners. At a phone store, he picked up two handsets: one to be used as Zalika's tracking device, the other for his own purposes. Then he went back to collect the suit trousers and the refitted Honda Civic, which he left in the darkest, least conspicuous corner he could find in one of Kowloon's underground car parks. Before he left the car, he opened the boot and spent a few minutes working with the rocket accessories, the acetone and the various bits of kit he'd brought from his Geneva toolbox. By the time he'd finished, Carver had both a getaway car and the means to destroy it, along with any evidence it might contain.

Satisfied with his morning's work, he called Zalika and met her for lunch. Afterwards, they took a cab up into the New Territories and found a spot where they could look down on to the Hon Ka Mansions and see the gaudy pink-painted home that was the Gushungos' Asian bolthole. It was one thing working on a mock-up, but there was no substitute for getting a first-hand look.

'Fine,' he said, once he'd committed the view of the house and its surroundings to memory. 'I'm ready. There's nothing to do now but wait.'

Zalika smiled. 'Not quite nothing.'

'No, maybe not.'

It was not easy for Moses Mabeki to smoke a cigarette. He had to hold it permanently to his mouth, his lips being too misshapen to grip it tightly by themselves. The drool in his mouth was apt to make the filter soggy. As he stood outside the Gushungo residence, slurping and sucking, blinking his eyes against the smoke, he made a grotesque, even bleakly comic sight. Mabeki could not have cared less. The sole purpose of his newly acquired habit was that it gave him an excuse to leave the house, within which Faith Gushungo had banned all smoking, and get outside. Once there he could walk to some quiet, unobserved corner, get rid of the cigarette and make phone calls in peace, without risk of being overheard.

He speed-dialled Zheng Junjie, and they spoke for less than thirty seconds, just enough time for Mabeki to give the precise time and location for the attack on Carver. 'I expect him to have made an effort to change his appearance,' he added. 'If so, I will of course update you. You will spot him easily enough. Have no fear of that.'

Mabeki's second call was made to General Augustus Zawanda, commander-in-chief of the Malemban National Army. Together they ran through a series of operations planned for the following morning. The conversation was notable for the unspoken assumption that even the most senior member of the nation's armed forces was junior to the President's unelected, unofficial right-hand man.

'Carry out your orders precisely as specified, and I will ensure that you receive a twenty-five per cent share of all the monies I will liberate from the President and the First Lady's private offshore accounts – accounts to which only I have the codes. Fail, or try to double-cross me, and I will ensure that your wife, your children, your mother, your brothers, your sisters and all your family die, very slowly. And all the soldiers in Malemba will not be able to save them.'

55

The Reverend Simon Dollond, rector of St George's Anglican Church in Tai Po, had faced an ethical dilemma when he discovered that Henderson and Faith Gushungo had bought a property in the Hon Ka Mansions development, within the boundaries of his parish, and wished to join his congregation. On the one hand, he could not turn away two people who wished to receive the sacrament of Holy Communion just because he believed they were profoundly evil. Dollond had served for a time as a prison chaplain. He had given communion to murderers, rapists and paedophiles. It was God's place, not his, to judge them. On the other hand, if the Gushungos ever turned up at his church on a Sunday morning they were liable to attract a great deal of unwanted attention.

Within days of buying their house, the Gushungos had set their bodyguards on to reporters and photographers who had attempted to get close to them. One reporter was taken to hospital suffering from concussion, a broken nose and two cracked ribs following a beating by Gushungo's thugs. Faith herself had lashed out at another newsman who had followed her on a shopping expedition, slapping and scratching his face, and had only stopped when physically hauled away, still screaming obscene abuse, by her own guards. Dollond ministered to a peaceful, respectable, family-friendly congregation. He did not need that kind of aggravation.

Nor, it had transpired, did the Gushungos. When Dollond and his assistant priest Tony Gibson were invited to meet the couple in their home, they were delighted to discover that Henderson Gushungo felt that for reasons of age and ill health he might not be able to manage the rigours of a full church service. Ignoring for a moment the many parishioners far more frail than Gushungo who managed to attend every week despite being blind or incapable of walking unaided, Dollond nodded thoughtfully and said that he quite understood. It was therefore decided that the Reverend Gibson would make a personal visit every Sunday after the church service was over to administer communion in the Gushungos' living room. There was nothing unusual about this: communion was often given in hospitals, rest homes and private houses to the dying or infirm. It was no trouble at all to add one more stop to Rev. Gibson's weekly round.

Shortly after nine o'clock on this particular Sunday morning, however, Simon Dollond received a call from Faith Gushungo's personal assistant informing him that the First Lady and President had both been afflicted by food poisoning and would not be able to receive communion as usual. Rev. Dollond sympathized with the Gushungos' plight, agreeing that few things were more unpleasant than food poisoning and assuring the PA that he would make sure Tony Gibson got the message and would not disturb them.

'I hope that the President and Mrs Gushungo feel much better next week,' Dollond concluded.

'Oh yes, sir, I am quite sure that they will be greatly improved,' agreed Zalika.

'That's the general idea, certainly,' Carver muttered under his breath.

'Now it's your turn,' she said, having put down the phone.

'God bless you, my child,' he replied.

Carver wasn't a big believer in elaborate disguises. He was blessed with a face that was neither pretty-boy handsome nor memorably ugly. His height was somewhat above average, but not so much as to make him stand out. He carried very little spare weight, so his jawline was not blurred by excess fat or sagging skin, and there was no bloating in his cheeks. When people described him, they could have been talking about a million other guys in their thirties or forties. The one feature that marked him out most clearly, the greenness of his eyes, could easily be dealt with using contact lenses. The combination of toughness, competence and relentless determination that gave his character its strength he camouflaged just as easily by hiding it below the surface of his personality like a shark lurking beneath the waters of a cheery tourist beach.

He'd entered Hong Kong using a Canadian passport in the name of Bowen Erikson, an alias he'd used for many years. For the job itself, though, he'd be using another of his identities, Roderick Wishart. It seemed right, somehow, for the character he had in mind.

Carver slipped on the grey wig and covered his eyes with brown contacts and the tortoiseshell spectacles. He put on the second-hand dark-grey suit and a black T-shirt, over which went an item of clothing he had bought at Vanpoulles: a dove-grey vicar's bib with a white dog-collar. Carver then slipped Wishart's wallet into the right inside pocket of his suit jacket. It contained the vicar's passport and a couple of his unimpressive-looking credit cards: it would take a lot more than a cursory search to uncover that they were directly linked to Panamanian bank accounts with hundreds of thousands of US dollars in credit. Three clean SIM cards were stitched into the lining of the wallet. Into the other inside pocket he slipped a small leather-bound prayer book. Its centre had been hollowed out to provide room for the Erikson passport and another set of cards. Carver never left home without the means to get anywhere in the world, fast.

Six days earlier in Tunbridge Wells, Carver had acquired a scuffed old briefcase with a flap-top secured by two buckled straps. Into it went a glass cruet – a glass flask with a silver screw top, filled with communion wine – and a silver-plate chalice from which to drink it. Whoever had owned the case before him had obviously not taken the trouble to screw his cruets tightly enough, because the fabric lining was dotted with purple wine stains, which gave off a faint vinegary smell. Then came a small, round silver box with a hinged snap-shut top, which contained twenty communion wafers. This was the pyx.

Carver had also bought a gold-plated crucifix on a plinth. It was about a foot high. A figure of Jesus hung on the cross. He'd been advised that it was normal to provide one of these to give a religious feel to the secular space in which the communion would be held. For himself, he had a red silk stole. It would be draped round his neck like a long scarf, reaching to his waist. A golden cross was embroidered at either end of the stole, with a red and gold fringe beneath it.

The last items to go in the case were a Book of Common Worship, which contained all the words of the prayers and responses he would require, along with A4 sheets of paper on which were printed the readings for the day.

Carver was sticking to his no-gun policy. He expected that he would be searched on arrival at the house: it was inconceivable to him that a man with as many enemies as Henderson Gushungo, protected by a sidekick as devious as Moses Mabeki, would not take such basic security precautions. Guns and knives would, in any case, be superfluous. If his plan was going to work, it would do so silently, quickly, before his targets even knew they had been attacked. Gunfire would be a mark of failure.

Carver made a final run-through to confirm that he had everything he needed. Zalika was still in the bathroom, getting ready.

'You done yet?' he called through the door. 'Because in exactly ten minutes I'll be going down the emergency stairs and out through the service exit. If you're not ready, I won't wait for you.'

56

The security guard at the main gate of the Hon Ka Mansions development waved Carver's car through without a second glance. It was Sunday morning. An Englishman wearing the costume of one of their clergymen had arrived to see the Gushungos. There was nothing unusual about that. If this one had brought a young woman with him that was none of the guard's concern.

Carver drove uphill along a winding drive that ran between two lines of newly built villas, each standing in its own grounds, discreetly hidden from its neighbours. Shortly before he reached the Gushungo property, he stopped and let Zalika out of the car. Then he continued up the drive, turned into the Gushungos' semicircular forecourt and parked his scuffed and battered old Honda next to a gleaming silver Rolls-Royce. From the way it sat fractionally low on its wheels, he guessed it had been given the full security treatment and was now as impregnable as a very fast, ultra-luxurious tank. It was a beautiful machine, all right, but it had been put to an ugly purpose that embodied the absolute contempt held by so many African dictators for their people's poverty. Carver thought of Justus and his children. They were sweating in prison cells, and here was Gushungo swanning around in a Roller.

Well, not for very much longer.

The front door to the house was raised a few feet and reached by a short flight of steps. One of the presidential bodyguards opened it and glared suspiciously at his visitor. He was half a head taller than Carver and fifty pounds heavier. His neck strained against the tightly buttoned collar of his white shirt. His shaved head glinted with sweat.

'Good morning,' said Carver, holding out a hand. 'My name is Wishart. I'm an assistant priest at St George's Church. I've come to give Holy Communion to Mr and Mrs . . . well, to President and, ah . . . well, the Gushungos, anyway.'

'Wait here,' the guard said, and disappeared into the house.

Half a minute later, Moses Mabeki was standing by the door, the guard looming massively behind him. Carver felt his skin prickle with a combination of tension and disgust. The memory of that night in Mozambique came back to him so vividly that he could not believe Mabeki would not know that he was the man who had caused his disfigurement. He had to remind himself that he had been wearing a mask over his face, that Mabeki could not possibly recognize him. And yet he could not escape the instinctive sense that Mabeki knew, by some force of intuition, precisely who he was.

If he did know, however, Mabeki gave no outward sign of it.

'Who are you?' he asked, not attempting even a veneer of civility.

'I'm Wishart, the Reverend Roderick Wishart if one's being formal. I'm afraid poor Tony Gibson isn't feeling terribly well this morning. Food poisoning. You know how ghastly that is . . .'

Mabeki gave no sign of knowing or caring anything about food poisoning, one way or the other.

'Well, anyway,' Carver continued, 'he couldn't make it, so Simon Dollond asked me to step in for him, as it were.'

Mabeki did not acknowledge Carver's words. He looked past

him at the car, studying it, assessing it as a possible threat. Carver thought of the Terminator films, the data flashing up before the cyborg's eyes as he scanned the world around him. Mabeki seemed barely more human.

He looked back at Carver. 'Come in,' he said. Then he glanced at the guard and said, 'Search him.'

57

An hour before dawn on Sunday morning, South Africa time, three black couples, dressed up to the nines and waving bottles of Dom Perignon in the air, came laughing and flirting out of the huge, opulent and achingly fashionable Taboo club on West Street in the wealthy Sandton district of Johannesburg. As they tumbled into a massive white stretch Hummer, they certainly attracted attention. But that was only because the young women were wearing exceptionally tiny dresses, even by the proudly sinful standards of Taboo.

The uniformed driver closed the limo door behind his last passenger and drove away. Behind the blacked-out windows, two of the women wriggled out of their frocks, as party girls do in the backs of limousines. There was, though, nothing remotely sexual about the way they undressed. The giggling had stopped, as had the pretence of being drunk. The party clothes and skyscraper heels were discarded and immediately replaced by black combat fatigues, bulletproof vests and rubber-soled military boots, handed out by the third woman from one of four plastic storage boxes that had been placed on the floor of the passenger compartment. The three men put on identical uniforms, taken from the second box. The third contained a variety of automatic weapons, all with noise-suppressors, knives and small-scale explosive charges. In the fourth and smallest box were radio headsets and night-vision equipment. Swiftly, without needing to be told, the five black-uniformed figures checked their weapons and tested their radios.

The car left the central business district and headed into Sandhurst, a top-of-the-market residential area where palatial mansions stood in grounds covering acres, on blocks that measured a quarter of a mile on every side. It was followed all the way by a dusty white minivan that remained at least a hundred yards behind it at all times. The two vehicles passed houses barricaded behind high walls and heavy gates, and watched over by CCTV cameras. Every property seemed to bear a metal plate by the entrance, stating that it was guarded by XPT Security. The company liked to boast that it had reduced the local crime-rate to zero, thanks to its combination of regular armed patrols and constant video surveillance. Its cars were a round-the-clock presence on the streets and its customers were assured that the company's response time, coordinated from a control room that operated for twenty-four hours of every day in the year, would never exceed six minutes, under any circumstances.

The white van pulled up in the moonshadow cast by a large jacaranda tree growing by the side of the road. Up ahead, the limo had stopped in front of a gate that would not have looked out of place outside a maximum-security prison. It rose at least twelve feet into the air and was made of thick stainless-steel plates, topped with four rows of barbed wire, angled outwards to prevent anyone climbing over the top. The gate opened by sliding across the entrance from left to right, from the point of view of the road. To the left-hand side of the gate, a guardhouse was built into the property's thick concrete-covered wall. South Africans drive on the left, so anyone driving into the property would therefore pass directly by the guardhouse and the gate would only need to be half-opened to let them in.

This was Wendell Klerk's principal South African townhouse. Its protective features befitted a man of his wealth, prominence and exposure to possible threat.

There were always two men in the guardhouse, working eight-hour shifts round the clock. One acted as the sentry and gatekeeper, watching the world go by through a thick plate-glass window; the other monitored the network of cameras, motion detectors and other alarms that covered the entire house and grounds. The feeds from all the properties' cameras were also available to staff back at the corporate control room. And just in case anyone should somehow get into the grounds, a kennel to the rear of the guardhouse contained three German Shepherds, bred for speed, strength and aggression. They could be released at any moment without the guards having to leave their post.

The men and women in the back of the limo knew all this, just as they knew about the maximum six minutes that would elapse between the first alarm sounding and the arrival of the XPT personnel, guns out and sirens blaring. They would be long gone by then.

One of the passenger doors opened and the woman who'd kept her party clothes on almost fell out on to the pavement. She was a fine-looking girl, and her micro-skirted, backless, halter-necked excuse for a dress revealed every inch of her toned, glossy-skinned figure. She paused for a moment on the pavement to gather her wits, then teetered towards the guardhouse, brushing away the tumbling waves of golden-brown hair extensions from her face then holding a hand to her mouth to stifle her giggles.

The two men in the guardhouse were entering the sixth hour of a shift in which precisely nothing had happened. The boss and his woman had stayed home. No one had come to visit them. Almost no one had even driven by. They were bored out of their minds, and their body-clocks were telling them they really ought to be asleep. When the guard on sentry duty saw the girl, he sighed, grinned cheerfully and waved his mate over to feast his eyes, too.

The girl tapped a finger on the window, smiled alluringly and started speaking. She appeared to be trying to ask some kind of question. Maybe she and her friends were lost: it was impossible to hear her through the thick glass.

The guard held a hand up to his ear and shook his head.

She shrugged her shoulders helplessly, but very prettily.

The guard had a bright idea. He gestured to her to come round to the side of the guardhouse where there was a window that opened, allowing staff to speak to anyone waiting by the gate.

The girl smiled and nodded then walked round to the window.

The guard slid it up and leaned out of the opening to get the fullest possible view of every inch of the woman in front of him. He was not disappointed. Putting on his most charming, debonair smile, he said, 'How can I help you, Miss?'

His pal was standing just behind him, peering over his shoulder to get a good look, too.

The girl gave a coy, embarrassed smile. 'We're lost.' She giggled.

'Ahh . . .' said the guard, nodding, his suspicions confirmed. 'So where is your destination?'

'Coronation Road,' she said. 'I have the address in my bag. Wait a moment.'

She was carrying a small gold sequinned clutch-bag. She opened it, rummaged inside and pulled out a Walther TPH pistol, a 'pocket-gun' barely five inches long that fires just six .22 calibre rounds.

The party girl used four of them to put a pair of head-shots into the guard closest to her, then shifted her aim and put two more in the one behind. From the first shot to the last took less than three seconds.

The only entrance to the guardhouse was at the back, on the far side of the gate. So the woman kicked off her shoes, pushed the first guard's dead body out of the opening and clambered through the window.

The .22 is a very neat bullet. Being such a small calibre, and especially when fired from a gun as modest as the TPH, it lacks the power to pass right through a human skull and instead ricochets around the brain. This causes appalling damage to the victim while avoiding the mess of bone, brain and blood-spatter caused by a through-and-through round. There was thus no obvious carnage for the woman to step through on her way to the guardhouse control panel. Not that she would have been put off if there had been. She had seen a great deal worse in her time.

She turned off all the alarm systems and opened the gate. The other five passengers got out of the limo, taking care to shut the doors silently behind them, and slipped through the gate, which closed behind them. The limo gently eased into motion and drove away. Then the road was silent again. As silent as the grave.

58

Carver had read a magazine story once about Ike and Tina Turner. Back in the late sixties, they bought a big mansion in LA and did it up in the kind of style Ike felt was appropriate for a legendary soulman and his red-hot wife. A guy from their record company came over one day. Ike told him the decorations had cost seventy thousand dollars, serious money back then. The guy replied, 'You mean you can actually spend seventy grand in Woolworths?'

The Gushungos' Hong Kong residence reminded Carver of that story. He was led down a hall floored with polished black marble tiles. They were edged in white and laid in diagonal lines, so that the white edges joined together to form a diamond-shaped pattern that criss-crossed the floor. Some kind of optical illusion made it look as though the white lines were raised from the black tiles, so that he constantly felt like he was just about to trip over them. Two glossy ceramic tigers, as tall as Carver's waist, sat on either side of the door, each baring its teeth and waving a claw in his direction. The walls were decorated with a paper that featured a swirling metallic silver pattern on a black velveteen background. Maybe it was the other way round. Maybe the black velveteen was the pattern. It was hard to tell, and Carver didn't bother to look closely enough to find out. He didn't want to risk getting a headache. He just looked dead ahead and thought about Jesus.

On the right-hand side of the hall, a staircase led upstairs to the bedrooms and bathrooms, and down to the servants' quarters. The main living room, however, was at the back of the building, looking out across a valley towards a jagged line of steep, thickly wooded hills. The land between Kowloon and Tai Po was mostly set aside as parkland, a rural oasis in the heart of the city-state, and the Gushungos' villa took full advantage of the stunning views.

The inside of the living room was spectacular too, in its own absurdly gaudy way. The floor tiles were the same as the hall, but the paper switched to a burnished gold colour. Carver looked to his right and saw a life-size double portrait of Henderson and Faith Gushungo, posing in their wedding clothes in front of an impossibly lush landscape of African savannah, teeming with wild animals of every kind – the kind, for example, that no longer existed in the arid wastelands of Malemba. The artist had taken about thirty years off the President's age and turned his skin the purple-black colour of an aubergine. He was standing with his shoulders squared, staring manfully into the distance, while his beautiful, submissive bride gazed up at him with adoring cow eyes.

Beneath the painting was a sofa strewn with richly patterned silk cushions. Its vivid purple-leather upholstery almost matched the mauve curtains draped on either side of the floor-to-ceiling windows on the far side of the room. The rest of the armchairs in the room were bright scarlet, and the light fittings were all gold-plated, as was the frame of the glass-topped coffee table, littered with copies of *Vogue* and *Architectural Digest*, that stood in front of the sofa. The other paintings scattered around the walls made the one of the Gushungos look like a masterpiece of aristocratic portraiture by Gainsborough.

At the far end of the room stood a bar with a white marble top. Beneath it, the side of the bar had been divided into three panels.

The outer edge of each panel was black. The inner heart of it was bright pillar-box red. The two colours were divided by a rectangle of white beading. The style was Nazi Nouveau.

'Do you have a cross?' Mabeki asked him.

'Of course.'

Carver reached into his briefcase and took out his crucifix. He regretted now buying one with Jesus hanging on the cross. It made him feel like he was being watched.

'Put it on here,' said Mabeki, patting the bar counter. 'Your colleague, Gibson, uses this as the altar.'

'Does he really?' said Carver. Either Gibson was too saintly to notice his physical surroundings, or he was taking the piss.

There was an ashtray sitting on the bar just a few inches from the cross, filled with lipstick-ringed cigarette butts.

'Could you move that, please?' Carver asked.

Mabeki gave him a bleak, spidery stare, then clapped his hands and shouted a few words in a language Carver could not understand. One of the bodyguards came in, was treated to a sharp burst of spittle-flecked orders, grabbed the ashtray and disappeared into another room. A few seconds later he was back again, this time with a colleague, to move the coffee table out of the way. More commands were issued. The two men hurried away and re-appeared once more carrying two ornate gilt dining chairs, which were placed about six feet from the bar, facing the cross.

'The President and the First Lady will take communion sitting on these chairs. The President's health makes it difficult for him to kneel. Other members of the household will kneel in a row behind them.'

'Will you be joining us, Mr...? I'm sorry, I didn't catch your name.'

'Mabeki. And no, I will not be taking part in this ridiculous charade.' He came right up to Carver, standing over him. Then he twisted his body so that his face was thrust towards Carver's, almost daring Carver to look away from the mangled wreckage of his scarred skin, twisted lips and glistening gums.

'Do I look like I should believe in a just and merciful God?'

It suddenly struck Carver just how all-consuming Mabeki's hunger for power must be, that he would choose to remain the way he was, with the effect that he caused, rather than have the surgery that could have repaired the worst, at least, of the damage. Mabeki actually wanted to look that deformed, that repellent. To him it was a source of strength.

'Well,' Carver replied, hoping that his face conveyed a suitable look of understanding and concern, 'it is not for us to judge God's purpose in afflicting us as he sometimes does. But you may be sure that he has one, and that it is filled with love and compassion for you.'

He ended with his face wreathed in a smug, patronizing smile and watched as Mabeki struggled to control the rage that constantly festered within him.

'Believe that if you like, Reverend. I do not. And if God exists, let him prove me wrong.'

'God does not have to prove anything, Mr Mabcki.'

Mabeki gave a dismissive grunt then took a pace back, breaking the tension between them. He took one last look at Carver – a man assessing the threat posed by another.

'Will you be taking communion as well?' Mabeki asked.

'Of course. The meal is shared between the celebrant and the congregation.'

'You will consume the same bread and wine as everyone else?'

Carver had been wondering when these questions would be asked. Mabeki was the kind of man who never, ever stopped seeing potential threats in everything and everyone around him. Would he now want Carver to taste everything to prove it was safe?

'Naturally,' Carver replied. 'There is one chalice of wine, shared by all. The wafers, too, are the same for everyone.'

'Who is the first to eat and drink?'

'I am. The celebrant is always the first to receive the sacrament.'

Mabeki thought for a moment.

'Is there a problem?' Carver asked, feigning bemusement at this line of questioning. 'I'm sure I conduct the service in very much the same style as the Reverend Gibson. The text is taken from the Book of Common Worship. The procedure is absolutely standard. Well, I say that, but of course there will be some difference between those who prefer the traditional form of words and the more modern version. Personally, I confess I hanker after the poetry of—'

'I get the point,' hissed Mabeki. 'Now, make your preparations. The President and the First Lady will be with you in five minutes.'

He stalked out of the room, leaving Carver with the two body-guards watching over him as he busied himself with his briefcase filled with holiness and death.

59

In Sandton, Wendell Klerk had woken early, keen to see the text flash on his screen that would tell him Carver had succeeded in his mission. He lay in bed with the lights off and curtains drawn, so as not to disturb the sleeping figure of Brianna Latrelle beside him, clutching his phone and snatching glances at its screen as anxiously as a nervous adulterer waiting for a message from his lover.

Because he was awake, he heard the sound of the .22 being fired. An average civilian could easily have mistaken those rounds fired in very quick succession for the popping of a backfiring engine. Wendell Klerk, however, was not an average civilian. He had fought in a vicious civil war and the instincts he acquired then had never entirely deserted him, even in his sleep.

He sat up in bed and listened for a moment. His gate had been designed and engineered to be as noiseless as possible, so as not to disturb anyone in the house. Yet he thought he could hear the soft sound of its rubber wheels rolling over the tarmac of his drive and the barely audible purr of an engine. Then nothing.

Klerk did not hesitate. He pressed the emergency button by his bed. He had always allowed for the possibility that his guardhouse might be overrun. The emergency button was linked by its own dedicated line direct to the control room at XPT Security's head-quarters, and it required immediate armed response. From the moment he touched it, the clock was running. Six minutes, maxi-mum, was all he now needed to survive.

He leaned across his kingsize bed and shook Brianna's shoulder. She moaned softly and shrugged his hand away. He shook her again.

'Go 'way,' she mumbled.

Klerk gripped more tightly and gave her a single, much rougher shake. 'Get up,' he hissed. 'Do it! Now!'

She raised her body on one elbow and peered at him blearily through the darkness. 'What's happening?' There was an edge of alarm to her voice.

'I don't know,' Klerk replied, 'but I want you to go to the panic room. Don't argue. Just go. Now!'

Brianna didn't make a fuss. She knew her man well enough to realize that he wouldn't give that kind of order without a very good reason. But as she stopped to grab the satin dressing gown she kept draped over the end of the bed, she asked, 'What about you?'

Klerk was out of bed now, too. He slept in a pair of pyjama trousers, worn for precisely this sort of occasion. He liked to tell dinner guests that he never wanted to be stark bollock naked when he came face to face with an intruder: 'I wouldn't want to frighten the bastard too much.' Now he walked over to Brianna, gave her a quick, fierce hug, kissed her cheek and said, 'Don't worry about me, worry about the other guy. Now get out of here!'

She raised a hand to touch his face, then sped across the room to her walk-in wardrobe. At the back, hidden behind her ballgowns, was a small touchscreen. She placed her hand against it and a hitherto-invisible door in the back wall of the wardrobe swung open, like the entrance to Narnia. It did not lead to a magic kingdom but a small chamber, roughly ten feet square, that was essentially an air-conditioned, bullet- and bombproof bank vault designed to safeguard humans rather then cash. When she swung the door closed behind her she was as safe as a gold bar at Fort Knox.

Wendell Klerk had never intended to use the panic room himself. The reason he gave in public – true as far as it went – was that he didn't want to be hidden away like a coward while someone was violating his property. It offended his manly pride. His private reason was never revealed to anyone, Brianna and Zalika included. He'd once been in the room just to see what it was like. He'd closed the door and suddenly found himself so overwhelmed by claustrophobia that it made his heart race, his body break out in a muck sweat and his chest heave as he desperately tried to breathe. The panic room felt to him like a tomb, and it scared him far more than any human ever could. Under no circumstances would he ever go in there again.

Once he knew Brianna was safe, Klerk switched his attention to the defence of his property. The panic room was not the only secret hidden in the walk-in wardrobe. On the single wall reserved for his clothes stood a large chest of drawers, in which he kept underwear, T-shirts, sweatshirts and sweaters. From the bottom drawer, hidden beneath two piles of neatly folded wool and cashmere jumpers, he removed a brutally simple, almost crude-looking black shotgun. Then he got out a circular drum magazine containing thirty-two twelve-gauge cartridges and attached it beneath the gun. What he now had was a fully loaded AA-12 automatic shotgun, capable of firing at a rate of three hundred rounds a minute.

Klerk had once met the man who'd developed it, a silver-haired engineer from Piney Flats, Tennessee, by the name of Jerry Baber. Baber hadn't minced his words when he described the AA-12. He'd simply said, 'It's probably the most powerful weapon in the world. There's no way that anyone within two hundred yards could face this weapon and survive it. There's so much lead in the air that it destroys everything in its path.' Klerk had immediately bought one for every property, yacht and jet he owned in the world.

Now, holding it in his hands, he felt like a human tank. As he eased open the door that led from the master bedroom suite to the first-floor landing, he heard a crash of glass from downstairs. A greedy, wolfish grin spread across his face. 'Bring it on,' he whispered to himself. He almost felt sorry for anyone in his path.

Wendell Klerk went back to war. He used his familiarity with the house to choose his killing ground and occupy the best firing position. He waited until his enemy, four of them, had come within range and then he hit them with overwhelming firepower.

He just didn't account for the possibility that there were five intruders in his home that morning.

60

Carver kissed the red silk stole and draped it round his neck. He took out the cruet filled with wine, the chalice and finally the pyx, the weapon with which he would carry out the killing.

As he took out his service book, Carver began to feel nervous for the first time; but these were the nerves any performer – actor, athlete or assassin – needs if they are to do their best work. They sharpened Carver's senses and honed his concentration. He had no doubt now about the rights or wrongs of what he was about to do. Once the decision to take the job had been made, the argument was over so far as he was concerned. He had made up his mind and he would stick with it.

From outside the room, Carver could hear the sound of footsteps and respectfully lowered voices coming down the stairs His stomach tightened. The action was about to begin. The door of the living room opened and the bodyguards snapped to attention as Moses Mabeki came in, then stood to one side to let his master and mistress through.

Faith Gushungo caught Carver's eye first. She was much taller than he had expected, at least as tall as Carver himself, her height exaggerated by a brightly patterned silk headdress. Her eyes were hidden behind impenetrable dark glasses and her mouth was set in a downward curve of stony disapproval.

'Why is Gibson not here?' she snapped, not waiting for any introductions.

Carver adopted the ingratiating manner of a meek and easily intimidated vicar. 'I'm awfully sorry, but he's suffering an attack of food poisoning.'

The First Lady gave a dismissive 'Pah!' And only then did Carver realize that she had so dominated the past few seconds that he had paid no attention whatsoever to her husband.

'The President of Malemba, the Honourable Henderson Gushungo,' said Mabeki.

The man who stepped forward, his hand outstretched, was as surprising in appearance as his wife, but in the opposite direction. Carver had expected a man exuding the same sense of power and malice as Mabeki, but magnified a hundredfold. This, after all, was the dictator who had maintained an iron grip on his country for three decades; who had torn down its economy around his ears; tortured his people, destroyed his enemies, outraged global opinion, yet left it impotent to harm him.

And all that was left was a wizened husk.

Gushungo's face was as wrinkled and shrivelled as a dessicated prune. Just a few thin tufts of curly silver hair clung to his scalp. His body had shrunk to the point where he wore his suit like a child dressing up in his father's clothes. The hand he offered Carver was visibly quivering. The other hand clung to an ivory-topped walking stick.

This doddery old geezer was the man Carver had travelled halfway round the world to kill.

For a second he wondered why he should bother. Gushungo's life expectancy could surely be measured in months, even weeks, rather than years. But then he thought about Canaan and Farayi Iluko, rotting in their Malemban cells, and realized that their life expectancies were shorter still.

In any case, it was clear that, as Patrick Tshonga had suggested, Faith Gushungo was now the real power in the room. She was his primary target. And then he caught something between her and Mabeki – a fractional turning of her head towards him; the faintest twisting of his lips – and thought, 'They're in this together.' And then other thoughts, half-formed, crowded into his mind, bringing with them a jumbled, inarticulate sense of danger, something not quite right. But there was no time to follow them because Carver was shaking Gushungo's hand, murmuring 'Mr President' and making his way to the bar, to stand in front of the cross, as Mabeki ushered the Gushungos to their seats.

The two bodyguards, joined now by another pair of men, took their places, standing behind the Gushungos. And then, even though it was still open, there was a gentle tap on the living-room door and a pair of young Chinese women wearing housemaids' grey cotton dresses and starched white aprons tiptoed into the room and formed a third line of worshippers behind the bodyguards. Carver recognized one of them as Tina Wong. She did not acknowledge his presence in any way. Either she did not recognize him through the disguise or, more likely, she was just as good a professional as she'd seemed when they'd met on the ferry thirty-six hours earlier.

Carver had to repress the urge to shout out, 'What the hell are you doing here?' It had never occurred to him that the Chinese staff would be required to take communion as well as everyone else. Was Faith Gushungo really that much of a religious maniac? Or were Wong and her colleague simply Christians themselves? It was possible, Carver supposed. Hong Kong had been British for a hundred and fifty years. Why shouldn't ex-colonies people choose to worship in the Church of England? He cursed himself for not thinking of that sooner.

Mabeki took up his position, standing by the door, watching over the service. He nodded at Carver to start.

'Good morning,' said Carver, trying to think of his next lines. His mind was momentarily blank. His concentration was awry. He had not yet even begun and things were already going wrong.

61

'Today,' said Carver, 'is the festival of Pentecost, or Whit Sunday as it is traditionally known in the Anglican Church, when we commemorate the appearance of the Holy Ghost among the apostles and its bestowal of the gift of tongues. I shall only be giving one reading, from Acts, if that is acceptable to you, sir, and will be using the traditional King James version. I find the poetry of the language far outweighs any loss of comprehension.'

Carver looked at Gushungo, who nodded his assent.

'Very well,' Carver continued, 'then let us now begin our worship.'

In the road outside the house, Zalika Stratten started walking.

Carver read the words from his service book: 'May grace, mercy and peace from God the Father and the Lord Jesus Christ be with you.'

'And also with you,' the congregation of eight replied, with a far greater intensity than the mumbled responses Carver was used to from his British churchgoing.

The next item in his book was referred to as the Prayer of Preparation. The Gushungos and their staff seemed to know it by heart, joining in as he declaimed,

> Almighty God,
> to whom all hearts are open,
> all desires known,
> and from whom no secrets are hidden:
> cleanse the thoughts of our hearts
> by the inspiration of your Holy Spirit,
> that we may perfectly love you,
> and worthily magnify your holy name;
> through Christ our Lord.
> Amen.

Cleanse the thoughts of our hearts, Carver mused. Now there was a line. How many people in the room could even pretend that their hearts were unsullied?

They moved on to the Confession, and Carver wondered what the Gushungos thought of when they told God that they had sinned against him and against their neighbours in thought and word and deed. Did they believe that? How could they then go right back and sin all over again? Perhaps the words were a sort of expiation, wiping the slate of atrocities clean and freeing the Gushungos to go back and commit more.

He read the collect for Pentecost, the special prayer dedicated to that day. It asked God to give his people 'the right judgement in all things'. Carver was about to act as judge, jury and executioner. Never in his life had he been in such close, intimate contact with his targets so soon before their deaths. Even for someone without much religious feeling there was something very special about the act of joining together in prayer. It made them all complicit, in some way he could not quite define. It made the cold finality of what he was about to do all the more stark in its cold-blooded calculation.

*

Zalika was at the front door now. She pushed it gently and it swung open noiselessly on hinges oiled earlier that morning by Tina Wong. Zalika was equally soundless as she made her way across the marble floor, heading for the stairs.

The reading for the day was taken from Acts, chapter two, verses one to eleven. It spoke of the Holy Ghost entering the building where the apostles were gathered.

> Suddenly there came a sound from heaven as of a rushing mighty
>   wind, and it filled all the house where they were sitting.
> And there appeared unto them cloven tongues like as of fire, and it
>   sat upon each of them.

Carver felt like a ghost himself, slipping into this house and falling upon its inhabitants. He was quite calm now, dispassionate, the nerves having begun to vanish as soon as he set about his business.

When the reading was done, he led them all in the Creed, that confident declaration of a belief he could not quite share. It spoke of Jesus coming again in glory to judge the living and the dead. As he read those words from the service book, Carver happened to look up for a second and catch Moses Mabeki's eye. There was a look of utter contempt on his face – the look of a man who had long since abandoned any concept of right and wrong in favour of calculation and expediency.

Carver was making his calculations, too. Very soon now he would have to find a way of killing Mabeki, independently of the rest. He assumed the guards would be carrying guns. If they were not, he would need another weapon. There must be a corkscrew behind the bar; held between the knuckles with its point slashing at Mabeki's skin, it could be a useful weapon. The curtains had tie-backs; wrapped round a neck and pulled tight they would serve to strangle him. Wherever Carver found himself, there were always weapons to be found if he looked hard enough.

He was thinking this even as he brought the Creed to a close with an invocation of 'God the giver of life', and at that point even he could not deny the sacrilege, even the obscenity, of what he was about to do. But that knowledge did not stop him, any more than the Confession altered the Gushungos' behaviour.

Now they were beginning the prayers that led to communion itself. Carver found himself laying a hand on the pyx filled with wafers, the chalice and the cruet of wine, to consecrate them. He led them all in the Lord's Prayer, almost wincing as he said some of the words: 'forgive us our trespasses . . . lead us not into temptation . . . deliver us from evil'.

Once they'd all intoned 'Amen', Carver said, 'We break this bread to share in the body of Christ.'

And the Gushungos, their bodyguards and their servant-girls replied, 'Though we are many, we are one body, because we all share in one bread.'

Carver opened the pyx and looked very carefully at the small round communion wafers inside it. He picked out one of the wafers, said, 'The body of Christ,' and popped it into his mouth. It was arid, flavourless, and stuck like a cream cracker to the roof of his mouth, forcing him to prise it away with his tongue.

Carrying the pyx, Carver stepped forward to the Gushungos' two chairs. The old man was sitting with his eyes closed and his hands held out, slightly cupped, in front of him.

'The body of Christ,' Carver repeated, placing another wafer into Henderson Gushungo's hands.

'Amen,' Gushungo murmured.

He lifted his hands to his mouth and consumed the wafer. And from that moment, the President of Malemba, the Father of the Nation, the most notorious dictator in a continent filled with psychopathic leaders, was, irrevocably, a dead man.

62

Saxitoxin, which has the chemical formula $C_{10}H_{17}N_7O_4$ and is named after the clam *Saxidomus giganteus* in which it was first discovered, is a neurotoxin or nerve poison produced by a small number of species of dinoflagellate phyto-plankton. These microscopic life-forms are ingested by other, bigger species such as shellfish and puffer fish, most commonly when the waters which the fish inhabit are affected by 'algal bloom'. This occurs when the population of algae, including the types of plankton that contain saxitoxin, multiplies rapidly, covering the water with a thick layer of red or brown scum. The fish eat the plankton, humans eat the fish, and then the humans are struck down by a condition known as paralytic shellfish poisoning, or PSP.

Saxitoxin is heat resistant, so cooking cannot nullify its effect. Once it has been consumed, symptoms appear within minutes and include any or all of the following: a feeling of nausea, followed by diarrhoea and/or vomiting and/or abdominal pain; tingling and/or burning sensations in limbs and extremities, including hands, feet, lips, gums and even the tongue; shortness of breath and choking;

confused and/or slurred speech; and loss of limb coordination. Someone who has saxitoxin poisoning could easily be mistaken for a drunk. The crucial difference is that a hard night's boozing will only give you a hangover. PSP, however, can very easily be fatal. In fact, saxitoxin is so dangerous that a single dose of 0.2 milligrams is enough to kill an average human. That makes it approximately a thousand times more toxic than sarin nerve-gas.

Naturally, the CIA became very, very interested in saxitoxin. Back in the fifties, its undercover operatives were supposedly given suicide capsules containing it, but in 1970 the agency was ordered to destroy its entire stock by, ironically enough, that most toxic of all presidents, Richard Milhous Nixon.

Saxitoxin, however, did not go away. Nature kept on producing it, and precisely because of its effects on the nervous system medical researchers discovered it could be an extremely effective laboratory tool. In time, scientists discovered how to synthesize it, using the methods described by Carver to Klerk. It had proved relatively simple for Klerk's people to replicate the process so painstakingly mapped out in the *Journal of the American Chemical Society* and then mix extremely high doses of saxitoxin, many times greater than that needed to kill, into the flour and water used to make communion wafers. The baking process did nothing to make the wafers any less poisonous. The intensity of the poison, however, ensured that its effects would be felt far more quickly than those of a naturally inflicted dose of PSP.

The timing was a delicate issue, though. It was absolutely vital that Carver reach the end of the line of communicants, dosing them all, before anyone realized that anything had happened. Ideally, he wanted a few extra seconds in which to attack Mabeki before he too was alerted. Finally, it was essential to coordinate the timing of everything he did downstairs with that of Zalika's theft of the diamonds upstairs.

Zalika was in the master bedroom. She had located the safe, hidden behind another portrait of the Gushungos. Now she was reaching into her canvas shoulder-bag and retrieving the envelope Tina Wong had given her. She opened it and pulled out a clear, sealable plastic sandwich-bag. Inside the bag was a thin latex glove, of the kind worn by surgeons. Zalika removed it and placed it on her right hand. Then she turned back to the safe.

Faith Gushungo accepted her wafer with uncharacteristic meekness. Then Carver moved on to the bodyguards kneeling on the floor behind. From the corner of his eye, he saw Moses Mabeki slip from the room. He thought he heard Mabeki's footsteps first in the hallway and then slipping up the stairs.

Zalika was up there, unarmed and unaware that she was in danger of detection.

But there was no way Carver could warn her that Mabeki was loose inside the house without blowing his own cover.

And if that were not enough, he had a more immediate problem to consider, the one that had struck him just before the service. And with every step he took, it was getting closer.

63

To avoid poisoning himself, Carver had placed two saxitoxin-free wafers into the pyx, as well as a dozen poisoned ones. That allowed one for the actual service and another in case anyone asked him to prove, in advance, that the wafers were edible. The two wafers were each marked with a very slight notch, to distinguish them from the rest. He had only needed one of them, leaving the second spare. But now there were two Chinese housemaids, one of them a woman who had gone undercover in this madhouse to help him, expecting communion.

Upstairs, Moses Mabeki was walking slowly but as inexorably as the angel of death down the corridor towards the master bedroom. As he moved, he reached into his jacket and pulled out a gun.

In the bedroom, Zalika Stratten was reaching into the safe and grabbing a green velveteen bag. It was heavier than she'd expected and there was a scrabbling sound of cold, hard surfaces rubbing against each other as she picked it up.

*

Carver was doing his best to be cold-bloodedly professional. His mantra had always been: don't worry about things you cannot control. It was Zalika's responsibility to look after herself. It was his to carry out the assassination. So think about that and come to the obvious conclusion: find the damn wafer, split it in two, and give them half each.

But the bloody thing had disappeared. It had become jumbled up with the others while he was serving the bodyguards.

Christ, had he given one of the guards the dummy wafer?

Carver told himself to calm down. There were still seven wafers left in the box. One of them, with any luck, was safe. Six to one: hardly needle-in-haystack time. So just look.

He riffled around the inside of the pyx with his right index finger. Tina Wong was looking at him with a quizzical expression.

'Close your eyes, my child,' Carver said.

She obeyed.

A cough came from one of the chairs behind him, the wheezing cough of an elderly man. It tailed away in a dry retching sound.

At last, Carver found the wafer he was looking for and halved it.

The Chinese girls were kneeling in front of him, Tina Wong perfectly composed, the other leaning to the side, eyes wide open, trying to see round him and find out what was happening up at the front.

Now Faith Gushungo had started coughing.

'The body of Christ,' said Carver, firmly, and shoved half a wafer into the hands of Tina Wong.

'Amen,' she said, and put it in her mouth.

Carver stepped a pace to one side, blocking the view of the second maid.

'The body of Christ,' he said.

The bodyguards were starting to suffer now. One was bent over, clutching at his guts.

'This bad!' the maid said, casting horrified glances at the

sickening men before throwing the half-wafer to the floor. 'You give us bad bread!'

'You're fine,' Carver hissed. 'Now get out of here.'

The girl didn't move, just knelt there.

'Scram!' Carver said.

Tina Wong jumped to her feet and started dragging the servant away, screaming at her in Chinese.

Carver spared them no more time. He could hear movement behind him. He spun round on one foot, uncurled his fist and punched the heel of his hand into the face of one of the guards, who had got to his feet and was clumsily trying to reach inside his suit for the handgun holstered to his ribcage.

The blow snapped the bodyguard's head sideways, straining his neck ligaments and sending his brain bouncing round his skull like a pinball against the bumpers. The guard reeled backwards, collided with Faith Gushungo's chair and landed in a heap on top of his mistress, who was physically incapable of resisting his momentum. The two of them collapsed on to the floor where Henderson Gushungo was already lying like a landed fish, gasping for air, incapable of any movement bar the occasional spasm of his body or limbs.

Moses Mabeki stood quite still a couple of feet inside the door to the master bedroom, watching Zalika Stratten. She had not noticed he was there. All her attention was on the bag. She had been unable to resist opening it and pulling out an uncut diamond the size of a quail's egg. It sat in her palm, the light glinting off its countless rough, irregular surfaces, just waiting for the diamond cutter's skill to bring it to full, sparkling life. Mabeki was happy to let her enjoy the sensation of holding such a magnificent gemstone. It was a pleasure to watch her and almost to enjoy the self-denial of delaying for those last few seconds before he took possession of her again.

Finally, he could wait no longer. He coughed quietly, as if politely clearing his throat.

Zalika spun round, her eyes widening as she saw Mabeki and the gun in his hand.

'I think you'd better give me the diamonds,' he said, quite calmly, watching the emotions play across her features as she took in the reality of his presence, and his actual flesh-and-blood appearance.

He crooked his right index finger and wordlessly gestured for her to come to him.

Even after ten years, the obedience drilled into her in Mozambique had not entirely gone away. The fiery pride and independence that had animated Zalika during the time she had spent with Carver vanished as swiftly as a desert mirage. She went to him without the slightest act of defiance.

'Put the diamonds in your bag and then give it to me,' Mabeki said.

She did as he asked. Mabeki slung the bag over his left shoulder and then, without warning, smashed the grip of his pistol, clasped in his right hand, into her temple.

Zalika was taken completely by surprise. She made a noise halfway between a gasp and a whimper and tottered unsteadily on her feet.

Mabeki grabbed her round the neck with his left arm. He pressed the gun to her head with his right.

'Come with me,' he hissed into her ear. 'Time we dealt with your boyfriend.'

64

Downstairs in the living room, the fourth of the guards was the only one still standing, although he was already losing his coordination. Carver slammed his left elbow into the guard's Adam's apple, let him follow the others to the ground, then crouched over him. He placed one hand over the man's throat, gently squeezing the already damaged airway, while his other hand felt for the handle of the man's gun and pulled it out of its black leather shoulder holster. He shoved the gun in his waistband and felt around on the other side of the chest. The ribs were moving as the guard made his last feeble attempts to breathe. His feet flopped about as he tried to kick himself free. Carver ignored all that. His only interest was the two clips of ammunition in the holster's second pocket. He took them out and placed them in his jacket pocket, then got to his feet.

Henderson Gushungo was silent and motionless now. In his last moments, he had coughed blood on to the marble tile in front of him. He had also evacuated his bowels and the stench of it was now hanging heavily in the air. The great dictator, dying in his own blood and shit. His wife, half her body trapped beneath her bodyguard's, made a weak mewling sound and with one last desperate effort reached out to grab her husband's lifeless hand.

From outside the room, Carver heard the sound of footsteps running down the stairs and into the hall. There was a high-pitched scream; the sound of two shots being fired; more screams, wounded ones this time; then two more shots.

There had been three women left alive in the house. Some, if not all of them, were now dead. But which ones?

Carver started to move past the twitching, gasping bodies of the dying guards towards the door of the living room, his gun out in front of him, ready to fire at any moment.

Then Carver felt something grab at his ankle. He stumbled to the ground, wincing as he cracked his kneecaps on the hard marble surface. He turned his head and saw that one of the bodyguards had somehow summoned the strength to reach out and wrap a hand round his leg. Carver kicked out with his other leg, hitting the guard's nose and feeling the crack as it broke beneath his heel. There was a gurgling sound as air left the guard's lungs, a final breath. But he did not let go. The dead fingers still had Carver in their grip.

Up ahead, Carver saw a shadow against the wall by the door as Mabeki's head bobbed into the doorway, then disappeared from view. Carver fired two quick shots towards the doorway then writhed desperately to change his position as Mabeki's gun-hand appeared.

Mabeki shot four rounds in quick succession. One went straight through the giant window on the far side of the room. Two ploughed into the marble floor, one so close to Carver that he could feel the stabs of tiny, needle-sharp splinters of stone against the side of his face. The fourth hit the glossy bald head of the man whose hand was clasped round Carver's ankle, entering just above his nose and blowing away the back of his skull.

The fingers jerked open with a convulsive twitch.

Carver jumped to his feet, ran to the wall next to the door and pressed his back to it. Then, with his newly acquired gun held vertically next to his head, he slid sideways along the wall towards the door.

That was when he heard the single word 'Carver!'

Zalika had survived!

Carver could make out the sound of feet scrabbling for purchase on the marble floor. Now he too had to move fast. He abandoned his cautious progress and dashed to the door, throwing himself forward into the hall then rolling to one side as Mabeki fired into the space where he had just been.

Carver came to rest by the body of Tina Wong. She was lying next to the other servant, so close that the blood from their wounds was mingling into a single pool on the floor. Wong's eyes were open, looking straight into his in mute accusation: 'I'm dead because of you.'

He looked up and brought his gun to bear. Mabeki was silhouetted against the light from the open front door. Carver's gun was pointing right at him. Or rather, it was pointing right at Zalika Stratten, who was standing there, directly in front of Mabeki, his arm round her throat.

Her eyes looked dull. There was blood trickling from a cut on her left temple. A decade after Moses Mabeki had first kidnapped her, he had her at his mercy once again. And this time Carver had no clear shot, no answer as Mabeki rasped, 'You try to shoot, she dies. You come after me, she dies.'

Zalika herself was silent now. But Carver could clearly see her mouth the words 'Help me . . . help me!'

Carver lay on the cold marble tiles, beneath the vulgar wallpaper. The blood from the two women's bodies was slowly spreading towards him. He cursed himself: why had he let himself be persuaded to bring an amateur, however capable, on a mission as important as this? Eaten up by frustration and helplessness, paralysed with fear for the woman he was supposed to have protected, Carver barely moved a muscle as Mabeki hustled Zalika out of the door. Only when he heard the sound of two car doors slamming shut and an engine coming to life did he get to his feet, hurdle the pathetic corpses in their blood-soaked grey dresses and start running frantically down the hall.

65

As he ran out of the house, Carver pressed 'send' on his phone's text-message screen and sent the 'OK' signal to the number he'd been given. It felt like a lie. Yes, the Gushungos were dead. But that was where the good news ended. Everything else was going more pear-shaped by the second.

Outside, the Rolls-Royce was cruising out of the forecourt with none of the frantic speed Carver would have expected from a kidnapper making a getaway. It paused for a second as a small white delivery van covered in Chinese characters pottered past the entrance to the property and drove away down the road. The Rolls moved forward again, still going gently. Even at this sedate pace, however, it would only be a matter of a second or two before Mabeki turned left and followed the little van back down the hill towards the main entrance.

Carver could clearly see Mabeki in the driver's seat, but there was no sign of Zalika. Either he'd shoved her down out of sight or . . . No, that wasn't it. Carver hadn't heard the sound of two doors closing. The first sound he'd heard had been the lid slamming shut. The bastard had shoved her in the boot. That was why Mabeki was going so gingerly. Any sudden movements and she'd be rattling around in there like a cat in a tumble-dryer. He didn't want to damage the goods.

Mabeki's caution gave Carver a fractional window of opportunity. He stood on the top step, just outside the front door, braced his legs and held the bodyguard's pistol out in front of him in a two-handed grip. It was a Chinese model, with a communist star stamped on the grip: a QSZ-92 with fifteen nine-millimetre rounds in the magazine. The Rolls was side-on to him now – as clear a shot as he would ever have, and as safe as it would ever be. This was his one chance to end it fast.

He aimed. His finger curled round the trigger, gently squeezing it . . .

Carver put the gun down. Firing a nine-millimetre round at an armoured vehicle was an entirely futile activity. The bodywork was impenetrable. Even the windows would repel a bullet without so much as a scratch. He would achieve nothing except make a lot of noise and attract unwanted attention.

Mabeki knew it, too. He turned his head, leaning forward in his seat and peering out through the passenger window. Then he wrenched his mouth into the closest thing he could manage to a broad grin, gave a brief mocking wave of his hand, and hit the accelerator. The Rolls's massive 6.7-litre engine did not exactly roar into life. A Rolls-Royce never does anything so crude. But, though the noise was not spectacular, the effect certainly was. The massive car leapt forward. An instant later, it had disappeared from sight.

Carver's instinct was to race to the Honda and give chase right away, but again he resisted the temptation. Instead, he went back into the house, past the two bodies in the hall, and returned to the living room. There, amid the lingering stench of cordite and shit, he gathered up the communion kit and put it back in the leather briefcase. No sense in leaving fingerprint-rich evidence if he didn't have to.

On the other hand, it did make sense to leave the gun behind where it could mislead police investigators. Carver wiped down the handle and trigger then, holding it by the barrel, his hand covered by a handkerchief, replaced it in the hand of the dead bodyguard. In total, he spent thirty seconds in the room before leaving again. Keeping the handkerchief over his hand, he closed the front door then walked briskly to his car. He got in and placed his briefcase with its flap open in the footwell of the passenger seat. Then he switched applications on his phone and, for the first time all day, gave a silent, heartfelt, entirely genuine prayer of thanks: Zalika's phone was on, and it was heading steadily up the road away from the estate. For the time being there was no need to panic. He could follow Mabeki at a distance.

Carver went back downhill to the main entrance and drove away. The road was little more than a twisting, narrow country lane, lined on either side by trees and heavy undergrowth, with no traffic to be seen in either direction. When he'd gone about a mile, Carver stopped the car by the side of the road and got out, taking the case with him. He looked around to check that no one could see him, then walked about twenty paces into the woodland and shoved the case into the heart of a large bush. Satisfied that it was completely invisible, he walked back towards the road, paused for a moment to listen for approaching engines, then stepped out on to the tarmac and round to the driver's side of the car.

He looked at his phone display and frowned. Mabeki had reached the Tolo Highway, but instead of turning right, back towards the city, as Carver had expected, he had turned left and was heading north, towards the Chinese border.

That could complicate things. Suddenly Carver couldn't afford to be quite so casual. When the Honda pulled away again, he had the accelerator down hard.

66

Nearly seven thousand miles to the west of Hong Kong stood the Malemban capital of Sindele. It still pretended, at least, to be the heart of a modern, functioning state. It had a central business district ringed by motorways. Their intersections led to broad four-lane boulevards, criss-crossing blocks filled with office buildings ten or even twenty storeys high. It had splendid government buildings left over from colonial times, lavishly appointed, department stores, banks with marble halls, and parks laid out with rolling lawns, shady trees and herbaceous borders.

These days, however, the roads were virtually empty, there being almost no petrol anywhere, nor spare parts for broken-down vehicles. The office buildings frequently lacked electric power or running water. The department stores were empty for want of goods to sell or customers to buy, and the banks had long since ceased to function in an economy bereft of meaningful currency. As for the parks, the lawns were now parched and bare, with just the occasional straggly weed or rusting soft drink can to break up the monotony of scorched earth. The trees had all been cut down for firewood and the empty herbaceous borders were indistinguishable from the rest of the barren terrain.

But Major Rodney Madziko of the Malemban National Army's élite Reconnaissance Squadron had no time to contemplate the passing cityscape or bemoan its decline. He was standing in the open hatch of an amphibious BRDM-1 scout car, an old Soviet model, bought second-hand from the Russians almost thirty years ago. Its body-armour was now more rust than metal, its engine propelled it in a random combination of lurches, kangaroo-hops and staggers, and its belching exhaust pipes created their very own black smokescreen. But the 7.62mm machine gun mounted above the front crew compartment still fired live ammunition, as did those on the four other scout cars that were following Madziko's as it made its way through the deserted streets of downtown Sindele.

It was half-past five on a Sunday morning, a perfect time to cross the city uninterrupted and unobserved. A perfect time for a coup.

Madziko's instructions were simple: on the 'go' signal, get to the headquarters of the Malemban Broadcasting Corporation, secure the building and hold it until Patrick Tshonga arrived at seven to make the simultaneous announcement of Henderson Gushungo's death and his own assumption of power on the MBC's solitary TV channel and all four of its national radio stations. His men had been ready since long before dawn. The signal had been received. So now, as the rising sun split the streets into long expanses of deep shadow and dazzling shafts of burnished gold, the Reconnaissance Squadron was on its way.

Madziko had sworn a solemn oath in the sight of God to uphold the state of Malemba and preserve it against all its enemies, foreign and internal. So far as he was concerned, he was upholding that oath more loyally now than at any other time in his fifteen-year career as an army officer. He had been raised to believe in the essential virtues of democracy and free speech. He did not accept that oppression was any more acceptable just because a black man, rather than a white man, had imposed it. To be in the vanguard of establishing true freedom in his country was thus, to Rodney

Madziko, the greatest honour he could possibly be granted.

Up ahead, he saw Broadcasting House, the MBC headquarters, named after the London home of the British Broadcasting Corporation in colonial times and unchanged ever since. It was a heavy-set, redbrick thirties office block that occupied three sides of a large courtyard, in the middle of which stood a modernist white marble fountain that had long since run dry. The fourth side of the courtyard consisted of a high metal fence that ran along the street, pierced by the building's main entrance. A guard-hut stood by a lowered barrier. The hut was empty, nor were there any signs of life in the building itself. It was, after all, first thing on a Sunday morning. Only the bare minimum of staff would be at work at this hour.

Major Madziko could easily have ordered his driver to burst straight through the barrier, but he did not want to act like a violent oaf. They were supposed to be there in the interests of a fair, law-abiding society. So he ordered one of his men to raise the barrier then led his troop of scout cars into the courtyard, the sound of their engines echoing raucously off the building's plain brick facade. They proceeded round the fountain, three to one side, two to the other, so that Madziko's vehicle ended up in the middle of a line of five, all facing the main entrance. He ordered the drivers to cut their engines and jumped down from his car. His men followed him, clambering out on to the tarmac courtyard until only the gunners standing behind their machine guns remained.

Inside Broadcasting House, another major, from the army's para-troop battalion, was watching events down below from the vantage point of a first-floor window. He was holding a walkie-talkie to his lips. He spoke very quietly into the mouthpiece, and a dozen windows slid open. From each, a round metallic snout slid forward.

'Fire at will,' said the major.

The moving window frames caught Madziko's eye in an instant, but the totally unexpected shock of impending disaster took him a couple of seconds to process. Too late, he turned back to his gunner, pointed at the dark interruptions in the facade caused by the raised glass and shouted, 'The windows! Shoot!'

By the time the first machine gun was raised, the triggers on the grenade-launchers had been pulled, the rocket flames were spurting and the grenades were on their way. A fraction of a second later, the scout cars were obliterated. The force of the blast and the thousands of razor-sharp shards of metal that filled the air blew Madziko and his men apart. In the time it takes to swat a mosquito, they were destroyed, and with them all hope of a peaceful coup.

The ambush was repeated with equal finality at the Parliament Building, the Central Bank, Police Headquarters and the President's official residence. Wherever Patrick Tshonga's forces went, government men were waiting for them. The rebels who had counted on the element of surprise were the ones receiving a rude and terminal shock.

67

Mabeki wasn't making for the border. He left the highway at the first possible interchange, turned hard left, almost doubling back on himself, and drove away to the southwest. He was driving smoothly, not too fast.

Carver unconsciously clenched his jaw as the tension and concentration built inside him. Where was Mabeki going? He mentally pictured the maps of Hong Kong he'd studied, and skimmed the books he'd read. A name came to mind: Shek Kong, a former RAF base now part-used by the Chinese air force. Private aviation was allowed there, which it wasn't at the main international airport. If Mabeki had arranged a plane to get him out of Hong Kong fast, on the first leg of the journey to Malemba, he'd very likely fly from Shek Kong.

Carver estimated that Mabeki was around three minutes ahead of him. If a jet was fuelled and ready to go, that was more than enough time to drive on to the tarmac, race up the steps, close the door and start rolling. Like Mabeki, Carver wasn't keen on driving too fast, but for different reasons. He'd never wanted to be convicted for murder, just because he'd been caught breaking a speed-limit. But he couldn't afford those niceties now. He had to narrow the gap.

The car showroom's mechanics had done a good job. The Honda might have looked like a piece of junk on the outside, but it had all the acceleration its reputation suggested, the steering was precise, and the suspension nice and tight. Carver was enjoying himself, revving hard and relishing the angry buzz of the overworked, tuned-up engine as he darted in and out of the traffic on the highway before swinging left on to an off-ramp painted with go-slower yellow stripes.

There was a roundabout at the bottom of the ramp. Carver swung left on to a road that cut through a sprawl of low-density suburban housing before heading out into the country, following the valley floor for a mile or so between two lines of hills. The road was undemanding, with long straight stretches broken by gentle corners that he could take flat out. He had no trouble keeping his speed above eighty miles per hour, sometimes touching a hundred as he overtook slower vehicles, leaving trucks, buses and crowded family cars in his wake.

Carver had to slow his pace slightly as he re-entered a more built-up area. There was another roundabout up ahead. The road to the airfield at Shek Kong was the second exit – straight across. It took him a couple of seconds to register the fact that Mabeki had not taken it. He'd swung left again, going due south now, back towards Kowloon. And he'd taken the most remarkable and most dangerous road in the whole of Hong Kong: Route Twisk.

It had been built in the early fifties by soldiers of the Royal Engineers to link the British Army's main base at Castle Peak in the Tsuen Wan district of the city with the RAF at Shek Kong. So the road was originally designated TW/SK, which soon became known as Twisk. Designed with inbuilt demolition chambers, which could be blown up to collapse the road in the event of a Chinese invasion, Twisk ran through some of Hong Kong's most rugged and spectacular landscapes, past its highest peak, Tai Mo

Shan. Barely four miles long, the road rose from sea-level up to twelve hundred feet and almost all the way back down again. It twisted and turned along and between the hills in a series of blind corners and hairpin bends. At the far end it was swallowed up by the urban highways and towering apartment blocks of modern Tsuen Wan.

By the time he got on to Route Twisk, Carver had cut the gap between him and Mabeki to a minute and a half. He wanted visual contact before they entered the maze of the city streets. Judging by the signal from Zalika's phone, Mabeki was a little over a mile down the road. He'd been doing about fifty on the first steep but reasonably straight uphill section of the road, then slowed right down as he hit a W-shaped sequence of bends that led to the tightest hairpin of all. That was reasonably good going. But it wouldn't be nearly good enough for Carver. He had no choice. He had to race all the way.

Ahead of him he could see the triangular peak of Tai Mo Shan rising like a huge grey-green pagoda against the clear blue sky. The road ran between two lines of shade-trees that for an instant reminded Carver of southern France: a gentle swing right, a nice stretch of straight road, then a quick chicane right, left and hard right again. There were a couple of motorbikes behind him, powerful ones by the looks of it, but up ahead the road was mercifully clear. So he could take the racing lines, cutting the apexes of the corners, barely applying the brakes at all and letting the gearbox and the accelerator pedal do all the work.

He jinked through the first hairpin and up a straight barely two hundred yards long before he had to hit the handbrake hard for the first time as he approached the first section of a tight double-S. He felt the car scrabble for traction as he kept the accelerator down, working the wheel and letting the car's rear axle drift, carrying it round the bend. Same again on the next bend, and then he was into the third section of the W, drifting round the apex, swinging right out into the oncoming lane, letting the rear end of the car break free round the outside of the bend in a sort of semi-controlled anarchy.

And there was a bus coming the other way, downhill, heading directly towards him.

Carver's instant reaction was not alarm but bemusement. The bus was a single-decker Dennis Dart, the doughty old stalwart of countless public transport services up and down the British Isles. And it was about to kill him on a mountain road in Hong Kong.

Carver could see the look of shock on the driver's face as he registered the presence of a car hurtling towards him in the wrong lane. There was an elephantine squeal of protest from the bus's brakes and tyres as he tried to check its momentum. But a Dart bus is around thirty feet long and weighs seven tons unladen. Basic physics dictate that it's a hard beast to rein in, particularly when descending a steep hill. The driver also had the corner to consider. He started turning into the bend, cutting across Carver's path, blocking off his escape route to the left-hand lane.

Now Carver had to make an instant choice. He could hit the brakes as hard as his right foot could manage and just pray that the car either halted or at the very worst collided with the bus at a sub-fatal speed. Or he could apply an equally powerful force to the accelerator on the outside chance that he could avoid the oncoming bus entirely.

He hit both.

First he yanked on the handbrake, drastically slowing the front of the car. The back end, however, kept moving, swinging round until the Honda was positioned sideways across the carriageway.

The bus was looming above Carver so close he seemed almost in touching distance. He had let go of his wheel and thrown his hands up over his face in an instinctive gesture of self-protection. As the bus, too, slewed round, Carver could see passengers screaming in terror. He couldn't blame them. He was tempted to scream too. He just didn't have the time.

He released the handbrake and hit the gas. The front wheels regained traction and the car shot forward, heading straight for the far side of the road . . . and the two motorbikes that had been riding behind him up the hill.

Carver heaved the steering wheel to the right, missed the leading bike by a whisker, hit the kerb on the side of the road and carried on over it so that his outside wheels actually rode up the earthen banking on the inside of the corner. The Honda tilted so far over it seemed on the verge of toppling on to its roof before Carver regained some measure of control and brought the vehicle crashing back down on to the road again. He took a deep calming breath, slowly exhaled, then raced away again.

Mabeki had gained a few extra seconds. But the chase was still on.

68

Patrick Tshonga had a safehouse, a detached villa standing in a half-acre of gardens, half a mile from the centre of Sindele. It was one of several he had used over the years as he moved from place to place, evading the attentions of Henderson Gushungo. Only his closest associates knew of its existence, and of these only the most trusted had any idea of its precise address. He had decided that this was the best place to be when the news came through that Broadcasting House had been captured and it was safe for him to make his first public appearance as leader of a free nation.

At 02.30 hours, a small detachment of Malemban special forces personnel had arrived in the streets that surrounded the safehouse. To their military training, patterned on the example of the SAS, they added their own, innate skills. They could run for hours at speeds no European could match; track human or vehicle trails over the roughest, stoniest landscape; and move as silently and invisibly as wraiths, so that their enemies died before they even knew they were in danger.

Just as the first grenades exploded outside Broadcasting House, two three-man teams blew the locks off the front and back doors to the house, entering through the front hall and kitchen respectively. A third team was positioned in the garden, waiting to cut off anyone attempting to escape from a window on the ground or upper floor.

The kitchen and hall were secured. There were two reception rooms on the ground floor. They too were checked. Both were empty.

Cautiously, each man, waiting for the first sound of a round being chambered or a gun being fired, dreading the impact of bullets into his own flesh, made his way upstairs. They had all seen copies of the plans. They knew there were three bedrooms, two bathrooms and a large storage area in the attic. None of them showed any sign of human occupation.

Only as the soldiers were leaving the building, feeling frustrated and even cheated by their lack of success, did one of them notice the tiny videocam positioned high up on the hall wall, just below the ceiling.

They knew then that Patrick Tshonga had been watching them. The unit commander immediately called his base to alert them to the likelihood that Tshonga had anticipated he might be betrayed. When the conversation was over, the commander summoned his men to gather round him.

'The traitor has escaped for now,' he said. 'He is laughing at us. But we will catch him and we will make him pay for that in blood.'

69

For all its magisterial size and dignity, a Rolls-Royce Phantom can be surprisingly nimble up a steep, winding road. Moses Mabeki was enjoying his Sunday-morning drive, staying well within the Phantom's capabilities and taking Route Twisk at a pace calculated to enable Carver to catch him if he pushed his car to the limit.

The pleasure was made all the greater by the updates from Malemba that Mabeki was receiving through his Bluetooth earpiece. The feeble attempt at a coup had been utterly crushed. Patrick Tshonga's escape was a considerable irritation, but all his allies had been killed or captured. Those in custody were being questioned by interrogators untroubled by any concept of human rights, or any squeamishness about the use of torture. It would only be a matter of time before one of them gave up the information needed to track Tshonga down.

The news in Hong Kong was just as satisfactory. Mabeki had already contacted Zheng Junjie and updated him on Carver's absurd disguise and the pathetically inadequate car he had chosen to drive.

In his jacket pocket, Mabeki had the phone Carver had given Zalika Stratten. He wondered what Carver would think if he knew it was no longer in her possession. He would probably be shocked; certainly surprised. But then, that was the least of the surprises Moses Mabeki had in store for Samuel Carver.

70

They played cat and mouse as Mabeki came to the end of Route Twisk and kept driving south. Carver followed him along an urban motorway between two long lines of tower blocks that rose on either side. The road fed like the tributary of a great river into another, even mightier highway that followed the coastline down towards the port of Kowloon. As he dodged between the thickening traffic, steadily closing the gap on Mabeki, Carver saw vast yards filled with rusting containers, and barges with cranes painted in vivid combinations of red, white, yellow and blue.

Up ahead towered the sixteen-hundred-feet-high ICC Tower, the tallest building in Hong Kong. It looked like a glass rocket, sitting on its launch pad, counting down to blast-off, and for a moment Carver wondered if Mabeki had somehow arranged for a chopper to pick him up from its roof: it was a suitably melodramatic location for a man who had chosen to live as the star of his own private horror movie. But no, Mabeki kept going towards the toll leading to the Western Harbour Tunnel that linked the mainland to Hong Kong Island.

As he approached the toll, Carver finally caught sight of the Rolls-Royce for the first time since it had left the Gushungos' driveway. It was about two hundred yards up ahead, caught in a line of cars all waiting for their turn at the tollbooth. Carver was close enough to get out and run. Every protective instinct he felt for Zalika urged him to do it. He'd surely reach Mabeki before he could get through the toll. But then what? The Rolls was virtually impregnable. He'd be left standing beside it, exposed to God knows how many witnesses' eyes, behaving like a lunatic and getting precisely nowhere. No, he'd have to bide his time.

Up ahead, Mabeki reached the booth, handed over the forty-five-Hong-Kong-dollar fee and sped away into the tunnel.

The seconds dragged by as Carver sat in the line of cars, his frustration mounting until he too reached the barrier, paid his cash and drove into the tunnel beneath Victoria Harbour. When he emerged on the northwest tip of Hong Kong Island, he was soon caught in the crowds of Sunday day-trippers. The traffic inched down Highway 4 along the island's northern shore, through the heart of Hong Kong's financial district and past all the bank head-quarters and corporate towers whose lights had flashed so brightly at him and Zalika two nights earlier as they'd stood by the rail of the ferry. Carver thought of her kissing him then looking at him with such tender, loving eyes as she said, 'You're a good man, Samuel Carver.' Well, he wouldn't be much good if he couldn't rescue her.

But what was Mabeki doing? Where was he going?

According to the tracker, he'd swung right off Highway 4 and was now heading south again. But then what? When Mabeki reached the south shore of Hong Kong Island there'd be nothing left in front of him but the South China Sea. Within the next three or four miles, Mabeki would come to the end of the line. That, for better or worse, was where everything would be decided. And Mabeki knew it too. Carver could see from the tracker that the Rolls was slowing down; letting Carver close the gap; leading him on. It didn't take a massively tactical brain to figure out that

Mabeki had some kind of plan. Maybe he was hoping to make an exchange: Zalika's life for his freedom. Or even Carver's life for Zalika's.

Forget it. Carver had unfinished business of his own. As long as Mabeki was alive, he and Zalika would never be safe. Killing him was simply a matter of self-defence.

Carver drove past the Happy Valley race track where vast crowds gathered to watch the horses and, far more importantly to a population obsessed by gambling, wager huge sums on the results. Then the road dipped down into another tunnel that ran beneath the hills of the Aberdeen Country Park towards Aberdeen Harbour itself. That made sense. If you looked as horrifically recognizable as Moses Mabeki it was safer to quit Hong Kong on a fishing boat or even one of the speedboats that bobbed on the waters of the Aberdeen Marina than risk the multiple security procedures of an airport.

As Carver emerged from the tunnel and headed into Aberdeen, the Rolls-Royce came into view once again. Mabeki was swinging off the raised highway down a ramp that seemed to lead right into the heart of the great clusters of apartment buildings where the boat people of old had been resettled. From up on the raised high-way, Carver could see that the towers were grouped in huge semi-circles and X-shapes, like fortified villages in the sky. He followed Mabeki down the off-ramp and saw his silver quarry up ahead, turning left into a side road. It wouldn't be long now, Carver was sure of it.

Then he, too, turned left into the shadow of the towers.

71

The street was crowded with cars and people: a few white tourists who'd ventured inland from the scenic harbour-front, but mostly locals bustling purposefully to and fro, or standing in groups, talking and gesticulating with a vehemence and energy that belied the clichéd image of Chinese inscrutability.

Mabeki had parked the Rolls-Royce on the left-hand side of the road, about fifty yards ahead. He was standing by it, watching Carver's Honda crawl towards him, hemmed in by cars and trucks, taunting Carver, challenging him to make the next move.

Carver pulled over to the left, double-parking and ignoring the horn-blasts and shouts from the drivers now half-trapped behind him as he got out of the car and tried to push his way through the crowds towards the Rolls-Royce. Mabeki stood quite still, just staring in Carver's direction until he'd caught his eye. Then he raised a hand, waved mockingly and walked away, heedless of the fact that he was turning his back on an armed enemy, his tall, twisted figure towering over most of the people around him.

And he walked away alone.

The question ripped through Carver's mind, driving every other thought from his head: what had Mabeki done with Zalika?

The Rolls-Royce was just ahead of him now, its boot pointing at him. Mabeki had left it unlocked so that it had opened a fraction. If Zalika was in there, she could get out, so why hadn't she?

He ran through the possible reasons. She was bound and immobile. She was unconscious or even dead. And then it struck him that Mabeki had left him an invitation. 'Open me,' the boot seemed to be saying. 'Open me and see what happens next.'

It would have been so easy for Mabeki to set a booby trap. Carver flashed back to the memory of Justus's prized VW van: the nylon line and the hand-grenade that had blown when the door was opened. Was that what Mabeki had in store for him now? Or was his real aim simply to buy a little time?

The longer Carver stood around wondering what to do, the further away Mabeki would get.

'Zalika,' he called out, 'are you there? You OK?'

There was no reply.

Carver moved closer to the boot, bent down and peered at the narrow opening, trying to spot any sign of a trap. Oh the hell with it. He'd had enough pussyfooting around. He grabbed the boot, swung it open with one swift movement . . .

And nothing happened. There was no explosion, no trap . . . and no Zalika.

But that was impossible. Carver had tracked the signal from her phone all the way from the Gushungos' house. Mabeki hadn't stopped at any point in the journey, apart from the delay at the toll-booth by the Western Harbour Tunnel. So where was the girl?

Frantically, irrationally, Carver opened the driver's door of the Rolls, leaned in and peered into the interior as if there was some faint chance that Zalika might be sitting there. She wasn't.

But her phone was sitting on the passenger seat. And it was ringing.

Carver picked it up. He pulled himself back out of the car, stood up again and looked down the street, searching for Mabeki, knowing that it would be his voice he heard as he pressed the 'receive' button and held the phone to his ear.

'Goodbye, Reverend,' said Mabeki. 'Or rather, goodbye, Mr Carver. You will not see me or Miss Stratten again.'

The phone went dead. Carver hurled it to the ground, anger and frustration getting the better of him. Then he looked up again and the anger was replaced by the chilly realization of imminent danger. There were five men walking abreast across the pavement, barging people out of their way as they made their way towards the Rolls-Royce. But it didn't take a genius to work out that it wasn't the car they were aiming for. Mabeki had indeed set a trap for him. And it had just been sprung.

72

Just across the road, Carver saw a grocery store. It was about as basic as a shop could get – a single room, open to the street, with steel shutters at the front that could be drawn across like garage doors at the end of the day. He made his way smartly towards it, aware that he was being followed, the men fanning out behind him to block any possible attempt to run his way out of trouble. The man giving the orders was walking in the middle of the line. He sported a scraggly goatee beard and moustache and was wearing an old olive-green army shirt, unbuttoned over a black vest. He was about thirty yards away now. At a steady walking pace, that gave Carver around fifteen seconds' start.

As he got closer to the store, Carver saw that a grey-haired old boy was sitting on a white plastic garden-chair to one side of the entrance. In front of him was a waist-high wooden counter. Cardboard boxes were piled up against the counter and along the side walls. Most of them were still taped shut, but the ones on the top row had been opened to reveal their contents. In the ones nearest him, Carver spotted a random collection of eggs – some regular, some pale blue, some covered in what looked like green mould – dried mushrooms, abalone and starfish, long-leaf Chinese lettuces in clear plastic bags, cooking sauces in glass bottles and folded cotton dishcloths. Above these boxes was an equally disordered collection of vegetables, dried goods and even sweets hung in plastic bags from hooks whose top ends were attached to metal rails suspended from the ceiling.

Behind the shopkeeper's head, so that he could not look in it without turning round and craning his neck, was a mirror in which it was possible to see almost the whole interior of the shop. Two narrow lines of bare metal shelves – dirt-cheap free-standing units, rising above head-height – stretched about fifteen feet back to front through the store, creating three very narrow aisles, one by each of the two side walls and the third down the centre. There was a door in the far wall, opposite the centre aisle. Carver was counting on that leading to a rear exit from the building. Without it, he had no way out.

He walked into the store and started assembling his weapons. He picked up three of the sauce bottles, placed them on top of one of the dishcloths, then closed the corners of the cloth over them and twisted the ends so that the bottles were tightly trapped in the cloth. Now he had a crude but effective club. Keeping it tightly clasped in his left hand, he reached up with his right and unhooked a large net filled with bulbs of garlic. Carver removed the net and was left holding the hook in his right hand.

The only other customers in the store were a couple of middle-aged women a few feet away, who were chattering over a display of dried chillis arrayed by the side wall of the shop. Without any warning, making the change in his demeanour as extreme as possible, Carver took two paces towards them, raised the hook menacingly and shouted, 'Bad men coming! Get out! Get out now!'

They glared defiantly at him and did not budge. One of them started shouting at him in Chinese. He got the feeling she wasn't exactly passing the time of day. Carver didn't have time to argue. He swept the hook along the shelf to his right, sending glass jars filled with something that looked like white testicles floating in brine crashing to the floor at the women's feet. The one who'd been shouting shut up. The other one gave a little scream. Carver raised his hook at them again and this time they took the hint, hurrying past him, neither of them even as tall as his shoulder, out into the street.

As he watched them go, he could see that the five men were closing in on the shop. They were barely five yards away, walking with the steady, purposeful gait of professionals going about their business. Carver saw the shopkeeper catch sight of them, too, glance back at him, then dive beneath the countertop. Very sensible, Carver thought. Now it was his turn to save his skin.

He backed away to his left, into the aisle furthest away from the shopkeeper's counter, letting the men come towards him. The aisle was so narrow, there would only be room for one man at a time to attack him.

Unless, of course, they came from two different directions at once.

The man in the army shirt pointed down the centre aisle and two men stepped towards it. They were going to try to outflank him. The leading man was dressed in jeans and a pale-grey hoodie top. The one behind him had on a black T-shirt and a pair of jeans from which a chain hung loosely. Wherever Carver went in the world, the punks always seemed to look the same.

Two more men stepped into the aisle where Carver was standing: a gaudy, short-sleeved floral shirt and a camouflage T-shirt. The one in the camo had his hair pulled back in a ponytail. His pal wore metal-framed aviator shades.

Carver backed away from them.

As he went, he glanced up into the mirror. The two men in the centre aisle, the hoodie and the black T-shirt, were almost level with him.

Carver kept moving back. The men in his aisle kept pace with him, not closing the gap, waiting for the trap to close behind him.

Out of the corner of his right eye, Carver was looking at the goods on the shelves beside him. There were jars of herbs; more jars of some indeterminate bits of beige gristle with a picture of a snarling shark stuck to the glass; tins of vegetables . . . none of this was of any use to Carver. He was being backed all the way to the end of the aisle. He didn't have any room for manoeuvre.

Then he saw packets of tea, racked from top to bottom.

Carver glanced back up at the mirror, stopped walking backwards and moved closer to the shelf till his right shoulder was almost touching the packets of tea. Then, still holding on to the hook, he smashed his right hand through the tea and out the far side of the shelf. He swung it forward and felt the impact as the end of the hook drove into the soft flesh at the base of the hoodie's neck. He heard a gurgling yelp of pain and pulled the hook hard back towards him, slamming the hoodie into the far side of the shelf.

One down.

Carver let go of the hook, switched the bundled-up sauce jars to his right hand and in the same movement swung his right arm like a tennis backhand at the ponytailed punk in the camouflage T-shirt. The guy swayed back, but not enough to evade the blow entirely, and Carver hit him just above the right eye, drawing blood and making him stagger backwards. Carver drew back his arm and swung again, in a brutal downward chopping motion, hitting the forearm the man raised to protect himself, hearing the crack of a bone and then driving the heel of his left hand into the side of his face.

That was another man downed, for now at least. But it was also the end of the good news.

Carver felt a throat-tightening, nauseating shock of pain on the point of his left shoulder and realized that he wasn't the only one smart enough to use a weapon. The dandy in the floral shirt and shades had flung one of the shark jars at him and was reaching for another.

Carver dived forward, rugby-tackling the dandy to the ground, then reaching out to grab his head and smash it into the shop's tiled floor.

Behind him, he could hear scuffling as the fourth man rounded the far end of the shelf and came dashing towards him. Carver rolled on to his back and kicked out, catching an oncoming knee with his heel. The man in the black T-shirt staggered back a couple of paces, giving Carver the fractional amount of space and time he needed to spring to his feet and leap upwards to catch the suspended rail above his head, swing forward and hit Mr Black T-shirt smack in the face with both feet, sending him careering into several boxes of iced seafood lined up along the back wall.

Carver kept moving, allowing the momentum of the swing to pull his legs forward and up, letting go of the rail and executing a backward somersault, like a gymnast dismounting a high bar. A gymnast, of course, aims to land in a perfect upright position, with his feet close together. Carver, however, stumbled when his feet hit the floor and fell forward.

That was what saved his life.

The fifth man, the leader of the group in the army shirt, had evidently tired of the low-tech approach. If he couldn't take Carver alive, he would have to take him dead. He'd reached round to the back of his trousers, pulled out the gun shoved inside the waistband and fired two shots that missed Carver's head by inches and instead hit his pal in the black T-shirt, who had just been extracting himself from the seafood display and was staggering to his feet.

The group leader didn't seem to care. He fired again, and Carver had to fling himself forward and scramble on all fours round the end of the aisle as bullets smashed into jars, ricocheted off the metal shelving and dug craters in the floor tiles. He got to his feet, came round the far side of the shelving, almost slipping on the blood that had spurted from his first victim's neck wound, then hurled himself against the nearest shelf-unit with all his strength, pumping his legs to overcome the dead weight of all the goods stacked upon it until finally it toppled over, deluging the man in the army shirt in a hail of jars, cans and cardboard packets.

The men who'd come to take him were all down. But not all of them would stay that way.

73

Carver dashed for the door on the far wall, wrenched it open and charged through. It led into a bare concrete passage that stretched for a good twenty yards in either direction, lit by occasional naked bulbs. Carver turned right and started sprinting, waiting for the sound of pursuit, his back prickling in dread anticipation of the first shot.

Up ahead, he saw a doorway. He glanced back. The passage behind him was empty: no sign of the man in the army shirt.

Carver kept running flat-out for the door. It was wooden, flimsy-looking, roughly painted in flaking blue gloss. He tried the handle, but it was locked.

He looked back again. Still no one in the passage.

Carver stepped back, kicked the door open and walked through into a store very like the one he had just left: more boxes, more shelves, but this time they all seemed to be laden with jars of herbs and strange-looking liquids. By the look of them, and the huge antique black cabinet divided into hundreds of small drawers, it was some kind of traditional chemist's or apothecary's. The counter in front of it was fancier than the one in the grocer's shop, fronted with glass and filled with brightly coloured boxes covered in Chinese script. The woman behind it was talking to two diminutive middle-aged customers who were competing to get their point across to her. Carver realized with a shock that these were the same women who had been in the grocer's store. They turned at the sound of the opening door, recognized him too, and raised the pitch and volume still higher as they pointed and shouted at him.

'Afternoon, ladies,' he said as he walked by as casually as he could, half-wondering if the old biddies might be crazy or angry enough to attack him as he went.

Once outside, he turned left and began walking back towards his car. Then he stopped. Now he knew why the gang leader had not followed him. He was heading for Carver's car, presuming that it would be his first port of call.

Carver took out his phone as he watched the man in the old army shirt walk up to the Honda, looking around as he went. Confident that Carver was not yet in the area, he leaned back against the car and took a packet of cigarettes from the chest pocket of his green shirt. Either he was a well-known local hardman or he simply carried an air of violence with him wherever he went, because the crowds seemed to part round him, leaving plenty of open space around the car – a good thing as far as Carver was concerned.

As the man tapped the bottom of the packet to punch out a cigarette, Carver tapped a key on his phone. He had always expected that he might need to do this at some point during the day, but it had only been planned as a means of destroying evidence, rather than taking out the enemy. Still, you couldn't complain about two birds with one stone.

The speed dial called up the number of the phone Carver had bought the previous day. The phone that was held down with zip-ties on to the piece of wood he had brought from Geneva. Two AA batteries were also tied to that piece of wood, as was the rocket sparking device. The two screws, their bolts and washers were also fixed to the wood, between the phone and the batteries.

Two crocodile-clipped wires ran from one screw to the batteries and from the batteries to the sparker. A third wire was clipped from the other screw to the sparker. Two much shorter lengths of plastic-coated electric wiring ran from the screws into the hole Carver had made in the side of the phone casing. Their bare ends were just a couple of millimetres apart inside the hole.

When he called the phone, the vibrator did its job and started vibrating. In so doing it touched the two bare wires together and completed the circuit that led to the batteries and the sparker. The sparker ignited the rocket engine, which in turn set off the acetone and then the petrol, and then the whole car went up in an explosive burst of flame, taking the man in the army shirt with it.

As screams and shouts echoed down the street and hordes of people poured out from shops, bars and restaurants to catch a glimpse of the drama, Carver walked ignored and unnoticed into a bar, and went to the men's room. Having made sure he was alone, he chose one of the toilet cubicles and locked the door. He took off his wig and glasses. He transferred the wallet with all the Bowen Erikson papers and cards from his jacket to his trouser pocket. Then he removed the jacket and his vicar's bib. He stopped, listened to make sure the men's room was still empty apart from him, then came out of the cubicle and stuffed all the vicar gear into a tall wire-mesh wastepaper bin that stood beside the toilet's wash-basins, covering it all up with paper towels from the dispenser on the wall.

As he walked back out through the bar, attracting no more attention than he had on the way in, Carver considered trying to find Mabeki, but dismissed the thought at once. By now he would have disappeared into the apartment blocks on the Aberdeen shore, or, much more likely, the boats crammed in its harbour. Wherever Mabeki was, there, too, Zalika would be. Carver could not believe he would kill the girl, not before he'd extracted his full helping of pleasure at her expense. And he wouldn't do that in Hong Kong, either; not when there was work to be done and power to be grabbed in Malemba.

Mabeki had known, beyond a shadow of a doubt, that the Gushungo hit was going down that day. He'd known, too, that Carver and Zalika would be doing the job. All that being the case, it followed that he'd known about the coup in Malemba. Carver was prepared to bet every cent in his offshore bank accounts that the coup had not succeeded – or not in the way he had been told about, anyway.

Someone had tipped Mabeki off about the entire plan, someone who had been willing to sell out Carver and Zalika. But who? Had Klerk been lying all along about his love for his niece? If Mabeki had offered him a better deal than Patrick Tshonga had done, would Klerk have put money before family? Carver didn't want to believe that, but he had long since learned the hard way that men who truly love money always value it more highly than any mere human affection. And what of Tshonga himself? Had he just been playing Klerk, leading him on with the promise of easy money, when all along he'd cut a deal with Mabeki? It would be an abdication of all Tshonga's principles to ally himself with Gushungo's right-hand man. But for anyone who really wanted power in Malemba that might be the smart, cynical move to make.

Whatever had happened, the answer to the puzzle lay in the same place to which Moses Mabeki was certainly travelling, and where he would hide Zalika Stratten until he had done with her: Malemba. Carver had no choice. He had to go there, even if it meant going alone and unprotected against overwhelming odds. He thought of calling Klerk and Tshonga, but decided against it. If one of them really had double-crossed him, letting them know he was on his way was the last thing he should do.

When he got back out on the street, Carver walked down to the harbour promenade. Taxis were dropping off tourists. He hailed one of them.

'Take me to the airport,' he said.

74

The timing had been split second, and even then it had been a close-run thing. But with the help of two of Fisherman Zheng's men, both armed and ready to use their weapons, Moses Mabeki had managed to get Zalika Stratten into the delivery van parked just outside the Gushungos' house before Carver came out of the building. From that point on it had been a simple case of mis-direction. He'd made a show of slamming the boot shut loud enough for Carver to hear, and standing right by it so that the Englishman would come to the obvious conclusion that the girl was in there. Then he'd taken the scenic route, leading Carver down Route Twisk, while the van went on the fastest possible highways from Hon Ka Mansions to Aberdeen.

It had gone straight to the waterfront where Zheng's men opened up the rear cargo, removed Zalika Stratten and led her down a flight of quayside steps to a small motorboat that was bobbing on the water below. She'd lost her ridiculous sunglasses as well as her phone. Her hair had come unpinned and now hung round her shoulders. She looked much more like her true self, but dressed more cheaply than usual.

The boat had sped away, jinking between the other craft crammed into the narrow stretch of water between Aberdeen and Ap Lei Chau island on the other side of the harbour. It had pulled up alongside the streamlined, dart-like hull of a Sunseeker Predator 52 performance motoryacht moored off the Aberdeen Marina Club. Once again, there were armed men all around Zalika as she was led aboard.

The motorboat had then sped away again, only to return fifteen minutes later with Moses Mabeki.

The Sunseeker weighed anchor, eased its way through the harbour and then, when it reached the open sea, the skipper opened up the throttle and it raced away westwards, hitting thirty knots as it ate up the twenty-five-mile journey to the former Portuguese colony of Macau.

The boat was one of Fishermen Zheng's favourite toys, and this voyage gave him particular pleasure. He had brought a diamond dealer along to inspect the stones Mabeki had agreed to sell him. The dealer assured him, in a Hoklo dialect incomprehensible even to the vast majority of Chinese, that they were worth almost twenty million US dollars. On Friday night, Zheng and Mabeki had shaken hands at six million, subject to delivery and acceptance. Now the money was paid directly into Mabeki's personal account in the Cayman Islands. Everyone was happy.

Mabeki made his excuses and went to the cabin where the next stage of the extraction plan he had agreed with Zheng was due to take place. A doctor – Hoklo, like all Zheng's associates, and thus guaranteed to keep his silence – injected Zalika with a heavy dose of nitrazepam, which knocked her out cold.

They were met at the Macau shore by an ambulance driven by two more of Zheng's men, dressed as uniformed paramedics. The ambulance took Mabeki and his unconscious companion to Macau International Airport, which is specifically geared to the private aviation needs of the high-rollers who gamble their money at Macau's twenty-eight casinos. There, a Gulfstream 550 ultra-long-range jet, equipped with medical facilities and with a doctor and nurse on its crew, was waiting to fly Mabeki and the comatose Zalika to a medical facility near Paris. No one enquired why she needed to travel so far for treatment. The airport's officials had long since become accustomed to the foibles of the rich.

An hour into the flight, the pilot was re-routed on to a new south-westerly course, towards Sindele airport, Malemba.

They were barely two thousand miles from their destination when Zalika Stratten began very groggily to wake up. She cast bleary eyes around the cabin and asked where on earth she was.

75

Gatekeeper Wu had been told very clearly where his duties lay. At half-past ten on Sunday morning, when the delivery van had first pulled up by the barricade at the entrance to Hon Ka Mansions, the two men inside had assured him that they knew precisely where he, his wife and three small children lived. They'd made it plain that not only his life but those of his family were at stake. If he wished to live, he would turn his eyes from anyone who came in or out of the development over the next ninety minutes. If he was approached by any policemen, he should play dumb and claim not to remember anything about any of the cars or people who'd gone past his post. It was made very clear that the boss for whom the men worked had contacts within the police who would tell him in an instant if Wu had told them anything of interest. On the other hand, his discretion would be much appreciated and his family would be greatly rewarded.

Wu had got the message.

The first police car had arrived shortly after midday. The officers inside told Wu they were responding to a report of gunfire. Wu assured them, truthfully, that he had heard none. One of the cops had shrugged and told him he didn't expect there was any reason to be concerned. The woman who had reported it said she and her husband had waited for more than half an hour before calling the police because they were arguing about what the sound had been.

It took the two cops almost ten minutes to determine that the noise had come from the Gushungo entrance and another five to decide they should force their way into the house. Twenty seconds later, they discovered the two bodies of the maids in the hallway, followed by the Gushungos and their four bodyguards in the living room.

The cops reported back to their station. The chief inspector, who was the senior duty officer, took the instant decision that he did not wish to be in any way responsible for the investigation of a head of state's violent death on Hong Kong soil. He got straight on to the Hong Kong Police Force's headquarters, where a chief superintendent went straight to the top, disturbing the Commissioner of Police, who was standing over a tricky putt on the fourth hole of the Ocean Nine course at the Clearwater Bay Golf and Country Club.

By happy chance, the commissioner's playing partner was the Secretary for Security, a member of the Executive Council that assisted the Chief Executive of Hong Kong in governing the territory. The two men immediately decided that every available police resource would be devoted to investigating the deaths at Hon Ka Mansions. They also agreed that it would be most unwise to alarm the public, or jeopardize the international reputation of Hong Kong, by making any statement whatsoever until the perpetrators responsible had been identified and, if possible, apprehended.

Around two in the afternoon, the first detectives came to interview Gatekeeper Wu. Like Zheng's men, they told him not to tell anyone about what he had seen if he knew what was good for him.

To any Chinese, a threat from a government official is at least as terrifying, if not more so, than one from a gangster. No gangster, after all, has killed even a tiny fraction of the Chinese citizens sacrificed by their own state over the past sixty-odd years. That night, Wu ordered his wife to gather together the family's pitiful quantity of possessions. On Monday morning they were getting on a train and heading back to their old fishing village, two hundred miles away on the coast of Guangdong province. The family Wu had had enough of Hong Kong.

76

Carver's flight got into Johannesburg at quarter-past seven on Monday morning. As soon as he'd made it through immigration and customs he sat down in an airport café with a double espresso and his iPhone. Then he logged on to the BBC news pages and looked for headlines about Malemba.

It didn't take long for his worst fears to be confirmed. The whole Gushungo operation had been blown and Tshonga's supposedly peaceful takeover had collapsed in a swift series of massacres. Meanwhile, there were rumours of a simultaneous attack on President Gushungo and his wife at their home in Hong Kong. The Hong Kong authorities were remaining tight-lipped, but neither the President nor his wife had been seen in more than twenty-four hours and although a local vicar reported that he had been told that they were suffering from a stomach-bug, some Hong Kong bloggers were suggesting that they were dead and that local authorities were engaged in a massive cover-up. Carver liked the sound of that. The more the truth was glossed over, the less chance there was that anything would ever be traced to him.

Malemba itself was now under the control of a self-proclaimed Committee of National Security, a group of senior military officers who had decreed a state of emergency pending the re-establishment of civilian government. The committee members, like the Hong Kong authorities, refused to comment on stories that Henderson Gushungo was dead. They preferred to focus on Patrick Tshonga, who was described as a traitor, an anarchist and a threat to peace. He was being hunted without mercy, one general stated, and would soon be cornered like a rat. In the meantime, a press conference was being scheduled for the following morning, Tuesday, at which time the people would get a chance to hear the committee's plans for the country.

The timing seemed about right, Carver thought. If Mabeki had flown direct to Sindele, he would have arrived at roughly the same time as Carver got to Johannesburg. He'd need a day to get his feet under the table, prepare the various bribes, threats and blackmails with which he'd bend everyone to his will, and then appoint whichever stooges would nominally run the country. He'd also have to decide what to do with Zalika. Assuming she was still alive.

In any case, Carver now had his deadline. His best, maybe only chance of killing Mabeki and rescuing Zalika was to do it before Mabeki had the chance to assemble and announce his new regime. Once that African Machiavelli had the full resources of the Malemban police state at his beck and call, he would be almost impossible to touch. It had to be now.

First, though, he had to confront Klerk. He leaned back in his chair, wanting to think through the best approach, one that would give him the flexibility to respond equally effectively, whether Klerk had betrayed the plan or not. Then something caught his eye, a copy of the *Johannesburg Star* discarded along with the empty coffee cups on a nearby table. The front-page headline screamed 'Slaughter in Sandton'. Next to it was a sub-head: 'Death toll rises to seven in billionaire mansion shoot-out'.

A nauseous sense of dread and apprehension clawed at Carver's guts. He reached across to pick up the paper. Two minutes later, he was on the phone to Sonny Parkes, Wendell Klerk's head of security.

'It's Carver,' he said. 'We need to meet. Now.'

77

Half an hour later, Carver was standing in the street outside Klerk's mansion while Sonny Parkes talked their way past the police guard manning the barricades and crime-scene tape round the entrance to the house. One look at Parkes told Carver why Klerk had trusted him so much. Sonny Parkes had a prop-forward's body, a boxer's nose, a balding skinhead's haircut and a redneck's complexion. Plenty of men who look like that are no better than drunken thugs, and that's on a good day. Others, though – the ones blessed with intelligence, courage and a sound temperament – are the warriors you want fighting beside you in the trenches. It's a common enough cliché, but Carver had been there for real, and he knew just by looking at him that Parkes had too.

'They pitched up just here,' Parkes was saying, 'at five-oh-two yesterday morning. Six of them, we reckon, with a seventh as the driver. The vehicle they used was one of those crazy bloody stretch Hummers: white, hired from a rental company on an account we've traced back to a shell company, registered in the Dutch Antilles. No way of knowing who owns it.'

'My guess, there's no need to ask,' said Carver. 'It'll be Moses Mabeki.'

'What, that ugly fucker from Malemba, the one who hangs around Henderson Gushungo? What's he got to do with this?'

The puzzlement in Parkes's voice was genuine. Klerk had involved his security chief in getting Justus Iluko and his kids the help they needed, but he hadn't been let in on the rest of the Malemban operation. That was useful to know.

'I'll tell you later,' said Carver. 'Just go on with what happened here.'

Parkes shrugged. 'One of the passengers, a young woman, gets out the car and comes over to the guardhouse over here, all giggly, flirtatious, pretending to be drunk: a real come-and-get-me act. We know this because it's all on tape from the CCTV camera up there. She persuades the guys on duty to come round to the side and open up the communication hatch here. Then she walks right up and shoots them, cool as you like. Double-tap to the head, both times.'

'The gun?'

'Walther TPH, a real lady's gun.'

'Professional's gun, too. Perfect for close-range work. No mess.'

'True enough, and she was a professional all right, a real cold-blooded piece of work. She took out both guards before either of them could even get their guns out of their holsters.'

'Or their thumbs from their arses.'

Parkes gave a short bark of laughter. 'Exactly. Then she climbed through the window, over the bodies and went over to the control panel. Can you see it in there?'

'Sure.'

'Well, that's where she switched off all the cameras and alarms and cut the feed to XPT headquarters.'

'So you weren't running the actual security operation at the house.'

'No, I was not.'

'If you don't mind me asking, why not?'

Parkes sighed bitterly. 'Outsourcing. Cost-cutting. All the usual corporate crap. The theory is that the organization has a helluva lot of properties around the world that it needs to protect. Not just Klerk's houses, but offices, factories, mines, you name it. It's cheaper and easier to hire local contractors for each of them, instead of hiring, paying and looking after full-time employees. I'm responsible for keeping tabs on all the different companies we use in this part of the world. And I've got a separate team of my own. We provide close protection whenever one of the Klerk household is out and about.'

'So XPT had plans of the house and the grounds?'

'Ja.'

'Who else?'

'The house is only four years old, so there are the architects, contractors and sub-contractors who worked on the place; the civic authorities, planning department and so forth – a lot of people, man.'

'And you think one of them gave the plans to whoever did this?'

'Someone did, that's for damn sure. Anyway, once the guards are dead, at least five people get out of the limo and come this way.'

'How do you know there were five?'

'You'll see.'

Parker walked through the gate, gesturing to Carver to follow, talking as he went.

'The gate closes behind them so no one outside can see what's happening. The limo drives away. We know this because a local resident who'd been out for the night drove past at around five past five and he's absolutely certain there was no white Hummer parked here.'

'It would be pretty hard to miss.'

'Exactly. Now, the five walk towards the house.'

As they came up the drive, Carver got his first proper view of the Klerk residence. It was a two-storey, flat-roofed modernist building, massed in a series of linked boxes. Plain walls of olive-grey concrete were pierced by wide expanses of floor-to-ceiling glass.

The geometric starkness of the construction was offset by the lush greenery all around it. Palms and other trees stood among impeccably trimmed hedges and brightly coloured flowers spilled from huge concrete planting boxes. The drive swept up to a formal entrance but Parkes ignored it and kept walking round the side of the building.

'They came round here to the back of the building.'

Carver followed him to an expanse of flagstones, framing the turquoise water of the house's swimming-pool. A set of steps ran from the pool area up to the back of the house. Parkes set off up the stairs. At the top, he stopped in front of a wall made up of wooden-framed glass panels, one of which had been smashed.

'They got in through the lounge area here. Just shot a couple of holes in the glass and knocked the rest out with the butts of their guns.'

'Must have made a helluva noise,' observed Carver.

'Damn right it must. But whoever they were, they didn't care about that. I get the feeling they wanted Klerk to know they were there.'

'Because they knew how he'd react?'

'That's what I think, ja.'

'But how could they know that?'

Parkes shook his head ruefully. 'I don't know, man, not for sure. But anyone who knows Klerk knows he's never, ever going to back down from a fight. They were probably trying to provoke him.'

'And it worked.'

'Oh ja, it worked all right. And now I'll show you where he found them.'

78

The lounge led into a dining area. Sixteen chairs ringed a huge hardwood dining table. There were more David Shepherd water-colours and drawings of elephants on the wall – studies, perhaps, for the huge oil painting at Campden Hall – and another set of tusks on either side of a modern marble fireplace. The room looked completely untouched. Carver wondered when he'd get to the scene of the action.

Then they walked into the kitchen, and suddenly they were in a war-zone. The solid oak kitchen cabinets had been ripped apart like balsa wood. Huge holes had been gouged in the walls. And every surface – walls, floors, units, even the ceiling in some places – had been spattered with dark crimson blood.

'Bloody hell,' Carver gasped. 'What happened here?'

'Are you familiar with the AA-12 automatic shotgun?'

'I've heard of it. Never used one.'

'Well look around, because this is what happens when twenty-nine twelve-gauge rounds are fired in quick succession in a confined area, hitting four human bodies at point-blank range: three male, one female, each with multiple rounds.'

'Klerk had an AA-12?'

'That's right: one in every house.'

'So he found the intruders, opened up, took four of them out. And the fifth?'

'Didn't come into the kitchen with her buddies but sneaked round another way, went into the hall, followed Klerk into the kitchen and took him out just like the boys down at the guard-house: two to the head from a Walther TPH.'

'Same shooter?'

'Can't be certain yet. The cops won't have the full ballistics report for two or three days. But I don't think so. I reckon the first shooter stayed where she was. This was a different one. But just as homicidal.'

'Ironic, isn't it? There's Klerk blasting away with an automated bazooka and he gets popped by a pea-shooter.'

Parkes looked at Carver coldly. 'If you say so. But the way I see it, my employer died on my watch. Ironic's not the word I'd use.'

'No, I suppose not. What did the shooter do after she'd taken out Klerk? Did she go looking for Brianna Latrelle?'

'Doesn't look like it. We reckon she went back out of the property, met up with her girlfriend and they both left, leaving the gate closed behind them.'

'How did they leave? You said the Hummer had gone.'

'I reckon there was another vehicle involved. I've got a couple of my guys with the police at the moment, going over the footage from every camera between here and the Taboo nightclub, which is where we think they came from, trying to see if we can spot it.'

'So they were gone by the time the first XPT cars arrived?'

'Uh-huh. Response time was actually five minutes and nineteen seconds, which is within their six-minute guarantee. But all the bad guys had skedaddled.'

'And Latrelle?'

'She was safe and sound in a panic room. Most of the big houses round here have one. She was majorly upset, obviously, and suffering from shock. They took her to hospital, just to keep an eye on her. But basically she was fine. She's upstairs now, if you want to speak to her.'

'That would be good.'

They headed into the main hall of the building from which a glass and steel staircase rose up to the first floor.

'So Klerk would have been fine if he'd just gone into the room with Latrelle, right?' Carver asked.

'Yep.'

'But somehow they must have known that he wouldn't do that because they didn't care about making a noise and alerting him. Just like they knew about the security systems, and the layout of the house . . . Hold on a minute.'

Carver stopped by the foot of the stairs. When he spoke again his voice was barely a whisper.

'Was Latrelle their contact on the inside? She may play-act the pretty arm-candy, but she's not stupid.'

Parkes nodded. 'I agree. You underestimate her at your peril.'

'She could have got hold of the plans,' Carver continued. 'She'd have known how Klerk would react to an attack. She knew she couldn't be touched in the panic room. Why not her?'

'She's a suspect, for sure. But I tell you, I got here yesterday morning a few minutes after the boys from XPT and I saw Miss Latrelle as they were getting her out of the panic room. I also saw her go to pieces when she caught sight of Klerk's body, just a glimpse of it as they were carrying her past the kitchen on a gurney. I tell you, that woman was falling apart. She'd have to be a bloody Oscar-winning actress to fake that. The other thing is, everyone knows she wanted Klerk to marry her. As his wife, she'd have first call on all his cash if he died. If she wanted him dead, why not wait till after the wedding?'

'Yeah, OK . . . I don't think Latrelle wanted Klerk dead either,' Carver agreed. 'She loved the old bastard, though she had no illusions about him at all. And I'll tell you something else. She was certain something bad was going to happen. She told me so, but I didn't take her seriously. Wish I had. But even so, I don't think she expected Klerk to be on the receiving end.'

Carver sighed as he weighed it all up. 'Right,' he said, 'let's go and talk to the grieving girlfriend.'

79

Brianna Latrelle looked wrecked. She was clearly exhausted, physically and emotionally shattered. Her face was bare of make-up, her hair scraped back in a carelessly tied ponytail, and her usually immaculate designer clothes had been replaced by a battered old pair of Levis and a plain silk blouse. The effect, however, was to make her seem more human, more vulnerable and to Carver's eyes infinitely more attractive than the painted doll who'd been on display throughout that weekend in Suffolk.

He was about to offer his condolences, one of those standard 'I'm sorry for your loss' platitudes, but she beat him to it.

'I told you,' she said. 'I told you there was something wrong.'

'I know . . . So who do you think it was?'

'I don't know. Maybe it was you. I get the feeling you could do a thing like this.'

'I was on the other side of the world. I didn't get into Jo'burg till seven-fifteen this morning. But if you're talking about the other people who met at Campden Hall, Zalika was with me and Patrick Tshonga was busy running for his life.'

Parkes butted in: 'Patrick Tshonga – what the hell are you talking about, Carver? And Moses Mabeki, the first person you mentioned when you got here. Why was that?'

'Because he has to be the person behind this attack,' said Carver. 'See, Klerk and Tshonga met in England earlier this month to finalize plans for a bloodless coup in Malemba – the same coup that went so spectacularly wrong yesterday. The deal was that Klerk would help Tshonga gain power and in return he'd get a big mining concession. Klerk admitted he was just in it for the money. He reckoned he was going to make billions.'

'And your role in all this?' asked Parkes.

'No comment. But I'll tell you this much. I knew yesterday morning that Mabeki had found out about Klerk and Tshonga's plan. He knew exactly what was going to happen. He was one step ahead of me all the way in Hong Kong and his people were ahead of Tshonga and Klerk here, too. The only thing I haven't worked out is whether he did a deal with one of those two guys and then double-crossed them, or the plan was leaked by someone else. I'd thought it might be you, Parkes. That's why I dropped Mabeki's name earlier. I wanted to see how you'd react. It could have been you, too, Brianna.'

'But it wasn't.'

'So let's concentrate on Mabeki. He's always going to stick to the shadows. He's not exactly got a face for presidential politics. But if you want to grab and keep power in Malemba, he's a good man to have on your side. So Patrick Tshonga, for example, might decide that this was a perfect time to keep his friends close and his enemies closer. That would also remove the embarrassing possibility of people finding out that he owed his power to a deal with a white man. That wouldn't play too well on the African street.'

'But none of this could happen without killing Gushungo,' said Parkes. 'I suppose that was your department?'

'As I said, no comment.'

'For fuck's sake,' snapped Parkes. 'I can't believe I'm wasting my time talking to you. I'm calling the authorities. They can sort it out.'

'I wouldn't do that if I were you,' said Carver matter-of-factly.

'Why not?'

'Well, in the first place, if I had killed anyone – hypothetically – I couldn't let you call the cops, could I?'

'I'd like to see you stop me.'

'And in the second,' said Carver, ignoring him, 'if you have any regard at all for the memory of Wendell Klerk and his family, then you won't go public with this. The scandal would destroy his reputation and wreck everything he ever worked for. But most importantly, you don't want to do it because any delay is going to make it more likely that Mabeki harms or even kills Zalika Stratten, if he hasn't done so already.'

Parkes frowned. 'Miss Stratten? What's she got to do with it?'

'Mabeki abducted her yesterday morning, while we were in Hong Kong. I tried to stop him, but he'd obviously got the whole thing planned while I was still blundering around like the proverbial one-legged man in an arse-kicking contest. I'm counting on the fact that he's brought her back to Malemba, and I'm hoping you're both going to help me get her back. Look, I know you and Zalika weren't exactly best friends for ever, Brianna . . .'

'You don't know anything about . . .' She seemed to run out of energy halfway through the sentence.

'About what?' Carver asked.

'Oh, forget it. I guess I'm just sick of all this. Why was Wendell trying to bring down governments just for some stupid mine, when he already had enough money to last him a hundred lifetimes? That's what he could never understand about me. I didn't love him for the money. I loved him despite the money. But look what the money's done to him . . . and to Zalika.'

'None of this is her fault.'

'You don't think so? Well, she was there at all your meetings, as I recall, looking down her nose at me while Wendell told me to go fix the chef's soufflés. She was right up to her pretty neck in it, so it's hard for me to feel too sorry for her now.' Brianna grimaced. 'Listen to me, I sound like a total bitch. Just let me pack and I'll get out of here.'

Parkes put a consoling hand on her shoulder. 'We'll leave you to it, Miss Latrelle. Come on, Carver, let's give the lady some peace.'

They went back outside, and Parkes sat down on the end of one of the upholstered sun loungers arrayed beside the pool.

'Pull up a seat,' he said, pointing at the other loungers. He took a packet of cigarettes from the chest pocket of his shirt. 'Smoke?'

'No thanks.'

'Suit yourself. So, tell me what you want to do.'

'Let's start with Mabeki. I don't think he's going to kill Zalika Stratten. Not yet. But she might wish she were dead, the things he's going to do to her.'

'I've worked with Zalika Stratten. It's not a nice thought, a girl like her with a sick bastard like Mabeki.'

'No, it's not. And I feel about it the same way you do about Klerk. She was taken on my watch. It's down to me to get her back.'

Parkes blew a long stream of smoke into the clear morning air. 'Ja, that I understand.'

'So then the question is: where's he keeping her? I can't believe he'd have her in Sindele. It's too risky. He doesn't want the outside world knowing he's got a kidnapped woman. But there is somewhere that makes perfect sense: the place where they both grew up, where Mabeki nursed his hatred and which he believes should belong to him by rights anyway – the Stratten Reserve.'

Parkes took a long drag on his cigarette. 'It's a helluva long shot, Carver. Malemba's a bloody big country. She could be anywhere.'

'She could, yes. But I'm certain it's the reserve. Hell, it's not just the Strattens that kept Mabeki from owning the land, Gushungo did, too. Mabeki killed the Strattens, then just when he was ready to claim his kingdom, his boss took it away from him. I know this bastard, the way he nurses his grudges. He wants that land. And if he can imprison Zalika Stratten, of all people, there, that'll just make taking it, and her, all the sweeter.'

'Let's suppose you're right. What do you plan to do about it?'

'Go there, free her, get her across the border. Then I'm going back for Mabeki.'

Parkes laughed. 'Sounds like you're planning a busy day. What are you going to do tomorrow, cure cancer? Bring peace to the Middle East?'

'No, that's not my job. Getting Zalika is. Sorting Mabeki is. So, you going to help me or not?'

Parkes stubbed out his cigarette on the paving, threw it into the nearest shrubbery, and immediately pulled another cigarette from the box. He took his time lighting it, then took another long drag, holding the smoke in his lungs before blowing it out equally slowly. At last he glanced across at Carver and said, 'Ja, I'm in. My men, too.'

'How well do you know the Stratten Reserve?'

'Can't help you there, brother. Never been there in my life.'

'Well that's a problem, then, because I haven't either,' Carver admitted. 'But I know a man who has. You happen to know what Justus Iluko is doing today?'

'Ja, I do, as it happens. He's got a court date this afternoon, his kids too. The lawyer's managed to combine all their cases into one. She wants to establish them all as victims of the same conspiracy. So now they've got a bail hearing. Not that they'll be offered any, of course.'

'How far is the court from the jail?'

'Dunno, man. But we can easily get a streetmap of Buweku and find out.'

'And they'll be taken there by car or truck?'

'I guess.'

'Then that's when we'll grab them. How soon can you get us to Buweku?'

Parkes almost gagged on the smoke as he burst out laughing. 'I'll say one thing for you, Carver,' he gasped. 'You don't fucking hang about, do you?'

80

'Hello, Mary, how have you been?'

Zalika Stratten smiled wearily as she greeted the woman she had last seen a decade ago. That day, the day her old world was destroyed, she had been a plain, gawky girl of seventeen and Mary Ncube a junior housemaid. Now Mary was the housekeeper, a plump, imperious woman who ruled her domestic kingdom with a warm heart for those who stuck to her rules and a tongue like a rhino-hide whip for those who did not. She had spent her whole working life catering first to her country's richest family and then to its president, his family and his guests. Over the years, she had developed an air of haughty self-assurance that made her seem almost grander than the people she served. But when she caught sight of Zalika Stratten, all that was overwhelmed by a wave of emotion.

'Miss Zalika!' Mary cried, frantically trying to wipe away the tears that were flooding down her round cheeks. 'It is so wonderful to see you again. Let me look at you.' She stepped back and examined Zalika through watery eyes. 'Oh, you are so pretty now.

But so thin, and with such dark circles under your eyes. And what is this?' Mary pointed at the scratches and bruises on Zalika's upper arm, left by the nylon straps that had bound her tight to the stretcher on which she'd been carried on to the plane in Macau. 'Have these jackals been mistreating you?'

Zalika looked wearily at the armed men, cradling their AK-47s, who were arrayed in a semi-circle behind her in the hall of the old Stratten house. 'I'm sorry about my new boyfriends,' she said. 'I can't seem to get rid of them.'

She tried to smile. It was supposed to be a joke. But her brain was numbed by exhaustion, stress and the after-effects of the drugs still working their way through her system.

'Pah!' Mary jeered, dismissing the men with a single, withering sweep of her eyes. 'Forget them. You come with me. I have made a bed for you in your old room. I am afraid it does not look the same any more. Our First Lady, Mrs Gushungo, insisted that she had to redecorate. But if you close your eyes, you can imagine that it is just the same, with all your tennis prizes and riding rosettes on the wall, and your pictures of pop stars who look like little white girls, even though—'

'That's enough!'

The slurring hiss of Moses Mabeki's voice did not so much cut across Mary Ncube's words as slide through them. But the effect was the same. Mary fell silent and the air in the room seemed to chill as Mabeki walked past his men and up to Zalika.

'I must go back to Sindele,' he told her. 'I have a government to appoint. A series of incompetent, gutless buffoons will beg me for the chance to become President. They will all be wasting their time. I have made my choice, and once he has been announced, I will tell him what to say at his first press conference tomorrow. As for you, my dear, I have my best men guarding you. They are all armed and will use their weapons without hesitation.'

He bent down till his face was alongside hers, his gnarled and pockmarked skin brushing against her soft, smooth complexion. Then he whispered wetly into her ear, 'Rest assured that I will be back, Zalika . . . my darling. I have spent the last ten years waiting for this moment, thinking of what I would do to you, planning every detail. I've got a very special night in store for you. And I want you to be ready.'

81

'Shall I tell you one good thing about my job? No one ever gives any crap to the one guy in the company who wears a gun to work!'

Sonny Parkes roared with laughter at his own wit, the four men he'd picked for the mission chuckled dutifully, and Carver managed a grin. It was plainly a line that got used on a regular basis, but he wasn't about to complain. Not when he was sitting in the cabin of the propeller-driven De Havilland Twin Otter that was currently flying him at a stately one hundred and ninety miles an hour over the southern African bush towards the Malemban city of Buweku.

'What did you tell them?' Carver asked.

'The truth, or as close as I could get to it. I said I was urgently pursuing a lead on Mr Klerk's murder. I also said that this was a matter that had to be handled independently. In our organization, Carver, the word "independent" has a very special meaning. And do you know who's responsible for that meaning?'

'No idea.'

'You are. When you went into Mozambique ten years ago and got Miss Stratten the first time—'

'I never thought there'd be a second one.'

'I'll bet. Anyway, Mr Klerk was very impressed. He realized that with Africa being the way it is – you know, total fucking chaos nine-tenths of the time – there was no point even trying to rely on governments and official authorities to, you know, protect you or uphold the law. A man had to be able to act independently.'

'Which is what you and your blokes do.'

'Correct.'

'Let's get on with the independent plan for today then. Were you able to get what I needed?'

Parkes grinned. 'You mean apart from the shower and the change of clothes? Man, you needed those. Smelled like a rotting warthog when you got off that flight!'

'Apart from that . . .'

'Yeah, I got most of it, and I got us a cover, too. Klerk's still got – sorry, had – businesses in Malemba. They're all run by locals these days, because that's the only way you can keep the government from seizing all your assets. But they're actually controlled by us through a bunch of shell companies and offshore trusts. Point is, no one in Malemba's going to connect them with Wendell Klerk, which is good for us right now. Same with this plane. As far as anyone in Buweku is concerned, we work for an independent security contractor and we've come to pitch our services to a potential client in Malemba. When we get to the airport, I'll show the customs people the flight cases containing all the fancy audio-visual equipment we're going to use for our presentation. They'll shake their heads and go tut-tut. Then they'll explain that it is against government policy to allow the importation of such products because it makes it harder for local Malemban industry to compete. Of course, there is no Malemban industry any more, but I will nod all the same and say that I quite understand, and would one thousand US dollars cover the import duty? We will then be waved through. And so will the weapons – including, you may be pleased to hear, a couple of AA-12s – that are hidden in the cases beneath the projector, the lights and the PA system.'

'You've got some non-lethal stuff, too?'

'Yeah, yeah . . . I can't believe you're so pussy. What's wrong with just blowing the bastards away?'

'Nothing, when they're the right bastards. But I don't want to kill innocent people. I leave that kind of thing to people like Mabeki.'

'That's a very noble principle. I just hope it doesn't kill you.'

'Hasn't yet. How about transport?'

'A minibus to meet us at the airport; one three-ton truck; some anonymous Japanese four-by-fours to get us in and out of the target area; and three drivers who know their way through every rat-run in Buweku. Yeah, we've got transport all right.'

'Outstanding,' said Carver. 'Right, let's go over that plan.'

82

Justus Iluko dragged the back of his hand across his brow to wipe away the sweat. His lawyer had bought clean shirts for him and Canaan and a floral cotton dress for Farayi so that they would all look respectable in court. But the back of the prison van was like an airless steel oven and its twelve passengers, crammed on to the benches down either side, were roasting in the heat. Outside, they could hear the sound of engines idling, horns tooting and angry drivers shouting at the crowded street as if their righteous indignation could somehow ease the congestion.

Justus smiled at his daughter as the van jerked forward and started moving down the road. 'Not much longer now, then we will get some fresh air.'

He waited for her reply, or even the faintest signal of acknowledgement, but none came. Farayi was sunk in depression so deep as to be almost catatonic.

'Don't be afraid,' Justus said. 'We are innocent. Even if the police will not admit it, the judge will know and he will set us free. I am sure of it.'

He wished he could reach over to stroke Farayi's head, the way he had when she was a little girl, but the chains that shackled his hands and feet made it impossible.

'You know that is not true,' said Canaan, bitterly. 'The judges are as bad as the rest. Even if they know what is right, they are too afraid to do it. They do not dare make Gushungo angry.'

'But Gushungo is dead.'

The words came from the only other woman in the truck. Her name was Winifred Moyo. She was a farmer's widow and she was facing trial for attempting to silence her crying grandson by cooking him in a pan over an open fire.

There were gasps of amazement around the van, then a voice called out, 'Do not listen to her! She is a madwoman!'

'He is dead, I promise it,' Moyo insisted. 'The guard told me this morning.'

'She is right, I heard this, too,' another man said.

'So who is in charge now?' asked Justus. 'Is Tshonga taking over? If he is, maybe we will get justice.'

'Not from Patrick Tshonga!' cackled Moyo. 'They are saying he is on the run from justice. He is a criminal, just like us!'

'Mr Tshonga is a good man,' Justus insisted. 'I am sure that—'

The van had come to a grinding halt again and the rest of his words were lost in another angry blast of horns. People were shouting up at the front of the van. Their voices were suddenly cut short, and then came the deafening percussive blast of an automatic weapon fired just a few feet away.

Farayi looked up, her eyes wide in terror. Winifred Moyo screamed, while male voices shouted for help and demanded to be let out. A second later, their wish was granted. There was another shot, and the inside of the door lock flew into the van and clattered against the bare metal floor. Then the doors were flung wide.

Two men were standing there. One of them carried a strange-looking black gun. The other clasped a vicious-looking pair of bolt-cutters. They were wearing facemasks and gloves but their eyes – one set blue, the other an eerie, clear green – made it obvious that they were whites.

'Please remain calm,' the man with the bolt-cutters shouted.

Justus frowned. That voice was familiar.

'You are quite safe. We are not, repeat not, going to hurt you. Just stay where you are and let us into the truck.'

The man with the bolt-cutters stepped up into the van while the other man covered him with the gun. Winifred Moyo was thrashing on the bench, desperately trying to wriggle free from her shackles. The man ignored her and went straight to Justus.

'It's me,' he said. 'I'm getting you out of here.'

'Car—'

Carver put a hand over Justus's mouth. 'Shh, no names.' He pointed at the two youngsters. 'Those your two?'

Justus nodded.

'OK,' Carver said.

He got to work with the bolt-cutters, snapping chains and setting the Iluko family free. They rushed to the end of the van and were helped out by the second man.

'Thirty seconds!' the second man called out, as Justus scrambled down on to the road. His voice sounded South African.

'Coming,' said Carver.

He looked around for the least panic-stricken face he could find: a middle-aged man with flecks of grey at his temples. Carver cut the chain that linked his leather-cuffed wrists then handed him the bolt-cutters. 'Free yourself, then pass it on,' he said. Then he too raced from the van.

83

As he blinked his eyes, adjusting to the dazzling sunshine after the darkness of the van, Justus took in a scene of total pandemonium. All around him, drivers had abandoned their vehicles. Cars were slewed across the road. Not far away, passengers were fighting to get off a bus. Pedestrians were running for the shelter of shops and offices, or huddling for cover behind parked cars. The reason for their fear was apparent: the four men positioned around the prison van.

Justus felt a hand grabbing his wrist and pulling it hard.

'This way,' said Carver, leading him round the side of the van.

In the front seats, the driver and guard were slumped forward, unconscious. A dart was sticking out of the driver's neck, exactly like the ones Justus had seen being used to sedate wild game when he worked at the Stratten Reserve. Up ahead, a truck had blocked the van's way, stopping just before a crossroads.

'Get in,' said Carver, gesturing at the passenger door of a large white four-wheel-drive.

'Where are my children?' asked Justus, fear in his voice as he looked around the interior of the car.

'Don't worry, they're safe,' Carver replied, getting in the front passenger seat.

Two of the gunmen got in the back, squeezing Justus between them. Up ahead, the truck began rumbling over the crossroads, oblivious to the traffic coming from either side, forcing its way through. Another vehicle pulled in behind it, a four-by-four like the one Justus was in, but with an extra row of seats. Justus could see Canaan and Farayi sitting in the middle row. He wanted to cry out to them but bit his tongue. They would not be able to hear and he did not want to seem ridiculous in the eyes of the men around him.

'Let's go,' Carver told the driver, and they set off, taking the third place in line, the speed picking up as they followed the truck.

Now they were racing through the middle of Buweko, passing modern office blocks and grand old redbrick colonial buildings, faster and faster, amid the roar of engines and the almost continuous blare of the truck's own klaxon up ahead as it urged everyone else on the road to make way.

They crossed two full city blocks, then five . . . ten . . . and then came the wail of a police siren. Justus twisted his head to see a police car come speeding out of a side street, almost losing control as it skidded round the corner, then gathering itself and chasing after them. A few seconds later, a second police car joined the chase.

One of the men next to Justus said, 'Cover your ears.'

The man turned in his seat and pointed his gun back down the road. Then he fired a single thunderous shot and the rear windscreen simply vanished as if it had never been. He rotated his head to ease his neck muscles, settled over the sights of his gun and pressed the trigger. As the noise crashed round the four-by-four, the drum magazine rotated, cartridges were spewed from the side of the gun and a gigantic hammer of flying lead hit the leading police car and obliterated it.

Justus had fought in a long and bloody war. He had witnessed more slaughter and destruction than any human being should have to face. But he had never seen anything like that before.

The police car seemed to stop dead in the road. The car behind went skidding into its rear. A policeman got out of the passenger seat and ran away with his hands in the air.

The gunman let him go. He stopped firing and slipped back down into his seat.

'Damn!' he said. 'That was fun!'

84

Half a mile up the road, the downtown area gave way to a district of low-rise industrial units, warehouses and open lots. The two four-by-fours pulled into a gated builder's yard on the corner of an intersection. Parkes's men spilled out and greeted one another with high fives and whoops of triumph. Justus ran straight to his children.

Carver let them be for a few seconds – enough time for Justus to be certain that his kids were unharmed – then put a hand on his old comrade's shoulder and said, 'I need a word.'

'Of course, of course!' replied Justus. 'I cannot believe that you came for us. I do not know how I can thank you.'

Carver grimaced. 'Well, that's the trouble. I do.'

'Anything, just say it.'

'I need you to let Canaan and Farayi go with Sonny Parkes over there. He's going to get them safely out of the country. I know you want to go with them. If you say that's what you're going to do, I'll understand. But I really need your help.'

The exuberance left Justus like the light from a bulb. 'What do you want?'

'Mabeki has Zalika Stratten again. I know, it's like some kind of sick joke: losing her once is a misfortune, twice looks like careless-ness. And I *was* careless. It's my fault. But the fact is he's got her, she's in danger, and without you I have no chance of getting her back.'

Justus did not waste time even pretending to reassure Carver. He got straight to the point: 'Where is she?'

'I think he's taken her to the old Stratten Reserve. In fact I'm sure he has.'

'But you do not know?'

'Not for certain, no.'

'And you need me because . . . ?'

'You can guide me in and out. We need to get to the house unob-served, then make a run for the border.'

'It's been a long, long time since I worked there. A lot has changed, I'm sure.'

'Maybe, but you still know more about the place than any of us. And the land itself hasn't changed. Look, I know this is a huge ask. But I'm not expecting you to get involved in any close combat. It's not right to risk your life that way.'

'So you want me to come with you, but you deny me the chance to fight?'

It took Carver half a second to spot the trace of humour in Justus's voice.

'So you'll do it?'

'Of course. I am in your debt, it is what I must do. And not just because of you. It is because of men like Mabeki that my beautiful Nyasha, the love of my life, is dead. For her sake, I must have my revenge.'

'You sure? Your children have lost their mother. I don't want them to lose their father, too.'

'They are almost grown now, ready to make their own lives, whether I am with them or not. Better that they should have the memory of a hero than the presence of a coward.'

'Then you'd better go and tell them that now. They'll be on

their way to the border in a couple of minutes. If all goes well, they'll be waiting for us when we get Zalika out. One way or the other, it'll all be settled tonight.'

Justus nodded and walked back to his son and daughter, passing Sonny Parkes, who was walking over to Carver.

'He agree?' Parkes asked.

'Yeah.'

'And it's just going to be the two of you? Because if you want me or any of my guys to tag along . . .'

'Thanks, but I'd rather you looked after the kids, make sure they get out of the country alive. I paid for their educations. I don't want my money wasted.'

Parkes smiled knowingly. 'Ja, that must be it. Don't worry, bro, we'll get them out in one piece. You decided on weapons? I've still got a couple of unused drums of ammo for an AA-12, if you want it.'

'No thanks. For this kind of job I need precision more than power.'

'Agreed, but I thought I'd ask, just in case the little demonstration back there made you change your mind. Anyway, I got you two M4 carbines with US Special Forces modifications: noise-suppressor kits and three thirty-round mags apiece. That's what we use on operations like this and we like the results. I got you an M11, too. I heard on the grapevine that's your handgun of choice. With a suppressor, of course.'

Carver nodded. 'Thanks.' The M11 was the US designation for the Sig Sauer P226. 'I always feel cosier with one of them around.'

'For me, what I like best is a good knife,' said Parkes. 'A nine-inch Bowie blade, black carbon steel, preferably. I assumed you and Mr Iluko would feel the same way. You may need them.'

Carver grimaced at the thought of a knife slicing through an exposed throat. There were few more horribly intimate ways to kill a man. But Parkes was right: there were also few more effective ways of silently eliminating one's enemy.

'The kit's all in that Defender over there,' said Parkes, nodding in the direction of a dusty olive-green Land Rover. It's got a full tank of gas and an extra jerrycan in case you need it. Believe it or not, that gas was much harder to come by than your weapons. Anyway, I've got you water, rations, and there's a winch fitted to the front bumper in case you need to pull yourself out of trouble.'

'Looks like you thought of everything.'

'Well, that's my boss's niece you're going after. Nothing but the best, eh?'

'I appreciate it. Thanks.'

'Don't mention it,' said Parkes. 'Well, I'd better get going. We've got a plane to catch.'

He turned to go, then paused for a second.

'Hey, Carver . . . good luck.'

'Thanks,' said Carver, 'but actually there is one thing you forgot.'

'What's that?'

'Beer, a cold one. It had better be waiting when I get across the border tonight.'

'Count on it,' said Parkes.

85

Parkes, his men and the two Iluko kids crammed into a Toyota Previa people carrier with blacked-out passenger windows, slipped out of a side gate of the builder's yard and joined the traffic heading out of town at the start of the afternoon rush-hour. It took a while to get on to the two-lane ribbon of cracked and potholed tarmac that constituted the main route to the South African border, and even then the going was slow. More than ninety minutes had passed before the driver took a right turn on to a much more basic dirt track that snaked away into the flat, featureless expanse of the bush.

A few minutes later, the De Havilland Twin Otter took off from Buweku airport without any passengers aboard. Barely ten minutes into its flight, less than fifty miles from Buweku, the pilot radioed the control tower, reporting multiple systems malfunctions. He said he would attempt to make an immediate forced landing and requested information about nearby landing strips.

The air-traffic controller hesitated. There was, indeed, a

full-length runway right under the Twin Otter's flight path. It was one of the many Forward Air Fields built thirty years earlier by the former white minority rulers of Malemba. Fighting a war in which the enemy could appear anywhere in the country, at any time, they'd wanted to be able to fly troops in and out of battle zones as fast as possible. Today, many of these airfields were derelict and overgrown, but the strips were still there, for all the plants that were pushing through them.

The controller wasn't sure whether the positions of the forward fields were considered a state secret. Of course, everyone knew where they were, but could one say so in public? In a government based on unreason and downright madness, it was so hard to tell.

'It is possible that there may be facilities close to your current position, but I am not at liberty to be specific,' he said, with painstaking caution.

To his surprise, the controller heard laughter in his headphones.

'Ja,' the pilot agreed. 'I have a feeling I may have heard of facilities like that, too.'

Seconds later, the Otter adjusted its course and began a rapid descent towards the crumbling remains of the airstrip.

'Bang on time,' said Sonny Parkes with a nod of satisfaction as he watched the Otter coming in to land.

Of the original two-thousand-yard runway less than half was still usable, but that was plenty for a plane with the Otter's short take-off and landing capability. It came bumping along the runway, swung through one hundred and eighty degrees and paused, engines still running, just long enough for its seven passengers to clamber aboard before the pilot raced back the way he had come and climbed into the dimming light of the late-afternoon sky. Then he banked to the south and headed for the South African border, some forty miles away.

Watching the Otter reappear on his radar, the air-traffic controller suddenly felt a lot less pleased with himself. He had been conned.

The plane had never had anything wrong with it at all. It had landed in order to make a drop or a pick-up. And since it had left Buweku empty, a pick-up was the overwhelming likelihood. For the past two hours he had been hearing snatches of news and gossip about the attack on the prison van. Several prisoners were still missing. Had some of them been spirited away on that plane? Men willing to commit such a crime in broad daylight, in the middle of Buweku's busiest street, would surely not baulk at such a dramatic escape. Well, they were not going to get away with it.

Feeling personally insulted, somewhat humiliated and very, very angry, the air-traffic controller got straight on the line to the air force.

In the aftermath of the coup, all of Malemba's armed forces had been put on an ultra-heightened state of alert. Everyone from the lowliest cadet to the highest-ranking officer knew of the glory and preferment that would be heaped on anyone responsible for capturing Patrick Tshonga, or any of his associates. They also knew of the terrible price to be paid if, by chance, they missed the opportunity to apprehend him. So three Malemban Air Force interceptors were airborne less than five minutes after the call came through from Buweku control.

They were Chengdu F-7 interceptors, a Chinese fighter plane based on the Russian MiG-21. They were twenty-year-old models of a fifty-five-year-old design, and as modern combat aircraft they were a sorry joke. They would have been as helpless as Wendell Klerk's clay pigeons against any twenty-first-century fighter. But the Malemban F-7s were not going up against an RAF Typhoon or an American F-22 Raptor. Their prey was an unarmed, propeller-driven passenger aircraft. And they could deal with that just fine.

Their turbojets blasted them through the sound barrier as they hurtled towards their target. There had not been time to arm the planes with air-to-air missiles, but each was equipped with a pair of thirty-millimetre cannons. The three pilots, all honed by years of combat missions during Malemba's participation in the Congo's endless civil wars, chattered happily on the radio. If modern rockets were not available, they were happy to do this the old-fashioned way.

86

In a cellar beneath a government building in the capital city of Sindele, Moses Mabeki watched the sight presented before him with eyes that glittered with greedy excitement.

The man whose arms and legs were currently being strapped to a long wooden board was a senior official in Patrick Tshonga's political party, the Popular Freedom Movement. He and Tshonga were known to be close friends as well as allies. He had thus been one of the first enemies of the regime to be rounded up when Mabeki initiated the counterstrike against Tshonga's attempted coup. For the past twenty-four hours he had been deprived of food, water and sleep. He had been stripped naked, repeatedly hosed in icy water and beaten savagely at random, unpredictable intervals, so that he remained in a state of constant fear of when the next agonizing assault might come. Now his interrogators, their skills honed by twenty years of experience working for a psychopathic dictatorship, were moving in for the *coup de grâce*.

This was a moment for connoisseurs, a display of artistry that was guaranteed to produce the desired results. Mabeki would not have missed it for the world.

The board upon which the man now lay was tilted at an angle of twenty degrees, so that his head was below the level of his feet and, more importantly, his heart. His mouth was covered in black masking tape so that he was unable to cry out. But his terror was evident in his bulging eyes, their lids stretched so wide apart that the whites were clearly visible right around the deep brown iris; the sweat that glittered on his forehead and ran between the veins that had distended beneath his skin; and the involuntary spurt of urine that was so cruelly and humiliatingly exposed for all to see.

Looking at the man, Mabeki thought that what was about to happen was probably superfluous. He was ready to talk, regardless. But it was always worth taking that extra little bit of trouble, just to be sure. Especially when the trouble was also such a pleasure.

Mabeki nodded to one of the men standing by the board. He, in turn, clicked his fingers at an underling, who handed him a white cotton towel. It had been soaked in water. With an almost tender solicitousness, the towel was draped across the face of the man on the board.

Another click of the fingers: a second towel, also wet, was handed over, and it was placed on top of the first.

The body on the board jerked from side to side, desperately struggling to break free from its restraints. The man's back arched in a taut rictus of agony. He tried to thrash his head, to shake off the towels, but strong, gentle hands pressed down and kept them in place.

Mabeki was fascinated by the perfect simplicity of waterboarding. A couple of planks, some cheap towels and a bucket of water were all it took to reduce anyone to a helpless wreck. The stifling press of the towels and the water that passed into the victim's nose with every inward breath created a perfect simulation of drowning. And if the towels were left in place long enough, the man would actually drown. Even if he tried to hold his breath – and only those with ice-cold nerves had the self-control to do that – he would have to breathe again eventually and the drip, drip, drip of water into his lungs would work its inexorable magic.

A minute went by. The thrashing body was reduced to feeble twitches.

Ninety seconds.

Mabeki gave another nod.

The towels were removed and the tape torn from the man's mouth. With a rasp like tearing canvas, he breathed again, dragging air into his starving lungs with desperate intensity.

'Again,' said Mabeki.

More strips of tape were stuck across the man's mouth. Two more wet towels were placed over his head. Another minute and a half went by before Mabeki signalled his satisfaction. This time the towels were removed but the tape stayed on, forcing the man to breathe through his nose.

Only then did Mabeki walk across to the board. He stood for a moment, contemplating his victim. Then, frowning thoughtfully, as though contemplating the possible outcomes of a scientific experiment, he placed his right thumb and forefinger over the man's nose and squeezed them firmly, shutting the nostrils tight.

Keeping that hand in place, Mabeki squatted down on his haunches so that his mouth was level with the man's ear.

'So, you snivelling, treacherous jackal, do you know where Patrick Tshonga is hiding?'

The man gave a series of rapid, frantic nods.

'And are you going to tell my colleagues here everything you know?'

More nods.

Mabeki let go of the man's nose and gave him a gentle, almost affectionate pat on the cheek.

'Excellent,' he said, rising to his feet. 'Console yourself with the thought that your last act before dying was to serve your country.'

Mabeki turned to the chief interrogator who had earlier applied the towels. 'Find out everything he knows. Inform General Zawanda. Tell him that I wish a detailed plan for Tshonga's capture to be drawn up as fast as possible. I want him taken before tonight is out. But no one is to make a move until I give the signal. Do you understand me? No one!'

87

'How far to the border?' asked Sonny Parkes. He was standing in the Twin Otter's cockpit, resting his hands against the back of the co-pilot's seat.

'A little under two minutes,' the pilot replied. 'One and a half if I push it.'

'So push it, then.'

'Ja, well, easier said than done. Top speed in this crate is barely two hundred miles an hour. It's a workhorse, not a racehorse.'

Parkes grunted dismissively and looked at his watch, following the second hand as it swept, or rather crawled, round the dial. Eighty seconds . . . seventy . . . a minute. They were almost safe, but still his back was crawling with prickly tension.

'There you go,' said the pilot. 'Look out of the left-hand side window, about five clicks up ahead – see those long lines of trucks? They're waiting to go through customs, either side of the border. We're almost— Shit!'

The noises seemed to come at once: the chatter of thirty-millimetre cannons, the shattering clatter of rounds tearing through the Twin Otter's wings and fuselage and the deafening roar of three fighter jets as they shot past their prey, throwing it around the sky as it was caught in the chaos of the displaced air they left in their wake.

'Hang on!' the pilot shouted as he flung his aircraft to the left, then plunged it into a precipitous dive.

Parkes was hurled against the side of the cockpit, then flung backwards, ending up on the floor, jammed up against a bulkhead and barely conscious, as the Twin Otter headed nose-first towards the ground.

Down they went, the windscreen filled with nothing but the onrushing earth. The pilot remained impassive as he maintained his suicide dive. But back in the passenger compartment, Farayi Iluko screamed with terror as the plane hurtled towards obliteration. For a few seconds her brother Canaan maintained the pretence that he was not equally terrified. But as the dive went on and on, and the brutal earth drew ever closer, he started screaming too.

Up above, the three Malemban fighters were coming to terms with an unwelcome consequence of the vast disparity between their power and that of their target. They were going so much faster than the Otter that they'd had very little time in which they could bring their guns to bear before they overshot it. Even so, their advantage was overwhelming.

The three planes looped up into the sky, twisting as they went until they were facing the way they'd come. Then they headed back towards the desperate evasions of the Twin Otter.

Now, at last, the pilot pulled back on the controls and shouted to the co-pilot sitting next to him to do the same, the two men leaning back, their arms, necks and faces flushed and contorted with effort as they desperately fought to bring the aircraft out of its dive.

It was too late. They were going to crash.

Sonny Parkes, for the first time in his life, understood the absolute certainty of death. His end was only a second away.

Canaan Iluko grabbed his sister's hand in a grip so tight it seemed her fingers must surely snap from the pressure.

And then the Twin Otter managed to grab some purchase against the onrushing air and haul its nose up, oh so slowly, away from the ground, until there was once again clear blue sky in the pilot's eye-line.

As the wheels of the fixed undercarriage brushed through the desiccated leaves of an ancient baobab tree, the pilot jinked right and sent the Twin Otter into a corkscrewing roll, its tumbling wingtips almost seeming to brush the ground before he spiralled back up into the sky.

And then the F-7s were on them again, coming in one after another and raking the Otter with armour-piercing rounds that ripped straight through the flimsy fuselage and out the other side, barely impeded by anything they encountered.

'Right engine's been hit!' shouted the co-pilot. 'It's on fire!'

They'd lost half their power and now the pilot faced another problem: the same burst of fire that had knocked out his right engine had also torn through the control surfaces at the rear of the wing. He was in danger of stalling. The plane was lurching drunkenly from side to side, and he could see the fighter planes turning for one last, assuredly fatal attack run.

When he looked down, however, there was hope. The border crossing was clearly visible just a few hundred feet below, little more than a mile ahead. Beyond the customs post on the South African side stretched a narrow black ribbon of highway and the safety of home.

If he could only reach it.

88

The pilots in the F-7s were like predatory raptors eyeing a dove with a broken wing. They wheeled and swooped in ruthlessly perfect formation, screaming down towards the Twin Otter as it limped past the first trucks on the Malemban side of the border. Down the fighters roared, and beneath them cab-doors and tarpaulins were flung open as drivers and passengers desperately sought to get away from the angels of death plunging from the sky.

Again the guns spat out a continuous hail of deadly shells, strafing the Twin Otter and the trucks and customs huts below it with indiscriminate malice. A petrol tanker bound for the thirsty pumps of Malemba's empty filling stations erupted in a ball of fire that seemed to swallow the fragile little plane before it emerged on the far side. Its wings and tail had been pierced so often they looked more like torn lace than solid metal. Its left engine had gone, too. All that its wounded, bleeding pilot could hope to do was bring a little control to the final glide as the Otter hit the top of a brilliantly painted bus, smashing several boxes filled with chickens that had been strapped there, bounced forward and crashed down on to the road surface as the F-7s roared by, less than a hundred feet above the ground.

The undercarriage collapsed, sending the aircraft skidding over the road surface, slewing round as it went. The right wing hit a fully loaded lumber truck and sheared off, but the Otter kept going, spinning like a Frisbee as it left the road, ploughed through a stretch of bare ground and then came to a halt in a cloud of thick black smoke and choking dust.

For a while, nothing moved. The crowd of people gathered on the roadside stood there motionless, too afraid to approach the crashed plane for fear of an explosion. But as the seconds passed and no eruption came, the first few figures made their tentative, nervous way towards it.

One clambered up on to the nose and peered through the cracked windscreen into the cockpit. Others tugged at the main passenger door, just to the rear of the battered remnants of the left wing and engine. Then they sprang back as the handle was operated from within the aircraft cabin.

The door swung open.

A white man was revealed in the open doorway, dressed in black combat fatigues. His face was covered in blood from an open wound across his forehead. He was only held upright by his right hand gripping the door frame. He tried to move his left hand, waving towards himself.

'Come here,' he croaked. 'Please help.'

A trucker dressed in a replica Manchester United football shirt helped the white man down on to the ground. Then he started shouting exuberantly, yelling at his travelling companions to come and assist him. Very soon the crowd could see what the excitement was all about as two slender black figures were carried from the plane. One was a young man in his late teens. The other was his older sister.

And they were both alive.

89

Justus Iluko tried not to think back to the night he had first met Sam Carver. But sometimes he couldn't avoid it, nights when his dreams were filled with images from a small town in Mozambique: the white-hot glow of a man leaning over a helpless girl; the shouts of drunken men and the giggles of prostitutes doing business in a squalid drinking den; firing guns and exploding grenades; the screams of wounded men; the clatter of an approaching helicopter; the dead weight of Captain Morrison's body as they dragged him back aboard. But above all the sense of chaos and confusion, the pervasive grip of mortal dread, clawing at his guts. He'd wake up in a cold sweat and Nyasha would have to calm him till the night demons had vanished back into the darkness. Now Nyasha was gone, and so, he supposed, was his bed, even the very house in which he'd raised his family and dared to dream of a better future for his children.

Here he was, though, still alive when so many others had gone, and now the nightmare that had cursed him for so long was being replayed in a new form. The night was quiet this time with just the chatter of insects and the occasional rustle of animals in the long grass to disturb the moonlit stillness. From his position behind a fallen tree trunk, Justus could see what he still thought of as the Stratten house no more than a hundred paces away, a low-slung building that nestled beneath a grass-thatched roof. The terrace where the Strattens had eaten so many of their meals and held so many parties, the African guides like Justus transformed into white-jacketed waiters for the night, was exactly as he remembered it. Even the woven palm-leaf sofas and chairs were still there. Yet Zalika Stratten was a prisoner in what had once been her home and the rest of the family were rotting in unmarked graves.

Now those chairs were occupied by armed men, four of them, sitting hunched over a table while they played games of cards. Though there were a few beer bottles on the table, these men had not let themselves get drunk. Their manner was sober in the extreme, the cards merely a means to pass the time between watches in the house, or out in the grounds. A woman appeared from time to time, but she was no prostitute, instead a respectable housekeeper who upbraided any man who dared put his feet on the furniture, even as she brought them their meals of thick maize porridge and stew.

Carver and Justus had arrived two hours earlier, having left the Land Rover hidden in the bush more than a mile from the house. They had approached their destination with extreme stealth, and Justus had been surprised and not a little impressed by the skill with which Carver selected his path, always avoiding soft ground; taking extreme care to move silently, without leaving tell-tale broken twigs or disturbed leaves in his path; regularly pausing to listen out for anyone who might be following them. Together they had reconnoitred the property and assessed the number of guards and the routine with which they carried out their assignments. There were eight in total: two inside the building, presumably standing guard over Miss Stratten; two patrolling the perimeter, walking in opposite directions; four resting between watches. Yet even these, the card players and beer drinkers, maintained their readiness.

Far in the distance, Justus heard the roar of a lion, a noise that struck a primitive, animal terror into a man, no matter how far away it sounded. Instantly, all four of the men stopped their game and looked out into the night, towards the direction from which the roar had come. As the sound of the lion subsided in a series of short, coughing growls, one of the men got to his feet and walked to the edge of the terrace, sweeping his gaze from side to side and causing Justus to fear that he had been spotted, even though he knew that no man had night-vision sharp enough to penetrate as far as his position.

All Justus had to do was wait. His job was very simple. As and when Carver emerged from the building, with Zalika in tow, it was his duty to lay down covering fire to suppress anyone who might want to stop them getting away. The orders Carver had given him were very specific. He was to remain exactly where he was. If anything went wrong, then he should melt back into the bush, return to the Land Rover and drive like hell for the border, which was less than ten miles from where he now stood. Under no circumstances was he to risk his own life in an attempt to save Carver's.

Justus wondered about that last point. He was by nature a man who obeyed his commanding officer. He also had a very good reason indeed to survive the night in one piece. Yet he had a feeling that if the moment came, he might for once be insubordinate.

But what about Carver? Justus could not see or hear him. He was out there somewhere, silently tracking the patrolling guards like a deadly spirit, his sharp, black-bladed knife in his hand.

90

Carver had already struck once, though Justus did not know it. The first of the sentries had been eliminated and his body dragged off the path on which he'd been walking. Carver had walked on a little further, towards the oncoming second sentry, and now he was invisible in the undergrowth by the side of the path, waiting for his next victim.

He was a young soldier who looked little older than the Iluko boy he'd rescued a few hours ago, and who carried himself with the nervous bravado of any squaddie in any army forced to mount a solitary patrol in the dark. It was almost too easy to let him go by and then slip out on to the path and approach the soldier from behind, place his left hand over the lad's mouth, pulling his head back, and then slide the blade in a single smooth stroke across the exposed neck, slicing through the trachea and feeling his body go as limp in his arms as an exhausted lover.

Slowly, with almost tender care, Carver lowered the dead soldier to the ground. Then he stepped back off the path and dropped to his belly to snake across the ground to his next position. When he got there, he pulled round the M4 carbine that had been slung across his back and found a comfortable shooting position. He imagined he was back on one of the stands at Campden Hall, waiting for his targets to be released. He thought of the sequence of shots he would be firing, the various adjustments he would have to make as he tracked from one target to another. He calmed himself, let every last dreg of tension be bled from his neck and shoulders. And then he got to work.

From where Justus was watching, what happened next had an eerie calmness, even a detachment, to it that made him wonder for a moment whether he was back in the world of his dreams. There were four gentle but quite distinct popping sounds, each less than a second apart. And then a spell seemed to be cast over the card players. The man who had just seconds earlier been looking so purposefully into the darkness fell to the ground without so much as a murmur of pain or surprise. A card player suddenly jerked backwards, his head resting against the back of his sofa, a bright-red hole between his wide-open, sightless eyes. The man sitting next to him was knocked sideways by the impact of a bullet in his temple. The third slumped forward over the card table, his beer glass still gripped in his right hand. As his head hit the table, his grip relaxed and the glass smashed on the stone-tiled floor – the first loud noise since the first shot had been fired.

Justus realized that the two sentries must also have fallen to Carver. Six men dead, and still Justus had no idea of where, precisely, their killer was.

The sound of breaking glass alerted the two men posted inside the house. From the first-floor landing it was possible to see right through the open-plan interior to the terrace where the four bodies now lay. Whoever had killed them was surely on their way into the house. Nervous fingers tapped out a number on a satellite phone, and the voice that spoke into the mouthpiece trembled with fear.

'We are under attack. At least four men are dead, maybe six. Please come quickly, I beg you, or it will be too late.'

In the back of the helicopter transporting him south from Sindele, Moses Mabeki felt a mixture of fury and delight. Carver's sheer effrontery was intolerable, and the possible seizure of Zalika Stratten was a nuisance, to put it mildly. But at least this gave him an opportunity to deal with Carver once and for all. It had been a mistake to expect a gang of Chinese peasant gangsters to solve his problems for him. From now on, Mabeki would rely on his own resources and do the job himself.

He checked his watch. He would be at the house in twenty minutes. He did not expect Carver to have got too far away by then.

Back at the house, the last two members of the unit detailed to stand guard over Zalika Stratten were not planning a desperate last stand to defend their master's chosen woman. They were climbing through a window at the back of the building, sliding down the thatched roof, falling the last seven feet to the ground and then running away as fast as their legs would carry them.

91

Carver was not a fan of the open-plan style. Not when it was fully lit and he had to make his way across a good fifty feet of living area, then up a single straight flight of stairs with flimsy wooden banisters and no decent cover anywhere. He came out of the dark with his M4 up and his eyes looking through the sights, ready to fire at the slightest movement or sound.

Yet none came.

At first he thought it might be a trap. He was being lured right into the property, the more easily to be caught at point-blank range. But the ambush he expected never came.

He took the stairs in half-a-dozen strides, three steps at a time.

The landing was deserted.

Carver turned right and made his way along the landing, stepping quietly, keeping his back to the wall until he came to the furthermost door. He paused to listen for any movement or noise from the room beyond it. There was none. He took a pace back, then smashed the heel of his boot against the door, crashing it open.

Nothing happened. The room was empty.

Carver checked around the bed. He opened the wardrobes and went through an internal door to the en-suite bathroom.

No one there.

He went back out to the landing and repeated the process in two more bedroom suites.

The main house had only ever had four bedrooms; guests were put up at smaller cottages in the grounds. When he reached the last bedroom, it was empty, just like the others. But the bedcover was pulled back, the sheets were crumpled and the indentation made by a resting head could still be seen on the pillow. A pair of jeans and a T-shirt had been left carelessly draped over the back of a chair. And there was something more, a lingering trace of scent in the air, a scent that went straight to his brain like a potent drug, triggering memories so powerful it was almost as if he were back in a hotel suite in Hong Kong with her body draped around his, his hand tracing a path down the curve of her spine . . .

'Zalika!' he shouted. 'Where are you?'

There were no words of reply. But he thought he heard a sound from behind the bathroom door, the whimper of a frightened animal.

He was there in a second, striding across the room, flinging open the door and saying it again – 'Zalika!' – when he saw her naked body curled up in the bottom of a huge stone bath.

He went to her and reached down to touch her, desperate to know that she was still warm, still alive.

'Are you all right?'

She nodded wordlessly and looked at him with wide, panicked eyes. All her hard-won self-assurance had deserted her, leaving just the broken husk of the girl he had first rescued all those years ago.

'The guards ran away,' she said. 'They were so scared. I just wanted to hide. I didn't know what was out there. I . . . I . . .' The faintest glimmer of an exhausted smile flickered across her face. 'I hardly dared hope it was you.'

'Come on,' Carver said, helping her from the bath, 'let's get you out of here.'

He hesitated then, trying to find the right words for what he had to ask next.

'Has he . . . has he treated you all right?'

Zalika pressed herself closer to Carver. He felt her nod against his shoulder. Then she pulled away a fraction and looked him in the eye as she gently ran the tips of her fingers down the side of his face.

'I'm OK,' she whispered. 'He hasn't hurt me. I promise.'

She pulled on her clothes and followed Carver out of the house, clutching him tight as they passed the four dead bodies on the terrace. Justus met them outside and they began the walk to the Land Rover.

Far away in the night, a lion's roar echoed across the bush once again, like a rumble of distant thunder.

92

The wardens called him Lobengula, after the last great warrior king of the Ndebele people. From the moment he was born, he was the biggest, most dominant cub in his litter. The two brothers and one sister that were born with him all died young, as most lion cubs do: one killed by hyenas, another by a snake-bite, and the third mauled by an older male. But Lobengula survived and swiftly grew to be the finest young male in his pride.

In time, as all male lions must do, he had left his birth-pride and become a nomad, ranging across the Stratten Reserve until he found another pride whose alpha male was past his prime and weakening. Lobengula had fought him, killed him and assumed his place at the head of the pride. For five years he had been the master of all he surveyed, a magnificent creature, standing almost five feet tall at the shoulder and measuring twelve feet from his muzzle to the tuft of his tail. In his prime he had weighed six hundred pounds, and the extravagant size and deep black-brown colour of his mane was a signal to all who came near of his physical prowess and regal status.

The male lion, however, leads a precarious existence. He is not required to hunt – his mane, acting like a massive scarf, causes him to overheat if forced to chase prey for any length of time – but he does have to fight. He must defend the pride against external threats and defend himself against other males seeking to take his place. In the end, a lion's career, like a politician's, inevitably ends in failure. He is either killed or forced to leave the pride and go back to a solitary, nomadic existence.

When Lobengula finally met his match he was still enough of a warrior to preserve his own life. But death in battle might have been a more noble end than the half-life to which he was condemned, wandering the bush, searching for carrion or particularly young or weak prey animals that he could bring down swiftly before exhaustion overtook him. But the shortage of food that affected the human population soon transferred itself to the animal population. Though the wardens of the reserve did their best to deter poachers, still the desperation of the people was so great that many of the wildebeest, bucks and even zebras were killed for their meat. And, in the end, unpaid and hungry, the wardens themselves joined the slaughter.

Every creature killed by human predators was one less for the animal ones. The lions grew hungry. Mothers could no longer provide for their cubs. And solitary males like Lobengula felt their muscles waste and their ribs press against their fur as starvation gnawed at their guts. But even a mangy, ageing Lobengula was still a very large, dangerous beast. He was also becoming more bad-tempered by the day; an angry, embittered old man with a grudge against his world.

Tonight he had been roaring his displeasure and frustration as he paced the bush, looking for something, anything, to eat but finding not a scrap. Now he was tired and hungrier than ever. So he lay down, as cats of all sizes will do, exactly where he pleased. And, like any other cat, once he had found his spot, he had absolutely no intention of moving from it.

93

For fifteen minutes the Land Rover made steady progress over relatively flat, open terrain. From time to time they came across game: a giraffe, some warthogs, even a female rhino and her calf, All made way for the car, disappearing into the bush at the sound of its engine and the smell of its exhaust. Carver was driving without lights so as not to give away his position, a skill he'd first been taught in the SBS. But for all his training, even the most docile bush country was still littered with hazards: potholes, boulders, tree-roots and thickets of tangled, thorn-bearing undergrowth. It was far better to temper his impatience, keep his speed down and stay out of trouble than risk going too fast and suffer an accident. Yet he knew it was just a matter of time before some kind of pursuit came after them and it took every ounce of self-control he possessed to resist the temptation to press the pedal to the floor.

Three miles from the border, the land began to rise towards a low range of hills. Now the going became rougher. The soil was thinner with many more boulders to be avoided. The Land Rover's four-wheel-drive and low gearbox ratio came into their own as

Carver let it roll down the precipitous bank of a dried-up river-bed and then up the other side. His pace slowed still further as the car made its way through tight gullies, the tyres fighting for purchase on narrow trails that fell away into ditches and ravines. What had been a straight line across country became a twisting course around blind corners and over humps in the landscape that gave no clue as to what lay on the other side.

Justus did his best to recall what lay in store for them, as did Zalika. But a long time had gone by since either of them had lived or worked on the Stratten Reserve, and their task was made no easier by the night, even if a three-quarter moon shone from the cloudless sky and the stars burned in the heavens as bright pin-pricks of billion-year-old light.

From time to time, Carver stopped the car and they listened for any sound of pursuit. Then, clutching his own rifle for security, Justus got out and tentatively walked on ahead, scouting out the way before returning to report his findings to Carver. As he stood outside the Land Rover, talking in a low, barely audible voice to Carver in the driver's seat, his reports were always calm and measured, expert assessments of the challenges they faced.

They were so close to the border now, just another few minutes' drive. The tension was still acute, the fear of capture ever-present. Now, though, for the first time, there was real hope, too. Carver had let himself imagine the beer that Parkes had waiting for him. Justus could almost feel the joy that would come when he held his children in his arms again.

But then, on his fifth sortie, when they were traversing a hillside along a narrow ledge, a rockface rising to the left of them, the slope falling steeply away to the right, Justus returned at a sprint, look-ing behind him as he ran. In his haste, he did not see the small hole in the trail ahead of him. His foot turned on the side of the hole, twisting his ankle and sending Justus crashing to the ground. In an instant he was up again, grimacing as he got to his feet and hobbling the last few steps to the car. He pulled open the passenger door, leapt up into his seat, the effort making him cry out in pain, and slammed it shut again before gasping a single, breath-less word: 'Lion!'

'Where?' Carver asked.

'Just around the corner, in the middle of the path. He is asleep. I don't think I woke him.'

'Then we'd better do it.'

'I don't think so.'

'Don't be daft. He'll soon wake up and get the hell out of there when he sees a bloody great lump of metal lumbering towards him.'

'I wouldn't be so sure,' said Zalika. 'Lions aren't like other animals. They don't move just because they see us coming.'

'We'll just have to make him move, then, won't we?'

The mutters of protest from the other two were drowned out as Carver started up the engine and moved the Land Rover forward. Its tyres crunched over dust and pebbles as it slowly drove round the corner. And there, exactly as Justus had promised, lay a very large, very sleepy lion.

94

Lobengula had encountered his first truck when he was still a cub. Over the years he had become accustomed to these loud, smelly objects and had learned that they offered neither a threat to him nor a meal. He was, therefore, entirely indifferent to their presence. So now, when the noise of the Land Rover's engine woke him, he reluctantly opened his eyes, glowered at the vehicle approaching him, then rested his head back down on his huge paws.

The metal machine came closer to him, so close that he could almost reach out his claws and strike it. This time when he raised his head, Lobengula's stare was a lot angrier and he gave a low, grumbling growl of disapproval. Then, determined not to budge, he lowered his head again.

'Why don't you give it a blast of the horn?' asked Zalika.

Carver almost thought he could hear a teasing tone in her voice, a return to her old, combative spirit. But then he recalled all the times during the drive when she had turned in her seat, looking anxiously out of the rear window to see if anyone was on her trail.

Whatever front she might put on, Zalika was all too aware of the danger they were still in.

'Can't risk it,' he said. 'If there's anyone out there, they'd hear it. Maybe we could shoot it.'

'You should only shoot a lion if you can kill it there and then,' said Justus. 'And if you kill this lion right here, you will then have to move its body.'

'That means getting a chain round it, using the winch – we haven't got time for all that,' Carver said. 'The hell with this.'

He revved the engine then slowly inched the car forward. Surely the lion would move once it felt the press of steel on its body.

Lobengula moved. He scrabbled backwards, got to his feet, gave an irritable shake of his mane and then, standing four square in the Land Rover's path, he growled again, a shorter, more clipped sound, almost a bark. It was his equivalent of a warning shot across the bows. The next time he'd really roar. And if that didn't remove this nuisance from his life, he'd have to start fighting.

Carver rolled his eyes and looked up at the roof of the car. 'Jesus wept.'

'There was another path, a couple of hundred metres back, pointing down the hill. Maybe we could try that,' Zalika suggested.

'Anything's better than pissing about here,' said Carver, pulling at his seat-belt. 'Strap in tight.'

The lion wasn't the only male losing his temper. The tension and impatience Carver had suppressed so efficiently for the past forty minutes burst through his tightly stretched composure. He wrenched the gear-stick into reverse, turned in his seat to look through the rear window and kicked the accelerator hard.

The Land Rover shot backwards. Carver turned the steering wheel hard to get back round the corner. Too hard: the rear corner of the car collided with the sheer rock on the upward side of the hill. Carver overcompensated as he pulled the wheel the other way.

'Watch out!' Zalika yelled.

But it was too late. One of the rear tyres had lost its footing on the edge of the road. Carver slammed on the brakes, but the Land Rover was out of control, skidding sideways and backwards over the edge, crashing on to its side and sliding twenty feet down the hill until it collided roof-first with the base of a tree and came to a crashing halt.

Carver turned off the engine, and as a cloud of smoke and dust drifted away on the breeze, silence returned to the hillside. The tree had punched a great trough in the roof of the Land Rover. All the windows down the driver's side of the car were smashed and the interior of the car was scattered with safety glass. The three people inside were hanging sideways in their chairs, suspended from their seat-belts.

The right side of Carver's head had smashed against the side of the car as it fell. It ached, and there was blood dripping from his forehead into one eye. Aside from that he felt bruised and shaken but otherwise in one piece. There were no broken bones, so far as he could tell.

'You guys all right?' he asked.

There were grunts of assent from Justus, who was hanging immediately above him, and Zalika in the rear.

And then she said, 'Now what?'

As the Land Rover reversed away from him, Lobengula's first instinct had been to get back to sleep. He was just about to slump back down on the ground when a scent came to him, one that had previously been masked by the stench of the exhaust: the smell of human being.

Lobengula had never been a man-eater. For the great majority of his life he had never needed to be. There had been plenty of game on the reserve and plenty of willing females to hunt it on his behalf. Now, though, times had changed. Humans might be unfamiliar prey, but they smelled edible, just the same. And Lobengula was very, very hungry.

Filled with the curiosity natural to his kind, he padded along the trail and down the hillside towards the ruined car.

95

Carver was busy working out the best way of getting out of the Land Rover. It was a right-hand-drive vehicle, so the door on his side was now pressed against the ground. There was a fist-sized hole in the windscreen directly in front of him and the rest of the glass was so cracked that one good kick would get rid of it. First, though, he had to find a way of delivering that kick, which would mean unstrapping himself and freeing his legs from the well in front of the driver's seat. Justus would have the easier way out if he could somehow open the passenger-side window or door and scramble up through that. Zalika would be able to do the same at the back.

Somehow, though, Carver felt that he should be the first one out of the vehicle. He was painfully aware that anyone for miles around would have heard the sound of the crash – a crash that was entirely his fault. He had got them into this mess. Time he started getting them out of it.

Justus, however, had other ideas. He was wriggling in his seat, trying to reach the handle that would wind down his window. He finally got hold of it and started turning it as fast as he could.

Then a low, purring growl reverberated round the inside of the Land Rover. Suddenly Justus began working the handle the other way. The lion was just outside. They could hear it snuffling at the upturned car, pawing the ground.

'Oh God, oh God . . . come on . . .' he muttered as Zalika shrieked, 'For God's sake, close that fucking window!'

Just then there was a thud up above him. The lion had jumped up and was now pacing along the overturned bodywork and peering in through the windows.

Zalika screamed. She unclipped her harness and fell down to the bottom of the car, away from the marauding animal. Justus lowered himself more carefully and crouched down next to Carver.

By now, Carver had drawn the pistol that Parkes had given him and pointed it up at the side of the car. 'Watch out,' he said. 'Fire in the hole.'

He punched half-a-dozen holes in the side of the car as he fired at where the great cat was standing. From outside came a squeal of pain. The lion half-jumped, half-fell down to the ground, gave another agonized grunt, then disappeared into the night.

For an entire minute, no one moved. But there were no more sounds from outside. No sign of the animal's return.

'Right,' said Carver. 'Time to go.'

'But the lion is still out there,' Justus protested. 'And as long as it is alive it is dangerous.'

'Yeah, the lion and Moses Mabeki. He's out there somewhere, too, and I'm not waiting for him to find us.'

'He might not find us,' said Zalika. 'Why don't we wait a bit longer, just to make sure the lion has really gone away?'

Carver was about to reply when he stopped, tilted his head to one side and whispered, 'Listen.'

The only sound to be heard in the Land Rover was very faint, but unmistakable: a helicopter, still a fair way off but getting closer all the time.

'Right, that does it,' said Carver. 'I don't care how many lions are prowling around outside, we're getting out of here.'

96

Moses Mabeki was up at the front of the helicopter in the co-pilot's seat, his eyes focused on the ever-moving pool of light created by the searchlight as it swept across the ground just a couple of hundred feet below. They were passing over hillier country now, where the shadows cast by the broken landscape made it harder than ever to see anything down below. His frustration was mounting. The border with South Africa was barely a mile away now. There was a very real possibility that Carver had eluded him and, just as bad, taken the Stratten girl beyond his reach. He was almost at the point where he would have to admit defeat.

And then something caught his eye. At first, he could not say exactly what it was, just an anomaly in the landscape. He tapped the pilot on his shoulder. 'Go back,' he said, pointing down at the ground behind them. 'I saw something.'

The pilot brought the chopper round through a one-eighty turn and retraced their course, more slowly now.

'There!' said Mabeki triumphantly, pointing down at the ground where the abandoned Land Rover lay. 'I knew it! Get us down. As close to that car as possible.'

Barely a minute later, Mabeki was standing at the crash site, running his hands over the punctured flank of the Land Rover, contemplating the significance of shots fired from inside the car and wondering where the blood coagulating in drips and smears across the metal had come from.

'Lion,' said one of his men. 'Big lion. See here.'

He flashed a torch at paw-prints the size of a large dinner-plate pressed into the earth around the car.

For a moment, Mabeki was nervous. 'Lion? Where did it go?'

The man looked down at the prints and the drops of blood scattered among them. Then he pointed away down the hillside, to the northwest. 'That way,' he said.

'And the people in the car?'

The man spent a few seconds examining the side of the hill before returning to Mabeki. 'That way.'

He was pointing back up the hill, towards the trail that ran about twenty feet above their heads. Towards the South African border.

'Excellent,' said Mabeki. 'Then let us follow them at once.'

Lobengula had indeed walked away to the northwest, but had not gone very far before lying down to ease the pain of his wounds, his huge frame melting invisibly into the undergrowth. In full sunlight, even an experienced tracker would have had a hard time spotting him. At night it was impossible.

The rounds fired by the M11 pistol would not have been recommended for the job by any reputable lion-hunter, and their trajectory had been impeded by the metal barrier through which they had flown, distorting their shape en route, before three of them hit Lobengula. So none of his wounds was fatal; not immediately so, at any rate. He had one round caught between two ribs, both of which were cracked as a result. Another had punctured his lower intestine. The third had worked its way into the muscle of his upper left hind leg, which he was now attempting to lick better.

He was in severe pain, which increased with every breath or stride that he took.

But Lobengula had been a fighter all his life. This was not the first time he had been wounded. Countless claws had drawn blood from his flesh before now, but none of them had finished him. And he was not finished yet. Slowly, wincing with pain, he pulled himself to his feet and went on his way again.

97

Carver was working out the odds. They were not far from the border now, as little as half a mile, maybe. All three of them were armed: Carver and Justus with their M4s and Zalika with Carver's pistol, which he had reloaded with a fresh magazine. But the going was getting tougher and their pace was slowed by the injury to Justus's ankle. He had found a sturdy length of fallen branch to use as an impromptu crutch and was not making the slightest sound of complaint. But Carver only had to look at the sweat bathing his face and the silent gasps and screwed-up eyes when he took an especially agonizing step to know that Justus was in trouble. The helicopter had landed barely three minutes after they had left the Land Rover. It would take Mabeki a while, a very short while, to work out what had happened and pick up their trail. But after that, he and his men would surely be moving at a faster pace. Somehow, Carver had to buy them some time.

They had been walking through a thicket of trees and bushes. At its far end, they emerged into a small open space, perhaps thirty feet across, that stood at the foot of a low cliff. Straight ahead of them, the cliff was bisected by a narrow gully that cut into the rock, rising as it went. At the base of the cliff, by the mouth of the gully, lay a scattered pile of large boulders – the result, presumably, of some long-ago rock fall. They made a perfect defensive position. This, Carver decided, was where he would make his stand.

He stopped and turned to face Justus and Zalika. 'I'm staying here,' he said. 'You two go on to the border. It's only a few hundred yards now, just the far side of this hill. All you have to do is keep going, and no matter what happens, or what you hear, don't turn back.'

'No!' cried Zalika. 'You can't do that. Come with us.'

'No point. They'll just get all of us.'

'Then leave me behind,' said Justus. 'I am the one slowing you down. I should stay.'

'No,' said Carver firmly. 'I promised I'd get you back to your kids. I'm not breaking that promise. Just give me your spare magazines and I'll be fine. Mabeki can't have many men with him. The chopper wasn't big enough. But they're coming this way. So go. Go now. And don't look back.'

Zalika stepped forward, as if to embrace him, but Carver pushed her away. 'No time for goodbyes. Just go.'

The two hesitated for a moment, then left.

Carver settled down behind one of the rocks. He wasn't too concerned. He had a decent amount of ammunition. His position offered him plenty of cover and would force his enemies to come at him across an open, moonlit clearing. Unless Mabeki had suddenly rustled up an entire platoon in the middle of the African bush it shouldn't be too hard to hold them off for long enough to let Zalika and Justus escape. After that he just had to find a way to disengage from the firefight and sneak away before anyone noticed he was gone. It was tricky, but not impossible. First, though, he had to cover the others' retreat. He reckoned he still had two or three minutes before Mabeki and his men arrived.

*

The first shots came much sooner than that. Two rounds, pistol fire, reverberating around the rocks – from behind his position. Christ, had they got behind him? Were the other two under attack?

Carver twisted round and peered back down the gully. There was something moving there, a deeper shadow in the darkness. It grew bigger and more defined until Carver could make out a figure carrying a handgun with arms extended, ready to fire, walking towards him. His finger tightened on the trigger.

And then he realized it was Zalika. He exhaled slowly, closing his eyes for a second as he contemplated how close he had come to shooting her. As he lowered the M4, he took his left hand off the forward grip and made a downward, pressing gesture with it, indicating that she should get down, under cover of the rock.

She kept walking.

'Zalika!' he hissed. 'What are you doing? Where's Justus?'

She did not bother to whisper, but in a calm, steady voice said, 'Put your gun down. Put it down, or I shoot.'

98

Carver did nothing. It wasn't out of any kind of bravado. He simply couldn't believe what he'd just heard.

'Put the gun down,' Zalika repeated. 'On the ground. Now.'

Very slowly, calmly, keeping his eyes on hers, he did as he was told.

'Now kick it away from you.'

Again Carver obeyed her. He could make out every detail of her face in the clear moonlight as she stood over him, pointing the gun down at his chest, the threat of the bullet pinning him to the spot like a butterfly on a pin. Now it was his turn to repeat himself: 'What are you doing? Where's Justus?'

'He's dead,' she said, so flatly, with such impersonal detachment, that he hardly recognized it as her voice at all. And then: 'I shot him.'

The information was so unexpected, so wrong, that Carver could not make sense of it. 'What do you mean, you shot him? Why the hell did you do that?'

Zalika looked almost surprised that it was not obvious to him.

'Why do you think? Because I had to stop him getting to the border. Just like I'm going to stop you.'

Still the words she spoke made no sense to him. 'Are you mad? We've got to get to the border. Mabeki's going to be here any minute. That's the only way of escaping him.'

'But I don't want to escape him,' she said, her voice beginning to rise as she taunted him. 'Don't you get it? All this time, you've been thinking he's the kidnapper. But he's not. You are. Those men back there, the ones you killed, they weren't there to keep me in. They were there to keep you out. I wasn't a prisoner. I wanted to be there, to be with Moses at last after all these years. That was why I had no clothes on when you found me. I was waiting for him.'

Carver had sleepwalked into a looking-glass world, where up was down, wrong was right and all his hopes turned out to be delusions. It seemed now that everything she had ever said to him was a lie that had meant the exact opposite of what he had believed. Everything she had done had been for totally different reasons to the ones he had assumed. He'd been fool enough to care about Zalika Stratten. He'd risked his life to save her. Had she really not wanted to be saved?

He made one last effort to try to preserve his own view of reality.

'Mabeki abducted you when we were in Hong Kong. He held a gun to your head. I saw him do it.'

'And I let him,' she said. 'Then, when we'd got outside, I ran to the van he had waiting, and they drove me away. I'd wanted to stay at the house, so that we could kill you together, Moses and me. But he said that was too risky. He wanted to be sure I was all right. And he'd already worked out a plan for dealing with you. All the time I was in that van I just prayed that he would get away from you safely, so that he could join me. And I prayed that you were dead, Sam. I prayed for that with all my heart.'

'And everything between us, that was . . .'

'Just a way of getting you to Hong Kong, so that you would kill the Gushungos, and then we would kill you.'

'So it was you all along, selling us out, telling Mabeki everything.'

'Oh yes.' She smiled. 'And it was him all along, telling me about the Gushungos. There were no old ladies at that church in Hong Kong. I didn't have to spend hours checking out their house. Anything I ever wanted to know, Moses just told me. We never met. But we talked on the phone, sent emails. He's even my Facebook friend. Fake name and picture, of course.' She laughed at the deceitful absurdity. 'It's been going for years. Did Wendell ever tell you how he got his bright idea to get rid of the Gushungos?'

'No.'

'Then I will. I went up to him one day and said, "I want revenge" in my best blank, moody, kidnap-victim voice. That got him thinking, just like Moses said it would. After that, all I had to do was drop the occasional hint and . . . well, here we are.'

Carver had a limited appetite for self-pity. The pain he felt was rapidly mutating into a cold, detached anger. 'Well I hope you're pleased with yourself. This country's lost the chance to be free. And your uncle's dead. Shot in the back. Did you know that?'

'Of course.'

'And it doesn't bother you? Wendell Klerk rescued you, gave you a home . . . the guy loved you like a daughter, and this is how you repay him?'

'Loved me? Is that what you think? He loved money. All I was to him was a way of keeping his precious business alive when he was gone. He only paid you to come after me in Mozambique because it was cheaper than paying the ransom.'

'That's not true. I know it's not. And how can you say you want to be with Moses Mabeki? The man's a psychopath. He killed your family. He tried to rape you. I saw him in that room, by your bed, half-undressed . . .'

Zalika's laugh was derisive, contemptuous of his stupidity. 'It wasn't rape. It was the most glorious moment of my life. I'd been in love with Moses since I was a little girl. I was willing to do anything, endure anything if it meant being with him. Finally, all my dreams were about to come true. Plain little Zalika, Mummy's problem child, the girl who wasn't pretty enough, or sweet enough, who couldn't get a boyfriend, who had to spend her whole life being compared to her wonderful, handsome, charming older brother . . . Finally I was going to get my man. And that's when Uncle Wendell's hired hooligan has to come charging through the door . . . And look what you did to him! Moses was so beautiful. He was like a God. But you took all that away from me. You bastard! I hate you! Every night we were together, I only got through it by telling myself I was doing it for him.'

She was unravelling, thought Carver. All the secret resentments she'd stored up for years were pouring out, toxic delusions that had driven everything she'd ever done.

'For Christ's sake, Zalika, listen to yourself,' he said. 'You've fallen in love with your captor. It's normal, the Stockholm Syndrome – happens to hostages, kidnap victims, even people who've been tortured. But we can get you help.'

'Help? I don't want help!' she screamed. 'There's nothing wrong with me!'

'He killed your family,' Carver said, emphasizing each word.

'Yes, he did. He killed my bitch of a mother and the brother I hated.'

'He killed your father, too. Did you hate him?'

For the first time he saw a sign of weakness in the wall of loathing and self-pity she'd built round her soul. 'My father . . . my father was a thief,' Zalika said. 'He owned land stolen from the people. He got rich by keeping Malembans poor.'

'Mabeki told you that, did he?'

'He explained it to me, yes, but—'

'And that was a good enough reason for your father to die?'

'There was no choice. That's how it had to be. I didn't like it, but Moses explained it and I believed him. I loved him. I still love him. And he loves me. He wants me by his side when he fulfils his destiny. He was born to rule Malemba. I was born to be his woman.'

'You deluded little bitch. You had everything and you threw it away. You betrayed the people who loved you, and for what? If you think Moses Mabeki loves you, you're as mad as he is. He just wants to fuck you. Fuck your family, fuck your class, fuck your race . . . it's not exactly subtle, is it? And once he's done it, he'll kill you, just like he killed the best of your people. Count on it.'

'You're wrong! You're wrong! He's coming for me now. Then I'm giving you to him. I'm going to watch him take you apart, piece by piece. And then we'll be together, the two of us, and—'

The sentence ended there. Zalika had seen something beyond Carver. She smiled, her whole face transformed by an expression of pure delight . . . and then the joy was replaced by shocked surprise as a burst of semi-automatic gunfire hammered out, puncturing her body with a three-shot ellipsis of wounds that flowered diagonally across her chest, exited explosively out of her back and flung her to the floor of the little ravine.

'She was deluded,' said Moses Mabeki, walking past Carver and stopping when he reached Zalika Stratten's body. 'A useful idiot who had outlived her usefulness. It would have been amusing to have had her, of course – had her again, I should say. But there are some things more satisfying than mere sex. I had total control of her. I determined whether she lived or died. Far better.'

It was then that Carver truly hated Moses Mabeki: hated him for the way he had perverted, exploited and then discarded a girl whose only real sin was to have loved him – or rather, loved a dream of what he might once have been. Carver hated himself, too, for not finishing this when he first had the chance. So much suffering could have been avoided, for the want of one more bullet.

'She was right too, though,' Mabeki said. 'I will take my time killing you. Get to your feet.'

Carver began to move. And then he frowned. There was something else moving out there, coming towards them down the same path Zalika had trodden. But this shadow was much larger.

Carver raised a finger and pointed past Mabeki. 'Behind you,' he said.

Mabeki raised his eyebrows and sighed. 'Please, don't insult my intelligence.'

And then there was a roar so loud that it seemed to reverberate inside Carver's body, liquefying his guts and filling him with a primal caveman terror that overrode all his years of training and combat.

Mabeki's eyes widened. He spun round. And the old lion Lobengula summoned up the remnants of his strength, leapt from fifteen feet away and hit Mabeki with the full force of his massive body.

99

Moses Mabeki screamed as the lion clamped his foreclaws on either side of his stomach, holding him tight in a terrible dance of death. Then his mouth opened, and even where he lay Carver was engulfed in the hot, fetid stench of rotten meat that hung on that carnivore breath.

Frantically, Carver rolled to one side, then scrambled away as the lion drove Mabeki to the ground, the gun falling from his hand as his outflung wrist snapped against the rock that had been Carver's shelter.

The massive, savagely regal head lowered over Mabeki whose screams rose to an even higher pitch. The great curved fangs tore into his shoulder and the base of his neck, ripping and gnawing at his flesh while the fur round the old lion's mouth became matted with hot, fresh blood.

From the far side of the rock came the sound of men shouting. Mabeki must have gone on ahead, wanting his own, personal moment of triumph. Now the rest of his people were catching up. More shots were fired. Carver heard the ricochets of bullets against the rock walls of the defile.

The lion paused for a moment, raised his head and looked with perfect feline night-vision towards the source of the disturbance. Again he roared, and now the men's earlier bravado was replaced by cries of panic and the sound of running feet as they raced one another to escape the presence of the man-eater.

The lion returned to his long-awaited feast. Mabeki's screams were now just barely audible whimpers. Carver looked on, mesmerized. This was the same beast that he had encountered less than ten minutes earlier. He could see the fresh bullet wounds in its flank and haunches.

And then, just a couple of feet beyond its twitching, hairy-tufted tail, Carver noticed his gun, lying discarded on the ground. He had to reach it without catching the lion's attention. With infinite care, keeping his movements as slow and imperceptible as possible, Carver wriggled his way across the ground.

Lobengula had switched his attention to Mabeki's right arm. Placing his front paws on Mabeki's chest, to keep it still and give himself some leverage, he dug his teeth in just above the man's elbow and shook his head to wrench the limp, unmoving arm out of the elbow joint, growling contentedly to himself as it did so.

Carver kept moving. He was almost there. Slowly, slowly, he reached out his hand and felt his fingertips touch the stock of the gun.

The lion's tail gave another impatient twitch, the brushy end swishing by just inches from his outstretched fingertips. Carver tightened his grip and gently pulled the gun towards him.

Lobengula was relishing the taste and feel of fresh, blood-warmed meat. His wounds were forgotten. There was nothing on his mind but the feast he had in store.

And then, out of the corner of his eye he noticed something moving by the tip of his tail. He raised his head from his meal and looked round.

*

Carver didn't wait to be attacked himself. He just switched his M4 to automatic fire and emptied an entire magazine into the lion's body and head. There was a part of him that felt sad, almost ashamed at the slaughter of such a magnificent beast. But there was another, far greater part of him that had no intention whatever of being the second course. There was a horrible moment when it seemed that even this might not be enough, when the lion's fighting spirit was so great that he attempted to charge through the torrent of bullets. But just as he seemed to be gathering himself for one last leap a round must have hit his heart, for his legs crumpled beneath him and he fell, stone dead, to the ground.

But even if the lion was dead, Moses Mabeki was not. His neck and shoulder had been opened up like a corpse on the dissecting table and his arm had been severed from his body, yet somehow the lion had missed his heart and his airpipe and he was still breathing. Just.

'Help me,' he whispered. 'For the love of God, please help me.'

So now, all of a sudden, you discover religion, Carver thought.

He discarded the empty magazine from his M4 and rammed in a fresh one. Mabeki was lying at his feet, his car-crash face and his twisted mouth and the white bones and torn muscles of his ripped and blood-soaked body clearly visible.

'Sure,' said Carver, 'I'll help you.'

Then he pressed the trigger, and once again he did not let go until the magazine was empty.

When the killing was done, an emptiness came over him. He looked at all the bodies and wondered what the hell the point of any of it had been. Zalika's lovely face was still untouched, and as she lay there in the pale-blue moonlight it was almost possible that she was waiting for him to come and wake her with a kiss. But hers was a sleep that would never end. Carver put a third magazine into his M4, more out of habit than anything else, and walked away down the gully.

He'd gone about a hundred metres when he heard the groan up

ahead. Carver's walk became a jog, then a run, then a flat-out sprint.

Justus was alive. Zalika hadn't killed him. And Carver was going to get him across the border if it was the last thing he ever did.

Six Months Later . . .

100

Samuel Carver finished a mouthful of butter-soft fillet steak – nice and bloody in the middle, just as he liked it – and took a sip of 2001 Jardin Sophia, a superb red wine from a vineyard in Stellenbosch, South Africa. He looked around the restaurant at the waiters bustling between close-packed tables. It was hard to believe they were all in Sindele, the capital of a new, democratic Malemba.

'Considering this country was starving six months ago, this isn't a bad bit of steak,' Carver said.

Brianna Latrelle laughed politely. She was sticking to mineral water. She had to. She was seven months pregnant.

'It was never really a starving country,' she replied. 'It was a prosperous, fertile country starved by a mad dictator.'

'Whatever happened to him, I wonder?'

This time her laugh was a lot more spontaneous. Brianna had quite a dirty cackle when she really laughed, Carver thought. It was one of the many things he was discovering he liked about her.

'Who'd have guessed it would turn out this way?' said Brianna.

'Tshonga coming out of hiding, demanding an election, with a fair count this time . . .'

'The guy's got a helluva nerve, hasn't he?' said Carver. 'You've got to admire him, really, the way he can talk about peace and democracy and keep a straight face.'

'Well, he truly believes in them.'

'Up to a point.'

'Yeah, OK, so maybe he slipped up once or twice. But be fair, round here that's nothing.'

'And it helped that there was such a handy scapegoat, who just happened to have been the only survivor of the Gushungo assassination, found conveniently dead on a hill by the South African border, his body having been used for dinner by a lion.'

'Couldn't have happened to a nicer guy,' Brianna said.

Carver raised his glass. 'I'll certainly drink to that.'

They ate in companionable silence for a while, then Carver said, 'So here we are, two directors of the Kamativi Mining Corporation. How did you think the first annual shareholders meeting went, Madam Chairperson?'

'I think it went well, Mr Carver,' she replied.

'Bizarre how it's all worked out, isn't it? I take the mickey out of Tshonga, but he kept his word about the deal.'

'Why shouldn't he? You fulfilled your side of it.' She smiled at Carver's quizzical expression. 'Yes, I know what your side of it was. Wendell told me when we were flying down to Jo'burg, that last time. We shared a lot more than he or I ever let on. You know I had a bad feeling about what went down, that weekend at Campden Hall. I told you then. But the mine was always a good deal for Malemba. So why shouldn't Tshonga keep to it?'

'I should have listened to you that time.'

'Damn straight you should have . . . and when we met at the house in Sandton. It's weird, looking back. I always sensed something had gone wrong with Zalika, even if I didn't know what. I used to tell myself I was being unfair, that I was just jealous of how much Wendell cared for her. I should have trusted myself more.'

'And I should have trusted her less.'

Carver didn't want to think about Zalika Stratten any more than he had to. Time to change the subject.

'So, the baby . . . did you tell Klerk about it?'

'Yeah, just a few days before he died.'

'He must have been ecstatic. He didn't think he could have kids.'

'I guess he hadn't found the right girl,' Brianna said with a melancholic mix of sadness and contentment in her voice.

'Well he found the right girl in you all right. I just hope he knew it.'

'He knew it,' she said.

Her eyes began to fill with tears.

'I'm sorry,' Carver said, reaching out to hold her wrist. 'I didn't mean to upset you.'

'No, it's all right, you didn't.' She took a deep breath, dabbed her eyes with her napkin and forced a bright smile. 'So, anyway, tell me about Justus and . . . what were those kids called again?'

'Canaan and Farayi. They're fine. Better than fine, actually. They got their farm back. Justus is rebuilding the house. He's got a new tractor.'

'Really?' Brianna said. 'That sounds expensive.'

'The man got shot doing me a favour. It wasn't a lot to do in return . . .'

'You know, Wendell was right about you,' she said. 'He always liked you, even when you turned him down. He used to say' – she lowered her voice into a feminine approximation of Klerk's bass rumble – ' "That Carver, he keeps his word. He does what he says he's going to do. And he can shoot the balls off a horsefly at a hundred metres." '

Once again their laughter lit up the table.

'I'd better write that down,' Carver said. 'It'll come in handy for my tombstone.'

Brianna smiled fondly. 'You're a good man, Sam Carver,' she said. Then a look of concern crossed her face as she saw him frown and twist his lips in an unexpected grimace. 'What's the matter?'

'Just that the last woman who said that to me tried to kill me three days later.'

'Don't worry,' she said. 'I have no intention of killing you.'

'Excellent,' said Carver, reaching for the bottle of Jardin Sophia. 'Then I'll drink to that, too.'

Acknowledgements

My thanks go, as always, to Julian Alexander and Peta Nightingale at LAW, without whom I would have neither contracts, nor manuscripts; to my editor Simon Thorogood – with special kudos for being such a gent over 'that difficult chapter' along with so much else – and to Daniel Balado-Lopez, who copyedited with such care and perception. In addition I must credit the original Flattie (you know who you are) for providing me with both a character and an ear for the rich and colourful obscenity of ex-Rhodesian Army conversation. The shooting scene would have been impossible without the technical advice and vivid imagination of Jonathan Irby at the West London Shooting School, not to mention the inspiration of Ian Fleming, to whose golf match in *Goldfinger* it is an admiring and respectful *homage* . . . Speaking of which, the character of Lobengula the lion was inspired in part by the many mighty cats that appear in the works of Wilbur Smith, for whose encouragement and support I remain enormously grateful. I should, however, add that the behaviour of a lion confronted by a truck when trying to get some sleep was taken directly from my own experience one memorable night in the Pilanesburg game reserve, South Africa – and you should have seen what the lion's mates and girlfriends were getting up to . . . Caroline Driggs sparked my imagination with her recollections of Chinese grocery stores.

David Hart's hospitality at his magnificent home in Suffolk was similarly inspirational, though I should say that he bears no resemblance whatsoever to the character of Wendell Klerk. Finally, I owe an enormous debt of gratitude to Jamie Allday, my office landlord, who has had to put up with me describing, acting out and asking for endless advice on scenes from this and other books. And of course, above all, to my wife Clare and my children, who have had to put up with everything, for ever . . .

TC, West Sussex, March 2010

Tom Cain is the pseudonym for an award-winning journalist with twenty-five years' experience working for Fleet Street newspapers. He has lived in Moscow, Washington DC and Havana, Cuba. He is the author of *The Accident Man*, *The Survivor* and *Assassin*.